. . . And Baby Makes Two

And Baby Makes Two

a novel

JUDY SHEEHAN

BALLANTINE BOOKS

NEW YORK

Published in the United States by Ballantine Books, an imprint of The Random House Publishing Group, a division of Random House, Inc., New York.

BALLANTINE and colophon are registered trademarks of Random House, Inc.

LIBRARY OF CONGRESS CATALOGING-IN-PUBLICATION DATA
Sheehan, Judy.
    And baby makes two : a novel / Judy Sheehan.— 1st ed.
      p.   cm.
    ISBN 0-345-48007-4 (alk. paper)
    1. Single women—Fiction.   2. Childlessness—Fiction.   3. Greenwich Village (New York, N.Y.)—Fiction.   I. Title.

PS3619.H439A85 2005
813'.6—dc22   2005040983

Printed in the United States of America on acid-free paper

www.ballantinebooks.com

9 8 7 6 5 4 3 2 1

FIRST EDITION

For Annie

Acknowledgments

Thanks, thanks, and more thanks, in no particular order, to:

Looking Glass Theatre, Justine Lambert, and Kenneth Nowell for letting me explore new ideas and then giving me deadlines—what a great combination. Everyone should buy season tickets to Looking Glass.

David Kaplan, my teacher and friend, you are largely responsible for expanding and twisting my old ideas about storytelling and I am forever grateful.

Myra Donnelley, my evil twin and my daughter's fairy godmother for being the madwright, for bringing my plays across the continent, and for the Wendy House.

The world of DreamMoms, especially my fellow travelers, Pat Nealon and Anne Marie Gussman, not to mention the adorable Sophie Nealon and the delightful Lucy Gussman, for all the playdates. And oh yes, remember that trip we took to China together?

Elizabeth Dennehy, Diane Vecchiarello, and Monica Rosenthal for moral support and more, and to Ryan-Joseph Nucum, for maintaining my sanity.

China Seas, Laura Cercere, Roberta Ferdschneider, and MeeMee Chin for the baby. I owe you one.

Deirdre Lanning, my extraordinary editor, who guided the book to a happy landing, and Lisa Lester Kelly, my scary smart copy editor.

My wonderful agent, Simon Lipskar, and the amazing Dan Lazar. I wouldn't be thanking anyone if it weren't for you two. I've still got bruises on my arms because I can't stop pinching myself. How did I get so lucky?

My sisters, Jeanne and Mur, for love, courage, and early manuscript reading.

My dad, who loves language and taught his kids the same. My mom, who was the hardest-working mother in the business.

Bob Gilbo, the best of the best.

Annie, my love, my turtledove. Mommy loves her work, but she loves you more. Thanks for being the most fun ever. Let's play balloon baseball.

. . . And Baby Makes Two

Chapter One

Jane walked out of her apartment building and saw the Christ Child. She was on her way to the gym when she saw a baby of such breath-stopping beauty she had to remind herself to inhale. He had gray-blue eyes, Nestlé cocoa hair, and was destined to have thick eyebrows after puberty. He had no pores. He had bliss. His mother held him on her hip in a swaddling sling that matched his eye color almost perfectly. She looked pretty happy, for a virgin mother, not that Jane noticed her. This glowing god-baby was the reason wise men traveled across deserts and little drummer boys drummed. He blinked, and Jane, a reasonably calm person as a rule, nearly wept. She had to talk herself down. She pretended to check her watch, and then she walked away. She only looked back at him four times. But he had already turned to perform other miracles.

Jane moved on. She really did. She was a grown-up, after all, so she went to the gym and climbed the Stairs to Nowhere. She showered. She tried to do something with that hair of hers, and why did it seem to have a mind of its own? And those roots. They were an evil announcement of her lack-of-youth. Jane was morally superior to her lack-of-youth, but she still hid her roots, as best she could.

Jane's life was pretty good for an almost-thirty-seven-year-old. She lived in New York City. She was of medium height and had pale skin, because she was afraid of skin cancer, and reddish-brown hair, of the Nice 'n Easy #110 variety. Her hair had given up being red all by itself years ago. At her age, it needed help. She still wore size six pants. She looked tense all the time, but she didn't know it. She walked fast, but always gave directions to tourists trying to find Broadway below Fourteenth Street.

Jane was lucky. She had a cool apartment with more sunlight than most people might expect in the East Village. The small extra bedroom used to serve as a darkroom, when she had been dabbling in photography. These days it was a makeshift office/storage closet/place to stash things when parents came to visit. She still took photos, but only on vacations or at family events where someone had to say, "I wonder when we'll all be together like this again?" And she had the Indian guy on Bleecker Street develop the pictures. He was nice, and always found one shot in the roll to praise as "Oh, very pretty, very good! You should take more pictures!"

Her family was in New Jersey, the exact right distance away. Different area code, so she could feel separate, but the same time zone, so they could all feel close. Perfect. Her friends envied her out loud.

So why was there an ache in her life? Why did it feel like there was a hole in her middle? Most of the time, she walked too quickly to feel it, but sometimes it howled, and when it did, she walked faster.

After all, Jane's life was pretty good for an almost-thirty-seven-year-old. The other side of the last cute decade of her life. She was starting to be not young anymore. Thirty-seven sounded old. Older. Agatha old. Too old to change her ways, find a husband, and make babies. Too late for that.

So Jane moved on. She really did. She had only twenty-three minutes to get to work, but she bypassed the subway and opted to walk. After all, it was a postcard of a morning in early May. Stray New Yorkers even smiled with late spring giddiness. She hit her stride and got a lucky stretch of green lights to keep the momentum. Nineteen minutes later, she would have just enough time to overpay for a double latte, smile as her elevator stopped at every floor, and then dive into the madness.

Jane always forgot to factor in the line at Starbucks for people who wanted to get brownie-coffee. And there he was. That same guy was there again. She had seen him last week, thinning blond hair, capped teeth. She noticed him noticing her. Why did she think he was an actor? And, even though Jane was going to turn thirty-seven in less than a week, he flirted with her anyway.

"Are you stalking me?" He grinned.

"Hey, a girl's gotta have a purpose in life. Or a hobby. Or . . ."

She grimaced. Her answer was too long. The Christ Child sighting was still visible in her head, and still so distracting. And could she still legally call herself a girl? She didn't schedule any time for a flirtation. The city was full of handsome, capped-teeth smiles, and here was another one, but she shouldn't be late for the Monday morning meeting.

The actor looked pleased and settled in to flirt with her. Did he know that he was blocking the door? He was smooth.

"This is, like, the third time I've seen you here. Do you live around here?"

"I work here. Not here, upstairs. In the building. I work in the building."

Oh, my God, she sounded like an idiot! His grin turned condescending, like he was George Clooney and he always had this effect on women, like he was taking pity on a stammering female fan. For Jane, it was time to move on. Really.

"My name's Richard. What's yours?"

"Jane. And I—"

"Really? Are you giving me a fake name or something?"

Did lots of women give him fake names?

"No. I'm Jane. Really."

He took her hand, nearly scalding it with his own latte.

"Look at us! We're Dick and Jane! We're, like, I don't know, something out of a baby book or something."

Jane smiled. This was no George Clooney, just a guy blocking the door when she had less than two minutes to get to her meeting.

"Me Dick! You Jane!" And he pummeled his chest Tarzan style. Jane smiled.

"See you in school!" she said and ducked around him.

"Wait!"

But she didn't wait. Instead, she took long ballet leap-steps to the elevator, into the conference room, and the workday took hold.

Jane had seven employees and nine consultants on her team. She liked to take care of them. She bought them zinc when they had colds, she held birthday celebrations and baby showers, and she listened to love life sagas. Nice work and she got it. She ran IT Support for the high-profile investment bank Argenti. Wall Street. The Street. The nerve center of the city, the country, the world. Decisions here reverberated throughout the universe, and Jane had to handle their latest Microsoft upgrade. And handle the eternal complaints about her Help Desk. And find a way to supply cheaper laptops to senior management. And phase out the old contact database. And integrate technology with the London firm Argenti had just acquired. And answer the e-mails she'd been ignoring. And make birthday plans. And get the latte stain out of her skirt. It was almost noon when Jane noticed that the actor had missed scalding her hand, but he had stained her skirt. Look at that . . .

· · ·

Jane wrote lists all the time. In the middle of a conference call, she'd add a stray item to the list. She lived by her lists and her schedules. She upgraded PDAs twice a year and had entirely too many opinions about them. Lists brought her order and comfort. Maybe lists could fill that hole in her middle. When it howled, she fed it lists.

See? See how much you have? Why are you greedy for more? Be happy. Stop aching and howling.

"Do you want anything from A.J.'s?" Her staff was always diligent about including her in their lunch plans, and she was equally diligent about declining. No one was going to intercept her almost-break at lunch. Outside, in the absence of fluorescent light, there were no PCs, or at least, not as many. When she felt brave, she ate from the local food carts, and when she felt braver, she ate at the expensive delis.

"Mommy! Mommy, please? I want fries! Please? I can have fries, please?"

It was a technicolor Shirley Temple, ringlets and all. Jane watched and listened. How did little girls get that bell-quality to their voices? And why does it disappear? Jane wanted to be some beautiful fries godmother and make the girl happy, but she suspected that the mother might have a minor objection or two. Jane moved on to the deli line.

You may not believe it, but the Dick-Richard-Actor was there. Same deli.

"Are you temping too?" he asked. "I'm at Sloan. I told them I smoke, so I get, like, five breaks a day. Hey. You got something on your skirt."

"Yes. Your coffee."

Richard overflowed with apologies, with seltzer, with salt. He betrayed no trace of enjoying himself as he pulled her out of line and attempted to rub the stain out of her skirt. He was all business, but Jane was still not taking him seriously.

She wished she had stayed in line. Just then, a pregnant woman entered the deli. Very pregnant, carrying her pregnancy so casually with an arched-out baby belly. This would have been unremarkable, but she was followed by a similarly pregnant woman. And then another. And another. In the end, there was a string of six pregnant women, waddling up to the counter for chicken salads, bagels with vegetable cream cheese, and soup. Jane had lost her place in line.

Dick-Richard was still babbling. He had a flier for a play—was he in it? Hah! He was an actor after all. She had been right. She was puffed with pride, and now it was time to move on. Again. Really.

"Would you look at that?" Dick asked as he pointed to the school of pregnant women. "What's in the water around here? I hope *you're* not drinking it!"

He was no George Clooney, remember? There was no call for stammering here. She just needed to tell him she was busy and she had to go now.

"Look. I'm really busy and I have to go now. It's Monday—it's a crusher day. You seem really nice, but I'm too busy to talk to you. I'm due. At work. I'm past due. I mean, I have to go now. Thanks for this."

She left the flier on the table and left the actor and the pregnant women in the deli, late for another meeting. Kendra, her manager, didn't speak English. She spoke only Corporate Speak, and though it took twice as long to say anything, she seemed to love it.

Kendra gave a five-minute speech about "levels of granularity as we ramp up the London integration" and suggested that Jane could "add value to this critical process." Jane translated it in her head and smiled: "We have programs, they have programs. Make them work together."

"I'm on it," Jane said, and it was true.

Kendra seemed confused by the brief reply. Didn't Jane know that she was at work? Why wasn't she using Corporate Speak?

Kendra talked about "server maintenance" and "time-sensitive issues." Jane sifted through the words and realized that Kendra was saying: server maintenance. Why the delays? It was a big issue, and they were going to have to schedule a power outage over the weekend. Saturday night? Jane, can you supervise? Of course she can. Jane's a team player. Go, Jane, go.

As the group shuffled out of the conference room, Kendra pulled Jane aside.

"You know, London offers lots of growth opportunities. If you're interested, I can escalate."

"Of course," Jane said before she finished translating. All it meant was "Wanna work in London?"

• • •

Jane phoned *The New York Times* where her best friend, Ray, would be stumbling into work right about now.

Ray was a theater critic, but people loved him anyway. He recently became a second-stringer for the *Times,* but still published in lots of tourist publications. Tourists loved his ability to identify which audience was right for which show, and publishers loved his ability to beat a deadline. His career expanded to include hosting seminars at the New School, where he interviewed the very people he had skewered in print. Lots of people attended just to see if there would be an ugly scene. Once in a while, they got their wish. Philip Seymour Hoffman spat at him, but Madonna hugged him. Go figure.

Jane loved Ray's broad appetite for the arts. Seated next to him, Jane saw gems and rip-offs. She shared his dislike of all those microphones, and she wondered aloud why there were always naked people on stage at The Public Theater. Ray explained that everyone calls it The Pubic.

"Hey, Ray. I have to work Saturday night. How did I let that happen?"

Silence. Why wasn't he clucking in sympathy, or trying to outdo her?

"Are you listening? Are you multitasking? No e-mail when you're on the phone with me. That was the deal, remember?"

"Janie. I'm not multitasking. I'm barely tasking. Auntie Mame's hung."

No one likes to say "Again?" when they hear that a friend is hungover, and no one likes to hear it. But Ray's latest boyfriend lived in a Ketel One world, and Ray wasn't up to the challenge.

"He's young. He likes to party. I try to keep up."

"He has more brain matter to spare."

"He had a gig at Arlene's Grocery, and it didn't go well. The audience wanted something more . . ." Ray couldn't finish that sentence. He didn't understand his boyfriend's music, so he really didn't understand his boyfriend's music's audience. So he said, ". . . else. They wanted something else. And then, there were all those sorrows to drown. Tell me about your wonderful, normal life, Principessa."

"They want me to go to London."

She could hear Ray sit up straighter.

"When? For how long?"

"Soon, I think. For forever, maybe. I don't have any details."

"Who needs details? Go. The London theater scene is *so* much more interesting than New York's. Go, and take me with you."

Ray described the last seven plays he had seen in London, while Jane multitasked and read e-mail. Ray could tell, and he interrupted her.

"Let's continue this conversation next week at that *Alice in Wonderland* we're going to see. Saturday night. No e-mail. You'll have to pay attention."

"Ray. I told you. I'm working Saturday night."

"Next Saturday. Pay attention, you dope."

• • •

Jane saved up all her fun, nice, friendly personal e-mails for a mini-break in the day. Here was one from her sister, Sheila. It was huge. 5MB. Wow. What had she attached?

It was called birthday.mpeg. A video clip. The file opened and presented a brace of frosted five-year-old boys dancing off a sugar rush in a green backyard. They belted out an off-key version of "Happy Birthday to me! I am so happy! Happy birthday, happy birthday, happy birthday to meeeeee!"

To finish the song, one of the boys ran loose-limbed to the camera. He became a blur of frosting and teeth and the clip ended.

To: stepmom@mynet.com
From: jane.howe@argenti.com
Subject: The little guys

Hey Sheil,

Wow! Did the boys eat that cake, or just wear it? Anyway, thanks for the clip. They are so adorable it should be illegal. I hope they like the little drum set I sent—and I hope you don't hate me for it. Hee hee!

It's so funny that you should send me that clip today. I'm seeing lots of babies today, and pregnant women. Hey, you're not pregnant, are you? Just kidding. I saw the most gorgeous baby this morning. The sun was bouncing off him in a very halo kinda way. How do babies do that?

Anyway, I gotta sign off. Work is completely insane, deranged & busy. How is life in the real world?

xoxoxo
Jane

She saw no babies on her way home. She walked, but at a much slower pace this time, stopping in Chinatown for dinner to take home. She was not sad, not lonely, not like you're thinking. She was definitely tired and would have preferred to be facing her twenty-second birthday, or even her thirty-first. She anticipated hating forty, but being all calm and wise at fifty. What was so bad about thirty-seven? Her life was fine, good, even wonderful, and only a real bitch would complain about this good life.

No, she wasn't sad. Nor was she stupid. All those babies and pregnant women must have been there all along, she knew that. She was just noticing them now because of some biological alarm that needed to be reset. The hole in her middle was at midabdomen. How annoying was that? The magazines and talk shows told her that she'd be fine on her own, but none of them told her about this ache. What was she supposed to do, become a single mother? Just do that? Just become a mother who was single?

A single mother.

She stopped walking. It sounded so plausible. She had a big apartment, she made a good living, and had a supportive family nearby. Well. She had family nearby. She was strong and she was loving. She could go out and get pregnant and have a baby and be happy. She could do this. She could have a baby.

Jane's life was a movie. (Isn't everyone's?) So, in her head, Jane tried to fast-forward to her life as a Single Mother, and the picture was fuzzy. There was baby food on her blouse, and she stumbled over Legos that were scattered everywhere. But she was smiling. Obviously, the fast-forward technique didn't work every time. She started walking again. Single Mother. That was crazy talk. Whatever phase she was in, Jane would ride it out until menopause. So there.

She fell asleep late, on the couch, in front of the television. She had a crazy dream that she was at a picnic, playing tug-of-war with a beautiful red velvet cord. She couldn't see her opponents, so she started following the red cord. She woke up before she could find them. The TV was flickering with some medical drama where doctors were urging a sweaty pregnant woman to breathe and push, and they could see the head! And then a six-month-old infant, playing the newborn, artfully smudged with goo, was placed on the mother's chest. She wept with joy.

Jane remained stoic. She brushed her teeth and went to bed without flossing, proving to herself that she was too irresponsible to be a single mother.

. . .

Dick-Richard was in Starbucks every morning, so Jane opted for the acidic coffee available in the pantry at Argenti, and then quickly converted to tea. After all, she couldn't go get coffee in a place where some temping actor-guy liked her and was flirting with her. The flirting could lead to dating and the dating could lead to love and the love could lead to marriage and babies. This temp could turn out to be the father of her child. Jane wasn't sure if she was afraid of him or of the theoretical baby. Better to keep this whole scary issue in limbo. Wait it out and drink tea.

The baby haunting continued through the week. Thankfully, some of the little ones were very unattractive. There was the red-faced toddler whose goal in life was to inflict his misery on all of Manhattan. There was the little cherub with the river of green snot oozing from her nose. There was a whole mess of running, screaming children in a playground that must have been there last week, but Jane had never noticed it. Jesus, there were a lot of children in a city that was really designed for adults.

Saturday came, and Jane made a pilgrimage to Bed, Bath & Beyond. It was jammed with Manhattanites who urgently needed more cookware, better towels, and storage solutions. Plus throw pillows and salsa. Jane was there for hooks, chic entranceway hooks to hold fashionable coats and jackets. She had ugly, boring brass hooks, and that would never do. Surely a big store like this would offer something more attractive—and it did. She carried two sets of hooks as she browsed the store: self-adhesive or needs-hardware. Oh, the suspense.

There was a special in-store demonstration on baby-proofing. Jane thought, for a moment, that this was a way to keep babies out of your home. She came to realize that it meant keeping babies from opening drawers.

She paced herself, well aware of the server maintenance that awaited her that evening. She would be required to supervise people who were doing something by rote. These people were already bored before they woke up. She was their overpriced babysitter. Jane browsed, she touched, she sniffed. Everything was bright and clean.

"Hey, Jane!"

Dick-Richard. It was Dick-Richard.

"Are you coming to my show tonight? I think we have, like, three reservations. You have to come and make it like four."

It's a big, crowded store in a big, crowded city. This sort of thing simply never happens in New York, except when it does.

"Oh. I'm sorry. I can't—"

A woman pushed her stroller between them. The sleeping baby taking the ride stirred, but continued to sleep. Jane lost her bearings for only a moment.

"I have to work."

"At night? Come on! You're, like, an executive or something, aren't you? What are you doing working on a Saturday night?"

A long explanation followed. Richard seemed to get some of it. He nodded and did lots of active listening, then launched into an animated description of the play, the company, the rehearsal process, his role, and what happened when he dropped a line last night and it was so funny and the audience had no idea.

Jane's mind wandered. She had always believed in signs. It was part of her Irish heritage. This guy was not sweeping her off her feet right away, but there was something to be said for the fact that she kept seeing him and seeing him. And babies. She kept seeing him and babies. She should be courageous, she should get out of limbo, and she should buy the hooks that required hardware. Brave girl.

She took his flier and his personal business card, which featured a grinning photo and a list of his union affiliations. She gave him her number. Her real number. Very brave girl.

• • •

Over the years, Jane had managed a lengthy series of repairs to her apartment. Once, she was a fix-it junkie. But this time, she went home and managed to decimate her wall attempting to insert the necessary hardware for her hooks. She left the new crater, and all the plaster dust, and retreated for the predictable safety of the office, where teamsters would never have allowed her to attempt this hook fiasco.

Server maintenance is not nearly as thrilling as it sounds. Oh, no, it's actually a tedious process, and Jane's presence there was somewhat ceremonial. If anyone had made a disastrous error, it would have been Jane's responsibility to contact powerful people and apologize. She had hours to kill and a search engine at her disposal. She sat at her computer and Googled.

She Googled Dick-Richard. Richard. She should really think of him as just Richard. She found him mentioned in a handful of reviews for Off-off-Broadway plays:

. . .

What Now, Chairman Mao?—a musical that was not well received

The Peanut Butter Plan—a children's play that was very well received

When You Comin' Back, Red Ryder—for which he did carpentry

Riverside Scene Night—wherein he performed a monologue by Christopher Durang

. . .

Jane couldn't make much of this. Did it mean that he was talented or not? Had he ever appeared on *Law & Order,* and how could she find out? She tried to find out about that program, but only learned that their upcoming episode was about a homicide over the custody of a baby.

Eventually, Jane's mind wandered to the phrase that had been rolling around in her head. Single Mother. She typed it in carefully, barely tapping the keys, and she Googled. She got 2,370,000 results in 0.26 seconds. She added "new york" to her search and was still sifting through 1,120,000 results.

There were articles, support groups, condemnations, personal essays, chat rooms, and dating services, and that was just on the first page. She kept looking, which was odd because she didn't actually know what she was looking for. An answer? A solution? To what, the baby haunting? She didn't mind the baby haunting all that much. She needed no exorcism. She liked babies.

She loved babies.

She wanted a baby of her own.

No, she didn't.

Did she?

Would the ache disappear someday, or would it expand and amplify the thump of her pulse and drive her mad, like a telltale heart? Jane stopped thinking and returned to her search. It didn't take her long to find a thread in the glowing, blue-underlined world of blogs. She clicked on one and followed it to the world of Choosing Single Motherhood. CSM. They offered the thing Jane craved: information. They were located in Manhattan, and they were scheduled to have a meeting next Saturday. Somehow that meeting got itself entered into Jane's electronic calendar. What was that—satisfaction? Joy? Progress? An endorphin rush?

Jane needed to breathe deeply. Typing this into her electronic calendar was absolutely not a commitment. It didn't mean anything, did it? It was a week away, and a lot could happen in a week. Maybe the Christ Child would appear again and give her a sign. Maybe Dick-Richard would give signs of an appealing future. Jane was good at extracting information from signs, even when the signs were vague and the information nonexistent.

She printed four articles and called for a car service to take her home. Work late—get a car home. What a perk. Jane pushed through the lobby doors, and there was Celeste, her favorite driver, waiting and waving. Celeste was as old as Jane's mother, but not nearly as cranky. Her laugh lines curved up to her forehead. Her baby-fine hair was dyed orange-yellow, and she seemed happily unaware of the bright pink lipstick she always wore on her teeth.

"Janie! You working late again? I'm gonna get you home, baby."

Jane put away her reading material for a cozy chat with Celeste.

"What you reading, Janie?"

"Oh, some articles. Stuff. About kids." This felt like an enormously brave step.

"Oh, yeah? You got kids?" Celeste asked.

"No. But I'm thinking about it." Jane felt drunk with the freedom to talk about this crazy idea, this motherhood thing. She could just spill the idea right there to Celeste! She even said, "I'm not married, but I have this feeling I'm supposed to have kids. I can't explain it, but I'm supposed to be a mother. I think I know it. Does that sound crazy?"

Celeste nodded and said, "Oh, darling. I understand it." There was no traffic, there were no pedestrians. Celeste could have driven faster and run a string of green lights, but she slowed down. She checked the rearview to watch her passenger in the backseat. Jane leaned forward.

"This makes no sense. I shouldn't want this. I'm probably being selfish or stupid or irrational. But I've had this urge before, and I'm starting to feel afraid. I'm almost thirty-seven, and if I wait much longer, I'll be in diapers along with the kid. You know what I mean?"

"Of course."

"You've never mentioned any kids, Celeste. Do you and Theo have kids?"

"No, sweetheart, my Theo and I, we always talked about kids, but that's not how you get them! And there was so much going on. He started the store and he was working all the time, and, darling, I do mean all the time. It was terrible. And then he got the blood pressure thing and then, I don't know, we stopped talking about it and a lot of time went by."

"And then?" They were two blocks from Jane's home.

"And then it was too late for me to make a baby. I went through the change, and that was the end of that. No kids. Not for Theo and me. And, of course, then he had his accident, and here we are."

Jane had already revealed something important about herself, so she felt safe in asking, "Do you ever regret it?"

A block away from Jane's apartment, Celeste suddenly pulled

the car over. Jane was pushed back and startled by the squeal of the brakes.

Celeste turned around in her seat, so that she could look directly at Jane and say, "Every minute of every day I regret it. Every minute. Every day. You understand?"

She waited for Jane to nod before turning back to the wheel and driving that last block. For Jane, that was The Moment.

• • •

Jane couldn't sleep until she'd read all her articles and made notes in the margins. Celeste's words and The Moment had seemed scary on the surface, but Jane was happy. A tumbler had turned and a lock clicked open. Gravity was pulling her toward her destination, and, oh, she was happy to have a destination that she could name. When she finally slept, Jane dreamed about fruit trees dropping apples that turned into pears, while her mother hissed in disapproval.

• • •

The next morning, Jane was too restless to sit and drink tea. There was a galloping feeling in her body, like something was on its way. An event. A change. She reminded herself about her birthday. That was the event/change, remember? Getting old? That's what's coming up. She pushed aside thoughts of Celeste and The Moment. Maybe The Moment was just a jarringly personal conversation and nothing more.

She sipped her tea and watched an episode of *Your Baby and You.*

She sipped her tea and reread her articles about single motherhood.

She put down the tea, took off her clothes, and looked in the mirror. See? Jane was a brave girl. Could you do that right now?

Jane saw her very good body. Strong legs, abs you could see (if you had the right lighting), healthy breasts. Uneven, but healthy. This body did what she asked it to do. But could it make a baby? It had worked so hard for nearly thirty-seven years—was she asking too much? Was that a gray hair down there? Oh, God.

When the phone rang, she jumped back into her shirt before she picked up. It was her mother.

"Janie, Janie, Janie. Next Sunday, darling. You and me. Another year older."

Jane's birthday came first—May 21, while her mother's followed on May 30. But Betty liked the expedience of mother-daughter celebrations, and this year, Jane's birthday fell on a Sunday. This Sunday.

"Who's going to be there?"

"The usual cast of characters, Jane. You, me, the pope. Who do you think is coming? Family. What a question. Your father, your brothers, the kids."

Family. Jane had two older brothers, Kevin and Neil, whom she still owed on a long-standing debt of Indian burns and loogies. She had never been close to the boys. Maybe it was because Kevin was already twelve years old, and Neil ten, when Jane was born. Maybe they were still bullies. They were not the whole family. Jane had always been close to her younger sister, Sheila, but Sheila would not be coming to the party. Sheila's name could not be mentioned, not in Betty's presence. In fact, it was probably a bad idea to think about Sheila too much. Betty might sense it and start yelling. Jane felt Sheila's image surfacing in her mind and grabbed the first words that pertained to something else.

"I'm just tired. I had a late night last night. Server maintenance. You know, these days we try to avoid power outages and . . ."

Betty didn't know what servers were, so Jane shouldn't talk about them. She remembered her Saturday CSM—Choosing Single Motherhood workshop. Jane shouldn't mention that either.

"Sweetheart, you can bring a date, if you like. Let me know if you're bringing someone, and I'll order a deli platter. I'm too old to cook for these things. Oh, did I mention that Kitty thinks she's pregnant—again? I mean, I don't know what they're using, but it's not working. Your poor brother looks so tired with three kids. How is he supposed to manage with four, I ask you?"

"Not exactly my business, or yours, oh mother of four children." Ouch. This was an indirect reference to Sheila. Conversations with Betty always took place on a tightrope.

"Three children. I have three children." An indirect way of declaring, once again, that Sheila was dead to her. The direct references had been shouted and sobbed. Now she turned to ice or steel when Sheila was mentioned, even indirectly.

"Mom."

"Janie, Janie, Janie. I'm just saying. Kevin's hair has gone all gray, and now he's going to start pulling it out. You'll see. And Neil and Linda still can't get the baby to sleep through the night. They finally closed on their house, and poor Dylan has to switch schools. This late in the year? What are they thinking? And next year, they're sending little Jason to preschool for eight thousand dollars a year. For preschool! None of you ever had preschool, and you turned out just fine. I never had to waste twelve cents for you to learn to finger paint."

"I think there's a compliment in there, so I'll say thank you."

After Betty finished the family litany, she reminded her daughter to bring that really good dip and that cheese that no one else can find. And a date.

"Will you have time on Saturday to pick up that cheese? What are you doing Saturday? Can you come out here and help me clean?"

Jane saw two truths in the front of her mind:

1. Turning down her mother's Saturday invitation to clean = a firm commitment to the Choosing Single Motherhood meeting. That looked, sounded, and smelled like a first step toward actually doing this.

2. Item #1 would require a convincing lie to her mother, which is, by definition, a quick lie. No hesitation. Show no fear.

There was no time to create any pro/con lists. Her synapses fired out a quick "Oh, Mom, I have to go into the office on Saturday. And then I have to go pick up the cheese—it's a busy, busy day. Look. I'll come by early on Sunday and help. Okay?"

Like millions of women before her, Jane took her first step toward motherhood by telling a lie.

Chapter Two

Jane unclenched her jaw a bit, though she didn't know it. She was starting to find the constant presence of babies to be a happy surprise, and she opened the door for official flirtation with Dick, who went by the name Richard, professionally. She had no intention of bringing him to the family gathering—what a nightmare of a first date that would be. No.

Jane had missed all six performances of his play, alas. But he was confident there would soon be another. His confidence was unshakable. He didn't know that he wasn't George Clooney, or if he did, he didn't seem to mind. This should have been a fairly typical event in her life: attractive woman flirting with not–George Clooney actor. But it wasn't, which leads to the question:

Why Didn't Jane Date?
1. She was busy.
2. She didn't meet anyone interesting or attractive.
3. She was getting to be thirty-seven.
4. She couldn't bring herself to bars, singles events, or dating services.
5. She didn't really care enough.

6. She didn't feel attractive enough to compete in today's market.
7. She didn't have the energy.
8. She had enough love in her life already.
9. She didn't want to shave her legs in winter.
10. She wasn't not dating; she was just in a dry spell.

All these sentences were true, but she knew that they didn't really answer the dating question. Jane had dated in the past. Not much in high school. She was reluctant to bring boys home to her bullying older brothers. But in college, she had freedom. And with freedom came everything she thought she wanted.

She was happy dating in college. She was. Okay, she found that she didn't love dating lots of boys. She didn't love dating a boy for just a few weeks and then being friends. And she wasn't alone in this, she knew. Jane's Irish parents had taught her to prize loyalty. She needed to be loyal to someone.

So what? This was a good time, by anyone's measure. Jane was so young she still believed that life was supposed to be fair. After all, she studied hard and therefore got good grades. Proof positive. And if she continued to be a good and loyal person, Jane would eventually find the good and loyal man she deserved. And she did. His name was Sam.

Sam was twelve years older than Jane. He had returned to school after several years in the real world. He was one of so many T.A.s, working on his graduate degree and scoping out the undergrads. Sam was the T.A. for Jane's favorite professor, Dr. Barbara Ali. She taught Comparative Literature in Translation, which was listed in the course catalog by its smirk-inducing acronym. The course examined great works of literature that had been translated from French into English. Sam would read the text in the original French, and Dr. Ali would pretend to swoon over his accent. He would bow graciously. Jane found his accent dreamy too. Not to mention his liquid eyes. Oooh.

Jane would sometimes monopolize the class, exploring the dark subtleties of Beckett. Sam seemed to appreciate that. Which meant that he wasn't shallow, right? Jane wouldn't have been loyal to a shallow man. She had her standards. She and Sam fell in love.

They never even discussed their plans for life after Jane's graduation. It was assumed that she would move in with Sam. For the most part, he seemed happy about this. They fought about stupid things. He was a little controlling, a little superior, a little high-handed when he explained things to her that didn't need explaining, and what did he think she was, an idiot?

Jane had whole weekends where these flaws were the tragic center of her life. "My boyfriend thinks he's the boss! Oh! Whatever shall I do?"

And then they'd make up. Sam would apologize and resolve to be more of a partner. She'd resolve to be more of a boss. He knew that it was too late to change their dynamic. He'd read enough French literature to know that his positive electrons and her negative ones would be drawn together like this forever. And it wasn't so bad. In fact, the more they did this dance, the gentler, more loving their steps became. They were together. Deserving. Lucky. Happy.

Sam had always been a bit of a geek. A little clumsy, a little book-ish. This was Jane's insurance policy against other women. They never made plays for the guy who dropped his fork. Dropped it twice. And hit his head when he tried to retrieve it. So many beautiful women didn't look past that to find the man who had so much patience. Who cooked. Who folded laundry with so much love. Who said things like, "Jane, you look so gorgeous first thing in the morning," and meant it. Who held her hand on their first date and never wanted to let go. It was easy to be loyal to Sam. Bossy Sam. Sweet Sam. Geeky Sam. Sam.

Then Sam got sick, and her loyalty became a measure of her character. He was diagnosed with amyotrophic lateral sclerosis, also known as ALS, but more popularly referred to as Lou Gehrig's disease.

The day they got the diagnosis, Jane went after information. Knowledge is power, she told herself. Get some power. She searched and researched. But Sam retreated. Like a dog, he circled the floor and looked for a place to die. He would never finish his doctoral thesis. He would never marry Jane—not in a wheelchair. He would never have children. Instead, he would drool, shit in his pants, and die. That was how he put it.

Sam never changed his mind about it. He didn't want to fight. He had no response when Jane brought him papers that studied elevated protein levels in ALS patients.

"But I think they're really on to something here."

He had no faith in thrombopoietin.

"I know it's still new, but look at these first studies. I mean, if they start clinical trials here in New York, you should definitely be part of it. You should."

She purchased a T-shirt that said COVERING ALL BASES WITH THE ALS ASSOCIATION. His motor skills were declining badly, but he still managed to give her the finger.

Jane met her neighbor, Ray, several times at the mailboxes. They had a very good nod-and-smile relationship. Years later, he would reveal that he referred to her as Tired Girl. One day, Ray knocked on the door and offered Jane a large piece of fudge, shaped like a heart. It had been part of the press packet for a show entitled *Love Is Bullshit*. It was a musical revue, and Ray hated it. He was also avoiding chocolate, in an effort to regain his lost boyish figure. And he supposed that Tired Girl could use some chocolate. She ate it and cried, despite her best efforts to do neither.

"Are you tired, honey?" he asked tentatively.

"Oh, God. So tired. So, so tired."

Ray suggested that Jane get some real help. He was right. And soon, Sam's mother moved in with them. She provided the real help Jane needed—she cooked, cleaned, shopped for groceries, and monitored medications. Jane worked in a word processing center from midnight to 7 A.M., the graveyard shift, and spent her days with Sam.

His mother, Kaye, was stoic and a bit bossy. So he came by it honestly. Kaye didn't complain, at least not openly. She didn't like New York, though. That was clear.

Jane would finish her seven hours of typing numbers onto a computer screen and squint at the rising sun as she rode home. But she stopped at the deli to pick up more juice before she came home. Wait. Maybe she needed bagels too. Maybe she should try that nice breakfast sandwich that Ray liked. She was stalling. She didn't want to go back to Sam and the sickroom. And that was a horribly disloyal thought, which prompted her to rush back to her apartment.

"Do you want more juice, hon?" she asked. "I picked up some of that white grape juice at the deli. You like that stuff, don't you?"

He spelled out "No" on his magnetic letter board.

Jane didn't want to hate him. She didn't like feeling angry at him—it was so disloyal. So she just plain put it away. Her resentment went into storage. She modeled Kaye's stoicism and even tried to do her one better.

It took Sam a long time to die, which surprised everyone because he wanted it so. Jane cried and Kaye cried, and the funeral was as sad and beautiful as they both hoped it would be. That was all due to Ray. He knew that funerals were theater, and he knew theater. He put together a catharsis, in quiet good taste. And then Kaye went back to her husband in Indiana.

Jane switched to the day shift in the word processing department. She liked the technology. It was logical and fair. She took classes to move up and on and out to a job at a law firm. She even went to a party at Ray's. A Breakup Party. This was Ray's festive way of sailing through heartbreak and fear. He cackled about his ex, "He put my copy of *Breakfast of Champions* away with the cookbooks!" Ray reenacted his ex's Perfected Precision Shaving to the delight of the party guests.

Jane stayed for a while, but it was too loud and bright. She slipped out the door. Ray followed her upstairs and told her to come back downstairs immediately.

"You've *got* to meet my friend Gerald. He's a director, and he's doing really well." How could such a kind and sensitive man try to fix her up so quickly after Sam? She reached for her flannel pajamas.

"Jane! It's not a fix up. It's a fixer-upper. An apartment. Downtown. He's leaving the city to go work in regional theater. The place needs tons of repairs and gallons of paint, but you're a visionary. And if you don't grab this place, I'll never forgive you."

Jane dropped the flannel. A month later, she moved in to a total fixer-upper apartment, closer to Wall Street, where she learned how to fix up. As she sanded and spackled, she thought about Sam. She turned him back into the geeky, sweet, but occasionally bossy Sam that she loved. He deserved it. She needed it. It was only fair.

It took more than a year, but she started dating again. She met a new lawyer at the firm where she worked. He was handsome and polished, and Jane just had to experience a date with him. She also had to experience sex again, and men who were verbal and self-sufficient. She fell for Dean. He took her to trendy nightspots, Martha's Vineyard, and bought her a bracelet at Tiffany's.

Jane thought that she had outgrown her youthful belief that life was fair. Didn't Sam's death teach her that and so much more? And yet, Dean felt like her reward for endurance and loyalty. He tried to write her a love poem. After four months of steady dates, he told her that she was his soul mate, and she rejoiced for days. Until he phoned her at 2 A.M. on a Wednesday night/Thursday morning and told her that she was rushing him, she was crowding him, she needed to back off.

She said she would, although she didn't know how. What had she done wrong? She racked her brain. Dean stopped calling. Jane was lost and afraid. Was she no longer his soul mate? He actively avoided her at the firm's elevator banks. It was like bad high school.

Finally, he e-mailed her:

To: howej@ashlandremnick.com
From: restond@ashlandremnick.com
Subject: boundaries

Jane,

I know this may seem cold, but I have to do it this way. We can't see each other any longer, effective immediately.

You seem like a good person, but you can't rush me into a relationship like this. It's not right. We're not right for each other. We're wrong.

Good luck in all your future endeavors.

Dean

The message was so wrong, so excruciatingly wrong, so obviously wrong Jane wanted to slide out of her skin. She quit her job. She drank. She rehearsed pithy replies to Dean, none of which were pithy enough, all of which were too long.

Jane remained underground until she ran out of money. She emerged from the dark and found a job at Argenti, where she worked at the Helpless Desk and resolved "user issues." She kept taking classes, and she worked conscientiously to keep up with the Wonderland changes in technology. She moved up. Promoted to associate, then senior associate, and then vice president, managing her own team.

Jane still dated a little, after she recovered from Dean. In her spare time, she took photography classes at the New School. She met some perfectly nice men there. She suspected that some of them took the class specifically to meet women, and what was wrong with that? So she dated them. But nothing stuck. Nothing worth e-mailing home about. After all, she was busy. She didn't meet anyone interesting or attractive. She was getting to be thirty-seven. She couldn't bring herself to bars, singles events, or dating services. She didn't really care enough. She didn't feel attractive enough to compete in today's market. She didn't have the energy. She had enough love in her life already. She didn't want to shave her legs in winter. She wasn't not dating; she was just in a dry spell.

And That's Why Jane Wasn't Dating.

She was pretty much the definition of Fine, except for that ache that told her something was missing. And don't count how she always cried on Sam's birthday. That was different. Jane's philosophy was: No one gets everything, at least not all at once. Jane had had a great love, and now it was over. Now she had exhilarating work, witty friends, reliable health, no money worries, and an apartment that caused more than a little envy. And isn't that a lot to have all at once?

· · ·

The week had a roller-coaster-climbing-the-big-scary-hill feeling. Something's coming, something big. Saturday morning, Jane located the Choosing Single Motherhood meeting place in a school basement in SoHo. The meeting was scheduled for ten, and Jane was early. She didn't like looking so eager, but too late for that. She was eager. She was curious. She was not afraid, and that made no sense at all.

Jane signed in and took some (thank you!) reference material. By the time she looked up from the table of books, resources, and lists of Web sites to investigate, dozens of women had formed a large circle of folding chairs. There were at least three babies and a gaggle of toddlers. A honey-voiced woman with two children stepped up and called the meeting to order. Jane found a chair and felt all momentous.

"Hi. And welcome to all of you new ladies. This is *Choosing Single Motherhood*. This is *not* the *Narc-Anon meeting*. We switched *places* with them because we needed more *room*. So, if you're looking for *Narc-Anon*, you need to go to the *third* floor, *room H*. Okay?"

A handful of women exited quietly, along with one very baffled-looking man.

"Okay, and in case you didn't know, this afternoon we'll be having a *Thinker's Workshop*. It's completely full. But if you're a *Thinker,* and you want to go to a *Thinker's Workshop,* just let me know. I'll give you the *schedule* of the *next* ones."

Following her announcements, the circle performed introductions that consisted of name and status: Mom, Pregnant, Trying (to get pregnant), Adopting, or Thinking. Jane soon learned that if you're not sure about anything, that means you're Thinking.

The host of the meeting had the large group break into smaller groups, based on their status as Mom/Pregnant/Trying/Adopting. The women rose obediently and shifted their metal chairs into smaller circles. Jane felt stuck to her chair, since there was no group for the Thinkers. So she made the most logical choice: She joined the Trying group, already in progress.

"So this guy walks in and he's gorgeous, and I do mean perfect! He says, 'Is this the allergy clinic?' And the nurse giggles a little bit because he's so damn gorgeous, and she says, 'Sir, this is a sperm bank.' And he blushes like a virgin, I'm telling you! And he has trouble leaving. I mean he starts to go through a door *where the guys go to do it,* and he blushes even more, if you can believe it. And he finally finds his way out, and all I want to do is say, 'Hey you! You wanna be a daddy? No strings attached! And we don't need a sperm bank—we can do it the old-fashioned way!' "

The women giggled. Jane was the youngest woman in the room. She couldn't help but notice it.

"Seriously, though. My cousin still has leftovers from a fabulous donor, if anyone wants any. I can get you the details."

A red-faced woman said, "I can't take these hormone shots much longer. They're making me crazy. Do we really understand what we're shooting into our thighs? Am I going to get cancer from this?"

There was a chorus of Nos and Don't Even Say Thats.

"I'm so frustrated. I'm losing hope. I want a baby so much. And every month, I go to Dr. Laskin and I say, 'Get me pregnant, Doc,' and every month I get my period again. What am I doing wrong?"

The red-faced woman had been trying to get pregnant by artificial insemination for seven months. She was about to give up, and was considering IVF—in vitro fertilization. The woman had been doing her research, so Jane paid close attention.

"Meanwhile, my mother keeps saying, 'Isn't it funny? I got pregnant if your father just looked at me funny. If you're having trouble, you didn't get it from me.' And my sister's due in a month, and I swear to God I'm happy for her. It's just . . . Anyway. My insurance will only cover three tries on IVF. I've already spent, oh, let's see, about twenty-five or twenty-six thousand dollars trying to get pregnant. The IVF is gonna be another twelve thousand, easy. This kid'll never get to college. If the kid ever gets born, that is."

Jane didn't know what to expect from this CSM meeting, but her nonexpectation had a pink and cheery hue. This was not it.

The red-faced woman accepted comfort and tissues from the group. She lasered in on Jane.

"How old are you?"

"I'm thirty-six. I'll be thirty-seven next—"

"Don't wait. Don't wait until it's too late. That's what I did. And now I'll probably never get pregnant. I'll go bankrupt and still have no baby to show for it!"

She folded her body over and sobbed. This time, she accepted no comfort.

The woman with the extra sperm tearfully related the story of her second miscarriage, and Jane started to panic. She could handle sobbing, and she knew about grief. But so many of these sentences scraped against her skin. She was in the wrong place. Wrong place. Wrong place.

"Remember," said the optimist in the group, "Susan Sarandon had babies when she was in her forties. So can we."

"Fuck Susan Sarandon," said the red-faced woman.

"Look, this is reality," someone was saying to Jane. "I'm about to hit my two-year anniversary of trying to get pregnant. So far, I've been through about a dozen inseminations, I've shot myself up with God knows what medications, I've been through hyper-stimulations, PCOS testing, I had to go on the Atkins diet, and I had a laparoscopy for endometriosis. But I draw the line at IVF. No way."

"Hey! A lot of good people have used IVF, and they have beautiful families to show for it. Who are you to judge?" shouted red-faced woman.

Wrong place. Wrong place. Get out. Leave. Was a baby a prize? Was she willing to put her body through all this? What was she doing here? Jane rose and wandered through the room. She needed quiet now, but the room was noisy and felt more and more like the school cafeteria it really wanted to be. Jane should have left the noisy room and gathered her thoughts.

Instead, she sat sideways in the first empty seat she found and kept herself quiet. The quest for pregnancy was a logical topic here, so Jane couldn't justify her desire to escape. She had been so stupid: All her research had focused on raising children with just one parent. She had been thinking about children, but had forgotten about pregnancy. She was stupidly surprised at the high jump of conception, the dangers along the way, the trauma of birth, the obstacles against recovery. And that was the short list.

"And this is my daughter."

Jane was sitting sideways in an extra seat in the Adopting circle. A petite woman in the chair next to her held up a snapshot of a three-year-old girl in a red bathing suit. The little girl was in midair, arms outstretched, mouth grinning. Nice shot. The little girl was Chinese.

The photo went around from person to person, and when it was handed to Jane, she turned her body around. The glossy paper vibrated with happiness. The petite woman, who was Italian by heritage, looked like her daughter, which made no sense to Jane at all. But there it was.

The petite woman was a lawyer, and her name was Maria. She handed out carefully formatted documents that described the process of adopting from China, in moderate detail. Jane started reading her packet before she finished handing over the balance to the rest of the circle.

She didn't look up to see who said, "Did you see that thing on the news last night? The couple who adopted that little boy when he was a baby and three years later the mother changed her mind and wanted him back? She won. They have to give him up."

Various women in the group said:

"Oh, God. That poor kid. Those poor parents. Oh, God."

After the Adopting group paid their respects to the Poor Family, Jane tried to steer them back over to China.

"You're single and they let you adopt?"

But the petite woman wasn't listening to Jane. She was on her cell phone, saying, "Mom. She's not allowed to have more than two cookies. Mom? Mom! Please don't!"

"I need some air," said Jane.

Images and ideas camped around her in no orderly fashion: sperm banks, IVF, adoption, custody battles, labor breathing, miscarriage, postpartum depression, China, breast-feeding, ovarian cysts, and red bathing suits.

Jane was stuck on the image of red bathing suits. The picture stayed in her head. She went back inside to find the petite woman who was the mother of Little Red Bathing Suit, but when she returned to the Adopting circle, the woman was gone.

"Where did she go?" Jane asked. The women explained that the petite woman had to go home and intercept Grandma's cookie bonanza, and doesn't that sound like the most fun ever? And who wouldn't love to do that?

The host of the meeting was standing at the center, announcing that the meeting was *over*, so would everyone please return their *chairs* to the *wall*. The women obeyed, but continued the conversations that had begun in their circles.

"I want to make Halloween costumes," said someone who would turn out to be named Karen. "I want to read bedtime stories and set limits and go to school plays and find out how to get chocolate ice cream out of natural fibers," she said as she folded her own chair and Jane's.

Karen was tall, with Lucy-red hair and an Irish complexion. She had an alertness, an energy that could have passed for a caffeine buzz. She wore a royal blue crinkly cotton sundress and comfortable sandals. Her voice was both vibrant and calm. She was snacking on sunflower seeds. She was up. She was awake. She had answers for Jane, who really wanted to talk to the petite woman.

"I really wanted to talk to that woman, Maria. Damn. I didn't see her leave."

"She's coming back. Look, why don't you go to the Thinker's Workshop? She's one of the speakers there. You can ask her anything you want."

"It's all full. I'll have to wait for the next—"

"Oh, you can have my spot. I don't need it. I'm done thinking. I've made up my mind. I'm going to adopt from China."

"Just like that? Don't you want to think about it a little?"

"I've thought about this for eight years and one hour. I'm going to the FCC meeting next week to find out how to get started."

The Federal Communications Commission? This was getting weird.

"Families with Children from China," Karen replied to the confused look on Jane's face. Jane wrote down the FCC meeting details as Karen asked, "Do you want to go to the Thinker's Workshop?"

"Yes. When is it?"

"Now."

Jesus, this was a little overwhelming. Did Jane have the mental energy for another noisy room full of weeping infertile career women? Here goes. She promised herself that she would sit near the door, and she could always leave.

Karen seemed to be reading Jane's mind.

"Look, you can go to the workshop or leave if it's not for you. You're just trying to find things out, right? I'm a little older than you. Okay, maybe I'm a lot older than you. For me, I know I have to take this leap now or I'll spend my golden years all bitter with regret. I'm ready to do this. I hope. Go, find out what you want."

. . .

Jane followed the parade of six Thinkers three blocks west and two blocks north to the office of a psychotherapist. The Thinker's Workshop was a much smaller gathering in a much smaller room. The Thinkers were joined by three actual moms, including Maria, the petite mother of Little Red Bathing Suit. It was quiet and almost claustrophobic. It felt like an intervention.

The psychotherapist hosted the workshop. A single mother herself, she had used donor insemination to conceive her son, who was now a teenager. Along the way, she founded Choosing Single Motherhood.

"If you're going to survive as a single mother, you need to be organized," she instructed. Jane was almost puffing out her chest. What a promising start.

"And, in my opinion, you need to have a few things in place."

Oh, boy! She was about to recite a list! What a good sign.

1. Financial stability: You need to pay off your debts, if you can, and have some kind of cushion, in case of emergencies.
   (Jane: check! She made a good living, and had zero debt. So far, so good.)
2. Career goals met: Maybe not all of them, but some of them. Because, for the first three years, you're not doing nothin' but taking care of your baby.
   (Jane: check! She had been promoted; she was in a good place for a few years. Yeah. Check on this. Two for two.)

3. A father figure: A brother, uncle, friend, someone who can fill that gap, and believe me, it's there. It's always there.
(Jane: check? Were her brothers a good answer here? Maybe. She'd have to see how they react. And then there's Dad, and her good pal Ray. If this was a test, Jane was passing.)

After the opening niceties, each of the guest speaker moms told her story. Mom #1 had an unplanned pregnancy that resulted in her delightful, chubby baby boy (photos, coos, aww). The older Thinkers in the room rolled their eyes. Accidental pregnancy, give me a break. The mom had sued her now ex-boyfriend for support and lived happilyish ever after on Long Island. She worked part-time now that her son was in school.

Mom #2 had endured the painful and expensive infertility treatments that had tortured the Trying circle. After eight months, she got pregnant and had her delightful, chubby baby boy (photos, coos, aww). She had a tough delivery, a C-section that refused to close for an extended period of time. But eventually she recovered and returned to work. She spent several minutes describing the importance of having a good nanny and a nanny cam. A topic Jane had researched!

At last, the group turned to Mom #3 and her adoption story. And Jane got to ask, "You're single and they let you adopt?"

Yes, they did. Each adoption agency is allowed a certain number of single parents.

"How do you know if you qualify to adopt?"

There are a few things that you must have: a steady job, a decent income, a home, no criminal record, and the ability to handle the paperwork involved in international adoption.

Most of the Thinkers wanted to know about Mom #2's infertility treatments, why she had a C-section, and how she chose her sperm donor. But Jane was not the only one drawn to Mom #3's story. There was a woman who would turn out to be named Teresa. She was wearing a pencil skirt, a silk blouse, panty hose, and heels. Rather buttoned-up for a Saturday, in Jane's view. Teresa had cropped, light brown hair and looked like old money. The pearls were probably real, and her teeth were perfect. She sounded authoritative, and the muscles in her face were taut. But Jane saw the spark of fear and worry in her eyes. That was the only spot where Teresa couldn't stop it from showing. She kept her legs crossed at the ankle.

As the group talked about hormone levels, Teresa said, "Look. I have a very senior position in the public relations industry. I can't just start . . . blossoming."

"But how can you miss out on creating life—the greatest experience of all time?" cried one of the Thinkers. This was someone who felt certain that her C-section would close properly, no problem.

Teresa explained: "I lived with Victor for twelve years. He and I started the firm together. We're partners. Everyone there knows about us. Way back then, he told me he didn't want to have children. Neither did I. But then something changed. Call it the biological clock, or call it what you will, something changed. I walked around feeling empty, and nothing could fill me up—not work, not friends, not shoes. I was empty because I needed to give . . . I don't really know what I'm saying here. Let's try again. When I met Victor, I was thirty. When I turned forty-two, I told him that I wanted to have a child. He packed his bags and moved out."

Frightened silence from the Thinkers and the Moms.

"Which is fine, because it's a great apartment, and now it's mine and I'm going to sell it for a pile of money. But everyone at work knows that we split up. And our clients know it too. We still work together, for the time being, anyway. And we're okay. We're mature adults. But I can't burst into the office with a big belly and milky breasts and say, 'Guess what?' " I can't. It's simply out of the question."

She turned to Maria.

"I never thought of adopting from China. I had thought, maybe

Russia. Maybe get a child who looks like me. But who cares about that? How can I find out more about China adoption? Oh. And I think this young lady wants to know too." She nodded toward Jane.

Jane nodded and said, "Please."

. . .

After all that Thinking about Choosing Single Motherhood, Jane joined Ray for an evening of *Alice in Wonderland* staged in a parking lot, which he was reviewing for *Big Apple Parent* magazine. In this version, a grown-up Alice was reading the story to her little girl. But the story came to life and the characters kidnapped mother and daughter and took them to Wonderland. Mother Alice had to stand up to the Red Queen in order to win her daughter and their freedom. Mother Alice won, of course, but then it all turned out to be a dream . . . or was it? The little girl fell asleep as the Cheshire Cat's neon grin glowed above her bed. Blackout. Applause.

The cast included several young children, because everybody works in this town. And Jane couldn't help wondering if the kids were staying up too late.

After the show, Jane and Ray had their traditional postmortem martini. Ray found the show creative, but too predictable. The child actors annoyed him.

"They're so trained and so cute in that 'sing out, Louise!' way. I can't stand it. As soon as I see that there are children in the cast, I can feel a black cloud spreading from the back of my head to the front. And did you see the fake crying that little girl was doing? She probably works her own mother better than that."

Jane put down her drink and said, "I've seen you around kids. I thought you liked them. Didn't you say you liked them?" Jane's voice was a few notes too high.

"I like real kids. I don't like professionals."

"There's a difference?"

"Jane. Where were you tonight?"

As a rule, Jane could tell Ray anything. He had been by her side through Sam, through Dean, and through a (mutual) case of food poisoning. She had helped him through a distressing number of bad boyfriends, so there was no reason not to tell Ray.

Reasons to Tell Ray About Doing Something That Will Result in Single Motherhood:
1. It was taking up two-thirds of her thought space, and so it was too hard to talk around.
2. He was a smart man who lived in the real, if theatrical, world. She might have a more coherent discussion with him than with the Infertile Career Women.
3. Talking about it with Ray would make it real.

Reasons Not to Tell Ray:
1. Talking about it with Ray would make it real.

"Ray. I did something crazy today."
"Wow. Who did you sleep with?"
"No one. Although I might have to. Or not."
She told him everything from the baby haunting to the red bathing suit, and she got sort of catty about the women and their outfits. She could do that with Ray.

Ray's breathing changed. It became very even, very serious. She couldn't read his face, but she was longing for his judgment. She started to babble.

"And I'm *still* seeing babies everywhere. And there's this one baby in my neighborhood. He always seems to have the sun right behind his head. I can hardly stand to look at him—he's so dazzling. I don't know how his mother does it. And out of nowhere, I met this guy and he asked me out. And let's be honest here: When's the last time that happened? So, what's going on here? Maybe . . . maybe everything just falls into place like that. Okay, the guy's an actor, but still. Maybe you pay attention to everything else and then, all of a sudden, you meet a guy and you make babies and it all just happens.

Maybe that's what all these signs are trying to tell me. Oh, God, Ray, please say something."

"Stop."

Stop talking? Stop going down this motherhood path? Stop what?

"Stop looking for signs. That's so crazy-Irish of you. You're too smart to be superstitious."

"I know. But am I crazy to want a baby? To even think about it? And is it crazy that I'm being haunted by babies like this?"

He took entirely too long to answer.

"Well," he said with a sigh. "Don't you think it's about time?"

Time meaning her age? Her biological clock? "Time for what?"

"Relax. I mean, you always had a mothering thing going on. Jesus, drink your martini and get your shoulders out of your ears. Do you need my permission to have a baby?"

"No." She didn't sound convinced. He knew what she wanted.

"Here's what I think: lucky baby. What a lucky baby to have you for a mom."

Her shoulders relaxed. All this stuff was now on the table. She could have a whole conversation with Ray. Once again, he was all caught up and knew everything about her.

"But—please don't rush this Dick-Richard actor guy down the aisle and into the delivery room until I've had a chance to check him out."

She promised. "What if I have to do this alone?"

"If anyone can, you can." Was he keeping his real worries to himself for tonight? Did Jane look a little too vulnerable?

"My mother will freak." Jane brought that one up.

"So? You're almost forty, Jane." Ouch. "You don't need her permission."

"I don't need her to freak, either."

Ray ordered another round and said, "Once she sees that sweet little baby in your arms, she'll melt like ice cream and say, 'my grandbaby!' and you guys will be fine. Her freak-out—if it happens—will be temporary."

The martinis arrived, and Ray raised his glass. "To Mama Jane." And they drank.

"What's wrong?" Jane asked. She'd caught a small bite of sadness Ray was sure no one could see. "Come on, Ray. Let's do you now. What is it?"

"Josh. He said an Awful Thing. He's twenty-five years old, but he's a musician, so that gives him the right to act like he's fifteen. I think I don't like him anymore."

He gulped his martini and said, "Josh says I'm too old to be a musician."

Except for Sondheim musicals, Jane had never seen Ray show any special affection for music. Why was this the Awful Thing? Ray illustrated his pain with a battered copy of *The Village Voice*.

"Look. See the musician ads? There's an age limit: twenty-eight. After that, you can't even try to join any of these bands. Twenty-eight. I'm a decade too old."

"But you don't want to be a musician, do you? Why did he even bring it up?"

"To be mean. I have to break up with him. He's too mean."

Jane hugged Ray, who signaled over her shoulder for another round of martinis.

"Don't play with mean boys. Okay?"

"Yes, Mama Jane. Oh, my God. You're going to be a mother. A *mother*."

"You're scaring me."

"Too bad. Right now, we need to do me. What am *I* going to be?"

Jane had no answer, and she still held a half-full or half-empty martini glass when the next round appeared before them.

"I'm just some guy. I write about what other people do. I date mean men. I have good real estate karma, and I can make a perfect omelet. But what am I going to be when I grow up?"

"Not a musician. We've established that."

There were muscles just behind his face that Ray could not control when he was deeply sad. He could only change the subject.

"And not an actor. And you! Don't put your daughter on the stage, Ms. Howe. What did you think of those weird little Tweedle Dum and Tweedle Dee kids? Why exactly were they so icky?"

As they talked about the play, Jane's impending motherhood became just another piece of the landscape. And that was enormously comforting.

Chapter Three

Sunday morning, Jane awoke and shouted, "Dip! Cheese!"

She was out the door in less than twelve minutes, sprinting to Mulberry Street for That Cheese and the ingredients for That Dip. No time to make it at home, she would prepare the dip at her parents' house and claim that she wanted to hang out with them in the kitchen and bond. And who were they to say that she didn't want that?

She knew the Port Authority bus schedule by heart. She did her best bob and weave through the crowd and collapsed into a smelly bus full of unhappy people. The Bus of Fools. The Bus of the Damned. En route to . . . New Jersey.

For two minutes, she feared that she had forgotten her mother's birthday gift, but she hadn't. There it was: a handmade wood carving of the Gaelic word *Failte,* which means "welcome." The letters were surrounded by Celtic swirls and designs.

Howard and Betty Howe still lived in the house where they had raised their four children. The top floor was shut off, notorious for losing heat to the outside world. Betty had recently redecorated the downstairs in pink and blue pastel stripes. It looked like an ice cream parlor.

When it was completed, she'd declared, "I can't wait to get started on our bedroom!" and Howard had shuddered but made no protest.

Jane kissed her mother hello and held up her offerings: dip, cheese, and a present. Mom pushed the gift aside without opening it.

"I don't need anything. I'm old. I'm done," she said at every birthday. She fingered a ringlet of her daughter's hair, absently, as she had done since Jane had hair. She related the tale of Jane's birth—so traumatic that "I had to stay in the hospital for nine days. I missed my own birthday. And all the doctors thought I was faking it. Just hiding from those crazy boys at home. But men don't know. They'll never know what we go through. Oh, Janie, Janie, Janie. You didn't bring a date, did you? For some reason, I thought you were bringing someone."

"And I did. Mom, this is my friend Harvey. Harvey, meet Betty Howe."

"I love *Harvey*. And don't make fun of Jimmy Stewart. It's un-American. By the way, false alarm. Kitty's not pregnant. I think she's starting menopause. And not a moment too soon."

Outside, brothers Neil and Kevin were laughing and drinking beer (already) as they fired up the grill. The backyard still had the same bald spots, rocks, and bumps, but a new generation of children now skidded over it all.

"Hey, Janie!" Kevin waved and tended the hot coals of his grill.

"Hi, Aunt Janie! What did you bring me?" asked Kevin's seven-year-old son. He and his six-year-old sister, five-year-old brother, and four-year-old cousin swarmed Jane. The sixteen-month-old toddled happily to her aunt.

"Let me see. I brought you . . . a *million dollars!* No. No, that's not it. I brought you . . . bubble pans!"

The children grabbed at the frying pan–sized bubble wands. Soon the backyard resembled some lunatic Lawrence Welk set.

"Don't get bubbles on the burgers!" shouted Kevin. "I'm not eating soap burgers!"

This prompted the children to bring the bubbles much closer to the burgers. Kevin went red, and his voice took on a jazz singer growl.

"I said, no!"

"Oh, now! Eating soap doesn't hurt you, Kevin," Mom volunteered. "It cleans your intestines."

"Oh, God, Mother!" Kevin exclaimed as he chased after children.

"You used to eat leaves!" she called after him, but he wasn't listening. Besides, she brought up that childhood tale whenever she wanted to overpower him as a parent. It had yet to work, but his mother believed in endurance.

"Right from that tree!" she added. Neil's wife, Linda, changed the subject. "The baby needs a nap," she said as she scooped up her toddling girl.

Betty sighed. "And that's why she doesn't sleep at night. Too many naps."

"There's my girl! There's my Calamity Jane!"

Howard Howe gave his daughter a gentle hug and kiss.

"Did you bring that cheese? I'm not supposed to have any, but this is a special occasion. The doctors will just have to zip their lips today."

The lazy Susan on the kitchen table was a pharmaceutical stockpile. If a 37-year-old was dizzied by it, how did the 37-year-old's parents handle it? Heart, blood pressure, blood sugar—were human bodies supposed to last this long?

"Janie, I bought some candy for the kids. I think it's in the living room," Betty said as she nudged Jane out of the kitchen.

That's where Janie found seven one-pound bags of mini candy bars. Underneath them was a stack of mail on one of the many decorative tables in the living room.

"Ma. You've got mail in here. It looks like birthday cards. Aren't you going to open them?"

"Bring in the candy."

Howard chimed in, "Never mind the candy. Where's that cheese?"

Betty had a pound of candy for each child, plus one "for a little snacking." Betty was diabetic.

"Mom. This is too much candy—for them and for you. Come on. What did the doctor say?"

"Howard, look at this." Betty ignored Jane and opened a refrigerator that was about to burst with too much food. A Land of Plenty image.

"I bought all this extra food—a whole deli platter—to go with the burgers and dogs. Why? Because, for some reason, I thought Janie was bringing a date. But Janie didn't bring a date. If only Janie had a date for the party. Someone to eat all this food. Right, Howard?"

"So my date was supposed to eat a whole deli platter? I've never dated a sumo wrestler, Mom."

Jane's mom usually didn't even mention her date-free status. In fact, she usually seemed so complacent about Jane's impending spinsterhood that Jane could manage to work up feeling hurt by all that apathy. She knew perfectly well that Jane wasn't bringing a date.

"Guess I'll have to fix this. As usual" was Betty's exit line.

Why was Mom smiling when she left? And where did she go? Jane took a Lamaze breath and went back to making That Dip. She had started the horrible bus ride contemplating telling her parents about Choosing Single Motherhood. By the time the bus emerged from the Lincoln Tunnel, she knew she wouldn't do it. Not today. Not yet.

She went outside and played Tickle Tiger with her nieces and nephews. This complex game involved chasing them, roaring, and tickling whomever she managed to catch. It was a favorite.

The oldest grandchild, Dylan, was sitting by himself and sulking.

His chin was covered with a large gauze bandage. He dangled his skinny legs from a lawn chair and watched the grass grow.

"Okay, time out! The Tickle Tiger needs a time out!"

"Awwww!"

And Jane collapsed on the grass next to Dylan. She laid down and looked up at him. He switched his gaze to watch clouds roll by. He let out a deafening sigh.

"What happened, Dyl?"

"Nothing."

It took several tries before he revealed that he had fallen off his bike and skidded along the curb chin first for a short stretch. He now had four stitches beneath all that gauze.

"Does it hurt?"

"Yes! And Mom doesn't think so, *But it does! It does hurt!*"

Jane's sister-in-law shrugged her shoulders from across the yard.

"You can probably have some aspirin, Dyl. That'll help a little. The stitches are really new, but they'll be out soon and they won't hurt anymore."

"Aunt Janie! Don't you even get it? Hello! I'm switching to my new school Monday. Like, *this* Monday? And I'm gonna walk in with this big white bandage on my chin and look like the world's biggest loser!"

His mom shouted from across the yard, "Oh, you are not!"

"You don't know anything!" Dylan was eleven years old, and it showed.

Jane couldn't bear to leave him like this. She had to fix it. Should mothers fix everything? Probably not, but Aunt Jane was going to fix this.

"Well. You know what you do? You lie."

"I can't lie—it'll be right there! On my chin!"

"No, no, no. You lie about how it got there. You tell them you got it when three guys jumped you in Chicago. One of them had a knife. But you got the others."

He paused.

"No one will believe Chicago."

"Okay. You tell me. What will they believe?"

It didn't take him long.

"That it's from playing hockey. A big hockey fight, and I won. It'll show that I'm tough and I'm good at sports."

Dylan came up with three more Scar Stories and was having trouble choosing among them. Aunt Janie assured him that he'd use them all eventually.

"This'll be your Harrison Ford scar, Dylan. You can make up zillions of stories to explain it, and they'll all make you look tough."

Dylan was about to have a sweet, hugging, thank-you moment when he noticed that the other kids had put down the bubble pans.

"My turn!" he shouted and flew into the kid-center of the yard.

"Jane!" shouted her mother. "Can you help us bring stuff out?"

Of course she could. She headed into the kitchen and found trays full of paper goods, every condiment known to the eastern seaboard, and the infamous deli platter.

"Can you go get the sugar bowl? I left it in the living room."

Of course she could. Jane didn't question why the sugar bowl was in the living room, or why a diabetic woman would be using a sugar bowl there or anywhere. She retrieved it, along with the unopened birthday cards.

"Here. I'll bring these out with—"

"Jane, this is Peter. Peter, you remember my daughter Jane, don't you?"

After thirty-seven years, this was the first time Betty had tried to fix her daughter up. Jane had no experience, no preparation. She stared. Her mouth fell open. She looked like a particularly stupid fish.

"Of course I do. Hi, Jane. Um, I'll carry the tray," said Peter. And, in a manly gesture, Peter lifted the heavy, condiment-laden supertray and brought it outside. Jane turned her mute gaze to her mother.

"Help him!" Betty urged.

"Who is he?"

Betty wrapped one of Jane's ringlets around a finger and calmly explained, "He's Peter. Peter Mandell." Betty searched Jane's face for a flicker of recognition, but Jane wasn't flickering. She was sure she had never met him before. Unless, of course, she had met him in—

"High school! He was in the class ahead of yours? Weren't you in AP Physics together? Or something like that? You were always so advanced. I figure you must have had some kind of class together."

Peter Mandell. AP English. Twenty years ago. Jane's appetite was gone.

"Mom. I haven't seen this guy in a couple of decades. I don't remember him. Why did you invite him?"

"His parents still live in that house on Albemarle."

"Why did you invite him?"

"He looks after his parents. He's so nice. When I saw him this morning, he was trying to figure out the trick windows. You know the little ones on the side? These old houses, I'm telling you. They should come with instructions, don't you think?"

Howard decided to help clarify things for Janie.

"Your mother had him over to dinner last week, and he was a very fine fellow. You should talk to him."

Betty disengaged from her daughter's hair and began rearranging napkins in a fan shape.

"Look, Janie, there's no harm talking to him. He works in the city. His mother makes it sound like he's doing pretty well. Where's the harm in talking to him? Worst thing that happens, you find a new friend. Do you have too many friends, Janie?"

"Mom, do you keep single men in your pocket in case of emergencies or extra deli platters?"

Betty looked up from her paper products.

"I wasn't planning to invite him—it was an impulse! You didn't bring a date, and I had all that food, and he was right there on his front porch, so it was like a sign. Like he's supposed to come to my party. *And* he's very, very, very nice. *And* he's good to his parents. But you're not being nice at all! He's outside and you're being rude. Go!"

Jane hesitated just long enough for Peter to return. He was back for more heavy lifting. He looked like he could handle it.

"Jane works at Argenti. Right in the thick of things," said Howard.

"No kidding. I work in the same building. I'm with Metro House."

"No kidding." Jane was trying to think scintillating thoughts, but the only thing that played in her head was "Oh, my God."

She managed to come out with "I'll get the napkins," and she headed out to the yard. The kids were having their burgers and hot dogs now, and her brothers had started singing. This mesmerized the kids and kept them in their seats long enough to finish a decent meal. The brothers were harmonizing on Betty's favorite song, "How High the Moon." Betty emerged from the kitchen, beaming with delight at her boys. She settled into a lawn chair. Their voices were similar, the harmonies perfect. Jane hugged the napkins and listened.

"Do you sing too?" asked Peter.

"Yes. I mean, I can."

"Why don't you do the next number? Do you take requests?"

Singing was the boys' province. Jane didn't sing at family functions. Come to think of it, Jane hadn't sung in a long time. She had no reason to.

"No, I don't want to crowd the boys. It's their show."

Peter turned out to be the fine fellow that Howard had claimed he was. A research analyst, very successful. Loved golf, which accounted for his tan and for the not-fake highlights in his sandy hair. She tried not to stare, but she needed to, if she was going to capture any kind of coherent memory of him in high school.

"You don't remember me, do you?" he asked.

"Of course I do. You're Peter. Peter Mandrell."

"Mandell."

"I suck."

"Burgers are ready! Grown-ups! Come and get 'em!" Dylan was shouting while he herded the grown-ups over to the table, as if he were a sheepdog. That done, he rallied the children for a game of tag. Grown-up dinner started with an awkward silence. Jane wished she were hungry.

"Did Peter tell you that he used to live in California?" Betty asked very energetically.

Peter smiled and said, "I used to live in California. Came back after my dad had a stroke. He's doing okay, but I just didn't like being so far away."

"Good children look after their parents. Peter's a good son."

"Except that I broke that trick window. That house may be charming, but it's falling down like a pup tent. I could spend the next two years trying to make all those repairs."

Aha! Jane found a conversational opening: fixer-uppers. She questioned him about his planned renovations. She offered advice based on her own experience renovating her apartment in Manhattan. Peter wanted to know where this wonderful space was located. As they narrowed down to her exact address, he laughed.

"I don't believe it. I live half a block away from you."

"I don't believe it."

Peter lived in the high-rise doorman building with the potted plants by the door, half a block away from Jane's prewar, walk-up, fixed-up apartment.

"Mom, did you know that?"

Betty shook her head and turned to Howard. "It's a sign," she whispered loudly enough for all to hear.

"Peter Mandell!" Jane shouted. The group stared and waited.

"Present."

"I remember you now. You played basketball. You were a total hotshot."

"I played basketball. With hotshot fantasies. And I'm afraid I don't remember what sports you played."

"Chess. And field hockey. And I ran the drama club. I directed *Our Town* the year that your team lost a big game. What was it, Pennwood High?"

"We lost a lot of games. We weren't a great team."

Betty smiled. This looked like success, right until Jane said, "You ruined my show."

"No way. I never did anything."

"You shaved your head."

Peter blushed as he remembered it. The team had vowed that they would beat Pennwood High, or they would all shave their heads. They lost. They shaved. Maybe that was why he wore his hair a little longer than corporate America dictated, Jane thought. He liked feeling a bit shaggy.

"How did my shaved head ruin your play?"

"It wasn't just you. All the men in Grover's Corner were bald. It was ridiculous. The audience couldn't stop laughing."

Jane's brothers were laughing. They remembered too, didn't they? The jerks. Jane knew it was stupid to get mad about something that happened twenty years ago, but did that stop her?

"Jane. Don't get mad about something that happened twenty years ago," said Peter. "Please."

"Even though it looked like Grover's Corner was next to a nuclear power plant." And with that, she eased into finding it funny, twenty years later. She tried to remember what Peter looked like without hair, but she only remembered him returning from summers at the beach, with hair as yellow as a Post-it note. If Jane had been a sensible girl, she would have had a crush on Peter in high school. Did he always have those dimples? They left parentheses around his mouth. Why did boys get such impossibly long eyelashes? Jane wondered. That's when she realized she was staring. She needed conversation items, and, hey, she could talk to her new neighbor about so many things, like: "the new Ethiopian restaurant" and how it was doing, or "that amazing store that sells chocolates and eyeglasses" that was doing very well.

And then Peter brought up "that children's store, the clothing place? They have shirts that cost more than mine, and I buy all of mine at the Barney's warehouse sale, so, hey, *I* can't even afford mine. Why do New York parents spend so much money on stupid things? Can a toddler really appreciate Betsey Johnson's sense of whimsy?"

There really was no escaping this baby haunting thing, was there? Peter went on to explain that he had overheard two mothers talking about how Betsey's sense of whimsy was conducive to language development. Suckers.

Jane had no defense for these foolish mothers, and she probably wouldn't have liked them if she met them. Still, she felt compelled to defend them. It wasn't easy.

"I guess, when you have kids, you can get caught up in any effort to help them. They may be suckers, but their motives are basically good."

Kevin and Neil pounced on the argument. After loyalty, Irish people love arguments. *Love* them.

"Janie-Painie, you know you're wrong. They're not helping their kids—they're pumping up their own self-image."

"We haven't even met these people, but we already know how shallow they are. Good for us." Jane should have backed down, joked it off, and changed the subject. Instead, she stood her shaky ground. Peter seemed impressed. Jane was misguided, but strong. He had no idea how true that might be.

"Are mealtimes always so lively around here?"

Neil answered for her. "Janie wouldn't know. She only visits under pain of guilt."

Betty shot him the Look. The one that warned him of airing family flaws in front of People. There are People here and they can hear you. Is that what you say around People? I don't think so.

Neil looked up and around. "Is that the baby? Did you guys hear the baby? I'll go check on her." Neil had a sixteen-month-old child who never slept for more than two hours at a pop, so Neil deserved some slack from the family. His wife usually made him get up at night, since she had the child all day. The baby was fast asleep that evening. Right up until Neil went off and—oh, God—woke his sleeping daughter when he shifted her into a more comfortable-looking position. Oops.

Kevin was older, warmer, friendlier. He sang the melodies, usually, while Neil harmonized above. Kevin had three children, and he insisted that his children all slept through the night within the first week. He and his wife, Kitty, were just naturals at parenting, what could they say? Some people just didn't get it. He felt sorry for Neil and his sleep deprivation. But he swore he couldn't identify.

"Janie-Painie, how's life in the big city? How do you stand it?"

This was intended as a compliment. He continued. "I never go to the city. I stay right here, right where I belong. Last time I was in the city was—"

It was Sam's memorial service. Please don't let him say it.

"God, I can't even remember how long it's been—"

Please don't let him say it.

"I think it was Sam's memorial service. And he's been gone, what, three, four years now?"

"Six."

And that's when Kevin figured out that Peter (People) was at the table, that he was some kind of fix-up for Janie-Painie, and that introducing the topic of her dead boyfriend was stupid. And everyone hates feeling stupid, not just the Irish. So he got mad.

"Jesus Christ, why are we still sitting here at this table?" he raged. "There's a cake, there's ice cream, there are presents and cards. It's getting dark. Let's get this show on the road, people!"

Kevin's face was red. He went inside and returned with gifts and cards. Kitty followed after him with a lumpy sheet cake. The children followed her, pied-piper-style, to the yard. Evening sunlight added a sleepy glow to the candles. Neil's daughter twisted in his arms for a futile lunge at the cake and the flames.

They sang, they ate. Betty loved her *Failte* carving and wanted Jane to hang it on her front door tonight.

"I'm old. I can't wait for these things."

Jane sat at her mother's feet, and Betty played with her curls while Jane opened the gift certificate from her brothers and the CD of Irish ballads from her parents. There were hugs and kisses all around. There was the stack of birthday cards, including one addressed to "Bitty" Howe. Betty's family had always called her Bitty. It prompted Ray to refer to her as Bitty-Betty.

The sun was setting, and the grown-ups all benefited by the kinder lighting. Jane had poor night vision but knew that she looked better in blur. When she looked at her mother, bathed in pink light and soft shadows, Jane could have sworn that Betty looked thirty years younger. Betty settled into her lawn chair and sparkled with each new gift and card.

Jane opened a card from her godmother, with a five-dollar bill enclosed. Jane blushed. Peter was stuck watching all this family stuff, but he didn't seem to mind. Jane realized that, polite as he was, he wasn't watching the Gift Rituals. He was watching the children chase fireflies.

Kitty had to explain, shouting, "*Cup* your hands! *Cup* them!" to the firefly-catching children. Apparently, there had been a few squishy casualties, and—

"Throw it away. Get it out. Out of my sight. *Take it!*"

Betty was up, moving faster than she had all day. She dropped a lavender envelope and a card on the grass. Jane retrieved them.

It was from Sheila. She hadn't written much beyond the preprinted birthday greeting. Her handwriting looked like her voice. No wonder Betty had bolted. She shouted clean-up instructions over her shoulder. Kitty and Linda exchanged meaningful looks and began to gather the paper plates, the plastic forks, and the children. The party was over.

Howard apologized to Peter. Betty was tired. Long day. Family business. Hope you understand. And he went off to tend to his wounded Betty.

Neil was the first to complain. "That bitch. She's not even here, and she managed to ruin the party."

Kevin took the high road. "She's desperate. She's sad. I feel sorry for her. I really do."

Irish loyalty is hard to manage. Jane was loyal to Sheila. And to her parents. And to her brothers, sort of. She watched and listened and took lots of notes in her head. But she didn't say a word. She was neutral. She was Switzerland. And everybody hates Switzerland.

"Okay, so, I better hurry off or I'll miss the bus. Thanks for everything."

Kevin and Neil nodded. Linda and Kitty were still hunting their children and gathering paper products.

Peter offered her a ride back to the city in his nice-smelling car. He always stayed in the city on school nights, and anyway, he knew where she lived. It's not like he had to go out of his way.

Clearly, Peter was raised by nice people. He chitted and chatted, but he never mentioned the mini-drama at the end of the evening. He waited for Jane to bring it up.

"Your brothers still call you 'Janie-Painie.' That's cute."

"No. Not if you're me, it isn't. They called my sister Sheilio. That was a much better nickname." There. Jane had mentioned Sheila, so she went ahead and said, "Mom's mad at my sister, Sheila."

"I gathered that. I know it's none of my business, but can I ask what happened?"

"She moved away. She got married. Eloped, actually."

Jane and Peter were sitting in the car, which was sitting in traffic, miles away from the Holland Tunnel. Jane wanted so badly to be back on her island. What better time to tell her family's story.

Sheila was the youngest in the family. She wore Coke-bottle glasses from the third grade and despised them forever. It was her excuse for being excruciatingly shy and awkward, which was her reason for staying at home. All the time. After high school, she attended the local Catholic college and commuted from home. She worked as a court reporter and commuted from home. She was a good cook, got stains out of anything, was quiet and neat as a pin. She learned to give Betty her insulin injections. She monitored her parents' growing array of medications. She chauffeured them to church, malls, grocery stores, and doctors' appointments. She might have considered surgery for her eyes, or maybe contact lenses, but it seemed a waste of money. She gave most of every paycheck to Betty.

And then, early last year, Sheila eloped. No word of warning, no dates with any gentleman callers, no preparation. She left a note for her parents, packed her quiet clothes, and left under cover of darkness. His name was Raoul. She met him in court. He was also a court reporter. They had lunch together every day. Sheila had been eating the exact same lunch for more than twelve years. Raoul offered variety. He was shy and quiet too. But compared to Sheila, he was Desi Arnaz.

But he had a lot of family in Florida, and he missed them. So the two quietly planned their elopement and their life together. Sheila made travel arrangements without saying a word. She never mentioned the elevator ride to the fourth floor of the courthouse, where she and Raoul obtained a marriage license. Betty and Howard never heard Raoul's name until they read it aloud in a note:

Dear Mom and Dad,

I'm sorry to disappoint you, but I am getting married. His name is Raoul Espinoza and I love him very much. We are moving to Miami. I'm sorry that this is such a shock to you. I knew I couldn't tell you. You need me so too much.

I love you, but I want to have my own life before it's too late. I'm sorry.

Sheila signed it with hugs and kisses. She attached a detailed schedule of doctors' appointments, questions for the doctors, and a medication schedule. A week later, she called from Florida, but Betty hung up on her. Howard tried to make peace, but Betty was having none of it. She was:

1. Insulted—she was never going to deprive her daughter of a life! Sheila had *chosen* to stay home. The letter clearly implied that Betty was trying to *enslave* her daughter!
2. Confused—how could this relationship have developed under her very nose, without a clue? Betty watched *The Young and the Restless* regularly and thought she knew just how sneaky people could be.
3. Lost—who was going to do the insulin injections? Who was going to make dinner? Who was going to drive them to church? How could Sheila abandon her parents to old age like this?

Sheila was dead to her parents. It had been more than a year, and Betty had stopped shouting and crying. She had moved into the ice age.

"No wonder your mother was so excited about me looking after my parents," Peter observed.

"Oh, my, yes. You scored big points with her on that. My family is very— My God, I've been talking about me and my family non-stop. Please, please, make me feel better and tell me everything you've done since high school."

And that's when Peter stopped the car in front of Jane's building.

"Next time."

"Well. Thanks for the ride—and the family therapy. Our time is up."

"It's been so nice seeing you again, after all these years. I hope I'll see you in the neighborhood—now that you've forgiven me for that head-shaving incident."

Jane almost touched him as she said, "You do look better with hair." But she pulled her hand back.

He handed her a slick business card. She wrote her number and e-mail address on the back of one of his. She worried about her handwriting and what it might reveal about her. She worried about Peter. There was something off about this guy, and it wasn't just that he was a fix up from Mom, or the second potential date in a week for a girl who didn't date. It was him. He was off. He had to be. How else would this handsome, kind, charming man still be single and preapproved by Betty? He must have some dark secret. Jane would find it eventually. For now, she climbed four flights of stairs to her sanctuary.

Just inside her door were two large shopping bags. Jane examined the contents. Doritos, Cheez Whiz, mini Snickers bars, cans of soda, and a remote control. TiVo. There was a note in the second bag:

If you love me, keep these bad things away from me. Love, Ray

Ray had keys to Jane's apartment in case of an emergency. She never expected him to use them to deposit snack foods.

• • •

You have two new messages.

"Hey, Jane. Did you come out to your family?" It was Ray. "Did Bitty-Betty freak? I trust you got the stuff I left for you. Look. Here's the thing. I'm going to the gym. Every day. You can choose to be a mom, and see, that's it. You made a choice. Well. So can I. I can choose to be—I don't know—healthy. Fit. A gym rat. A hunk. Right? That sounded better before I said it out loud to be recorded for all time on your machine. Anyway. This weekend, I'm going to drop off my fat clothes. This is the new me. There's no going back. Call me tomorrow. I'm seeing a late show tonight."

Beep.

"Happy B-day, Janie. Tomorrow's your day." It was Sheila. "And guess what? The Gods of TV Programming are taking good care of you. The classic movie channel is showing one of your favorites, so let's watch it together on the phone. Didn't they show it last year?"

Beep.

Yes, they did. They showed Jane's favorite movie on her birthday, three years running. *Bringing Up Baby.*

Chapter Four

"Now watch. This is where Cary Grant is gonna rip her dress."

"Sheila. That's later. When they're outside."

Rrrrrrip.

"See?"

"Sorry. So, how does Katharine Hepburn not feel that breeze?"

Jane and Sheila were watching *Bringing Up Baby* together, but apart. They were on the phone in their own homes. They had ridiculous long distance bills. Raoul knew better than to complain about it. Sheila had five-year-old twin stepsons who provided occasional background noise for the movie/chat.

"Too bad he's fictional," Sheila complained.

"Who?"

"Cary Grant."

"Yeah. Too bad."

They ate pizza and tried not to talk until the next commercial. When the first ad blasted out, Sheila regressed to thirteen and giggled. "So? Is this Peter guy cute?"

"Yes. In a handsome kind of way. I don't trust him."

"Why? Because all beauty is evil? Because he was

nice, and we can't have that? Or is it because he's Preapproved by Mom? You shouldn't hold that against him. Mom would probably like Raoul, if she ever met him."

"Look, Sheil. I was thinking I'd go out with that actor guy. Dick-Richard."

"So?"

"This is a weird time for me. I'm thinking about my life and where it should go. There are some things that I know. I think. And anyway, did I tell you Peter was in that whole head-shaving conspiracy in high school?"

"It wasn't a conspiracy. It was just— Oh! They're back."

Jane wasn't paying attention to the glittering people on her screen. She should tell Sheila about these baby plans/thoughts/ dreams because:

1. Sheila was her sister, best friend, and most reliable confidante.
2. They had survived a childhood of Irish superstitions, unspeakable bridesmaid gowns at family weddings, and Betty.
3. Sheila had two little boys and would therefore be loaded with joy and good advice.

Three good reasons. Perfectly good. Wonderful, even. So why the hesitation?

Jane should not tell Sheila about the adoption because:

1. Sheila never told Jane about her elopement. She just eloped. Yes, Jane knew that Sheila was dating Raoul and that it was getting serious. But that was all Jane knew. She learned about the elopement from Betty. It was a memorably ugly phone call.

Maybe this was a test. If she didn't have the courage to tell Sheila about the thought of a baby, she definitely failed the test. And anyway, couldn't Jane tell Sheila anything? Loud commercials blared. Go.

"So, Sheila? I wanted to tell you something. Here goes. I keep seeing babies everywhere, and thinking about babies and actually, maybe, wanting to have a baby . . . of some kind. I went to this meeting and there were all these women who were trying to get pregnant and these other women who were trying to adopt, and there was a picture of a little girl in a red bathing suit."

Sheila didn't say anything. Not a good sign, right?

"Look. I don't think I can explain this or justify it or anything sensible like that. Sam and I used to talk about kids before he got sick, and I guess I always assumed that I'd be a mother someday. And I think that this is the sort of thing that if you don't do it, and you need to, you go crazy. Anyway, there. You're a mother, so tell me the truth. Am I insane?"

Silence. Really awful sign.

"Oh, God, Sheil. Is it that horrible?"

One of Sheila's stepsons, who wished to remain anonymous, had run through the room and disconnected the phone. It took several minutes for either of them to figure it out. Jane now had a sign that she shouldn't say anything yet. When they finally reconnected, Cary Grant and Katharine Hepburn were hunting the wrong leopard in Connecticut.

"Sorry, Janie. There's a cute little boy here who wants to play outside in the rain at night, but it's not going to happen. Yes, I mean *you*, Tyler! You should be in pj's, shouldn't you? It's late!"

Cary Grant and Katharine Hepburn caught that wrong leopard.

"Hey, I was trying to ask you before. Did Mom get my card?"

And Jane was pushed off track, just like that. She dug her pinky nail into the soft flesh of her hand until it hurt.

"Sheila. She was too surprised—you should have told me. Next year, send it to me and I'll give it to her."

"How bad was it? I guess I was kind of hoping I could make a little peace offering. Sorry."

For months after the elopement, Sheila cried over the phone to her sister. There was a lot of "I've wrecked my life!" and "I miss my parents!" and "Florida is really hot!" conversations. And every conversation ended with Sheila apologizing for her grief and her intrusion.

But Raoul was patient with his new bride. It was hard to know what scared her more: her new family or her old one. The little boys were moody. In the morning, they would order four different breakfasts from their weary new mother. They invited her to play, then slammed her to the ground and jumped on her. Motherhood stretched Sheila and nearly broke her. Always a pale, slight person, she thought of herself as mousy. Her voice was thin; her hair was wispy. The twins liked her, but they smelled her fear and took full advantage. Over the phone, Sheila's voice had sounded farther away than Florida. She sounded lost and at sea. Jane wondered if Sheila would retreat to their parents' home.

One day, little Tyler caught his hand in a door hinge. Sheila cradled the boy while Raoul extricated his hand from the door. She tended his wounds and nurtured him with a healing bowl of ice cream, medically proven to prevent or heal broken bones. Tyler clung to her for the rest of the day. His brother followed obediently.

After two and a half months, the conversation sounded like this: "I made Cuban pork rolls today. I think they were only okay, but Raoul's mom said they were good, and everybody ate them." And then it was "Tyler kissed me good night for the first time. I almost started crying. Did I tell you that already? Sorry."

Sheila's voice deepened. She swore (not often, and only in Spanish) and talked about the kids and her spicy adventures in cooking. She no longer wept when she asked about Betty and Howard, but sighed noisily and sometimes she apologized again.

Tonight, Jane offered a very soft, very edited version of her mother's reaction to the birthday card.

"It's okay. I thought I'd take a shot, but *Dios Mio,* I didn't mean to cause a scene."

It was okay? How could it be okay?

"Look, Janie, I'm not defending Mom here, but I do sort of get it.

The bond between a mother and kid is so intense. If you feel like your kid betrayed you—how do you come back from that?"

"You didn't betray them. You got married."

"I know. But Mom doesn't get it. She'll never see it that way. I was supposed to take care of her, and instead I abandoned her. Anyway, I'm not defending her. I'm just—I have no idea what I'm doing and *so help me, Tyler, you will not live to see six!* Sorry. Hold on."

Sheila put the phone down and had a big scene with Tyler. Jane heard little remnants. She fingered the gift and card she had received from Sheila. She opened it, since the Tyler scene might take a while. Sheila had cross-stitched her a *Bienvenidos* wall hanging in vivid colors. So gorgeous. She would hang it in the entranceway, right over the wall craters. Sheila had stitched her initials in the bottom right corner: SHE. Sheila Helen Espinoza.

"Sorry, sorry, sorry. I'm back. What were we talking about? By the way, did you open my present yet?"

"I just did. It's gorgeous. Gorgeous. How did you do this?"

"It was fun. I did it during the boys' naps. It's really relaxing."

"I love it. Hey, Sheil—"

"*Tyler!*" Sheila covered the phone, but Jane could still hear, "Listen to me, mister. If you get out of that bed again, I'm taking Batman. I mean it!"

Katharine Hepburn was climbing a giant dinosaur. It toppled, and then Cary Grant pulled her to safety. She told him that he loved her, and he said, "Oh dear . . ."

Jane paid attention to signs and knew that this was the wrong time to tell Sheila about her plans. The credits were rolling. It was time to hang up and go to bed.

"Sheila, I want to have a baby."

"Sorry?"

"I want to be a mom. I want to have a baby. And I'm looking into it. Just thinking about it. Trying it on for size. So. What do you think?"

"Um. I think it's wonderful. It's a wonderful idea. Sorry. I have to make sure the boys are in bed. I better go. Sorry. Bye. I love you."

Jane was damned by silence. She felt cold. Why was she assuming that Sheila would be supportive? She closed her eyes and tried to picture her sister's face. It had been too long since they had seen each other. She gave up. A minute later, the phone jangled her out of her melancholy. It was Sheila. Jane couldn't see Sheila shaking her head in Florida, waving her husband away, and settling in for a long hard talk. But that's what happened.

"Janie. You know I love these boys. I really do. I'm their mom, forever and ever. But it rained here for six days in a row, and I swear I wanted to throw us all out the window on the fourth day. Only, we live in a ranch house, and we would have landed in the hedges and gotten a twisted ankle or something. Anyway, I didn't do it, but the point is—it's so hard that these horrible thoughts can actually get time and space in your head."

Jane closed her eyes, sat on the floor, and pictured Sheila and her family in the hedges.

"And, Janie, my guys are kids—not babies. Everybody says that those first baby months are so awful. Remember how Mom always complained about when you had colic? And her episiotomy? I can't even think about that—I need to cross my legs."

Sheila's voice dropped low. Secrets.

"You want to know the best thing about having the twins? I'll never have to get pregnant. Instant Family. In fact, I've even thought about asking Raoul to get a vasectomy, but I want to wait 'til I'm sure."

Jane laid down on the floor and pictured Raoul in a hospital gown.

"I told you how his ex-wife went kind of crazy after she had the kids. She was really traumatized by the birth, and she had to go into therapy. I'm not supposed to tell you that, by the way, so you don't know it. And she never comes around. She says that she never bonded with the boys because she had so much trouble recovering.

I kind of understand her. A little. Janie, what if you had twins? I mean, I can't imagine getting through that recovery all alone with those babies. Even if there had only been one, I couldn't have done it alone. No way."

"So I shouldn't have a baby? Or maybe I should just visit yours? Sheila, I'm having trouble following your logic."

"This is not about logic. Look, I can speak two and a half languages, and I don't know any words to describe how hard this motherhood thing is. That's why I don't even try to put it in words. I'm sorry, honey. I know this isn't what you wanted to hear, but I'm gonna say it. Don't go through with this."

Jane curled into the fetal position and pictured a red octagonal Stop sign.

"Maybe you should get a cat."

Sheila went too far. Jane sat up straight. A cat? What the hell?

"I don't want a cat. I don't think a cat can go to school or learn to ride a bike or talk or become a full-fledged, independent human being. But I can research that."

"Jane."

"Do you wish Raoul's ex would come and take custody of the boys? Do you wish you weren't raising them? Do you? Don't even pretend to be funny about it, because you love them. This is a decision that I know in my spine: I am supposed to be a mother. And it's so arrogant to tell another person that it's too hard for them. Me. That it's too hard for me."

"Jane."

"And since when is 'easy' the criteria for doing things? Was it easy for you to break away from Mom and Dad? Was it easy for me to take care of Sam? No. But I'd do it again. I'd do it tomorrow."

"Jane."

"Don't underestimate me. That's always a mistake. Remember when you thought I couldn't learn to swim? You're so good at seeing everybody's point of view—why can't you see mine?" Jane's voice was high and shrill.

"Jane. Honey. You could be a great mother—but not alone. It's just too hard. You need a partner. And this is not just about you, Jane. I don't think anyone can do this alone. I've been a mom for more than a year now, so I know what I'm saying. It's hard for two people. It's impossible for one." Sheila's voice was low and quiet.

Jane was silent. If she spoke, she would start weeping. Sheila sounded so right.

"I'm sorry," Sheila continued. "Look, you're catching me on a bad day. Can we talk about this tomorrow?"

What choice did she have? Jane had to let her sister go, and let the ghosts of her words dance around the living room. Sheila was right. Jane found herself longing for the pre-Raoul Sheila—the one who was quiet as a mouse. The one who would never have said all these things.

This was a sign. This was an argument she had lost. She tried to replay the argument in her head. She gave herself extra time to come up with zingy replies. There were none. Sheila was right. Single motherhood was a bad idea. Any fool could see that.

• • •

Jane finally went out with Dick-Richard. If she wanted motherhood, she was going to have to attain wifehood first. They went for dim sum in Chinatown. She made sure that she thought of three things to ask him about, so that she could keep the conversation going. She shouldn't have bothered. Dick-Richard needed no drawing out. He was both talker and topic. Before the first dish arrived, she learned that he had recently been living with a girlfriend but had moved out when she started "using the M-word."

A small alarm went off in Jane's head. Two small alarms, in fact. One alarm responded to his running away from a live-in girlfriend who was looking toward marriage, and another alarm sounded because he used the expression "the M-word."

He had just started temping, but he didn't like it. He was going to go back to telemarketing next week, where he could make his own hours. It was important to be available for auditions.

Another alarm. Does anyone like telemarketers?

Oh, don't worry. He didn't *sell* things over the phone. He took surveys and helped companies identify potential customers so that someone else could call and sell things. But he assured her that he was going to make it as an actor. He had come to the city from the bad streets of Nebraska, and had given himself two years to succeed. That was eleven years ago, and he now realized how immature his timetable had been.

He described a handful of roles he had played. He gave a detailed description of what it's like to be an extra in a Woody Allen movie. Apparently, Woody doesn't talk to the extras. What a snob. He reenacted his entrance in a play, and everyone in the restaurant stared at him.

Jane wondered if dating had always been such a trial. Could she add this night to the long list of reasons why she didn't date? Should she call or e-mail Peter from high school? Would he be just as annoying?

It was eight-thirty. She was free to eat quite a lot and to study Dick-Richard. For a few minutes, she thought of him as a potential, unwitting sperm donor. What if she slept with him and—oops—got pregnant? Was that an honorable goal—to be a victim of some accidental twist of fate? Maybe he would be a willing sperm donor. She could take her temperature a lot, and when it reached fertilization numbers, she could have sex with this guy. But should she? And would he be a good donor?

"Ouch. Too much ice in this drink. I have rotten teeth. I was jinxed—both my parents had bad teeth—and blind as bats too. It's so unfair."

Done. She wanted nothing to do with this man or his gene pool. She wanted the last two hours of her life back, starting with the part where she tried on three different blouses for this date.

Dick-Richard kept talking. It didn't seem possible that there was more to say, but he was resourceful.

Jane didn't steer the conversation. She couldn't. But somehow, he started talking about children. It may have been a response to Jane observing a family gathering at a nearby table. The children switched easily between Chinese (Cantonese? Mandarin?) and English. The adults spoke only Chinese. The children were restless, but not unruly. They seemed happy. Jane may have been staring at them, she wasn't sure. She knew she hadn't spoken for a long while.

Dick-Richard saw his date looking at children and announced, "I don't want to have any more children."

Any. More. Which word jarred her more? Hard to say.

And that's when he started talking about a woman he left behind in Nebraska. A very young woman who told him that she was on the Pill, but wasn't. She lied to him. She got pregnant and tried to get him to marry her. He fled to the big city instead, and pursued his dream of stardom.

"I've never met the kid, and I don't want to. People say that women should have a choice, fine. But what about me? Why didn't I have a choice? Where was my choice?"

Jane might have answered him, but that would only have prolonged the evening.

He finished digging his grave by describing how the awful mother used to put her weeping child on the phone to him. When the child said, "Hi, Daddy," Dick-Richard hung up on him.

Jane signaled for the check. It was 9:15, and if she hurried, she could salvage this evening with a bubble bath.

Richard studied the check, all serious and mathematical.

"Let's see, you owe a little more, since I didn't have any dumplings, so it's—"

"I thought we could just split it."

"I didn't have any dumplings. You ate them all. I really wanted one. I wasn't going to say anything."

Jane smiled for the first time all evening. He wasn't going to say anything? Not say anything? As in, "not talking"?

"Richard. Allow me."

She paid the check, left a hefty tip, wound her way through the tables and out of the restaurant. If she'd had a hat, there might have been a Mary Tyler Moore moment here. She was free. She was happy. She wasn't just free from Richard, either. There was a calm inside her that Calgon could never have created. Jane was going to be just fine.

"Look, you don't have to get all huffy about it. I'll split the check with you. After all, it's our first date. Or, were you expecting me to pay? That is so sexist, you know. Just because I'm the man and I make more money and I rape and I plunder and blah-blah-blah. You say you want equality, but you women are all just talk."

She kissed him on the cheek.

"Good night, Dick-Richard. Thanks for a lovely evening."

Chinatown's streets are too crowded to allow a happy girl to skip, so Jane was skipping on the inside. The joy sustained until her cell phone rang. How could it be good news? Had she given Dick-Richard her cell phone number? Was there a crisis at work?

"Hi, it's me, Ray. Whatcha doin'?"

"Oh, I just finished my date."

"It's nine-thirty. Which means . . . Oh, dear. Martini?"

"Yup."

• • •

They met at their favorite bar, Necessary Evils. Ray wanted help writing a review of an expensive production of Ibsen's *Ghosts*. He wanted lots of ways to describe "bad." A fun drinking game for Jane & Ray:

Mary Kate & Ashley Do Ibsen!

Made me think fondly of that bout with salmonella. Good times.

Theater as only Helen Keller could have appreciated it.

He had the clap. We had to clap. The end.

And then they got silly. Ray called a halt to the process when they started to write the entire review in Dr. Seuss rhymes. That's never a good sign.

He prodded her for details about her date and heard enough about Dick-Richard's career to know that he didn't really have one. Clearly, he was not worthy of our Jane. He ordered her another.

"Ray. You're making me drink martinis, but, hello, what are you drinking?"

"Celery soda."

Ray explained that he was abstaining from alcohol, carbs, red meat, sugar, fat, dairy, radio, and television.

"What does that leave you?"

"Ibsen and celery soda. I didn't know being beautiful was going to be so dull. No wonder models all look so vacant. They live in a bubble. A quiet, flavorless bubble. But I'm not complaining. I want to make a real choice here. My body is a temple and yeah, okay, whatever. I was thinking that it might be great to grow up to be that guy who eats tree bark, never catches a cold, and has perfect, glowing skin. Does that sound realistic?"

Jane sipped her martini. Ray had gone through several romantic crises before, and even the occasional career crisis. But Jane couldn't remember any previous identity crisis. Ray was always Ray. A human collage of good qualities plus a bitchy sense of humor.

"Wait." Jane worried about how worried she sounded. "Does this mean you're not allowed to mock bad actors, crappy writers, and pretentious directors anymore? Because I need you to do that for me. I need you to be mean about these glamorous, beautiful people. Please promise me that you'll never get so healthy that you'll be all serene and generous to them."

"Never. It purges toxins."

• • •

Ray walked her home because he wanted to be sure that no Dick-Richard-Actor was waiting for her. He wasn't. Ray often thought that Jane was a perfect candidate for a stalker: kind, bighearted, pretty, and lacking in peripheral vision.

"Are you disappointed that this guy was such a disappointment?"

"No. The heart, she is intact. I was just sort of hoping."

Ray groaned. "Oh. Hope. That's the worst. You bruised?"

She wasn't. She hadn't raised her hopes about this one date. Okay, it was the first one in a long while, but she was sailing along.

"I just keep looking for signs, you know? About the baby. About whether or not I should really be doing it. Meeting a nice potential-daddy would have been a good sign, don't you think?"

"You know, I've been thinking a lot about this whole baby thing too. And I have to ask you: Does the whole universe have to put up big, flashing neon signs saying, 'Jane, go ahead and have a baby'? I mean, is that necessary?"

"Absolutely."

"Here's my sign to you: Do it. I really hope you go through with it. And I hope . . . Can you include me too?"

Jane hugged and hugged and hugged him.

• • •

Jane took a break from work to look through the notes she had taken at the CSM meeting. Maria had given her a document entitled, "So You Want to Adopt From China." Karen had given her details about a Families with Children from China meeting that would take place tonight, on the Upper West Side. If she rushed out of work on time, she would make it.

Jane walked past the community center three times before she saw the dripping sign announcing an FCC meeting. Jane shook off the rain and located Karen by her red hair. She was sitting in the front, perched at the edge of her seat. She had a small, pastel note-book and pen. The meeting hadn't started yet, but she was ready to write down anything interesting or useful. She was jumpy.

Jane sat down next to her and wondered about Karen's caffeine intake when she leaned over and whispered, "Hey! Jane! So glad you're here! They'll be starting soon! I'm so jazzed!"

Jane didn't see Teresa step in late, and slip into the seat directly behind her. Despite the rain and wind, Teresa looked perfect. Her hair never frizzed, her lipstick in place. Teresa had control. She tapped Jane on the shoulder and mouthed "Hello."

The demographics for this meeting included married men and women, and some children. During the welcome speech, someone passed around (hooray) brochures, literature, and fun fact sheets. There was a duplicate of Maria's "So You Want to Adopt From China" document. The place felt chaotic and warm. Jane took it all in.

Tonight, there would be two speakers, both women. One was a married woman with two bio(logical) kids and a little girl she had adopted from China. The other was a single woman who had just recently returned from China with her baby.

Married Mom spoke first. Her baby ignored the small audience and climbed all over her mother. She pulled at Mom's ears, clothes, and noisy necklace. Mom multitasked.

"I take it some of you are thinking about adopting from China, and—"

Karen piped up, "I'm not thinking. I'm decided. I'm definitely doing this."

"Oh. Kay."

Jane missed the next few sentences. She studied Karen, but then looked away when her staring became obvious. Married Mom was relating her adoption experience:

"We had a great adoption agency. They really held our hands and made everything easier. And the whole process is so regulated. You assemble this series of documents, called your dossier. If you're a reasonably organized person, you can do it. Then you get all your— honey, don't pull Mommy's earring—all your documents notarized and certified and authenticated. You send it off to China. You wait. You wait and wait and wait, and then you get a referral. That's when your agency calls you and tells you that China has matched you with a baby. They send you a picture and a medical report. You make travel arrangements, you go—you pick up your daughter, get her a visa, and fly home. And that's when the real fun begins."

Jane wanted the meeting to stop so that she could think about this for a minute. She wanted to stand up and say, Oh, come on! Does anyone honestly think that it's this easy to get a baby? If it were this easy, people would be doing it all the time.

"Any questions?"

Karen shuffled through her notes, almost frantic but not quite. She mustn't let this golden opportunity for questions pass her by.

"Yes? In the back?"

It was Teresa.

"I'm new to the whole China adoption world, so please forgive my ignorance. Why are there so many babies? And why does it sound like they're all girls?"

Karen's hand shot up. She was the girl in the front row at school and she had the answer. Married Mom smiled and let Karen take the floor.

"It's an overpopulation thing. See, Chairman Mao told everyone to have big families—seven kids was the ideal. But China couldn't feed that many people, or house them or anything. Big overpopulation problem. So then they started the one-child policy. You're only allowed to have one child. That's the policy."

"Okay. But why are all the girls up for adoption? It doesn't sound like they're planning ahead. Aren't they going to need some girls eventually?"

Karen had no answer. She deferred to Married Mom.

"It's mostly girls who are put up for adoption. In China, boys marry but stay with their parents and support them. Girls marry and move in with the husband's family. If you need someone to take care of you in your old age, you need a son."

You need a Sheila, actually. A Sheila would be better than any son because she was so obedient, and such a good cook. But then,

China probably didn't have any Sheilas. They're very rare. This was not a good time to be thinking about Sheila.

"It's almost unheard of for a woman to remain single in China," Married Mom continued.

"Not here!" Karen snorted.

And then Married Mom described the act of abandonment.

"The girls are left in public places, so that they will be found quickly, and then they're brought to an orphanage. Sometimes, they are newborn, umbilical cord still attached. Sometimes, they are weeks or months old. You hear stories about older girls left in a market or near a police station. But it's usually an infant that's found. It happens a lot. China doesn't tell us just how many babies are abandoned."

Jane pictured swaddling babes, like the Christ Child, nestled in a big box of ginger.

"It is illegal to abandon a baby. So the government runs an ad in the paper, searching for the baby's parents. Are they ever found? Who knows. If they were found, they'd be treated as criminals. The women who do this, the men and women who give up their children, they're brave. They're risking a lot, they're facing heartbreak, all so that the child can have a life. A better life. Does anyone have any questions about the adoption process?"

Some audience members started throwing around acronyms and terminology that Jane didn't understand. Even Karen seemed puzzled. She stopped taking notes. She had a glassy, overwhelmed look that Jane found comforting. Maybe glassy and overwhelmed is an appropriate response to so much emotional information.

Single Mom spoke up. She was a very large woman who had some trouble making her way to the front of the room. She settled into a chair with her sleeping baby in a stroller nearby.

"I've only been home for a month. This is my little treasure, Kaitlyn."

Sleeping children rarely appreciate the oohs and aahs that they generate. Single Mom's style was much tougher, much more direct than Married Mom had been.

"First of all, you have to have a great agency. Ask them questions. You've got to really work with these people, so you have to trust them. You have to know who you're getting into this with, right? Am I right?"

Karen nodded. Jane blinked a lot.

"Second of all, like she said, if you're reasonably organized with paperwork, you can put together your dossier, no problem. The waiting is the hardest part, like the song says. I chose China because it was so clear and straightforward. And Korea doesn't let fat ladies adopt. That's right, I'm too fat for Korea. But anyway . . ."

It should have been comforting to hear the tale of Single Mom. After all, she adopted this beautiful baby, didn't she? Success, right? Jane struggled to keep up as Single Mom reeled off the list of documents that are contained in a dossier, as if everyone in the room were familiar with the list. Wait. What was that fourth one? How do you get it? She kept talking. She described a celebrity sighting that occurred when she was fingerprinted. Hold on. Who fingerprints you? How do you get that done? She made the audience gasp out loud when she told them that she lost her job a month after submitting her dossier to China. And finally, she described that day in China when her baby wasn't there.

"They brought the crib in to our hotel room and told us that the babies would arrive that afternoon. Everyone in my group got ready. And then our facilitator came around and said that the babies weren't coming 'til tomorrow. I thought I'd die. I took pictures of the empty crib. I told my sister, I said, 'Kaitlyn's never going to get here! I'm never going to be a mama!' But the next day, she was there, and she was so beautiful. Of course, she was totally freaked out, but we bonded eventually. So don't worry about that part."

This led to a series of questions about children and their bonding habits: what to expect when the child is first placed in your arms, various reactions from children of different ages, and some disturbing health questions.

"Look. Let me be the crude one in the room," said Single Mom. "I chose China adoption because I knew that at the end of it, I would have a healthy baby girl. I didn't know how long it would take, exactly, but I knew—guaranteed—how it was going to end. That helped my stress levels a lot. *A lot.* And when I had trouble finding a job after I was DTC, I knew I could just pull the plug on this and do it again later. I could. I didn't want to, but I knew I could."

Jane was recording it all in her head. Later, when she understood more about China adoption, she'd play it back and say, "Oh, DTC means Dossier to China. So that's what she meant. She lost her job after she had sent her Dossier to China. What's a dossier?"

If she had stopped there, Jane would have gone home happy and serene that night. But Single Mom had one more thing to say.

"The paper chase may get complicated for some of you, but it's nothing, absolutely nothing, compared to motherhood. And I want to aim this at the women who are thinking about becoming single mothers. It's not about being organized or keeping track of lists of documents."

Jane wondered if there was a spotlight on her. Single Mother continued.

"It's about being a superhero, every day of your life. And it's forever. If you think you can't do it, you're probably right."

She may have said more, but Jane missed it. This was a sign, just for her: Don't do this.

"Questions?"

It was Karen, asking, "What's step one?"

All heads turned, tennis match style, to Single Mom.

"Call the INS and get an appointment for fingerprinting. Step two: find an agency, a good one. No, a great one. They'll hook you up with a social worker who'll do step three: your homestudy so you can get started on your I-171H. Then start working on your dossier and get it out there. And then, bring your daughter home."

"Bring your daughter home" was a loaded sentence for people who were experiencing baby hunger. And she said it with an angelic infant sleeping by her side. Karen continued her note taking through loud sniffling.

If she had had time for it, Jane might have wondered how the Infertile Career Women group might have responded to that sentence. Jane was still stuck, however, at the way Single Mother seemed to know that Jane was simply not up to the task of single motherhood.

"Here's the number," said Single Mom, and she read out the 800 number for the INS. Karen wrote it down. Everyone wrote it down, except for Jane. She seemed to be the only one not writing the ten digits. She noticed Karen noticing her not writing it down.

Jane, Karen, and Teresa left the meeting together. The rain had slowed to an active mist. No one remembered who initiated it, but they decided to have coffee and talk about this whole single mothers adopting from China situation. First, they did a pulse check.

Karen was already rolling up her sleeve for the fingerprinting. She was go-go-go ready. She painted a picture of three cherubic Chinese girls singing "Ring Around the Rosie." She had already started a college fund. It had only $12 in it, but it was a start.

"You know what my mother said?" Karen asked. "She said, 'All mothers are single mothers.' Now, okay, that's really cynical, but then she's a very damaged person. Still, she thinks I can do it. And she's so stingy with praise and support, forget it."

"What do you do for a living?" Teresa was fact-finding. Jane could appreciate that.

"I teach soft-skills." Blank stare. "Management development. Time management, stress management, things like that. I see a lot of single parents in my work."

"Have you chosen an adoption agency?" Teresa pointed her question at Karen.

"No, but I've been doing tons of research. It's a key factor. There has to be a chemistry there, a reaction. Something. Hey, I couldn't find Mr. Right, but I'm going to find Mr. Right Agency. Or Ms.

Right. Right?" No more coffee for Karen. The more she giggled, the quieter Jane became. She wasn't going to go through with this. No.

Teresa must have noticed Jane's quiet when she said, "There are a million ways to get this motherhood thing wrong. And without a husband to help share the load, well, it all sounds kind of selfish, doesn't it? Still. I want to find out more, and I can't explain why. So I won't try."

The active mist had retreated. They exchanged phone numbers and e-mail addresses. Jane felt separate from them. Different. They were already walking down this road. She was standing still. She didn't see herself joining them. She didn't see anything. She was not going to do this. It was crazy. Irrational. A phase.

• • •

You have two new messages.

"Hi, this is Peter Mandell. Your friendly neighborhood . . . neighbor. I seem to recall you know how to do lots of fixing-up kind of stuff. Well, I just bought a bureau-type item from Ikea, and I can't get past the first page of instructions. Is this the sort of thing I can ask you to help me with? Am I totally out of line? Anyway, I'll buy dinner, and who knows, it could be fun."

Beep.

"Hey, Jane, it's me." It was Sheila. "Look, I take back about eighty percent of what I said the other night. I was PMSing big-time, and the boys were really on a tear. It was just bad timing. Call me. Please don't hate me. I'm sorry."

Beep.

• • •

Sheila. I'm not going through with this. Probably. I mean. Okay, yes, I want to have a baby. I've always wanted to have kids, but then, after Sam died, it just wasn't going to happen. It was too hard and— wait. I'm getting off the topic. Sheil, I've been doing all this research and looking around, and I was thinking about adopting from China.

But I can't do this alone. I can't. I'm not strong enough. I met these women, and they're strong enough. Or, at least, they think they are. And good for them. But I'm not. I'm pulling the plug on this whole crazy thought process. Forget I ever said anything.

She thought it sounded lame and needy. Jane kept trying to polish the speech before she dialed Sheila. In the end, she dialed the phone and said, "Never mind. I was just kidding."

"You don't have to be. Oh, Jane. I've always pictured you with kids. You could do it. If anyone could, you could."

"No. I'm not doing this. Forget I ever said anything. Okay?"

Chapter Five

Dutiful daughter Jane phoned her mother nine days after their joint birthday party.

"Sorry, honey. Your mother isn't feeling well. She picked up some kind of stomach bug," said a very weary Howard.

Great way to turn seventy-two. Poor Betty.

"Is she still upset? I mean about the card? From Sheila?" Jane wanted something hopeful to report on her next Sheila call.

"She has a stomach bug. She'll be okay. I'm taking her in to see Dr. Crosby today."

"Can I help? Do you need me to bring crackers or ginger ale or something?"

"We have all that and more, Janie. Right here in New Jersey."

And Howard had to go. A man who only drives fifteen miles per hour needs a lot of lead time to get to a doctor's appointment. The strain of taking care of Betty was beginning to show on him. If only they still had a Sheila.

The Irishness in Jane made her good at loyalty, with the occasional desire to argue, and a careful observation of signs (from God, the Universe, Somewhere). Jane's

Irishness also gave her a healthy dose of guilt. This was free-floating guilt, which was the worst kind. Hey, it's not as if Jane were responsible for Sheila's elopement or her upsetting birthday card. Okay, so she had been toying with the idea of single motherhood. But she wasn't following through. It was just a phase. She dropped it. So it wasn't her fault that her mother caught a virus. Was it?

Of course it was! Oh, Jane was a terrible daughter. She tried to remedy that with a call to NutraWorld. They sold diabetic sweets. She sent a one-pound Nutra-Sampler box with a get-well card. She checked her reflection. Yes. She was still a terrible daughter—and a foolish one who was sending chocolates to a woman with a stomach flu. Maybe she should follow her mother's advice and hook up with Peter. Maybe that would make Betty happy. Maybe Jane should ignore that little alarm/warning/danger-danger sign in her gut and call him back. And besides, the notion of yet another date gave her an adolescent sense of smugness. The smugness was amplified by the fact that she could help him solve his Ikea problem.

"Hi, Peter. So you went Ikea, did you? I'll help you put it together. And then you'll have it. All put together. And I guess that's all. Call me when you get this. Bye."

She was still a terrible daughter, but she had run out of ways to fix that.

. . .

It's not easy to dress for a date where you'll be assembling furniture, but Jane found a way.

Peter lived in Vincent van Gogh's apartment, if Vincent had lived in a Manhattan studio. It was spare. Very. He had bare parquet floors, a bed, a chair, a table, a big box that said IKEA in bold blue letters. There was a photograph of his parents (aww) on the table, but no other personal touches. Pretty much the height of spare. There was nothing here to help her figure out who this Peter guy was.

"Come on in. Can I get you something? All I have is water. But it's filtered."

"I brought my own tools," Jane said brightly. And she held up the screw gun and the wood glue. As she entered the vacant apartment, she was relieved that she had thought to bring them.

"Oh, good. I don't have anything like that. I use this old computer battery for a hammer." He proudly displayed the battered battery. Jane smiled and wondered if she should have brought her own chair.

"So," said Peter. "Um. What can I get for you?"

He may have meant filtered water vs. not filtered water, but Jane said, "Bowls. I'll need some bowls or plates or something. To sort the hardware. That's the best way to start. It looks like I'll need about seven bowls. Okay?"

He only had two plates.

"Sorry. But, hey, I can fix this. I'll order dinner and ask them to send extra plates. Sorry, I don't have real food in the fridge. Just bachelor food. Oh, wait, there's root beer. And all my take-out menus. Would you prefer pizza, Indian, or Chinese?"

She Mona-Lisa-smiled and said, "Chinese."

They sorted hardware, ate mu shu, and started to work on assembling his bureau-thing. Jane took charge, all the while trying to figure out that danger-danger feeling in her ribs. She failed. No one can assemble Ikea furniture and divine the secrets of a Mystery Man at the same time. Everyone knows that.

"Here. Put this part—this is the back—put it over here. And hold it steady. No, steady. No. Don't let it move around." Jane was trying to hammer it to some wobbly side pieces, but Peter kept letting it slip, and Jane hammered at the air.

"Oh. You mean, steady. Got it."

The first thing they did was put the back on backward. The second thing they did was assemble the drawer fronts upside down. The third thing they did was lose the crucial hardware under Peter's bed. Jane cringed. Peter laughed.

"I could have gotten it wrong all by myself, thank you very much."

He laid on the floor and extended his reach to the far end of the floor under the bed to retrieve the wayward hardware. That's when Jane realized that he smelled good. Not perfume-good. Men's colognes usually made her sneeze. Peter had a good smell all his own. She leaned in a little to take it in. She jumped up when Peter emerged victorious, dowels in hand.

"Got it!"

Despite the Dowel Victory, Jane knew they had lost this war.

"We have to remove the drawer fronts and do them over," she announced.

Peter wanted to do no such thing. He decided that they should just build the whole thing upside down. Jane was studying the Swedish directions, though she didn't speak a word of Swedish.

"I don't think that's going to work, Peter. I think we have to go back, fix what's wrong, and then finish the rest of the assembly."

"Why?"

Jane was still working on an answer for that one when the phone rang. She paused for Peter to go answer it.

Instead, he said, "Aren't you going to get that? Or are you screening?"

It was Jane's cell phone that was ringing. Jane leapt to it before the call was lost to voice mail. Emergency at work? Ray having a crisis? What?

"Jane, honey, it's me." It was Betty. Jane blushed crimson. Her mother was calling her while she was on this date where she was ruining the Mystery Man's furniture. Don't you hate when that happens?

"Mom? How are you feeling? I heard about the flu and all." She smiled sheepishly at Peter and tried to move toward privacy, but there was none to be had. Empty apartments offer no refuge, and echo loudly.

Peter tried his best to give her privacy by immersing himself in the assembly project, or maybe by just pretending to.

"Oh, Janie, you almost got a call inviting you to my funeral. I wanted to die. I just wanted to die."

"Don't say that, Mom. It's so morbid."

"It's true. I was telling your father, I said, 'Shoot me now and put me out of my misery.' I did. I really said that."

"Well, I'm glad you crawled away from your grave."

"Crawled is right. I crawled. And I wanted to say thank you for the dietetic chocolates. I can't eat them yet. I'm still living on Saltines and ginger ale. It's a little bit like being pregnant."

"Okay."

"I think it was that card from your sister. It put me over the edge."

"That's crazy talk."

"It did. It upset me, and it lowered my resistance—just in time for my birthday. Thanks a lot for that."

Peter was done studying, so he resumed the assembly. He was going with the upside-down bureau idea. It would have legs on the top and a flat surface bottom. Jane shook her head and tried to signal to him to take apart the drawers. He waved her away.

"What are you doing, Janie?"

"I'm helping—or at least I'm trying to help—Peter assemble this bureau-thing. I think I got it horribly wrong, and he's just going with that—which is wrong. We can still fix it. It's not that hard."

"Peter?" There was so much delight in Betty's voice. "Really? Oh, I knew it! I knew you two would hit it off! A mother knows these things. You'll see."

"What? Mom. Please, I just want to— Peter, take this out and reverse it. Really. You'll be glad that you did."

He waved her away.

"You're building something? That doesn't sound very romantic. And you know, you're not supposed to do that sort of thing at night. You do it on the weekend. That's when the pieces are ready to be built. Everyone knows that."

"Mom."

"What's he wearing?"

"Mom."

"Well! It says a lot about a man—how he dresses on a first date."

"It's not a first— Mom. It's— Can I call you back? I need to finish this thing."

"Get him to tell you about the Peace Corps! You like the Peace Corps. And he was in it. Did he tell you?"

Jane gave up. Betty was going to have this ill-advised conversation. Resistance was futile.

"He's a good one, Janie. He's really looking after his parents a lot. He's got them doing all sorts of social things in the city. Me, I'd never buy into any of that. I don't like the city. I don't know how you stand it. And you know, after you and Peter get married, you should have kids right away. I mean, right away. You're not getting any younger, you know. And then you'll come live out here, and we'll have dinner together every night, practically. Oh, Jane, you've made me so happy! I can't even tell you! You're going to get to experience the miracle of childbirth! And all the pain too, but that's part of the job, right? It'll be wonderful. You'll see."

Jane was dizzy.

"Mom? Catch your breath. I'll call you from the delivery room, okay?"

They said their good-byes, and Jane went back to the doomed bureau. Peter looked concerned.

"Delivery room?"

"Long story. Look, you don't want to do it this way. You want it right. Let me."

"I like it this way."

So now Jane tried to interpret the instructions upside down. And they actually made more sense that way. Jane had a feeling for how to put it together, and the feeling filled in the blanks. But she still didn't have a read on Peter. He was so nice. Mr. Root Beer. Mr. Filtered Water and No Dishes. He was too nice. Jane became suspicious. Maybe Mr. Bachelor Food was planning to hide bodies in the bureau. Or body *parts*! Aha! She started a deliberate study of Peter. Peter the Puzzle.

"Is your Mom okay?" He sounded so cheerful—he had to be a sinister character.

"Oh, yes. She's fine. She had a flu, but she's okay now."

They worked a bit more, and then Jane said, "So, that must have been weird for you, getting pulled into a family birthday party—not to mention all the family dramas. Sorry about that."

"Your family is fine. I like the way your brothers sing. I like the way your Mom *is* with you."

"Is?"

He described how Jane sat at her mother's feet, and how Betty had curled her daughter's ringlets around one finger. It must have been a nice picture.

"She used to do that when I was little, and I loved it." Jane's voice was soft. "Then I turned twelve, and I'd freeze every time she did it. And then I went through my hair-straightening phase. No curls to curl around her finger."

"How frustrating."

He knew too much. He was going to write a Howe Family Exposé for the *New York Post*. He was going to tell all their family secrets in front of People. Jane tightened a corner of the bureau and realized that Peter was behaving exactly the opposite of Dick-Richard. He was drawing her out. Asking her questions. She knew almost nothing about him. Time to turn the ready-made table on him. And if he refused to answer her questions, she could confirm that he was hiding something.

"So, why don't you have any dishes? Do you live on take-out food?"

"I work such long hours, and there's only me here. Why bother cooking?"

"I know what you mean. Sometimes I get scared that work is completely taking over my life. I think about it too much. I like my job, but I resent it creeping around my whole world. Here. Put glue in these holes and then hammer in the dowels. I'll get the other side ready."

It was starting to look like a bureau—from Willy Wonka's Factory. Jane had messed up this project, and she was also turning out to be a lousy detective. She still hadn't figured out Peter the Puzzle. She needed cleverer questions. And then it happened.

She was reaching for the screw gun while he was reaching for a dowel with his left hand. A band of gold on his ring finger. He was wearing a wedding ring.

Had he been wearing that before? Did her Mom know this? Why hadn't Jane noticed it before? Where was the wife? *Was it her body that was going in the bureau?*

Jane lifted a piece of pressed wood over her head. It was lighter than she had expected it to be, and she knocked down the photograph of Peter's mother.

"Oh, God, did I break it? I'll replace it. I'm so sorry!"

"It's not broken. It's fine. Don't know your own strength, huh?"

They were both looking at the photo, and Jane was speed-thinking: come up with a not lame way to draw this guy out.

"You don't look like your mother." Lame.

Peter smiled and nodded. "Don't look like my dad, either."

This would be the part of the movie where he reveals his alien/robot self, wouldn't it?

"I'm adopted. So is my brother. We don't look like each other, either."

Jane moved slowly and quietly. Adopted. What next?

"My wife thinks I look like Brad Pitt, but I don't see it."

Adopted and married. What is his story?

"What is your story?"

"I don't think I have one." Peter sounded so truthful. But Jane was still stuck, so she kept talking.

"My mother thought she was fixing me up with you. Are you telling me that my Catholic mother would fix her daughter up with a married man? Has she met your wife? Where is your wife? Answer that one first. Where is your wife?"

"My wife writes travel books. She bought this apartment before the neighborhood was cool, and she paid practically nothing for it. She's so smart."

"Where is she?"

"Oh, right. She's living in L.A., but she's only there for a few months out of the year. So here I am, living in her old place. It kind of sucks. I miss her a lot, but I guess this works for us. We really get to appreciate the time we have together. She's so great."

And now, of course, Peter was looking very handsome and desirable in a neglected-husband kind of way. Information overload. Jane needed to go home. Maybe she could teach him how to finish the bureau and then go home.

"Jane, did you think this was a fix up? Did you think tonight was some kind of date?"

She blushed before she could answer. Damn that pale skin—it always gave her away.

He was apologizing while she was busy faking that everything was fine. And now she felt obligated to finish his damn Willy Wonka bureau before she could go home. She worked quietly. One more table leg on top and she could go home and tell Ray or Sheila all about this. Maybe she'd do a three-way call and tell them both at once.

"So, do you have kids?" she asked without looking up.

"I wish. I mean, no. We don't. I thought we were going to adopt someday, but my wife sort of changed her mind about that. And this would be a tough way to raise a kid. She's right about that."

He was trying to sound very matter-of-fact. Trying not to reveal himself, or so it seemed to Jane. But she heard the sadness behind his voice. The regret. Jane was having trouble concentrating through it all. She nearly sliced her finger with the screw gun.

"Want the last dumpling?" he offered. She smiled and took it.

"Thanks." Nice guy. Damn.

· · ·

"Sheila, he was such a nice guy."

"Damn."

Jane looked like a teen in *Bye Bye Birdie*. She was on the floor, wearing a baby doll nightie, with her feet up on the couch. She played back the evening in complete detail for Sheila to analyze. Sheila, never an optimist to begin with, foresaw doom and gloom in a teacup.

"Janie, stay away from Mr. Married. He's just looking for a little something-something to keep him happy while his wife's away, and she is away *way* too much."

Jane's arguing gene surfaced.

"He never made a move on me. Not one. I think this was a simple misunderstanding. I thought it was a date. He thought it was a home repair."

"Married men have no business hanging out with single women. End of story. And I hope I said that loud enough for Raoul to hear. Oh! Oh-oh-oh! Maybe he's not really married! Maybe it's like one of those old movie tricks where he pretends to be married so he can avoid commitment."

"We watch too many old movies. I think he really is married."

"Jane? What about adoption? Are you going to try it?"

Jane wasn't sure, but she wanted to be, so she said, "No. Not on my own. No."

"Honey, were you thinking of Peter as potential Daddy material?" Sheila was very gentle.

"Yeah. Sort of."

"I'm sorry."

· · ·

Talking with Sheila didn't fix the knot in her stomach. As Jane pictured the mess she could make of her life entangled with Mr. Married, she barely realized that she had started tidying up her home. It evolved into a vacuuming and scrubbing the tub. And it actually helped—or wore her out too much to maintain the stomach knot. It was untied until she saw the flashing light on her answering machine.

You have one *new message.*

"Tell Janie to call her mother when she gets home." Betty. "Is she still out? I guess so. That's a good sign. Howard! I got her machine."

Beep.

Jane hesitated, then dialed.

"Hi, Mom."

"I called ten minutes ago. Did you just get back?"

"I was cleaning. I didn't hear the phone ring. Over the vacuum cleaner."

"Jane. No one vacuums on a weeknight. Everyone vacuums on Saturday morning. That's when the dirt is ready."

"Okay. I'll do it again on Saturday."

"So? Tell me? How did it go? Has Peter called you?"

"Are you serious? I just left his apartment two hours ago. So, no. He hasn't called. And even if he does . . . I don't want to see him again. Mom, he's married. Did you know that?"

"I know."

"I thought you were fixing me up with him. I thought you wanted—"

"Jane. He sees his wife maybe thirty days out of the year. If that. She keeps an apartment in Los Angeles so that she can travel around the Pacific. She has their dog, Jane! Their dog! She's got her dog with her, but not her husband. I mean, come on! This is no marriage. This is a sham. He's a nice fellow. He deserves a real life, and a real family."

Jane was mute. How often does a mother encourage a daughter to break up a marriage, excluding Joan Collins?

"He wants children, but his wife doesn't. And, Janie, a good son like him would make such a good father."

"He told you he wants children?"

"Yes. In so many words, yes. He did. Even the Catholic Church would give him a divorce. In a New York minute, they would!"

"Mom. I'm not going to break up his marriage. I wouldn't know how."

"Watch my soaps. I'll tape them for you. Take a few tips from Erica Kane, and you'll know what to do."

"Good night, Mom."

"Just picture it. You could live right here by me in the house on Albemarle. And you could stop by here every day. Every day! Oh, Janie. I want you to have a family. I want you to be happy, that's all. I love you."

Jane thought of telling her how she was haunted by babies. She thought of telling her mother about Choosing Single Motherhood and Families with Children from China. She thought of telling her about Little Red Bathing Suit, and how she had backed away from it all, too afraid, to awed, too overwhelmed.

"I love you too."

• • •

The phone rang at 5 A.M. Jane sprang out of bed, heart in her throat. It was her father.

"Janie. I'm afraid I have bad news. Your mother. She wasn't feeling well last night, after she got off the phone with you. She went to bed, but then, a few hours later, I heard her. She was calling to me. She was on the floor next to the bed. She was in a lot of pain. I called the ambulance."

Jane tried to push the words away. She knew what was coming.

"They said it was a heart attack. They got her to the hospital, and the doc said she was stable. They sent me home. They told me to go home. I didn't want to leave her there, but they told me that she needed to rest. So I came home."

"Oh, Dad."

"They just called. Just now. They said she had another attack.

This one was worse. They couldn't save her. She's gone. She's gone, Janie. What am I going to do?"

. . .

Jane walked out the door and saw the Christ Child in front of her building. The sun had been up for hours, but Jane couldn't make herself go to New Jersey. Not yet. She couldn't let this day move forward. She went outside because she thought she'd be more reluctant to cry in public. It was true until she saw Him. He seemed more active, more animated this time. He waved his arms, as if performing manic miracles. His mother seemed to have a cold, but He hadn't cured it. He saw Jane and shouted, "Adaa!"

Jane felt herself splitting open. Afraid of alarming mother or Child, she managed to say, "I'm sorry. I'm so sorry," while she gulped through her tears. Mother and child remained unfazed. She ran back upstairs and called Ray.

"I'm coming over. Don't move."

He must have flown to her apartment—he was there so quickly. He sat her down, made a pot of tea, and proceeded to make enough scrambled eggs for a platoon. He sat with her, ate, and practically spoon-fed Jane, who seemed oblivious to everything around her, until she said, "I thought you didn't eat eggs anymore."

Jane sniffled as she ate.

"Oh. That. Well, things change," Ray replied. "It's important to evolve as a person, and not get caught up too much in the physical world. You know? All that vanity is bad karma."

"So now you're a Buddhist?"

"Sort of. Maybe. Yes." Ray sounded a little embarrassed. "If you take enough yoga classes, you start to realize that the physical plane is not the most important thing."

"Are you giving up on being a perfect physical specimen?"

"Did I sound that stupid? Sorry. I don't know what I'm doing exactly. But I think that it would be better for me to pursue my identity on a spiritual plane, instead of a physical one. Let's face it. The body is mortal."

Jane put her fork down. Ray gasped and said, "Oh, God. I did not just say that. I'm an idiot. Please, Jane. I'm so sorry."

"It's okay. And anyway, it's true, isn't it?"

. . .

Ray stood by as she called Sheila. Jane repeated Howard's early morning phone call, word for word. Sheila cried quietly, almost from the beginning.

"Oh, Jane. I didn't want it to end this way." She was already disintegrating.

"Please, Sheil, please. Come to the funeral."

"Mom wouldn't want me there."

"I'll make it right with Dad. I'll stay with you the whole time. I'll be with you. Please be there."

"I'm scared. What are the boys going to say to me? And what about Dad? I can't go."

"She's *your* mother too."

Jane ate cold scrambled eggs with hot sauce. She called into work and let them know she would not be in for several days. Maybe a week. A death in the family. She found a dozen unimportant tasks that needed doing. She knew she was stalling, and Ray didn't rush her. Finally, Ray accompanied her to Port Authority.

That afternoon, she arrived at her parents' house, hereafter known as her dad's house, to find that the funeral would take place in three days. Flowers, music, prayers, reception, coffin, headstone, mass cards—everything was arranged. Kevin was playing alpha male and wouldn't part with one detail. She pretended to be angry that everything was done, all the work "taken." But in truth, she had dreaded making any of these decisions. Sam's funeral had convinced her that when her time was up, she should disappear from the planet and the body should never be found.

"Have you picked an outfit for her?" She should at least do something. She should figure out what Mom would want to wear forever. Jane pictured Betty's signature cardigan sweaters, chunky cotton and colorful. She had a big collection of them, so it would be hard to choose. Definitely include one of these, so that Betty would look like Betty.

"I already picked out a dress. That black gown that Mom wore to the anniversary party. The one you missed," Kevin replied.

Betty had worn black maybe three times in her whole life. She used to reprimand Jane about her urban propensity for black clothing.

"Janie, black clothes attract everything but men and money," Betty used to say. Used to.

Jane had to take Howard aside and let him know that Sheila might be coming. He was true to all the men of his generation, strong and firm-jawed.

"That would be fine," he said. Thank God.

• • •

The funeral started with a viewing, which is a terrible event that has a wonderful effect on the people who attend it. Everyone gathers in the room with the body, looks at it a lot, then moves on to the funeral and reception. It sounds awful because it is. Still, the viewing is a big help because it puts everyone face-to-face with a dead body. And there is no denying, no pretending, no kidding yourself. She's dead. That's not her. She remembered Ray's description of a Buddhist custom: Mourners stay with a dead body until it is so decomposed as to be unrecognizable. Embalming speeds up that process for the mourners. One look inside the casket and you know: Betty did not reside in that waxy husk. She was gone.

If Betty could have pulled a Tom Sawyer and seen it all, she would have loved her funeral. At least, she would have loved the viewing. She had a big turnout. A nice mention in the local paper.

She would have loved the flowers. She would have preferred to wear one of her colorful cardigans. It was a lovely viewing.

And then Sheila walked in. It took Jane three beats to recognize her. Her sister was tanner, blonder, fuller in every way. Was she wearing contacts? She looked like the old Sheila, but different. This was Sheila happy. It seemed inappropriate for a funeral.

Howard embraced her, as if she were a titled cousin. Familiar, but formal. Close, but distant. Still, he had done the Big Acknowledging. The boys would have to follow suit, and so would their wives.

No, they wouldn't. Kevin shook his head and sneered. Neil stood protectively by the casket. No one spoke. The viewing resumed, and Jane hooked her arm around Sheila's. The crowd may have resumed speaking, but not to Jane and Sheila. The sisters walked cautiously to the coffin, and Neil stepped aside. The daughters said silent good-byes to the mannequin in the satin-lined box. They did it again, later, when there was really nothing else to do since no one would speak to them. When the funeral director instructed the mourners that it was time to pay final respects, Jane and Sheila faced it together one more time. They had already had two practice runs, so you would think it would have been easy, but it was not. This time, Jane could not see, could not speak through her tears. She felt Sheila against her left arm, shaking with grief. They stepped aside. Howard and his sons paid final respects as a team, and then they closed the coffin together. Jane turned away before it was finished. There are images no one wants.

The funeral mass was surprisingly tear-free. Jane expected to lose control when she heard a familiar hymn, but it didn't happen. The graveside service was only a brief farewell. The sisters never even made it to the front of the crowd. They saw nothing and heard only every fourth word. Then came a reception at a local restaurant that Betty had frequented. Jane and Sheila retreated to the ladies' room.

"Almost done, Sheila. Thank you for coming. I couldn't have gotten through this without you."

"Thanks for making me. How are you holding up?"

They recharged each other, then returned to their table. Some distant cousins had sat at their table while they were gone, but when they realized their mistake, they immediately relocated. Radioactive table. Jane and Sheila smiled and kept the large table to themselves.

Howard entered the restaurant, and Kevin and Neil called to him.

"Dad! Over here! We saved you a seat!"

Howard waved to his sons, and then he sat with his daughters. Just like that, Jesus sat with the lepers and the prostitutes. Neil looked furious. Kevin looked shocked. But not as shocked as the leper and the prostitute who basked in their father's glow.

Neil rose and used a big voice.

"Folks, I'd like to make a toast. This has been a tough, tough day for us all. And we wouldn't have gotten through it without the help of the man of the hour."

Jane and Sheila smiled at their father and prepared to make room for him to rise and bow. Neil continued.

"Ladies and gentleman, let's hear it for my brother, Kevin."

Everyone was surprised by this, but everyone applauded politely. Kevin rose and bowed.

Howard didn't eat the gray food that was put before him. He made very very small talk with his daughters. Sheila knew better than to mention Raoul's name. For these few hours, he didn't exist.

"Your mother is a wonderful woman. She had a hard life, you know." Howard was still mixing past and present tenses when he talked about Betty. Jane and Sheila saw his skin turn a bit red. Even if he didn't allow himself to cry, his Irish skin would give him away.

"Your mother loved"—he swallowed hard before he could continue—"being a mother. It was the greatest joy of her life. And, oh, was she good with babies. You wouldn't believe it. Other mothers in the neighborhood would bring their babies to her when they needed a rest or some help. And she always said yes. No matter what else happened, what problems she had, she knew she did a good job raising you kids."

"Yes. She did." Jane was a little surprised at how calmly Sheila said this. Howard was on a roll.

"Motherhood was the siren call of her life, you know? She didn't need a lot of money or a fancy house. She never cared about clothes—except for those sweaters of hers. No. She found real satisfaction this way. As a mom. Oh, the joy she took at watching you kids grow. She taught you all how to read, and it was a national event when you mastered the silent *e*. She'd jump in the air. She was happy. Really happy."

Her father's words made something open in Jane's heart. Why was she thinking about Little Red Bathing Suit? Why was she dreaming about adoption? She shook her head and came back to the funeral.

Sheila took Howard's hand. He patted hers and changed the subject. He wondered if Betty would have liked the flower arrangements.

Jane wished she smoked. She wished she could stay at that table for a week. But it ended. She and Sheila had to leave. Howard walked them to the door. She looked back over the chatting crowd in the restaurant. Kevin was staring daggers at his sisters. Neil was actively ignoring them.

And that's when Jane spotted Peter, near the back of the restaurant. He was sitting with his parents and with Jane's weird cousin Kyle, making what appeared to be polite small talk. Jane froze. Peter saw her and came over to her.

"You must be Sheila," he said. He introduced himself and offered condolences to the sisters. Then Peter spoke to Howard.

"Mr. Howe, I'm so sorry for your loss."

"Thank you. Thank you so much."

"I didn't know Mrs. Howe very well, but she seemed like a spectacular mother."

Howard's eyes betrayed him. He must have wanted so badly to cry.

"That she was," he managed to say. He hugged both of his daughters. Both of them. And Jane felt sadly, darkly hopeful about Howard and Sheila.

"I'd best see about your brothers now," said Howard. "You girls take care. I love you."

Howard joined his sons, while the girls stepped outside to the brutal sunlight. Peter followed them.

"Would you like a ride back to the city?" he offered.

Jane nodded and smiled. He put his arms forward, and Jane collapsed into them. She hadn't meant to, but he offered a shoulder, and she cried on it.

Meanwhile, Sheila had a car waiting to take her to the airport. She hugged her sister one last time and whispered, "I take back everything I said before. I like him."

Chapter Six

You have three new messages.

"It's me, Ray. Are you okay? Hey! Someone put a rhyming curse on me. Shit. Anyway, I just wanted you to come home to a not-awful message. And I hope there's one on this machine. Love you. Think you're swell."

Beep.

"Jane. This is Richard. What are you doing tonight? I'm in a scene night at the Actors' Collective. I sent you a flier, but I must have gotten your address wrong. It came back to me. But you need to know, I'm doing this scene from *Bette and Boo,* and it is *so* hysterical. You'd love it."

Beep.

"Hi, Jane. It's Karen, from the Choosing Single Motherhood meeting. Listen. I don't know if you got the number for the INS. In fact, I don't know for sure that you're really going through with this adoption. By the end of the night, you sort of looked like motherhood was maybe not the path for you. And that's fine. But if you want it, you should call them soon. This part of the process can take a while."

As Karen read the number, Jane's whole body lunged for paper and pen. There was no hesitation, only paper and ink. She wrote the number as neatly and prettily as she could. Jane smiled and thought, In the beginning was the number, and the number was toll-free . . . She needed that number. She was beyond thinking, planning, and making lists. She was going to make that call. Soon. She was going to adopt a baby. Soon.

· · ·

The city seemed too bright and noisy after the funeral. It felt disloyal to Betty (and to Howard) to get back into the swing of things. But it was so compelling. There was no resisting the pull of daily life. Jane was back in the swing inside of two days.

Argenti's London acquisition was complete. Her staff walked around saying, "Pip, pip, cheerio," and suggested that they all go out for bad food. There was a kind of comfort in the return to daily life. Today always included tomorrow. And tomorrow included a trip to the gym.

· · ·

"Ray. Please. I know you're the next Dalai Lama and all, but don't you care about muscle tone? I'm going to be lugging a baby and a baby's stuff up all those stairs. On a spiritual level, I'm going to need lots of upper body strength."

"Please. I'll never look like one of those Chelsea boys, so why bother? I'll be deep instead."

"Can't you be deep with biceps? And keep me company?"

"I'm so tired of sweating. But for you . . . Okay."

Jane got Ray to join her at the gym early. Really early. Oh, so early. He had been up late the night before, writing a scathing review of a new musical about a pair of homicidal twins. Jane was already keeping a good pace on the treadmill when he stumbled in.

"Come on, Ray. Your body is a temple."

"My body is a temporary vessel. And this is a pointless activity. Hilarious, from an existential point of view."

"Oh."

"I can't outrun you, babe, but I can out-Buddha you."

And that's when Jane saw Peter, across the gym, climbing the Stairs to Nowhere. She missed Ray's speech about his karma manifesting itself as love handles. She fixed her hair. She stood up straighter. Peter waved. Ray was still talking about his previous life when Peter came by and said, "Hi. Right. So. I guess you live in the neighborhood, so you go to the neighborhood gym. Right. I guess."

Why was he being all shy and awkward? In the gym mirrors, she could just barely see Ray smirk.

"Yes. Right here in the neighborhood. Yup," Jane replied. Clearly, no one could salvage this conversation. Ray's smirk turned into a giggle. Peter was holding in his stomach, and Jane was distracted by how handsome Peter was, in a tousled, early-morning way.

"I'm Ray," he said, waving to Peter and shaming Jane for forgetting to make introductions.

"I'm Peter. Do you live in the neighborhood too?"

"Sort of. Jane and I are old friends. So. How's your wife?"

Jane flinched and increased the speed on her treadmill.

"She's fine. She's great. She's wonderful. Writing in Australia at the moment. Well. I'm off to work," said Peter. "Gotta go. I'm going to shower first. Then go."

"Right," said Jane.

Jane and Ray were silent until Peter was completely gone. They spoke at once:

Jane:

Ray:

"How's your wife? God! That was so rude! How could you embarrass me like that? I thought you were supposed to

"He's married! Ma-a-a-a-a-rried! Wake up, Jane. And he isn't all that gorgeous. I think he wears

be all karmic holy or something? tinted contacts, and what else
Doesn't that exclude catty does he wear? Oh yeah, I
scenes like this?" remember: a wedding ring!"

They ran another mile. Jane burned off her temper, and then Ray said the obvious.

"It's not my fault he's married, sweetie."

• • •

Oh, sure, it looked like an ordinary phone call. Just another 800 number. No one in any of the offices around her would know that this was actually a first step. All this thinking, talking, reading, all amounted to nothing. Jane's unique set of fingerprints would start the process that would lead her to motherhood. She gulped and dialed. As she listened to the automated menu, she reminded herself that she could pull the plug on the adoption any time she wanted to. She wouldn't have to go through with it. Jane could hang up at any time. So she did, and then retreated to a list. She needed to know why she was doing this. She typed:

Why Am I Doing This?
1. I don't know.
2. If I don't do this, I think I'll get sick or go crazy.
3. I think I have to.
4. I don't know.
5. I want to.
6. I actually believe that I can do it.

As lists go, this one was a bit thin. What was it in her father's words that had lifted her off her feet and pointed her down this road? She tried to remember. It was lost. Jane looked at her thumb while she dialed the INS. She made her request. This request resulted in an appointment day. Just a day, not a time. She could arrive and be fingerprinted at any hour of the day. How convenient. This anytime appointment would launch her legal, out loud request to adopt a baby. Those prints would travel to Albany, Washington, and Beijing. Jane examined her thumb more closely. And then she got her first e-mail from Karen:

To: <chinamoms>
From: karen51@ournet.com
Subject: INS Fingerprinting

Just came back from my ordeal at the INS.

Learn from my pain. First—don't enter on the avenue, enter on the cross street, or you'll never find the right room. Second—get there as early as you possibly can. I mean it. The line is long and it just gets longer. It took me forever and a day.

Have you guys found agencies yet? I'm still looking. Oh the pressure!

Fingerprinting takes a long time? Why? Jane couldn't take an undefined, long morning off from work. Could she? She'd never done it. Never tried. She wasn't the kind of person who did that. This wasn't the kind of firm that allowed it. Jane wasn't sure if she should interpret this as a bad sign or as a test. These things are never obvious. Let it be a test. Mothers sometimes need to take whole mornings off from work, don't they? So. Go to the INS.

Jane never managed a true list of the pros and cons of motherhood. It's not a step that works well on paper. She never finished questioning herself about proceeding, but she proceeded anyway. It was like color soaking into fabric. Little by little, it clung to her, until it was part of her.

• • •

At 8:30 A.M., there was already a long, long, long, long, long line of people at the INS. They snaked around stretch-o-ropes and out into the hall. As she was promoted through the line, Jane could see that there were four or five cubicles where tired people would fingerprint everyone on that line, but never look at them.

While she was waiting, and clutching her appointment letter, Jane noticed a blurry color television with a built-in VCR. The INS showed movies to those waiting in line. Jane hadn't noticed the television at first. But when a fingerprinter came over to put in a new movie, Jane groaned. Did this mean she would be waiting for two hours? Or more? What if they showed *The Godfather*? Did that mean an even longer wait? Was she expected to leave before Michael Corleone became head of the family?

They played *George of the Jungle*. When scantily clad George bonked into a tree and fell down, Jane heard a throaty giggle. Teresa was on line, six people ahead of Jane. She was easy to spot. She wore the most expensive clothes Jane had ever seen.

"I canceled lunch with a client, just in case this runs late. You?" Teresa asked.

Jane had canceled a staff meeting. And her staff had looked entirely too pleased about that.

They chatted through the other people on line. From time to time, they watched George fall down again. Teresa wondered aloud if this is what kids watch these days. It didn't seem educational. But eventually George found true love, and Jane and Teresa found the front of the line. Teresa's formality never faltered.

"I came here this morning with an out-clause in my head. I keep telling myself that this is all still theoretical, this adoption, this child." Teresa seemed to be talking to her shoes. She spoke slowly and never looked up.

"But this isn't theory. I'm going to do this. I'm hungry to do this. I'm starving. I'm adopting a baby from China. I'm going to be a mother." Still talking to the shoes. Nice shoes. Awkward pause. Jane needed to state the obvious.

"This is hard."

"Yes. I'm narrowing down my agency search, but honestly, I can't tell why one agency would be better than another. I suppose it's a personal reaction to the individuals? I don't know."

Jane made a mental note: start agency searching.

The fingerprinting process was very high-tech. It involved computers and glass screens. No paper and ink. Jane studied the ridges and whorls on her hands until Mr. Fingerprinter grabbed her thumb and started the process. It took only a few minutes, and then he turned his back on her. Jane was lost. What happens next?

"Excuse me? What happens next?"

"What are you doing?"

"I'm asking you a question. What happens next?"

"No. What are you doing?"

"I'm asking you a question. What happens next?"

The supervisor stepped in.

"What are you doing?" he asked Jane.

"Well, I'm trying to ask a question."

"No. Why are you being fingerprinted? What are you doing with the prints? Getting citizenship? What? Let me see your letter."

He took two seconds to read it, then said, "Your fingerprints will go to the FBI for clearance, then back to the INS with your paperwork. Good luck, Mommy. Next!"

· · ·

Jane returned from the INS, sat at her PC, and Googled adoption agencies: "adoption agency," "China," "single mother." The results spilled out with blinding blue underlines. Each "welcome" sounded the same. Each offered the same instructions and advice. Some were more religious than others. Some assembled the dossier for you and charged a hefty fee for doing it. Some dealt only with China adoptions, some were multinational. And then she saw an agency called Founding Mothers. It specialized in helping single women adopt. Founding Mothers. She gave the site a quick read, and that was it. She had chosen her agency. Done.

Jane planned to lie about how she chose her agency. She would never admit to this slipshod research. She would fake a story about a detailed list. She looked for their phone number—it was a Brooklyn number. She found a link to e-mail the agency. She composed a formal and formidable introduction and request for documents to initiate an adoption. Her e-mail read like a letter of introduction to the King of Sweden. Just in case they were judging her by this initial contact, they would have to take her *so* seriously. And their reply would give her a sign about whether or not she should proceed, whether or not this was the right agency for her. Did Founding Mothers know how much pressure was on their reply? Within the hour, she received this e-mail:

To: jane.howe@argenti.com
From: b.ali@foundingmothers.com
Subject: Re: Request for Documents

Dear Ms. Howe,

I'll send you our documents through the post office today. I can stop by there after I pick up my daughter from school. BTW, she's originally from Hunan Province.

I have to ask: You wouldn't be the same Jane Howe who used to spend hours finding all the nuances in Beckett, would you? Before I started this agency, I used to teach a class on Comparative Literature in Translation and I remember a Jane Howe in my class, but this was years ago. If that's you—Hi! If that's not you—Hi too!

Later!

Barbara Ali
Agency Director

Yes, Jane was that same Jane Howe. And now, Jane Howe had her agency.

To: jane.howe@argenti.com, karen51@ournet.com
From: teresa.fenno@reedpr.com
Subject: Dossier

Ladies,

I've begun work on the dossier. My agency sent me a very helpful checklist to guide me through the process. Planning to assemble photos of family and home, as this is part of the dossier. Heard that one adoptive mom hired a "bug wrangler" to assemble thousands of ladybugs for her photo. Apparently, Americans think that Chinese think that ladybugs are good luck. Do the Chinese know this? At any rate, the mom-in-question arranged for the ladybugs to be released from their cages just as the photos were snapped. And they're going to give a child to this person. Oh my.

To: teresa.fenno@reedpr.com, karen51@ournet.com
From: jane.howe@argenti.com
Subject: Re: Dossier

I hope I get a list from my agency. Where did you hear about the ladybug lady? I love that.

We're supposed to include photos of us along with our families, and a good look at our home. I always take pictures, so I'm not in any of them myself. So, this weekend I'm going to have my friend Ray take pictures of me at the Chinese Scholars' Garden. Is that too cheesy, too "look at me I'm all into your culture"? By the way, what agency did you choose? I chose Founding Mothers. They're small, but I actually know the founder. Talk about signs!

Jane

To: jane.howe@argenti.com, teresa.fenno@reedpr.com
From: karen51@ournet.com
Subject: Re: Re: Dossier

Jane,

No way! I chose Founding Mothers too! I liked the name. I like the woman who ran it. Oh my God! Maybe we'll end up traveling together! Maybe our girls are in the same orphanage! Wow! I'm getting chills!

Karen

To: jane.howe@argenti.com, karen51@ournet.com
From: teresa.fenno@reedpr.com
Subject: Re: Re: Re: Dossier

Ladies,

I don't mean to give anyone here chills, but I may have no alternative. I chose Founding Mothers as well. I wanted a New York-based agency that knew how to handle single mother adoptions and had reasonable fees, a good track record, and a few other factors.

   That said, do you know the odds against us traveling together? And Jane, you haven't started your homestudy yet.

   T

Jane returned to the gym, while Ray claimed to be home meditating. She chose to believe him. She quietly rejoiced that he wouldn't be able to ask Peter about his wife again. Not that she was thinking about Peter. Ever. In fact, she was actively not thinking of him when she packed her clothes for the gym: her tightest yoga pants, her littlest midriff. She wore her hair in a bouncy ponytail. She put on makeup. She looked fake, like an advertisement for a gym.

She sprinted on the treadmill until boredom set in. She went over to find her weights. She studied the selection of shiny weights, opting to start with a low, low, easy size, and suddenly there was Peter. He wore shorts and a NYC Marathon shirt. Had he run a marathon? Did he want Jane to know? Were those tinted contacts or were his eyes really green?

"Where's your friend?" Peter asked.

"Home. He's a better person than me. He doesn't need the gym."

"Well, I do."

Jane decided that his eyes were really green like that. No contacts. He looked like a fast-forward of Brad Pitt with engraved laugh lines. They said something positive about his character, didn't they?

Peter was using heavy weights, so Jane chose a larger weight than she really wanted, did two bicep curls, and exchanged them for a lighter weight.

"Don't move your elbow like that," Peter advised. He placed his hands gently on her elbows. She tried not to flinch.

"Keep your elbow at your waist. Like this. Don't jerk your arm up, or you'll hurt yourself. Form is really important with weights."

"Got it." She looked in the mirror. They looked like they were ready to sing a song in a Rodgers & Hammerstein musical. They were a picture.

"So, Jane. Since we work in the same building, maybe we can hook up for lunch sometime."

Jane wanted so much to say yes. That's why she said, "No. I usually eat at my desk. But thanks anyway."

"Or dinner. There are so many restaurants in our neighborhood that I really want to check out. And I hate to go to restaurants alone. What do you say?"

"Oh, I don't know. I mean. No. Thanks, but I don't think it's a good idea."

"Oh."

He went back to his weights, and he looked a little angry. Jane didn't think that Mr. Married Peter had any business being mad. He shouldn't be asking her out on a date, right?

"I'm not asking you out on a date, you know. I'm married."

"Yes, I found that out. Eventually." Now Jane sounded a little angry.

"I just thought that we could be friends. Why can't you be friends with me?"

Because you're gorgeous and smart and charming and nice and warm, and I like you way too much. And I want to have a child, and I'm even working on that, and you look like such good Daddy material, it makes me want to break my own teeth. That's what she wanted to say. She couldn't think up a polite lie quickly enough. So Peter continued.

"Dinner buddies. We could be dinner buddies. We both have to eat. Please? You're looking at a guy with no dishes and a big appetite. Look at me. I'm hungry. I'm wasting away. You can help me out, or you can turn the page."

She smiled. She relented. They would become dinner buddies.

• • •

The Founding Mothers DTC checklist came with a bright red folder on which Barbara had written, "Building a Family" in gold letters. Jane could check off five columns of progress: Obtained, Reviewed by Founding Mothers, Notarized, Certified, Authenticated. A list with levels. Ooh. Her dossier would contain a big pile of paper.

1. The Homestudy—this scared Jane the most. A social worker must come to her home and inspect it, her, three letters of reference, and her life. This verdict would sway the entire process.
2. State Report—this required her to give Albany a list of every

address she had inhabited since she was eighteen, and it would prove, on a state level, that she was not a crook.

3. Police Report—this meant a trip to police headquarters and another fingerprinting. It would prove, on the city level, that she was not a crook.

4. Financial Report—this was a form provided by China where she listed her debts and assets. She needed only to be above the poverty level to qualify.

5. Medical Report—this was another form provided by China. It required a general checkup and tests for HIV and TB.

6. Letter to the China Center of Adoption Affairs (CCAA)—this was a sort of cover letter to the dossier. There was no template to follow, but she absolutely had to gain China's trust, convey her personality, and explain why she had chosen to adopt, why China, and how well she would treat the child. All on one page.

7. Photos—this would be two pages of photos that showed Jane, her family, her home, all captioned, colorful, and happy.

8. Birth Certificate—easy.

9. Passport—easy.

10. Proof of Employment—easy.

11. Marriage Certificate or Divorce Decree or Letter of Single Status—a little embarrassing. This was a notarized letter, stating that she was, in fact, unmarried. Never been married, still not married. Sincerely, Jane Howe.

12. Document I-171H—This would prove, on a federal level, that Jane was not a crook. It could take months to receive. A copy would be sent to Jane and to China and to all the twelve apostles, maybe.

Still, Jane's heart sang. A list! Lists are so specific and possible.

• • •

Karen and Teresa had already begun work on their lists. They were ahead of her. They would get to China before her. Jane had to catch up. So she scheduled a homestudy right away. She tried to imagine how it would go. Some large, suspicious person would interview her and probably run a white-gloved finger over the top bookshelf, the one Jane couldn't reach. Maybe there would be an elaborate lie detector involved. Dr. Ali, who really wished Jane would call her Barbara, encouraged Jane to complete the homestudy as soon as possible. The FBI's approval of the fingerprints would combine with the homestudy in an INS office and transform into the I-171H. The magical result of bureaucratic alchemy. Hard to obtain. Very Holy Graily. But once it was received, Jane would be ready to send her dossier to China. Jane could not see anything beyond the Dossier to China date. The DTC, as the folks on the listserv called it. Jane was learning the lingo.

Jane enlisted Ray's help with the cleaning. He could reach the top shelf of the bookcase. Jane reorganized her very organized sock drawer. She grimaced at the thought of the spare room—she couldn't call it a baby's room yet—being inspected. It looked like a warehouse in hell. Ray talked her down.

"You know, babies make messes. They're not known for their neatness."

"This is an inspection. I had to gather three letters of reference that make me sound like the savior of western civilization. I'm not leaving anything to chance. Please tell me that the place doesn't smell too much like cleaning chemicals."

It did.

"Please, please, please let me cleanse the place with a little burning sage?" Ray was practically begging. His eyes looked big.

"Babies. Fire. No."

She opened the windows and tried to whoosh all the chemical smells out to the city.

"Ray?" Jane asked while she whooshed. "You'll come with me to China, won't you?"

He kissed her cheek.

"Darling Jane. Just try and stop me."

By the time social worker Donna Dupree-O'Reilly arrived at Jane's home, it would have met the standards of the worst obsessive-compulsive in Martha Stewart's family tree. Clean, but warm. Safe, but lived-in. Happy, but stable. Good, but great. This was to be the actual judgment of her fitness to be a mother. She buzzed Donna into the building with maternal warmth and firmness.

Donna seemed to like Jane in advance. She had a list of questions that she had to ask, but they veered off topic easily. Donna had two teenagers and talked fondly of the baby years.

"Jane, you have a second bedroom? Wow! Most of the people I interview are still kicking themselves for buying a one-bedroom, you know?"

"But the room is kind of small."

"So are babies."

Donna wasn't judging or inspecting. She was chatting. She offered advice on the baby's adjustment to the U.S. She shared good and bad experiences in child care. She never even glanced at that top bookshelf. Jane forgot about being nervous. The interview lasted an hour and included two cups of decaffeinated tea.

"Now, I take all this stuff, the letters, the financial stuff, and I turn it into a homestudy," Donna explained. "You and your agency okay it, and there'll be two copies: a long version for the INS and a short version for China."

"Why does China want a short version?"

"They've got to get this all translated, and they need a more condensed version. The long homestudies used to really slow them down. They've got a lot of homestudies to read. A lot."

There was so much to know. Jane worried that perhaps she had used too many American idiomatic phrases, and her homestudy would be impossible to translate. Donna reassured her that all would be well. Jane raced to the phone and relived the entire evening for Ray. He was, as always, an attentive audience.

Chapter Seven

"Barbara, tell me the truth. Can I do this alone?" Jane knew she was asking for a passing grade, permission, and a psychic prediction. She also knew that Barbara was too smart to provide any of the above.

"Jane, sweetheart, no." And didn't that sound like a failing grade?

Barbara continued. "No one can do it alone. It takes more than a village to raise a child, Jane. It takes a whole hemisphere. Let's make sure you stay connected."

And so Barbara invited all her adopting Moms to dinner in Chinatown. There were other single women who were following this same crazy path, beyond Karen and Teresa. The restaurant was noisy, but the women found one another easily. There were lots of new faces.

"I'm Greta. I'm halfway through my dossier. And you?" Greta was short and heavy. Jane thought she looked like a mushroom.

"I'm Charm. C-H-A-R-M. My parents thought it would be cute. I promise you, I'll give my kid a normal name. Not Charm. I haven't started yet, on the dossier, I mean. I'm still thinking about it." Charm was a pretty brunette with a thick New York accent.

"I'm Megan. I'm waiting." Megan was rail thin, with an ex-punk look to her.

"For what?" asked Charm. Jane wondered if Megan waited for signs too.

"For my referral. My dossier went to China, like, six months ago. So I'm watching the Web like crazy. We all keep track of what each agency is saying about timing. And the referrals usually come in monthly batches. So you watch a whole mess of people get their referrals, and you know you're one step closer. Don't you watch the lists?"

You would think that a Web site commonly referred to as "the lists" would have had a special appeal for Jane, but so far she had avoided them. She had lists of her own. It seemed like adoption was an entire world beneath or around this one. She had just never noticed.

Barbara arrived late, with her daughter, Rachel, in tow. Rachel was six years old, with pigtails and a Catholic school uniform. She was lethally gorgeous. There was too much to react to. The baby hunger awoke in the table of women, and Rachel sensed it immediately. They all looked ready to snatch the little girl and take her home. She clung to her mother.

"She's not usually so shy," Barbara apologized, then got down to business. "Ladies, one of the reasons I've brought you all together is this: I'd like to hold a couple of seminars or discussions that I wish I'd had back when I was paper-chasing." The women glowed. It was like free money. Or shoes.

"But I'll need someone to organize the materials, schedules, and such. Any volunteers."

It looked to Jane as if every woman at the table was trying to shrink. Jane shot her hand up. This was a job for List Woman!

"Jane. Of course. I should have known. Let's talk about this separately, okay? I'm so hungry. Rachel, honey, I've lost all feeling in that arm. Can you relax a little bit?"

Eventually Rachel sat and ate and colored the dragon picture that the waiter had given her. She started her own pictures on the side, a parade of Disney villains.

Jane took a chance. She pointed to a black and white woman on Rachel's page and said, "Cruella De Vil."

"Uh-huh."

Jane sang, "If she doesn't scare you, no evil thing will. To see her is to take a sudden chill."

Rachel lit up. She stopped drawing and gazed at her new American Idol.

"Cruella, Cruella De Vil."

Why Jane knew all the words to this song, she could never explain. But they had taken up space in her brain, and now they were connecting her with little Rachel. As they sang greatest Disney villain hits (Jane got a little carried away and shimmied as she belted "Poor Unfortunate Souls" from *The Little Mermaid*), Jane realized that she was missing all the helpful hints that the Chinamoms were sharing around the table. She should have stayed in the grown-up conversation.

"Do you know the Gaston song?"

Jane did her best baritone and kept singing.

• • •

The women helped one another with the dossier work:

To: <chinamoms>
From: jane.howe@argenti.com
Subject: Police Plaza

What a frustrating morning. Here's the deal:
1. You don't need to wait on that long line at the lobby/reception area. You can go right into the waiting room.
2. You need to bring a money order to pay the fee. That's right, no cash, no checks, no credit card. I had to leave, get the money order, and come back. It was so annoying.

Also, here's a MapQuest link for anyone having trouble getting there.

To: <chinamoms>
From: meganr@hotlink.com
Subject: Timing

Things are moving so slowly in China. Barbara just told me that I probably won't get my referral for another month, month and a half. I'm miserable. If anyone is free, please call me and talk me in from the ledge. How can I wait another month and a half oh God!!!

Megan, Mom-to-Be

To: <chinamoms>
From: teresa.fenno@reedpr.com
Subject: Ow

Ladies,

I have just returned from getting my medical report completed. My GP will sign the form after the tests are back. Can't describe how much the TB test hurts. It involves wiggling a needle under the skin, causing it to bubble and hurt. Does anyone else remember those little tine tests we got in school, or does that go back to the days of leeches? Why did those tine tests go away? Not painful enough?

Is anyone else considering hepatitis vaccinations before traveling? If so, please do contact me.

T

Saturday morning. Jane was still half asleep, or so she thought. She wanted to sleep in. She blinked at the chair in her bedroom and saw her mother. Sitting, smiling, and looking about thirty years younger. Jane blinked again and sat up. The chair was empty. Of course.

. . .

Jane received her homestudy in the mail. It was surprisingly cold. It listed pertinent dates about Jane's life. It listed her family members. It noted the recent death of Betty. It gave a sketchy description of her job, her apartment, her appearance. It listed her assets and her lack of debt. It was so impersonal. But then it stated that Donna, a social worker qualified to make such judgments, recommended Jane for adopting a child. There. She was catching up with Karen and Teresa. Wasn't she?

. . .

Another Saturday. She should really sleep in while she can. Time would come soon when she wouldn't be able to. And there was Mom, standing in the doorway, keeping the thirty-years-younger look. A good choice. Jane followed her out of the bedroom, to the far end of the apartment.

"Janie? What are you going to do with this extra room?"

"The darkroom? I'm changing it. You'll see."

"No, dear. I know that's the baby's room. I meant over here. See? You have a whole extra room you've never used. See?"

She guided Jane through a hidden door and into a large room, off the kitchen. Had it always been there? It was a rough space. Dark and musty. It would need a lot of work. A lot of fixing up. But Jane could do it. Oh, look. It needed new windows. And maybe she should break through the wall here and—

She woke up and laughed at herself. Every New Yorker's dream—discovering extra space in your apartment.

. . .

"This is such a powerful dream," Ray told her over drinks. "Let me look up some of the symbols in my book and I'll give you a full interpretation."

But Jane didn't want it interpreted. It was about mother and baby and real estate. That was enough. Besides, she was late for meeting Peter, her dinner buddy.

"You really think he just wants to be friends with you?" Ray could not hide his cynicism.

"Listen, if he wants more than that, I'll scare him off with my baby plans. A married man looking for a little something-something doesn't want that kind of complication."

"Speaking of baby plans—have you told Howard yet?"

No. She hadn't. Jane visited her father, but it was more difficult now. Her brothers wanted nothing to do with her. They kept the children away, made dramatic exits, and stayed away until Jane was back on her island, Manhattan. Jane had allied herself with Sheila, the traitor, and the Irish boys' sense of loyalty to their mother locked Jane out in the cold. So Jane did not visit often.

"He looks so exhausted these days. Don't yell at me, but I'm waiting for a sign—for the right time. For timing. I'm waiting to tell him."

"Hey, who am I to lecture? I had a hard time coming out to my parents too. You'd think my Judy Garland album collection would have clued them in, but I still had to do it. And so will you."

Jane hadn't been paying close attention to Ray while she took care of the great paper chase for her dossier. But today, she looked at him and saw a change. Was it his skin? His eyes? Was he really getting something from this new phase he was in?

"Ray. You look gorgeous. You look, I don't know how to describe it, happy."

"That's right."

Jane kicked herself for being so self-involved and missing this change in her friend. Ray was happy. Ray. Happy. Anything was possible.

He was still smiling, still quiet, still happy. Jane squirmed with curiosity.

"Ray? Talk to me. What happened? How did you manage this?"

"How to be Happy in Ten Easy Steps. Is that what you want to hear? Come on. I'm happy, Jane. That's all."

"Wow."

Jane sat, chastened and silent, for at least three minutes. Didn't she look so shallow, with her martini glass and obliviousness. But then, chaste silence didn't suit her relationship with Ray. She giggled and said, "Is he cute?"

Ray smiled like the Grinch. "So cute. So, so cute. His name is Burton, such a movie star name. He introduced me to this great meditation class. I pondered his cuteness until I found that I really liked the rest of him too."

"Wow."

. . .

Jane met Peter at an Argentinean restaurant. She was prepared for an evening of awkward conversation and prolonged pauses. After all, this date/nondate may well have been forging new territory in the relationships between married men and single women.

Peter, however, was bursting with energy and conversation. He seemed delighted to have a dinner partner. No, he seemed delighted to have *Jane* for a dinner partner.

"Did I tell you I ran into Chris Aiello? He was the guy who made us all shave our heads when we lost that game in high school. Anyway, he's totally bald now, so you get some kind of revenge there, I guess."

"I guess."

Then Peter did a dead-on impersonation of their high school principal, which left Jane laughing harder than she wanted to.

"Announthment: Any theniorth who thkip clath will be thuthpended tho thwiftly it will make their headth thpin!"

When Jane caught her breath, she begged him to impersonate

the paranoid biology teacher who could speak without moving his lips.

"It's time to dissect the frog. Hey. You. Put down the knife. Why do you smell like formaldehyde? Hey. Hey. Hey. Get out of my class!"

"Oh, Peter. I wish I'd had you in my class. It would have been a lot more fun."

They ordered too much food and ate it all. Jane wondered if she should tell Peter about her adoption plans. Instead she asked about his parents.

"I got them into this City Seniors Social Club—can you imagine our dear old principal joining that? Anyway, I didn't think they'd go for it. But they like it."

"What do they do?" Jane asked.

"Oh, they go to museums, shows, restaurants, all sorts of things. It's been great to see them make new friends and get out more. They love their house, but isn't it good to visit the city sometimes? The whole reason I moved back here was because I was worried about them, but now I'm not so worried. Hey, maybe your dad would join it. He might like it."

Not likely. Jane knew that Howard shared Betty's dislike of all things city. He was also not ready for a change. Not yet.

"It's been kind of hard to visit with Dad. My brothers and their kids are there. I don't feel all that welcome. Family drama. It's kind of complicated, and very stupid."

"At least he has his grandchildren around. My folks really want grandchildren. They don't say anything, but they don't have to. It's the one way—the only way—that I know I've disappointed them."

This was as close as Peter would come to mentioning his marriage that evening. Jane had to let it go by. If she started criticizing his marriage, they couldn't be dinner buddies. And suddenly she knew that she wanted to see him again and again and again.

. . .

The larger group of Chinamoms met for dinner every Monday night, but Jane, Karen, and Teresa remained a subset of the group. The three went to a gallery opening where Teresa represented the artist. The artwork included a lot of disturbing pictures of clowns. Karen was very sensitive to the evil within the clowns and hit the free Chardonnay a little harder than she should have. Jane and Teresa escorted her to a restaurant.

"It doesn't seem real to me yet. Does it seem real to you?" Karen asked. That would have been a confusing question for anyone else, but Jane and Teresa knew what she meant.

"My doctor didn't approve," Jane revealed. When she had her exam for the medical report, he scowled when she told him what this was all for.

"I told my ex." Teresa knew she was dropping a bombshell.

"And?"

"Tell us!"

"What did he say?"

"He got mad. He got really mad. Like I had trumped him or something. Like I had made him useless. And then he got ugly. He said something so mean—"

She probably should not have continued.

"He said that when he had his midlife crisis, he just bought a car. Chinese babies might be a trendy accessory, but I'd send her back within a year."

That line hurt them all. Jane wondered if Teresa repeated it just to unload some of it. Here. Now everyone could have a portion of this hurt.

"Do we know why we're doing this?" Jane ventured.

"He said that a mother can't be the disciplinarian for a kid the way a dad is. So my kid is destined to be spoiled rotten."

"Not mine," said Karen. "Nobody can be spoiled on my salary."

"He forgets." Teresa sounded mad. "My dad had a gun collection. But my mother was the one I was afraid of. She was tough as nails. And faster than a speeding bullet. I never crossed her. I still don't." Teresa sat up straighter when she talked about her mother.

"My mother had lots of issues back then," said Karen, "and now she has a lot of different issues. But now she gets to be all Sweet Grandma, spoiling the kids. She's so excited about having another grandchild."

"Mine too," said Teresa. "But I'm still ticked off at my ex. I mean, he sees me working there day in and day out. In fact, I showed up for work the day after he left me—just to prove a point."

"Wow," said Karen.

"Yes, wow. You're right, wow. Big Huge Wow. I'm one of the three most disciplined people he knows, and he doesn't think I can do this?"

"But how can you guys keep working together?" Jane asked.

"We have to. We have a business. Part of me thinks that he's waiting for me to get terribly upset and walk out. I know I'm waiting for *him* to get terribly upset and walk out. He wasn't happy about me planning a Family Leave, I promise you that."

"I only get three weeks leave, then I'll have to go back to work," Karen mourned.

"Do we know why we're doing this?" Jane repeated.

"I can't believe I almost forgot this. I got you guys a little something," Karen said as she pulled a pair of colorful paperbacks from her large canvas sack. She had gotten all three of them a book entitled, *Fun Shui: The Art of Joyous Baby Rooms.*

"I'll have my decorator refer to this when he starts work on the baby's room," Teresa said without a hint of sarcasm.

Karen lived in a one-bedroom apartment that Realtors called "cozy." She planned to share her room and her bed with the baby. She cited several parenting experts on co-sleeping.

"It accelerates the bonding process. And there's something really deep about that vulnerability, you know? You're asleep. She's asleep. You know?"

Teresa wanted nothing to do with it. "My daughter will get her own bed, and I've already picked out the Calvin Klein crib sheets. She'll be happy. And she'll be in her own room. Trust me."

Teresa was about to move into a large two-bedroom apartment.

"Don't move yet," Karen advised. "Not until you get your referral. It's bad luck. And I hope you haven't chosen a name for her yet."

"My dear, I've already closed. Paying the mortgage on a place I'm not living in is even worse luck. I'm moving. It's done. It's a good location, and we're already waitlisted at two private nursery schools. She won't need luck. She'll have me."

"Do we know why we're doing this?" Jane tried one more time.

Karen and Teresa looked at Jane as if she were an alien. Karen was speechless, but Teresa sighed.

"Jane, Jane, Jane, Jane, Jane, Jane, Jane. Try to keep up."

To: jane.howe@argenti.com
From: peter.mandell@metrohouse.com
Subject: Hungry!

J,

Can we eat early tonight? You know the big meeting I had this morning? Well, it ran right through lunch. Just ended. So, not only do you win the bet (again), but I'm dangerously hungry. Feel like going to Chinatown?

The gym says they're getting a machine that stretches you. Doesn't that sound like a medieval torture device?

P

To: <chinamoms>
From: teresa.fenno@reedpr.com
Subject: I-171H!

Ladies,

It came in the mail last night! I have cleared my calendar. I'll visit the downtown offices to get these notarized, certified, authenticated and off to China. My dossier is now complete.

Teresa

To: <chinamoms>
From: karen51@ournet.com
Subject: Re: I-171H!

Me too! Call me. We can go to the offices together. Oh my God! My dossier is done!

K

They were done. Jane was still waiting. Burning. Was it possible that Karen and Teresa understood something about this adoption process that Jane didn't, and somehow the FBI knew that and they were withholding her I-171H until Jane became enlightened?

The three friends attended an FCC event to celebrate the Autumn Moon Festival. Legend has it that a woman drank a magic potion in order to escape her abusive husband. She landed on the moon. There may or may not be a rabbit up there with her. The Autumn Moon was the one time of year that she was visible to all of us on earth. And until they made her story into a Lifetime Movie, she was happy and safe. Meanwhile, the rest of us eat gooey, sweet mooncakes in her honor.

Megan came bursting into the room. She'd confirmed her ex-punk look by adding magenta highlights to her short hair. She looked bright.

"I got my referral! Look! There she is! There's my girl!"

She held up a tiny picture of a tiny baby bundled in a huge, padded snowsuit. Her cheeks were quite red. She looked dazed. There was an aggressive painting of pandas and bunnies behind her.

Megan was a celebrity. She told the story of Barbara's phone call, which started with "Hi, Mommy." This evoked joyful noises from her audience. And now, post-punk Megan was in a mad dash to buy baby things. She clutched the photo and declined to eat any mooncakes.

"All this time I've been waiting, and I didn't buy one pack of diapers!"

She expected to travel in a few weeks. She glowed. She floated through the room. She was all joy.

Karen and Teresa got to tell people that they had a Dossier to China/DTC date. Jane got to say that her dossier was thisclose to being done. Karen picked up on Jane's jealousy almost immediately.

"You know, Jane. In China, they say that there's a red thread connecting you with the people you love. And it doesn't matter how much the thread is pulled or stretched, it will never break."

Teresa made an attempt. "If I may, I think that Karen is saying that you and your child will be together. You will. It's done."

Jane liked both versions of consolation. But managed a complaint or two.

"If I don't get my dossier to China this month, I won't travel with you two."

Karen didn't see the need to worry, since it was only September 20.

"But I don't know when I'll get it. And yeah, I'll be fine, no matter when it gets here. I'll get to learn from your experiences and yay for me. But still, I worry that this delay is some kind of sign that I'm not supposed to do this. Maybe the universe or the FBI is trying to tell me that I'm not supposed to be a mother. And it sounds so much stupider out loud. Oh, God."

Teresa didn't believe in signs. Karen believed that we all made our own signs.

"And you give off tons of Good Mother signs."

"Like what?" Jane really wanted to know, but there was no time for an answer.

"*Cruella De Vil!*" a chirpy voice shouted. It was Rachel. She darted through the restaurant and threw herself into Jane's arms. Once again, Jane missed out on the latest gossip from the Internet, useful networking, and other tips for adoptive parents. Instead she played her new game with Rachel, called Let's Change All the Words to the Songs.

• • •

A week later, Jane received her form. It came in a boring brown envelope, with no ceremony. In fact, she had to study it to figure out that she was holding the Object of Desire. The magic word, I-171H, was so tiny, tucked away in a little corner of the form. As if to say, "Oh, and by the way, you are approved to adopt an orphan. Whatever."

Jane raced around the judicial offices of Manhattan, then dropped off the small mountain of paper at the Chinese Consulate for authentication. It hurt to leave something so hard-won behind. In an effort to catch up with her friends, she took more time off from work so that she could hand deliver the completed dossier to Dr.—Barbara.

Barbara's apartment was a warm, messy sanctuary. Rachel was sprawled on the floor, finishing her homework about opposites.

"This is baby stuff," Rachel complained. "I know this already. Hot-cold, up-down. I mean, come on! Hey, wanna sing the Captain Hook song with me?"

"Finish your homework, Rachel, then you can have a concert. I'm going to look through Jane's dossier here in the kitchen."

They drank tea and looked through it all. Jane feared that she'd have to throw herself in front of a train if there was a problem with this dossier. But it was fine. Her dossier would go to China tomorrow. Tomorrow. It would arrive at the China Center of Adoption Affairs no later than September 30. She had squeezed into the month after all.

Jane sprang for pizza so that she and Rachel could complete their Disney concert. Rachel had a magnetic mind, pulling in dialogue, choreography, and facial tics for the songs and characters she liked. She corrected Jane a lot. A whole lot. She knew her Disney stuff.

It was getting late. Rachel pitched a minor fit when Jane moved toward her coat and the door. Jane wasn't just flattered; she was having too much fun to leave. She stuck around for bath time. She read to Rachel at bedtime and kissed her good night. Jane floated out of the room as Barbara stepped in and had a quiet snuggle with her daughter. She could hear them singing a lullaby together and chatting quietly about the day. After a while, Barbara emerged from her daughter's bedroom.

"The nighttime routine is getting more and more complicated. If I do something one night, I'll have to do it for the next six years! This is what it's like every night. You'll see."

Jane's heart was bursting. Did Barbara have any idea how exquisite this evening was? And she got this every night? Night after night? Did she know that she was rich beyond measure? Okay, maybe she did. So Jane didn't say anything about that.

"Janie, Janie. You've changed so much since your old school days."

"Really? How?"

"Back then, you were all about the footnotes, not about the body of the work. You know what I mean?" Jane didn't, but Barbara continued. "And I remember, you had a thing for lists. I'll tell you right now. I thought it was a little weird."

The bright red fire in Jane's cheeks gave her away. Barbara talked a little faster.

"And then you met Sam. I think he fell for you on day one. He was always trying to get your attention, but you were always writing lists. It took you forever to notice that he was completely smitten with you. Once you two got together, I knew you'd be okay."

Jane hated the turn this conversation was taking. If she talked about Sam too much, would she end up crying? And if Sam had redeemed her, then what was to become of her now, in a post-Sam world?

Jane took a breath, looked in Barbara's eyes, and said, "Sam took me dancing."

Jane described Sam trying to dance. She did a perfect reenactment of his awkward, hardworking dance. It caught her by surprise and made her cry.

"I'm sorry," Barbara whispered. "I shouldn't have brought him up. I won't do it again."

But Jane was almost glad to cry for Sam one more time.

"He should be here. We should be doing this together," Jane said.

"Jane. He is here. And you'll be a perfectly smashing mother. You'll see."

• • •

That night, in her dreams, Betty and Sam were playing gin rummy in the baby's room until Jane came in and told them that it was time to get to work.

Chapter Eight

The Wait. The Weight of the Wait was enormous. Everyone on the listservs knew that the wait to be matched with a baby was a painful process. Even Jane had gotten that warning. Once they completed their dossiers, Jane and her friends could only wait and wait and wait for that moment of supreme joy, also known as the Referral, when China would reveal the new combinations of babies and parents. It could be difficult to predict how long they might have to wait for a referral— six months, nine months, a year? More? Everyone watched the latest Wait Statistics: how long from your Dossier to China date, to your Date of Referral. In the land of adoption acronyms, everyone wondered how long from DTC to DOR. How long, how long, how long? It was important to find a useful and productive way to fill the Waiting Time.

Teresa was renovating her new apartment and building up her portfolio, already preparing for Ivy League tuition. Karen was taking a class on holistic motherhood. The three of them still sent e-mails, if only as pulse checks or to giggle over entries on the listservs. But their intense paper chase was over, so there was less need to lean on one another. That need would revive, soon enough and strong enough. For now, they prepared. Jane threw herself into her work, determined to get one more promotion before motherhood. With her austere new work budget, she was spinning straw into gold. Management had to be impressed. Jane was.

And she threw herself into fitness. Every time she pictured herself climbing all four flights of stairs with a baby, a stroller, and a diaper bag she felt a little wobbly. She pictured a speck of dust landing on her shoulder and collapsing in midflight. It scared Jane into the gym five days a week. She wondered if anyone would look at her funny if she put a twenty-pound weight in a Snugli. She didn't do it, but she did wonder.

Peter was always at the gym before Jane got there. And Jane was always wearing cute yoga pants and very bare midriff tops. But she promised herself that it wasn't about Peter. Peter? Peter who? No, that outfit forced her into good posture. She was all about posture.

"Jane, I have a confession to make. I did something terrible."

You told your wife you were in love with me? Jane kept climbing. Peter took a deep breath and said, "I ate a half a box of Mallomars last night."

Peter looked so forlorn. Jane giggled.

"Well. I guess you were hungry."

"No! That's just it. I wasn't hungry. I had just eaten a stromboli the size of a human head. But the Mallomars were there, and I ate the whole box."

"I thought you said you only ate half."

"Oops."

Peter laughed at himself. He needed company to keep him from eating like a twelve-year-old boy. He had a long list of restaurants they should try. Jane felt warm and surrounded.

The good angel on Jane's shoulder made her pick up the heavier weights. The bad devil on her shoulder made her go to dinner with Peter that night. Again. It was her new favorite habit. And dinner was so much fun it easily evolved into a movie. So Jane listened to the bad devil on her shoulder and shoved an olive in the good angel's mouth. And anyone who saw them together would think that they were a couple.

"Action movies require extra popcorn," Jane reasoned as they studied the overpriced concessions.

"Oh, yes. And at least one chocolate snack—to balance the salty and the sweet," he informed her as he waved his giant box of Raisinets.

He popped a handful of them into his mouth, just in time for Jane to ask, "Doesn't it feel like you're eating chocolate-covered bugs?"

He grimaced. The image wouldn't go away.

Jane giggled like a girl. "Sorry. Did I ruin those for you? Guess I'll have to finish the rest of the box, huh? Oh, well!"

But Peter finished his candy and said, "No. Whenever I eat bugs, they crunch. These just go *squish!*"

She had shaved her legs, even though it was winter.

• • •

"One martini and one club so—"

"Two martinis. Extra olives." Ray corrected Jane. She studied his face. The happy phase was over already. Much too brief.

"Cheers." He clinked her glass but had no cheer. "Tell me about your love life."

It was Jane's turn to scowl. She didn't have a love life. Did she? But Ray didn't wait for an answer. He drank, he sighed, he slumped over the bar.

"I have to review this new play at Manhattan Theater World, and it's so awful I can smell it from here. It's going to be three hours of bloodless, pointless talk, talk, talk. I wish I were young again. I wish I could still do drugs."

"Sweetie, you've endured bad plays before. Is this one going to be extra-terrible? Can you at least have a little fun with it? A *Legs Diamond* kind of thing?"

Ray didn't answer. He knocked back the martini and looked at his hands.

"Ray?"

"So. Any word from China?" This was the wrong question to ask Jane. She had a long wait in front of her. It would be months—an indeterminate number of months—before she would hear from China. Ray knew that. Had he forgotten?

"No. No word from China. Are you okay? Is it the guy from the meditation class? Did you have a fight?"

"No. Burton and I are fine, thank you. No fighting. All blissful. Am I so shallow that my state of being is completely ruled by my boyfriend? What am I, a fourteen-year-old girl? Or are you?"

"Hey. Don't" was all Jane had to say, and Ray swallowed the rest of his catty remarks with his martini.

"Sorry. And as a matter of fact, Burton is more than fine. He's wonderful. Still cute, still peaceful, still everything. Okay?"

"Glad you're so happy." Jane lifted her glass. Ray smiled for the first time all evening. There was something gray about his skin. She wanted to take a washcloth, remove that film, and find Ray again. He looked large, almost hulking, but she knew he was not a large man. There was a padding around him that increased him and deterred her. She didn't like it. She tried again.

"Do I have to beg? Come on, Ray. What's wrong?"

"Ask me one more time."

"What's wrong?"

"There. Now you've begged, and now I can answer. And the answer is nothing. Nothing really. It's all so petty and stupid."

Jane was fully prepared to argue with this dismissal, but she didn't have to. Ray kept going. He described the wonderfulness of Burton, the peacefulness of meditation, and the general goodness of his life. Then he told her, "I didn't get to go to London."

Oh. London. For the last three years, his editor had promised him that he would be the one to review the opening of the theater season in London. Every year, his editor contrived a different excuse to send a senior reviewer. Ray understood enough about the food chain of the paper of record. He knew that he had to wait his turn. This year was to be his turn. He earned it. Instead, they turned around and gave the assignment to—

"Mannings Porter! He's an idiot, and he makes us all look bad. Remember when he liked that god-awful production of *Medea*? I mean, even the actors knew it sucked. When they were in Hartford, I remember Eric Callendar—he played Jason—he actually called me and told me what a stinkburger the production was. All that wailing, all that ululating. He was living on a diet of ibuprofen. And then Mannings Porter comes along and calls it brilliant, and the damn stupid thing comes to Broadway. When I saw it, I wanted to stand up in the middle of the play and shout, 'This is horseshit!' but I didn't. *The New York Times* gave its blessing to this piece of crap. I wanted to throw up."

Jane knew the *Medea* story by heart. She was with him when he wanted to stand up and shout. She had been the one to stop him. She listened to all the details about the bad *Medea*.

"Mannings Porter is deficient. I think he was held underwater for a long, long time. But not quite long enough. His writing makes me want to throw myself in front of a train. He splits infinitives every day. He's going to need a translator in London. How can they send that total moron to represent us in London?"

Ray had gotten a bit loud, and his gray face turned pink. Jane had no idea what to do, so she did nothing. Ray presented further evidence of Mannings Porter's essential cluelessness: his clothes, his backpack, and his irrational fear of Indian food.

Jane knew that he had to run out of words eventually. And he did.

"Why are they sending this guy to London, and not you?"

Ray slammed his third drink down a little too hard. Jane had to check that it was still intact. It was, but Ray was large and angry again.

"Well, they offered it to Ana, but she had too much school stuff going on with her kid and she didn't want to miss that. Okay. Fine. She's been there longer than me. Longer than *I*. But then she suggested—*she* suggested—that they send Mannings Porter! Did I mention that I don't like him? That he's just a wee bit stupid?"

As the story eked out, Ana felt that Ray was much less ambitious than Mannings. Especially lately. Ray let go of plum assignments with a serenity rarely seen at a daily newspaper. But Mannings displayed the ambition of a virus. He wanted. Ray didn't. Mannings got London. Ray got mad.

"If I get any more spiritual, I'll turn into a poltergeist. No. Worse than that—I'll lose my job. My mother was so proud when I got this gig—she almost made me cry. Let's face it, this is the place to be. This is *The New York Fucking Times*! And here I am, in my lotus position, completely blowing it. I can't have that. I have to change it. I have to."

"Then you will." Jane sounded almost meek. After a silent goodbye to the Zen Ray, she began to worry that Workaholic Ray wouldn't have enough time for little things like food and friends and sleep.

"Ray, honey. Try to keep some kind of balance in—"

"Shit! I'm late. I can't be late. I'm *The New York Fucking Times*."

. . .

Jane went to bed that night wondering what she should have said to Ray. Wondering what she would say to Peter the next day. Wondering when China would call and turn her life upside down. Wondering when she should tell Peter about China. Wondering why she even wondered.

Peter was beside her. He touched her chin and lifted her head gently, as if he were examining her eyes. She studied his. She felt his hand at her chin. Slightly calloused. He smelled good. He felt solid. He kissed her, briefly at first, and then not briefly at all. She promised herself that this was real. This was not a dream. He kissed her again and held her for a long, long time. In the dream, she told herself that this was not a dream. This must be real because she could feel his shoulders beneath his leather jacket. Wait. Peter didn't own a leather jacket. She woke up.

To: <chinamoms>
From: teresa.fenno@reedpr.com
Subject: Concert

Ladies,

I've been out of touch, what with apartment renovations and a busy work schedule. Sorry about that.

Would anyone like to come to a concert at Alice Tully Hall? I've got a block of seats, for next Thursday evening. I think that we should all hear grown-up music before we sing the ABCs about three million times.

To: <chinamoms>
From: karen51@ournet.com
Subject: Re: Concert

Count me in. I've been working like a mad woman, trying to squirrel away as much money as I can. Don't love this, I can tell you. I miss you two. I feel like we're all working too hard.

To: <chinamoms>
From: jane.howe@argenti.com
Subject: Re: Re: Concert

Sorry, but I have dinner plans Thursday night. An old friend from high school, who moved to the city. Peter. So. Have fun without me . . .

Jane

Jane and Peter both loved dessert as much as they loved dinner. She firmly believed that any dessert that included trace amounts of fruit could be considered healthy. He believed her and thanked her for the delusion. Meanwhile, Peter introduced her to dark chocolate, for which she would never forgive him.

"Milk chocolate is for kids. You're all grown up now. Try it."

She extended her hand, but he held back. He wanted to feed her. Her heart skipped a beat. He fed her a silky piece of chocolate, and she couldn't hide her pleasure. She blushed. The bad devil laughed with glee, while the good angel choked with fury.

"See?" he said. "That's for a woman, not a little girl." He continued to smile right at her, but she had to look away. She changed the subject. What was going on with the economy lately? Hmmm?

She introduced him to black-and-white movies. He had always resisted them because he suffered from Cary Grant envy, but then, who doesn't? They settled in to her living room with too much takeout and a bottle of wine. When Cary Grant brought Ingrid Bergman to South America, Jane realized that she was cold.

"Sorry. They haven't turned on the heat yet," Jane complained. Old buildings required a lot of patience. "I'm freezing." Before she could rise and search for a sweater or a blanket, he tugged at her hand. She flinched just a bit.

"Here," he said. And he wrapped his arms around her. She wasn't cold anymore. Nope. Cold not happening at all. Pretty much not cold at all. Feeling quite warm, as a matter of fact. Toasty, even.

"Is this okay?" he asked. She didn't answer. She took in all the body heat. And there was that good smell again. His face was just above hers. Inches away. She couldn't form thoughts as words, just smoky jumbles. If she turned and looked at him now, they would kiss. She knew it.

So instead she said, "I'm adopting a baby." She wanted to take herself into another room and ask herself why she just blurted that out. If only she could. He was stunned into letting go of her. He sat up. Jane felt a chill.

"Your mother never told me."

"She never knew. I never got to tell her. I mean, I never had a chance to." This was a lousy time to tell a lie. "I never told her. And I didn't know she was going to die like that. I only made the decision after. Right after."

He looked like he was running through flash cards in his head, considering twenty other things to say before he said, "Congratulations. I was adopted," he added.

She knew that. He had told her before.

"You knew that. I told you before, didn't I? My wife and I, when we got married, we said that we were going to adopt someday. Only we're never in the same time zone for very long."

"That'll change." Jane sounded a bit smug. "The old biological clock will beep really loud one day, and she'll be pushing for a baby, rearranging both your lives around it. You'll see." Jane was afraid that she sounded like someone on Fox News.

"I don't know about that. Did I tell you that she's fifteen years older than me? Yeah. The biological clock has come and gone. I don't think it's going to happen."

What? Peter and Jane were about the same age, give or take, so that made his wife, what, do the math in your head, fifteen years older.

Jane could only say, "Oh. Kay."

"We haven't talked about it for a long time. The last time I brought it up, she said, 'Why would we mess up our lives with a kid? We have a great life together.' And then we had this fight, and then she went back to L.A. She likes it out there." Jane was trying not to stare at him as he said these things.

"My mom said you wanted to have kids" was the best Jane could do.

"Did I tell her that?"

"You didn't need to. That was my mom. She knew when I snuck in late, even though I never told her. She knew stuff."

· · ·

Teresa and Karen were immersed in the listservs, which left Jane feeling a bit out of the loop. Jane clicked on the list and found a flame war in progress. It started when a pair of proud parents-to-be announced that they had stitched a sampler for their daughter-to-be. They could hardly wait until she was in their arms enjoying the beautiful stitchery. Yes, this sampler is for you, Elvista Priscilla. They had contemplated naming her Lisa Marie, but they felt that this would be intruding on the King's territory. And Elvista might mean something pretty like "The View," which was a favorite program. So, win-win, right?

No one objected to the hideous moniker. A few people objected to naming a child in advance because it was bad luck, incurring the wrath of the Naming Gods or something. But there was a flood of objections over the absence of anything Chinese in Elvista Priscilla's new name.

It started when one person posted, "What about her Chinese name? Are you going to keep it?" No, they weren't keeping her Chinese name. It had never occurred to them to do so. How cold! How insensitive! Obviously, the child will grow up with no sense of her Chinese heritage. Elvista will have no contact with any culture, Chinese or otherwise, will she? Hey, this is America, where you can give your child any ugly name you want. Chinese names are optional. On and on it went. A Flame War.

Jane was so absorbed in watching the new postings come in she nearly missed a meeting. It was like Betty and her soap operas, but these faceless people (who couldn't spell-check) were real. Elvista's mother-to-be wrote:

My hands are shaking so bad while I type this I can hardly type this. You people are so mean to dash a mothers heart when she has stiched her fingers to the bone for her little girl in China who she loves already and wants to go get her right now and bring her home where she belongs and love her forever and be her Mom.

Just for the record and not to make any of you happy I am quiting this list. I don't need this and who does. I hope your not in China when I am their because I don't want to see any of you ever in person because that would be to much for me and my family and we are all about love unlike you.

Godbye forever to you all.

Jane felt guilty about giggling before.

Finally, a moderator interrupted the drama. There would be no more messages about names, Chinese or otherwise. There would be no more judgments about anybody's choice of name for their daughter.

The messages slowed for a while, then someone started a faux-war, questioning whether the song is "Itsy Bitsy Spider" or "Teensy Weensy Spider." A few souls played along, and the rage subsided.

Karen and Teresa had been following the online jihad and drew their own conclusions. Teresa vowed never to post anything resembling personal information to the list. Karen purchased copies of a baby-naming book, Name Your Child's Destiny, for all three women. And all three quietly decided to keep some form of Chinese name for their daughters.

Jane kept Peter informed of the ongoing drama as they walked to dinner.

"If I ever had a kid, I would name it after my parents," he said. "None of these trendy, made-up names for me. I like the idea of honoring my folks and making that connection. That's important. I was named for my uncle who died in Korea. I'm proud to have his name."

Jane actually, physically bit her tongue. Why was he married to someone so far away? Why wasn't he going to have children? Didn't he see how much he wanted to be a dad?

Jane looked peculiar with her tongue between her teeth. Most people do.

"Are you okay?" he asked.

"Oh. Yes. It's just—names. What a responsibility!"

They were walking quickly. The leaves danced around them, along with newspapers and other litter.

"So, Peter? You're really never going to have children?" Maybe she was free to ask this while they were moving.

"No. I guess I'm not going to. I'll be okay, though. Nobody gets everything."

"But what about your parents? Don't they want grandchildren?"

Jane had ventured into a very sensitive area for Peter. She was half expecting a big "none of your business," but Peter was too kind to say such a thing. And oh, yes, his parents wanted lots of grandchildren. They were wary when he brought home his older girlfriend, and tense when he married her, but always confident that they would soon be spoiling their son's babies.

"They wanted grandchildren, sure," he said. "But nobody gets everything."

"You said that before."

"Sorry. But it's true. Everyone needs to know it. And I understand why my parents were upset. I wasn't completely thrilled, either. But then they started prying into my marriage. They don't understand how much I really do love her. And need her. She's my wife, and that's never going to change. I got really mad at them, actually. I told them that this is *my* marriage and it's none of their business. They got the message."

So did Jane. She got that this speech was aimed at her—and she even doubted that he said any of this stuff to his own mother and father. And with that, she set up a rule for herself: She must not comment on his marriage. Instead, she said, "Names. What a responsibility," and gracelessly changed the subject. "Want to see the new Alec Baldwin movie next week? I hear he lost weight."

"Can't. Bianca's coming out here for the holidays, and we'll be staying out at my parents'. We really can't stay in the city together.

That studio is way too cozy for an old married couple, you know what I mean? Hey. You're visiting your dad for Christmas, right? Maybe we'll see you out there. Wouldn't that be great?"

Jane kept a fake smile stapled to her face as she said, "Yeah. That would be great."

She worried that her eyes betrayed her panic. She snapped her holiday plans into place: "But we probably won't see each other. Because I'm leaving. Early. I'm just going to be out there for a little while. And then I'm coming back to the city. So. Ya know . . ."

"Got it," said Peter. "We won't see you at Christmas."

Was he hurt? Was he making a promise to Jane? Was he actually understanding that Jane would require advanced pharmaceuticals if she had to tolerate a visit with Peter and his wife? Did it matter? She had succeeded in preventing the visit. Done.

· · ·

Jane's favorite name story was about the woman on the list who named her biological son Trey, inexplicably forgetting that his last name was Lohr. Trey Lohr was one miserable kid on the playground. Then there were the people proposing traditional names, Mary, Cathy, and a lot of Juliets. Then there were the people proposing names like Champagne and Turquoise. These girls were destined to join Trey Lohr on the playground as Champ and Turkey. Maybe it was Peter's influence, but Jane knew that she couldn't escape her daughter's name. It was settled. It would be Elizabeth. For Betty.

But not Betty. She wasn't going to call her Betty, oh, no. She was going to call her Elizabeth. Which, okay, might be too long for a tiny child to say, and that's exactly how little girls end up being called Betty or Bitty. Or Beth. She could call her Beth. This faraway little girl, who seemed like a fantasy most of the time, took a giant step toward reality the moment Jane said the name Beth out loud. She would be Beth Chinese-middle-name-extracted-from-the-baby's-name-at-the-orphanage Howe. Beth.

. . .

The Chinamoms were a growing group. Every Monday, they gathered at the Melting Pot, a Midtown restaurant that allowed everyone an easy commute. On this particular Monday, they would say a special farewell to Megan, who was about to travel to China. The first of their number to do so. She would be home just in time for Christmas. Baby's First Christmas. Pangs all around.

A new woman, Arlene, sat quietly at the end of the table. In fact, she sat silently. It was hard to sit next to her and have a conversation. She was small, with long dark hair, an oak complexion, and a tiny mouth. Charm was still working on her dossier. She described every detail of her process. Jane felt almost sentimental. Was her paper chase really so long ago? Greta completed hers two weeks after Jane.

"Barbara says that we might travel together!" Greta exclaimed. "We should hang out and everything. I'm thinking of bringing my parents and my niece and my brother with me to China. What about you? Who are you bringing? Are you going to move? You can't have a baby in a walk-up. What if you fall and break her head? How would you live with yourself? I'm getting the hepatitis vaccinations. Are you? You should. I mean, you could lose your liver if you don't. You want my fries? I'm trying to do Atkins, and I can't have this on my plate."

Greta kept talking. And talking. Jane gripped Teresa's arm. She didn't want to travel with Greta, please God. Post-punk Megan, Mom-of-the-Moment, entered and you could see the hurricane swirling around her. She was here, there, and in China all at once. She was packing. She was preparing. She was terrified. She was leaving in nineteen hours.

"Take my advice." It felt like a deathbed pronouncement. "Don't wait, like I did." The advice sounded familiar. "I don't know if I'm going to make it to the plane tomorrow."

"What do you need?" Teresa asked. She sounded calm and smart.

Megan needed help. She needed to track down medications that, so far, two drugstores didn't have. She needed to start packing some clothes. She needed to make copies of her dossier. She needed to have some food stocked in the refrigerator for when they came home. She needed different nipples for her bottles. She needed a new camera battery for the most important event of her life. She needed the changing table pad replaced and the whole table cleaned and the folding part kept falling off and was that dangerous? Was it? Oh, and she needed to pack some clothes. Did she mention that?

Teresa solicited volunteers, and even silent Arlene managed to raise her hand. No dinner could ever be as exciting as finding the right nipples for Megan. In a matter of hours, everything was complete. Except for the changing table, which required a little more work. The group settled into Megan's apartment while Jane repaired the changing table.

"Hand-me-downs suck," Megan pronounced.

"This is going to be as good as new." Jane tried not to grunt as she tightened the bolt.

Everyone sat on the floor, except for Teresa. They edited Megan's packing and promised hours of babysitting. By the time they left, Megan was physically and logistically ready for China. You can imagine the other levels of readiness that she needed. To Jane, those all read as fuzzy static. Megan would return to this room in two weeks, with her daughter. They left Megan, post-punk adoptive mom, to finish her other levels of readiness.

They found a diner and sipped coffee and tea. They talked about the buzz of Megan's excitement. Teresa wondered aloud what the Chinese would think of Megan's pink highlights. Out of nowhere, Jane told them all about Peter and his faraway wife and their almost-kiss. More blurting. She was becoming such a blurter.

Teresa felt certain that he was not really married, and therefore even more despicable. Karen worried about Jane's karma and explored the possibility of a relationship between Jane and Peter in some previous lifetime that had echoed in this one.

Karen justified her otherworldly approach. "It's possible. It's the only explanation I can find for Artie, my last boyfriend. He was a relentless, brooding jerk." But Jane found no tangible help there. She still wanted Peter. She wanted him so badly.

"Push him," Teresa advised. "He *wants* to leave her and go to you—if she exists, that is. So give him a push. Can't you see it? He's practically begging you to push him. Push him!"

These women were big on advice. Karen advised Jane to give Peter a set of time boundaries. This sounded like a soft way to say "deadline" or "ultimatum," and Jane shied away from both. And then Arlene spoke, at last. Hers was the advice that got under Jane's skin and stayed there.

"You want him. You can't have him. Walk away."

Chapter Nine

No one got good Christmas bonuses, and Jane had the privilege of telling everyone precisely how little they were getting. Hers was slashed, beaten, and barely breathing. The London acquisition had strained the firm's resources, and everyone had to share the burden. But Jane got a card from Barbara. It contained an official warning, on behalf of Founding Mothers, stating that this would be the last holiday season where she could tear up the town. Next year, life would be unrecognizable. Next year, she would celebrate Christmas with her baby.

Jane overspent, especially on her dad. No one in the world was going to have a tougher Christmas than Howard. Betty had always loved the holidays and found ways to gild lilies and then add lights to them. Jane tried her best to re-create her mother's heavy touch in decorating.

"Do you want me to put the singing snowman on the porch or next to Rudolph?" This was one of many questions she tried to frame seriously. He kept the cocoa coming, and she kept putting up lights, holly, and crèches. But no amount of staple-gunning could make it look like Betty was still there.

On Christmas Day, Kevin, Neil, and their wives and their kids seriously outnumbered Jane. But she had the Christ Child on her side. The original one, not the one from her neighborhood. They knew they would lose valuable moral high ground if they said anything harsh to Jane today. So they said nothing. This was just like having People around. You didn't talk about things in front of Christmas.

The children were bigger and louder. They were more thoroughly inducted into pop culture than ever before. They quoted prime time and MTV. Jane, aka Margaret Mead, studied their aggressive behavior. She saw Dylan slinking off to call his girlfriend. She saw the little ones topple their parents' ability to say no. Jane promised herself that her child would be more pure of heart, and she was going to disconnect her cable TV immediately.

Kitty and Linda managed to re-create Betty's Christmas dinner perfectly, and anyone with good sense would have to wonder why. Betty openly despised cooking. For years, she had been inventing the fully microwavable Christmas. She invested in an industrial-size microwave oven, for maximum efficiency. It was her moment of triumph when the turkey emerged from his plastic tray, ready to serve.

"No one can tell the difference!" was her battle cry.

Howard always made appropriate *mm-mm-mm* noises, and the family followed suit. Kitty and Linda always had hot dogs or Lunchables for the little ones. The first Christmas without Betty would be no different. Kitty sat in Betty's seat, so as not to draw attention to her absence.

After dinner, the adults exchanged presents while the children fought over which DVD to watch first. Kevin, Neil, Kitty, and Linda had pooled their money to buy Howard a watch. It was a classic gold pocket watch, engraved "from your loving children."

Jane's blood ran backward. Your loving children? We left out the un-loving children, Jane and Sheila, because, hey, they don't love you. Jane said nothing. You can't say anything in front of Christmas, remember.

Jane's gift was a collection of PBS DVDs on history topics that

Howard loved: the Revolutionary War, the Civil War, World War I, World War II. Wars in a digital format. It looked stupid and shallow next to the gold watch from the loving children. But Howard was no fool. He crowed with excitement over his gifts from Jane. He put Sheila's gift under the tree for later. Much later.

Jane needed to tell Howard about the baby because, from an adoption point of view, she was beginning to show. She looked for an opportunity to get Howard alone. On Christmas. With the whole family around. It wasn't easy.

Howard, Jane, and the Loving Children all endured a constant stream of visitors. Everyone who was anyone in northern New Jersey wanted to check on newly widowed Howard on his first Christmas without Betty. By midafternoon, Howard had received a year's supply of holiday cookies and a stack of fruitcakes. Some guests talked about Betty, some talked around her. But every guest seemed to study Howard for a sign of sadness that they could heal with their baked goods. Howard twinkled good-naturedly and allayed all fears and worries.

These were truly nice people, weren't they? Jane thought so. That's why she had to stop wishing them all to start sneezing a lot and urgently need to go home so that she could have some time alone with her dad. She didn't have the power to inflict sneezing fits, so she would simply have to wait out all this niceness. She'd have to tell him later.

Night was falling, and the visits stopped. Perhaps she could sit with her father on Christmas night and tell him everything, everything. It sounded like a good plan in Jane's head.

It sounded even better when her brothers gathered the tryptophan-drowsy children and departed for home. It was late, and Jane had missed the last bus back to the city. She would have to stay over. Good. She went upstairs, theoretically, to find a toothbrush, but instead she sat in her old room, which had been painted into a taxi-yellow guest room, and tried to rehearse a Dad-I-Made-a-Big-

Decision speech for Howard. She'd be fine, as long as there weren't
any more—

"Janie! Come down here! Look who's here!"

Visitors.

Jane walked into the living room, and there he was: Peter. He
stood up when Jane entered the room. It was definitely Peter. And
that had to be her. Next to him. His wife. Bianca.

"Merry Christmas!" Howard said before Jane could speak. When
she saw the pair approaching her, she wanted to run, wanted to
hide, wanted to be home already.

Howard was smiling, Bianca was smiling, but Peter wasn't. Did
this have to be Bianca? Couldn't it be a cousin? A sister-in-law?
Somebody else? Please?

Jane made sure her mouth was closed as her father said, "You remember my daughter, Jane?"

Peter's smile looked like a grimace. Good. At least he was suffering here too. He reached out and shook Jane's hand. Shook her
hand!

"This is my wife, Bianca."

Jane may or may not have shaken Bianca's hand. Later, she
would try to recall it. Bianca brought some kind of traditional
Swedish noodle dish. Jane took it (heavy!) to the kitchen, gave herself three seconds to breathe deeply before she returned to the living room where Howard was chatting about the cold, the day, the
season with Peter and Bianca.

Bianca. She was small and spare. Jane thought she looked like a
good athlete. She wore a Hillary-style hair band. She was blond.
Maybe even sun-bleached. Lines were imprinted deeply on her
forehead and around her mouth. She was bouncing with energy.
Her voice was high and sparkly. She was perky. Perky, perky, perky.

"How are your parents doing?" Howard asked Peter. "I would
have dropped in to visit with them today, but we had quite a lot of
guests today! Didn't we, Jane?"

Jane felt the tension in her neck as she nodded a little too quickly. She heard Bianca speak.

"They would have come with us, but this is a little too late for them! Peter here kept making us wait and wait and wait to come over here. I told him, I said, 'I think we're waiting too long to visit anybody,' but he kept making us wait!"

Because of Jane? Because he expected her to be gone by now? Because she told him that she would be gone by now? Oh, why wasn't she gone by now?

Jane heard conversation floating around the room, but found herself tongue-tied. Christmas. Travel. Work in the city. Later, she would try to revise the evening in her imagination. She could have gone to the kitchen and hand-washed the dishes she had loaded into the dishwasher. She could have gone outside to turn the decorations on. Or off. She could have claimed to be tired, which she was, or ill, which she wasn't. She could have missed all of this. But the conversation rolled along without her. "The city. The village. Neighbors."

Jane surfaced completely as she heard Bianca exclaim, "Oh, you're *that* Jane. You're the one who's adopting a baby from China. Good for you! I think that's super!"

Howard sat up and looked at his daughter as if he were looking at a stranger. Peter must have understood, because he said, "Oh. Did I say that? I may have gotten confused. I work with so many— I mean, Jane is kind of a common name, and, I think you're confused and . . ."

Bianca's perkiness overrode him.

"No. It's Jane. Your neighbor. And she's adopting a baby. Aren't you? Aren't you adopting a baby?"

Jane had been holding her breath since Bianca first said the word "baby." Howard's face looked like it belonged on Mt. Rushmore: large, gray, and cold.

Peter looked at Jane helplessly, while Bianca said, "Single motherhood! Wow! You know, I was raised by a single mom. My aunt. She taught me how to be independent, and I've never regretted it. And won't it be nice to have a kid to keep you company? Super!"

There was a long silence. Bianca looked at the sad and angry faces around her. Howard stood up and said, "Company? You're going to have a child to keep you company?"

"No. Dad. I'm not. I never said that. I mean—I am adopting a baby. That part is true."

Howard was shaking his head. Peter rose quickly.

"It's late, and I think that maybe we should head home." Yes, their work here was done. It was time to leave.

Howard saw his guests out the door and went directly to bed without another word on Jane's adoption. Jane retreated to her room. She stayed awake in the aggressively shiny room and decided that it was now legal to hate Bianca, or at least actively dislike her.

. . .

The next morning, over stove-cooked eggs, Jane urgently needed to talk to Howard. She had the Dad-I-Made-a-Big-Decision speech polished and ready.

Before she could start it, Howard said, "Jane. About last night— tell me it isn't true. You can't be considering adopting a baby? From China? You would never do anything so foolish, so selfish. Tell me I'm right, Jane."

Breakfast was starting to burn. Jane's hands were damp. She dumped the eggs onto a plate, but half of them missed. She tried to focus on the cleanup. Howard was studying her face. He was stern. Jane made more of a mess as she cleaned up the eggs.

"Dad. I am. I've already sent my dossier to China."

"Well. I don't know what that means. But I know that this is a mistake, Jane. A very grave mistake. But you don't have a baby yet, so it can't be too late to put this notion away and stop it all."

"I don't want to."

"I'm sorry, Janie. I know this isn't what you want to hear, but you shouldn't go through with this adoption. You mustn't."

She couldn't speak. He could.

"Have you really thought this through, honey? After all, you're an unmarried woman. All alone. You don't know what you're getting yourself into."

Jane still couldn't speak. He took her silence as a kind of agreement, and so he went further.

"And I'll let you in on a little secret: The rewards of parenthood are not all they're cracked up to be. Look at your mother and Sheila. They used to be thick as thieves, then Sheila went off and did what she did. Do you think we deserved that? I don't. But that's how it is when you're a parent. It's grossly unfair, the whole package."

"I didn't know you felt so"—she searched—"un-rewarded."

"That's not it. Not at all. You're proving my point, Janie, if you could just hear yourself. Being a parent is all about giving and giving and giving. It's hard work and it's arrogant to think you can do it alone. I love you too much to stay quiet about this. Tell me you'll think about this, Janie. Just give it some thought."

"Dad. This is not for you to decide."

"I wish it were. I'd make a better decision than you're making."

His voice was gentle and quiet. He sounded right. And he sounded reluctant. She wanted to quote his speech about how much Betty loved being a mother, but she was undone. Her bones were mush. Her teeth were jelly. He had the Irish-arguing gene too, and he was good at it. He'd had more practice. If this were a debate, Howard would have been the winner, Jane the loser. And so Jane returned to the city, bathed in pain.

• • •

Sheila called to thank Jane for the extravagant gifts. The kids were wildly excited about Christmas. They had made a special "I Love You" wreath for their stepmother, and Sheila was overcome with delight.

"I think they really do love me. I can feel it. Or maybe it's just how much I'm loving them. Either way, it's so great. Oh, Janie, I can't wait until you're a mom too, and we can talk about this stuff. This is the best Christmas of my life."

Jane said nothing about her Close Encounter with Peter & Wife, nothing about Howard's lecture/argument/judgment. Not today.

. . .

Jane, Teresa, and Karen had exchanged gifts at Teresa's very swanky holiday party. All three friends gave each other picture-frame ornaments for next year's trees. It was their "Gift of the Magi" moment. Karen read great meaning into this overlap. They made plans to visit Megan and her baby as soon as they could locate some frankincense, gold, and myrrh.

Karen visited first, and announced, through e-mail:

To: <chinamoms>
From: karen51@ournet.com
Subject: Little Stella

Megan's little girl is even more beautiful in person!!! And Megan
is so amazingly in tune with her daughter, she anticipates her
every need and has got this whole motherhood thing going on!!
You've got to go visit her soon!!!!!

XXOO—Karen

"Can we come over? We have a present!" We. Peter was a "we." And Jane—"she"—had no handy excuses. Of course they could come over. They.

They showed up at her door. And she—Bianca—looked even tanner and perkier than she had before. It made her eyes brighter. Peter smiled at Jane as if this whole scene were just the most natural thing in the world. Didn't he always bring his wife over? Didn't he?

Jane fussed with glasses and coasters and snacks and napkins, in order to maintain balance and speak like a reasonably mature mother-to-be. She was faking it.

Bianca said, "Peter tells me you fixed this place up yourself. Good job! Good for you!"

"Thank you."

Jane struggled to prevent an awkward pause, but Peter saved the day when he asked, "Did your nieces and nephews go crazy on Christmas morning? Must have been quite a scene with all those little ones."

Jane nodded, and Peter sounded a bit gushing as he continued.

"That's what Christmas is all about: kids. Without them, it's really kind of selfish and weird. Don't you think? Are you going to spoil your daughter at Christmas? I hope so."

And that's when Jane saw Bianca roll her eyes. But why, exactly? If only Jane could ask.

But Bianca changed the subject and said, "We would have brought your present at Christmas, but Peter was so sure you wouldn't be there!"

"Yes," Peter said. "I figured you'd go back to the city. I thought we'd missed you. Didn't you say you were going back to the city?"

"Wrong again." Bianca sounded so cheerful when she said that. "Peter says I spilled the beans about your adoption—"

"You did, and we're so, so sorry—"

"But I think he's just trying to be gloomy. It was a nice visit, wasn't it?" Bianca rolled right over him.

There were no awkward pauses until Jane sat down and tried to smile. And then an angel passed over. Jane searched her mind but had nothing socially acceptable to say. Finally Bianca made a chirpy sound and said, "Your present! We almost forgot!"

She reached into a bag and grinned slyly.

"Okay, maybe this doesn't really count as a present, but we thought you might like it." She retrieved a paperback book, probably four inches thick: *The Insider's Guide to Mainland China* by Bianca

Hartley. Jane had forgotten to put China guidebooks on any of her lists. This was actually helpful. This was a great present. Damn.

"I wrote this right after Hong Kong was handed back to China, and I got to travel everywhere. Remember that, Peter? We had an e-mail marriage for, like, six months. Remember?"

Peter nodded. It looked like he remembered.

Jane thumbed through the book. It looked so thorough and smart. Damn.

"Thank you," Jane said. "I really needed this. It's great."

"I know the editor who does all those 'baby in the city' books. I can hook you up with some of those too. But you're not really going to stay in the city, are you? And climb all those stairs with a baby? Really? Maybe you should move in with your dad! Wouldn't that be super!"

Jane felt so invaded she didn't manage an answer. But Peter did.

"I think she'll move out when she's ready to move out. We don't need to push her."

Bianca flinched. She had been looking steadily at Jane through-out the conversation, and she kept her gaze on her hostess, even as she answered her husband.

"I know. I'm not pushing her. I'm just saying, it's way too hard to raise kids in the city."

"I know. I'm agreeing with you. But this is Jane's decision. It's her baby."

"I know. But I'm saying, it's way too hard to just *live* in this city."

Were they starting to fight? And would it be wrong to enjoy that? Bianca kept talking.

"Look, I did my New York City time, and I got it out of my sys-tem. All done. I mean, that's why I told *Everyman Guide* that I didn't want the editing gig out here. Forget it. The city ages you two years for every one year you live here. Stress, stress, stress."

Peter kept looking at Bianca, who kept looking at Jane.

"You turned down a job?"

Bianca was busy snacking on the edamame Jane had placed on

the table. She nodded her head and couldn't have seen Peter clench his jaw and look up at the ceiling. But Jane saw it.

"No offense," Bianca said to Jane. "But tomorrow morning I am getting on a plane, and I can hardly wait. And you want to know the truth? A married couple in a studio? Bad idea. Much too confrontational."

"You turned down a job here in the city? And you didn't even tell me? Bianca?"

Jane watched the show but offered no visible reaction.

. . .

At the next Melting Pot dinner, Jane wished that she could empty the restaurant and have Barbara all to herself. She needed to take Howard's Conversation of Doom off her shoulders and hand it to someone else. She wanted someone to make sense of Married Peter for her. Barbara would know what to say to make it better.

But the table was full. Arlene nodded a lot, but still kept her conversation under twelve words. Charm was excited because Megan had promised to try really hard to come to the restaurant with little Stella. Teresa summoned a high chair for the table. And once again, Jane and little Rachel sang Disney tunes. Karen was late, and so was Greta.

"Actually, I don't think Greta is coming tonight." Barbara tossed this off as if it were nothing, really nothing, no big deal. The group ordered their food (Rachel wanted fries with a side of fries) and complained about winter. No big deal.

Greta did arrive, and Barbara was surprised to see her. They talked quietly, off to one side, and Jane missed it all. They were having a Scene. Barbara returned to the table, and Greta soon followed.

"Look, everybody, I think I have a right to say what I'm going to say, so I'll say it."

Jane only heard, "Say . . . say . . . say it."

"You have no clue what you're getting into. I mean, *I* didn't. But I spent last Sunday with Megan and baby Stella, and I wanted to throw up and die. She cried all day. She shit all over the couch, and that was a good couch, I could tell. But not anymore. Now it has a shit stain."

"All babies cry," Barbara said in a telephone-lady voice. "And they all move their bowels."

"She cried *all the time*! And she shit her own weight on that couch. It was huge. That couch is ruined. She'll never get that out. It was huge."

The man at the next table gave a pained look that he hoped would say so much. Greta didn't notice.

"And Megan smelled awful. She hurt her back, because Stella doesn't like to be put down. She can't put her in the stroller—she has to carry her everywhere. All the time. And she cries even louder if Megan takes a shower, so forget that. So Megan just smells. And I mean, I have never seen so much actual shit in my whole life."

The pained-expression man cried out, "We're eating!"

Greta didn't hear him.

"And sleep? She doesn't sleep. She can barely manage to eat whatever food she can find in the fridge. She has no life. I don't know how she'll make it back to work in one piece. It was a nightmare. It was an eye-opener. Is this what you want for your lives? I don't. I don't care what I've spent. I don't care if I wreck the Chinese government. I'm canceling my fucking dossier. As of now."

The food arrived and Greta departed. Pained-expression man applauded, but the Founding Mothers table was silent. Finally:

"I don't think she should swear in front of a kid." It was Arlene.

They ate for a little while before Barbara spoke again.

"Greta's right. She's right to quit now, before it's too late. I hope that you all know that you can stop this, if you want to. All you have to do is call me. But please, you don't have to ruin dinner for an entire restaurant, okay? Rachel, you can't eat just fries, honey."

Jane focused her thoughts on the child who might have been matched with Greta. What will become of her now? She quietly started a bet with herself: Who among these three friends, this trinity, would quit? It would require some study. Jane wrapped this evening up with her father's Conversation of Doom and put it away. It was like a tumor.

. . .

Peter—just Peter—"he" had yet another gift for Jane: a deluxe baby wipes warmer. She didn't have this item on any of her lists. She didn't know what it was. But he did.

"What if you're changing her diaper in the middle of the night and you go to wipe her bottom with a cold wipe? She'll cry and resent you, and then she'll have to have years of therapy. But this little invention will keep the wipes warm, and she'll love you and make sure you get into the really good nursing home."

She smiled at his logic.

"Thanks for sealing my fate. I'll think of you when I'm old and drooling." And then she kissed him. And he kissed her. It lasted for three Mississippis, which is just long enough to be exciting and scary. They pulled away from each other.

"I'll put this away," Jane said to the wipes warmer. She tried to walk like a normal human being. She could hear her own heartbeat. She wondered if Peter heard it too.

Alone in the baby's room, Jane felt the echo of that kiss. Just a brush of his five o'clock shadow against her cheek. She resolved to march right back out there and kiss him again. She found him in the living room, ordering dinner over the phone. His voice sounded a bit choked.

"Brown rice, right?" he asked. She nodded. Opportunity lost. Damn.

They were already pretending that there had been no kiss, although it seemed to Jane that the entire apartment had turned red on the second Mississippi. They ate dinner and watched *Yankee Doodle Dandy*. Jane sat next to him, but then decided that she was sitting too far away for another kiss to happen. But how could she shift closer without being obvious? Could she find an excuse to get up, then sit back down in a more kiss-friendly location? She shook her head at her own foolishness, sat back, and said, "Bianca left for California?"

"Oh. Yes. She did. Sorry we had a little fight. I didn't know about the job out here."

"Oh."

When was he going to kiss Jane again? Now? Tonight? Soon?

"The thing is—she's older than me, and maybe she sort of pulls rank on me. She makes every decision. She wins every fight. I gave up a lot to be married to her. When is she going to give up something for me? And that's why I need to ask you—"

For another kiss?

"—to forgive me. It was kind of awkward to have Bianca visit you, wasn't it?"

"No. It was fine. It was really fine and . . ." He looked at her sideways, and she knew she had to drop the Fine act. "Okay, it was a *little* odd."

"For me too. Somehow I couldn't talk her out of visiting. And I tried. Anyway, I'm starting to feel like . . . like . . ."

Like kissing Jane again?

". . . like I miss her so much," he continued. "It gets me into trouble sometimes. Like just now. That kiss. Sorry about that."

Sorry he kissed her. Sorry. So. She let it drop. He missed his wife. Let him go. Let him go. They were quiet for a long time. James Cagney was dancing down the steps of the White House. A very athletic buck and wing. Jane smiled and closed her eyes. Let him go. Let him go. If he's sitting here missing his wife, then just let him go. She was belly breathing. She was calm. She was asleep.

And so was Peter. He fell asleep first, and she followed soon after. She eased into sleep, her head drifting to his shoulder. Their breathing synchronized. She surfaced in the predawn hours when his chin brushed her forehead. She raised her head and looked at him, peaceful and vulnerable. He opened his eyes and quietly pulled her toward him. They lay down on her couch and slept until the sun woke them for the day.

In the morning, he held her for a while.

"Thanks for letting me crash here."

"You're welcome."

"This is getting confusing." It was, but Jane didn't want it to be. Everything she wanted was in her grasp. This lovely, warm, good-smelling man, who could be a father to the daughter whose face would be revealed one day soon. It was all so close.

After a lingering hug and a forehead kiss, Peter said, "I really should go." But he didn't go. Jane said nothing. It was all so close. She held on to him. He was holding her closer. She forgot to think. She kissed him.

"Jane."

"Don't say anything. Not now. Not if you're going to say no."

"No. I mean, no—I'm not going to say no. Jane. You have to know how I feel."

"I don't. I only know that you're married." Jane squeezed her toes under. Why did she say that?

He answered, "But here I am. Falling for you. This is impossible."

"Falling for me? That's impossible?"

"Falling for you was easy." This time, he kissed her. And Jane's helium heart floated out of her body and into the morning sky.

• • •

Somehow Jane managed to concentrate on work that day. A little. And when the clock said that she could leave, Jane decided that she could not commute like a normal person, on the subway. She wanted to walk through the icy streets of the city. She wanted to move her long legs and own the city she walked on. The Irish would call it a good stretch of the legs.

You need to factor in the wind when you're getting your good stretch of the legs. Parts of Manhattan are genuine wind tunnels. Once or twice, she thought the wind might swoop her into the middle of the street. She picked up her pace.

She had lists in her head. Work lists, project lists, e-mail lists. And the Über-List, a list of all of the lists that she needed to roll around in her head. Maybe her lists would anchor her to the ground until she could see Peter again and—

Jane took a giant step, but her foot slid forward and up into the sky. She had a sharp intake of breath, and a slice of pain in her leg. She saw the gray sky and then saw bright white. She opened her eyes to find strangers hovering around her, shouting to one another. Soon, she was rumbling along the street, on a stretcher, inside an ambulance, paramedics shouting numbers to each other, moving equipment and cracking gum. She closed her eyes, then opened them again, hoping for a better picture.

"Lady, you with us? You okay? She's back. She's here. Okay, what's your name? Can you tell us your name?"

Her leg was giving her a lot of pain. Her left leg, down near the foot, it hurt more and More and *more. Oh, my God, the leg!*

She pulled herself up on her elbows and assessed the damage. She relaxed when she saw that her leg was, in fact, still there. It felt shattered, but it appeared to be intact. The paramedic read her mind and laughed a little.

"You slid on the ice. You blacked out for a minute when you hit your head, and I think you sprained your ankle. It looks pretty bad, but we won't amputate. I promise."

Great. Now she was an idiot in pain.

"Now, what's your name?"

Jane was referred to as Head Trauma & Sprain. She stayed overnight in the hospital because of the concussion. Noisy people in soft cotton clothes woke her up on a regular basis. She wasn't sure if they intended to or not. They entered the double room Jane shared with Colitis and simply continued loud conversations that had begun outside. Jane had an ugly lump on the back of her head. It kept time with her pulse.

Peter came to the hospital the next day. Peter taking time off from work was no small gesture, and Jane knew it. Removing himself from work was one of the most selfless gestures in his vocabulary. He wheeled her to a waiting car and drove her home.

Home. Four long flights of stairs up and up and up and up. And Peter carried her. She tried not to think of Scarlett O'Hara, and he never grunted, though he did refrain from speaking until after they were inside her apartment and he finished a glass of water. Jane had been trying to think light thoughts the whole way up.

"Do you want to be on the couch or the bed?"

"I'll take it from here."

"Sure." He put her on the couch. He made her a pot of tea, angled the television, brought the phone, the laptop, the paper, the sugar for the tea, the PDA, the remote, a box of tissues, the crutches, the milk for the tea, the other remote, some crackers, a spoon for the tea, some juice, her medication (just ibuprofen, no real street value there), and a sweater. She couldn't bear it anymore. She wanted him to sit and be romantic, but that wasn't happening. He had fallen for her. He said so. Right over there, by the door. Was he experiencing kisser's remorse? Jane didn't realize that she was scowling.

"Sorry. Am I in the way?" he asked.

"No." Yes, he was. And if he was going to continue in this servant mode, then please, let him have a break and go back to his office. He finished his tasks and he left.

She spent most of the first day combing through real estate ads. She needed an elevator building. It would solve all her problems and make motherhood a breeze. By the end of the day, she was running out of ads. There was nothing she could afford. And why was Peter so unromantic?

"Janie? Your voice mail at work says that you're home? You're laid up? What happened?" It was Howard.

"It's nothing, Dad. A twisted ankle. I slipped on the ice."

"How are you managing?"

"I'm great. I'm fine."

"You can't get outside, can you? Is someone there for you? Oh, Janie."

"Peter lives right nearby, remember? I'm fine. It's nothing, Dad. It's absolutely no big deal." She left it at that. Nothing about falling in love with Peter. After all, Howard was not a young man, and Peter was still a married man. One shock at a time.

Howard wasted no time. "How would you take care of a baby like this? Are you even able to walk? What would you do?"

And that was why Jane kept combing the real estate ads. If she had an elevator, she could get outside. She could feel competent. But she needed to find something affordable. Something that allowed room for child care, taxis, tuition, and emergencies. So far, it didn't exist. And that was why Jane was surly with her dad.

"Look, Dad. I am still going through with this adoption." She thought she heard him wince. "You can help out or you can just not call. Was this conversation supposed to make me feel better?"

It was supposed to make her change her mind. That little tumor got bigger.

• • •

Peter returned the next day. He brought movies, chocolate, and glossy magazines. He did everything that needed doing, which left Jane morose. Why was Peter so unromantic and utterly incapable of eye contact? Was he going to apologize again? If he did, could Jane find a way to hurt him back?

"Let me paint your toenails," he offered, and he meant nothing kinky, unfortunately. He retrieved a gaudy, glittery nail polish and proceeded to paint her toes. His hands were warm. He cared about doing it right. Jane regretted that she was still wearing yesterday's sweatpants and flannel. Her toes caught the light, and Peter seemed pleased that he had finally gotten her to smile.

Before he left, her kissed the top of her head. The last time he kissed her, there had been a good deal more passion and more declaring of feelings. Maybe her sweatpants killed romance. Maybe this was how people made the switch from friends-who-flirt to lovers-who-love. Maybe he was about to say something great.

Peter smiled and said, "I'll take out the trash. It's starting to stink."

"Peter? Is something wrong?"

"Well, yes. Your ankle. It looks like an alien is going to come out of it."

She didn't have to say much. She just had to force him to look her in the eye. She had to keep from blinking. He got it. He got her.

"Jane. I'm still married. And I'm Catholic. And I'm in way over my head. You have to give me some room here. And some time. Please."

She blinked.

· · ·

Ray brought Burton to Jane's place to check on her. Burton was at least six feet four, but, oh, so gentle. He had a thick swatch of salt-and-pepper hair and a matching beard. He brought Jane a homeopathic balm for her sore ankle. It smelled like cloves, and so did he.

"You know, Jane. There are no accidents," said Burton. "This was the universe telling you to slow down."

"Please," said Ray. "This was the city not clearing the streets properly. Where's Peter?"

"It's the middle of the afternoon, so I'm thinking he's at work," said Jane. "In fact, maybe he's sitting at his desk right now, and he's on the phone with his parents, and maybe he's telling his parents that he's going to leave his wife for a nice girl who's adopting a baby. And maybe they'll be happy for him because they want grandchildren and they want him to be happy. And hey, we even have my mother's blessing, from beyond the grave."

Ray looked tired and serious.

"It's nice how you're so grounded in reality."

Jane pulled herself up on the couch. She relived the Bianca/Peter spat for them. For an encore, she detailed her own love scene with Peter. And she repeated that Peter said he was falling for her. For emphasis. Falling for her. And then she revealed, "So after all this dreamy romance, what does he mean when he says he needs room? What? You're a guy. Translate, please!"

Ray translated, "It usually means, 'let me find a graceful way to get out of this.' At least, that's what it means in my world." Jane wasn't prepared for so much honesty.

Well, there it was. Ray was easing her into the Inevitable End. She couldn't speak, so Burton did.

"Wait and see. Maybe he'll have a great follow-up."

Jane looked at her glittering toes. Her voice changed.

"That's just it: There won't be any follow-up. He changed his mind. I . . . I don't know what I should do."

"You're heartsick. You should eat!" cried Burton. He overwhelmed Jane's tiny kitchen. "Where's your rice maker?" he called out. But Jane didn't have one.

She whispered to Ray, "Burton's so nice. So? Things are good with you two?"

Ray smiled for the first time all day. "Yes. Still. Can you believe it? Of course he hates my new work schedule. I never thought a yoga teacher would be so full of complaints."

Burton entered with tea and miso soup.

"For our patient," he said. Ray continued as if he had been talking about work all along.

"And I'm going to write an Op-Ed piece about the NEA and religion in the arts."

Ray was working, earning, expanding, climbing. Jane felt like Tiny Tim next to prolific Charles Dickens himself.

"But have you booked the flights for Texas yet?" asked Burton. Jane was in the dark. What flights? Where?

"No. And there are no accidents, are there, Burton? My parents want us to come visit them. In Texas."

Jane perked up. "You guys are up to the 'meet my parents' stage? That's so good. Why aren't you smiling? I'm smiling, and I'm not even you."

"Ray doesn't think that there'll still be an 'us' to go to Texas. And he doesn't want to do anything that isn't work, that isn't furthering his earthly career. Why bother visiting your family of origin with your life partner? After all, there's a bad play you have to say nasty things about. There's a reason why you're never home. You don't *want* to be home." Burton's shrill voice didn't match his grizzly appearance. Jane shrank back while the two men had their fight.

"Why can't I have a career and a boyfriend at the same time?" Ray asked.

Burton smiled. "Women have been asking that since the dawn of careers and boyfriends. So, meanwhile, why don't you use your power more wisely? You could get involved in the gay community."

Ray's face went red. Jane wished she could leave the room and give them privacy. But she couldn't.

"Don't talk to me about the damn gay community. I'm sick of that line. And where is their community center, anyway?"

"I can*not* talk to you when you're like this. Jane. I hope you feel better. Ray. I hope you grow up soon." He made a quiet but dramatic exit. Ray seemed more sad than embarrassed.

"So. Did we make you feel better? We'll do another show at eleven."

"Poor you. Are you guys going to be okay?"

Ray thought a long time before he answered that one. It was as if he could create the answer he wanted, but he had to work so hard for it.

"Yes. We are. We just are. I'm tired of being just me. I want a partner. A family. You understand that. You're adopting a baby. I want to be part of something bigger. And don't start on the gay community, please. I want my own little world, my own little family. Am I asking for too much?"

Jane wanted to get off the couch and hug him a lot. Just then, her door buzzer buzzed. Karen and Teresa were downstairs, and Ray let them in. Karen was shaking from a street drama in which she had just starred. She had encountered not one, but two ex-boyfriends on the way here. Two! And both of them awful. Meanwhile, Teresa was so traumatized by the climb up the stairs, she didn't speak for several minutes.

Finally she said, "Karen. I see my ex every day. Every single day." She sounded like a superhero.

"How can you stand it?"

Ray agreed. "I can barely stand to see my current boyfriend every day. But an ex? Never. I had an old boyfriend who was the house manager at Roundabout. Half the time, our encounters were more dramatic than the plays."

And that was how they launched Bad Boyfriend Rehab. They opened a bottle of wine, realizing that they were in for a long haul. Teresa told them about how and why she and Victor had split up. She had talked about him before, but this time she included lots of dramatic details. She knew that he cheated on her, and that made it easier to part with him. But twelve years was too much time to dismiss. She kept a photo album of their trip to Greece, one of their first trips together. It was important to remember how happy they had once been.

Ray once dated an NFL football player, who still called him.

Karen had a boyfriend, or rather an ex-boyfriend, for every situation, every problem, every city block.

"For a long time, I thought it was so important to be open to the experiences that life offered me. But then, I don't know. I got tired. Bad boyfriends can really drain your energy."

The purge of bad boyfriends required another bottle of wine and very little encouragement. Ray had evil nicknames for all his boyfriends. Mr. Toenails. Mr. Plaid. Mr. Rogaine.

"He thought he wasn't being unfaithful if he never knew the other guy's name."

The women joined in:

"He used to steal my underwear, and he thought I didn't notice."

"He wrote me all these dirty limericks. I still have them."

"He left me. The son of a bitch left me."

"I left him so fast. So fast!"

"I miss him."

"I don't miss him."

Yes, some of the talk was venomous. But you'd be surprised how much of it was venom-free. There were girlish giggles and a few fond sighs. Bad Boyfriend Rehab did not require bashing. Not all the time.

"Will you ladies date again, after your babies come home?" asked Ray. This stopped them all cold.

"No." Teresa sounded certain.

"Maybe," said Jane. She wondered if she could tell them that she was now semi-officially dating Peter. Ray read her mind and gave her a look that told her "Not yet."

"Yes," Karen countered.

"If you wanted to date as a single mother, your life would have to be so very together. You'd have to have every duck, every dotted *i*, every crossed *t*, every-everything," Teresa insisted.

"So, what does it take to have your life together as a single mother in New York City?" Ray asked. As they shouted out their ideas, Jane saw a beloved list in the making. You need:

1. A two-bedroom apartment. (Even Karen endorsed this.)
2. With an elevator.
3. In a cool neighborhood with restaurants very close by, and all public transportation nearby too.
4. And zoned for good schools. (Clearly, the apartment list would be appended, so they moved on.)
5. A good nanny who can work late sometimes.

6. Enough money to take taxis whenever you need to.
7. An expansive wardrobe so that you can easily change into another fabulous outfit after the baby pukes on your blouse.
8. The ability to remove stains from anything. (They remembered Greta's shit-stain speech with a shudder.)
9. Two single-mom friends: In case one of them is busy, there is always someone who understands your life's dilemmas.
10. A male person/father figure to take the pressure off you and your daughter.
11. Good luck. Lots of it.

This was only a starter list, Jane realized. She would revisit this list a lot in the months to come. Ah, lists.

Chapter Ten

Sheila sounded awful.

"The thing about kids is they're all about germs. They're little walking petri dishes. I should send the boys to school in matching Haz-Mat suits. Would the other kids make fun?"

"I would."

"And they know I'm sick, so they really walk all over me. They told me that Raoul wants me to give them lots of chocolate and free money. Little con men. They're not good at it yet, but they just need practice. Oh, God, I feel like crap."

"Oh, Sheila. You're sick. I'm wounded. We match."

"Sisters, sisters," Sheila sang as best she could. "There were never such devoted sisters . . ."

Jane was not talking about Peter. She had stopped telling Sheila, after her sister declared, "This is going to end badly. It's like one of Mom's old movies. Remember? The girlfriends who go to the city to find fame, fortune, and husbands? The one who hooks up with a married man is the one who ends up with a concussion." Jane looked at her sore ankle and changed the subject. Permanently. After she hung up, Jane complained to the mirror.

"What's up with Peter? Why is he being so standoffish? Has he been replaced by an evil twin or a pod person? He's acting like he's providing a service to a friend with a sprain, not starting a new relationship and changing his whole life. Why? Where is he? Isn't this going to happen?"

The mirror offered no answer, but Jane saw how pathetic her sad face was. She contorted it into an Elvis twitch and a growl.

"Oh, grow up," she said to herself and limped away.

• • •

Ray was out of town, missing the second act of Jane's drama on crutches. This justified Jane's dependence on Peter. Didn't it? Sure, it did. Jane e-mailed Ray at his parents' home in Texas and tried to describe what life was like for her now.

To: raylite97@thenet.com
From: jane.howe@argenti.com
Subject: Tiny Tim

Oh Ray,

I'm still hobbling about in the snow on crutches, and am considering selling matchsticks for extra income. By the time you return, I'll be all better. Peter still brings me soup and even watched three episodes of *Buffy the Vampire Slayer* on one of the rerun channels. If that's not love, what is? And yes, I know he's still married, so don't start with me. Don't even. He's been noble and good through this whole mess, and how else was I going to get up the stairs? Riddle me that one, Rayman.

Sort of seriously, I want to know how I would ever get up all those stairs with a baby and a stroller and a diaper bag plus any kind of physical injury at all. Forget the "sort of" part, Ray, tell me, seriously, what would I do?

J

He wrote back in a matter of minutes:

To: jane.howe@argenti.com
From: raylite97@thenet.com
Subject: Re: Tiny Tim

How would you get up the stairs? Silly girl, you would call me, and I would get a plane or a boat or a taxi or whatever I needed, and I'd be there to swoop you up the stairs.

Re: physical injuries and diaper bags. Please. You can't solve problems you don't have yet, so JANE, STOP THIS CRAZY THING!

I, on the other hand, have a real problem. My Dad has bought a used car, fixed it up and given it to me as a belated Christmas gift. And I really am grateful. It was generous and thoughtful and he practically rebuilt the thing. (It was Mom's idea so she could get him out of the living room. She hates his retirement, so far.)

Mom and Burton are in the kitchen—bonding and cooking all the livelong day. He gave her an aromatherapy facial. Should I be grossed out?

Anyway, as an extra-added bit of special, we're going to drive it back to the city. Together. Me, Burton, Mom, Dad and thousands of miles where we can re-e-e-e-ally get to know each other.

God Bless Us, Everyone.
R

PS: Promise me you'll never do this to your kid.

Jane quoted Ray's e-mail at the next Melting Pot dinner. Karen and Teresa decided that Ray was Jane's husband-substitute. A good man, minus sex and laundry. Arlene let that simmer a bit, then corrected them.

"He's her hubstitute. And now her in-laws are coming to visit."

That was absolutely right.

"So, you guys," said Charm. "I saw Dr. Laskin again."

Oh, no. Another mutiny? Another Greta speech? Jane braced herself.

"Who's Dr. Laskin? Your boyfriend?"

"He's a fertility doctor," said Charm. "And he thinks he can get me pregnant. I mean, I don't know how menopausal you guys are—"

How menopausal did they need to be?

"But I'm not. And I can't give up trying. And my dad said that he'd pay for two IVFs. I can probably talk him into more."

If she got pregnant, she would stop the China adoption. Another casualty. Jane couldn't decide what to hope for. She couldn't justify why this news upset her, but it did.

Karen smiled gently. "If you're asking for our permission to conceive, then I think you should ask yourself why."

Charm looked very confused and a little bit hurt, and none of this was Karen's intention. So Karen tried again.

"You don't need our permission, Charm. Do what's right for you."

"Who here is in menopause?" Charm asked this quite loudly and several other tables paid attention.

"I was hoping to save this for a press release, but I'm perimenopausal. For more than a year now. Do you need details?" said Teresa.

Charm declared that menopause created a significant divide between Teresa and herself. How could anyone justify adopting when there was still a possibility of conceiving?

"I can't give up." Resolute Charm.

Teresa signaled the waiter for another glass of wine. Charm continued.

"Jane, you're still a little bit young, aren't you? Don't you want to know what it's like to have a child grow inside your body? Don't you want to experience the miracle of life?"

Jane had wanted those things, once upon a time. Where had that desire gone? It looked like an insane thing to want now. Insane like choosing single motherhood?

"I had a hysterectomy," said Karen. This was what it was like to make friends with people who already had a history. Massive explosions at the dinner table got a mini-synopsis.

"Cancer. A long time ago. I'm feeling much better now."

Charm steamrolled right past this. She wanted an answer from Jane.

"You don't want to get pregnant, but you want to be a mother? I think that's so weird. I don't understand it. Why don't you want to get pregnant, Jane?"

"Because—and this might sound odd, but maybe Dan Quayle was a little bit right."

Karen gasped. Teresa put down her wine. Arlene stared. Dan Quayle was Satan Incarnate at this table. He was the Anti–Single Mother. Arlene shook her head, full of pity for poor Crazy Jane.

"Hear me out," Jane said, suddenly aware of the hostility that was waiting to silence her. "I'm just saying that maybe he was a *little* bit right. I mean, aren't you guys as scared as I am about doing this alone? And Charm, you want to add labor and delivery to all that, and I say, 'Wow.' This is big, this motherhood thing."

"How was Quayle right?" Teresa really wanted to know. She may have voted Republican in the last election.

"He said that two parents are better than one. And he's right. They are. They just are. Someone to stay home with the child, or two incomes—that all sounds good to me. Two people to counter each other. Two people to pay twice as much attention and give twice as much love. Two is better than one."

"Then why are you doing this?" Teresa lost a bit of vocal control, sounding a tad screechy.

"Follow the math. If two parents are better than one, then one parent is better than none. There is a baby in China who has zero parents. And maybe, like the Chinese say, maybe there is some kind of red thread connecting me to her. And I'll be her one."

Teresa eased up. Charm looked perplexed.

"Oh, that sounded so great. Okay, maybe I'll cancel Dr. Laskin."

Jane pictured Charm, seventy years old and well past even high-tech child-bearing, cursing that damn Jane Howe who talked her out of conceiving and she never got to experience childbirth. That bitch.

"Oh, my God. Charm. Sleep on it? Please."

That night, Jane slept well. She had more real estate dreams. This time, she dreamed that Teresa sold her amazing new apartment to Jane, and the apartment transformed into a house. It had hidden rooms and corridors. And Teresa was selling it for a tiny fraction of its worth. Jane found a storage room filled with old furniture. She found a door that opened to the street. She was facing Peter's high-rise building. The sun was in her eyes. She woke up.

. . .

Jane was fully mobile. The stairs took her a long while, and the subway was still intimidating. New York is not a city for anyone who can't walk fast. Peter managed to watch over her without looking at her very much. He looked at food, movies, and every book on her shelf. Jane watched and waited for him to be Peter again.

"Tonight, let me cook for you," Jane offered. "I'm not a great cook, but at least I can stand up in my own kitchen. And I have plates. I'll make pizza. What do you think?"

Peter shook his head. "You're a nut. That's the single easiest thing to have delivered. Why would anyone ever make pizza? You *order* it. You don't make it."

He drank wine while she made the dough. He drank more wine while she made the sauce. Instead of looking at Jane, he was studying the Village outside her window. She refilled his wineglass after every few sips. She wondered if she was trying to get him drunk, and why.

He thanked her properly, ate his food slowly. Part of her thought that she should let this quiet polite man eat his dinner in peace. But that part lost out to the part fantasizing about slugging him. She pictured herself shaking him hard for a long, long time. Then she remembered: You want him. You can't have him. Let him go.

She gulped her wine like she was in a Mountain Dew commercial. She reached out and touched his face. He looked young.

"So, Peter. All this time, I've been thinking that you and I were starting some kind of a romance. A relationship. Something."

He stopped eating.

"Why? Why did you think that?"

And just like that, she had her Irish up.

"I've seen *Gaslight* about fifteen times, so don't, just don't *don't* do this. I have a bunch of good reasons. Including the fact that I can feel it. I know it. I don't walk around the city thinking that everybody loves me. But *you* do. I can feel it."

He looked like he was searching for notes. He was unprepared. Too bad. Jane kept going.

"I'm going to be a mother in a few months, so I have to know: Are you staying or going?"

He couldn't find his notes, if they ever existed. He stood up and said, "I better go. I have to go." He sounded definite.

"Fine. Go." She couldn't hide the crack in her voice. She tried to get mad about that too.

"I can't do this to my marriage. I can't be someone who does this." He was putting on his coat. "Why can't things go back to the way they were before. Okay? Please?"

"It's too late. My time-travel machine is broken." The crack in her voice grew wider.

"Jane."

"Get out. Now."

His exit was awkward and fumbling. She couldn't say any more because her voice had become an open crevice. She stared at the door in disbelief. It was all so close. How could it have slipped away? She needed to call Sheila. She needed to call Ray. She needed someone to slap her for falling in love with a married man. In love. She whispered it. She couldn't take it back. She loved him. She was wrecked.

Jane stopped staring at the door and started to assemble that list of shoulders on which she could cry. And then she heard the knock on her door.

"It's me, Peter. Open the door? Please?"

She hesitated. She didn't need a long speech to go with the rejection. She didn't want to hate him. Then again, a little hostility might heal her vocal chords. She opened the door, already working on her fury.

"Did you forget something?" she snapped. "A jacket? Umbrella? Your wedding ring?"

He stepped inside and framed her face with both hands. He kissed her with no hesitation, no doubt, and no restraint. Jane needed a second to catch up, but then she matched him. Her skin flushed against his. He was open to her. It was all right here. She saw the word "finally" in her head. The second kiss lasted longer. She had a feel for him now. He was a good kisser. She missed kissing. They kept kissing. Her body awoke. Was this a first? Had it always been asleep? He was holding her with a hand on the small of her back. She didn't need oxygen—she needed another kiss.

Jane didn't know how they made their way into the bedroom. She thought she heard fabric tear as they uncovered each other. This was all too fast. At the same moment, they both slowed down to savor all the new skin. Peter finally spoke.

"This changes everything."

Jane knew he was right. She had been biding her time, wonder-

ing when they would ever turn this corner. Now that they were turning, she wanted to wait.

"What's going to happen to us?" She took a gamble that her
words wouldn't ruin this, wouldn't stop the momentum, wouldn't
take him away from her.

"I care about you, Janie. I really kind of love you."

Her muscles twitched. She sat up. Was she supposed to like that
kind of declaration? She didn't. And she was ready to turn hostile at
a moment's notice.

"Peter, make a choice. Either be married to your wife or be with
me. I can't do this for you. I can't help you here. What do you want?"
She didn't wait for an answer, and maybe she should have, but she
kept talking. "I know what I want. I want a family of my own. I want
to be a mother. I want to raise my daughter and be good to her and
be happy and grow old and get into that really good nursing home.
Tell me you don't want to be part of that."

"I do. But I can't just leave Bianca." *Eek!* He said her name!
"We've been together for twelve years, off and on. We have a life and
a history—"

"And three thousand miles between you. Teenagers who are
going steady see more of each other than you do." Jane opted for
hostility.

She found her shirt and tried to make noise as she pulled it on.
She locked her teeth. Peter looked a wretched mess, his head in his
hands. Jane had never noticed the little scar on his earlobe. Did
Peter once have an earring disaster? How long ago? Half-dressed,
half-empty, she was free enough to touch the small shadow near the
tip of his ear.

"Peter. Should I just walk away? If you were my friend, what
would you tell me to do?"

"I want you."

"How much? Look, I can't play junior high anymore. Staying or
going. Make a choice." Jane was still looking at his ear.

Peter stood up, forcing her to let go of his dimpled ear.

"Staying. I told you: I want you. I want this. I want to be there in China when that baby is put in your arms, and I want to be there when she learns to read and learns to drive. I want this whole life right here."

She saw the word *"finally"* in her head once again. He was choosing her. Finally.

"But look at where I am. I need to work this out with Bianca before I say anything more. And before I do anything more. I have to be fair to her, you know."

She hated that he was right.

"I'll talk to her soon," he continued. "She doesn't know anything. This is going to blindside her. And my parents. They can't know about this yet. Oh, God. Look. We can't be *us* until I take care of that. I need to go to L.A. and talk to her. Can you wait? Because this is big. This is huge."

He was so right.

. . .

Ray's parents. Jerry and Rita. Try to remember that they meant well and had never been in a situation like this before, and that they really really meant well.

Ray set them up with a full agenda. Tickets to big splashy musicals, to serious, edgy dramas, and a handful of cabarets. He insisted that they ride a double-decker tour bus and spend the day hopping on and hopping off. Ray kept them busy while Burton doubled his usual quota of meditation.

Ray, their only child, beloved son, would be accompanying Jane to China to adopt a baby. That little girl was the closest they would come to grandchildren. They wanted to meet Jane, and they really did mean well, as you know.

Jane invited them over for brunch, and included Karen and Teresa, to keep things lively and to give her a good context. If other women, perfectly respectable single women, were adopting, it added to Jane's sense of legitimacy.

Mr. and Mrs. Whittier took so long coming up the stairs that Jane began to worry.

"You okay down there?"

"Whoo! Yeah! Give us a few minutes, here! Whoo!"

Teresa sympathized. "Those stairs are just awful. Maybe you should go help them."

"How? I can't carry them up."

"How are you going to have a baby in this apartment?" Wow, Teresa was becoming so blurty too. Jane couldn't answer because she had no answer and because Ray's parents made their entrance.

"How are you going to have a baby in this apartment?" Rita asked, following a few Whoos and Oh, Mys.

"You must be Jane! Hi!"

Ray made introductions all around, while his mother gulped water and his father mopped his forehead with a tissue. Jane apologized for the stairs and began to feel that she was living in a tree house. Once the Whittiers recovered from their mighty climb, they settled in and stared at everyone in the room.

"How was the drive?" It seemed like the obvious ice breaker, but the pained looks among the Whittier family revealed an incomplete conspiracy. They had never settled on a party line to describe the torturous drive.

"That car gets wonderful m-m-m-m-mileage. I think we made it through the C-c-c-c-carolinas on one tank of g-g-gas." Ray never told Jane that his father stuttered.

"That's important," Karen chimed in. "For the environment."

Jane had assembled her favorite brunch of bagels, smoked salmon, and all the fixings. She set it up as a buffet. As part of a cleansing preparation for motherhood, Karen was abstaining from meat. She was a little vague about her new diet restrictions, but she was absolutely going to have this salmon. It may have been alive once, but now it was smoked.

"Is this sushi?" Rita asked Teresa, who always seemed to be the one in the know.

"Well, technically, it's sashimi, but we call it lox."

"I've had sushi. Made me sick. Don't care to try that again, thank you very much."

But they made it through the meal. Back in Texas, Jerry and Rita had access to television and the Internet, so there was nothing about New York that was so surprising that they would have to sit down. It might not look, sound, or feel like Texas, but they coped with it just fine. And the bagels in New York were really much nicer than they were in Texas. So big. So fresh. They had a lovely brunch.

"When Ray was a baby, he didn't sleep through the night until he was five years old. I always said that was why he was an only child. We never had a chance to make another one."

Ray braced himself for the same stories of his potty training, odd eating habits, and stuffed animal friends that Burton had endured. Jerry and Rita obliged.

"He wore diapers at night until, oh, gosh, I think he was in kindergarten, was it?"

"Remember the way he hated ch-ch-ch-ch-cheese?"

"I think we still have Mr. Jumbles, the bear. You know, I found that thing under his pillow the morning he left for college? Isn't that sweet?"

Ray endured. He looked at the clock. They had a three o'clock matinee to attend. He could endure anything if he knew when it would end.

The mimosas went to Rita's head and made her all too comfortable with her almost-daughter-in-law. She settled in to have a real talk with this lovely girl.

"Jane. You're a lovely girl. I wonder if we could have a real talk."

"Mom."

But Jane let the real talk happen. She knew about the matinee and had the same sense of endurance that Ray had. The finite was infinitely manageable. And she anticipated Rita's idea of a real talk: a series of personal questions. If she thought of this as a list, it felt cozier.

"When will you go to China?"

Jane hated this question more than you might think. She didn't know if she would hear from China in a month or three months, or how long it would take to get travel permission. No one liked the haziness of the answer, including Jane. So she said, "In the spring."

"Will you take some time off from work?"

Rita had stopped watching the news in 1989. Jane got to fill her in on Family Leave. Some firms offered paid leave, some offered unpaid leave. Argenti, a big player on Wall Street, offered full pay for three months.

"How does your employer feel about all this adoption business?"

Jane hadn't come out at work yet. She was waiting for a sign. So she said, "They're fine." And began to feel guilty about lying to these nice people, here and at work. She would tell the truth on the next question.

"How much money do you make?"

Ray groaned loudly. "Mother! You may not ask that! Try again. Sorry, Jane."

Jane wondered if she could postpone the truth to another question.

"Are you going to stay home with the baby?"

Jane was planning to hire a nanny, and to be the nicest employer any nanny ever worked for.

"Can you afford that? And who's going to climb all those stairs for you every day with a baby and a stroller and God knows what else?"

Ray shot her a look.

"I'm just asking."

Jane didn't have an answer. She hoped she'd find some very fit person who really wanted to stay that way and saw in Jane's building the perfect workout.

"You know what, Mom? Jane doesn't know where her daughter is going to go to high school, or college, or what she'll wear on May thirtieth seven years from now. No one knows all the answers. We let you ask a bunch of questions that were none of your business, but now you're going to be late for your show. And look outside. It looks like it's going to rain soon, so let's go."

"We traded in those t-t-t-tickets. We wanted more time with y-y-y-you and Jane."

The unmanageable infinite. Oh, no.

Teresa and Karen were watching the launch of some horrible new reality show: Watch Your Friends Squirm. They spent a lot of time wrestling with the moral dilemma of staying vs. leaving. The longer they wrestled, the more they got to see. But there would be a price to pay.

"Do I understand this right? You're all adopting? And you're all single?"

And it began to rain. Karen and Teresa should have left while the sun shined.

"Why? I mean, why are you adopting a yellow baby? Can't you get a white one?"

Ray was imploding. Jane wanted to take care of him. So she did her best. She answered the question.

"I don't really care if my daughter resembles me or not. That isn't important. And I guess I chose China because I knew China wouldn't reject me. They would let me adopt a baby, even though I'm not married. And it's all so regulated and proper. No black market, nothing devious going on. That's Communism, for you, right?"

"So, China just lets single ladies adopt their b-b-b-babies? Just like that? Don't they care about fathers? And w-w-what's the deal, do they just hate girls or what?"

Jane decided everyone needed more coffee/tea/juice/water/

anything in the kitchen. She let Karen and Teresa testify for a while. Ray followed Jane into the kitchen and stayed in there, washing dishes as loudly as he could. When Jane returned to the living room, Teresa seemed to have things under control.

"So you see, if Dan Quayle was right, then one parent is better than zero parents." She smiled obligingly at Jane as her footnote. Jane nodded back. Rita and Jerry seemed satisfied with the answer. Rita leaned in and spoke quietly.

"Tell me, what would you do if your little girl came home from college and told you that she was becoming a gay? That's what happened to us, and I think we handled it as well as anyone. Have you met Burton? Nice man, but he's so hairy! We all went to the pool and—"

Ray had finished washing the dishes, so Rita leaned back, using her full voice once again.

"I know we've been intruding, and I'm sure Ray already told you that I'm a busybody and a snoop and he wants nothing to do with his mom and her nosy old questions—"

"You're close!" Ray shouted from the kitchen, where he was still hiding.

"But I thank you for talking to me like this. You don't know me from Adam, and all I really wanted out of this trip—aside from seeing Katie Couric—was the chance to get to know you and find out about this whole China baby thing. Yes, I'm a nosy old lady, but you're all such sweethearts. Thank you."

This made it sound like it was over. And it almost was.

"Can I ask one more q-q-q-question?"

Why not?

"Why aren't any of you ladies m-m-married? I'll tell you, if you moved out of this big city, you'd catch a husband as fast as you please. The fellows here all have the eye for each other, and I say that with all d-d-due respect." He nodded gravely to his son.

"Jerry's right. You're all pretty enough—you shouldn't have to die old maids."

It was Karen's turn.

"We all follow our own path, Mrs. Whittier. I think that, perhaps, in another life, I had a difficult marriage, and that's why I avoided it this time around. I needed to work on myself."

Jerry and Rita didn't understand Karen's answer, and didn't want to lose this last opportunity to find out.

"But why don't you at least have a b-b-boyfriend?"

Karen described her last seven boyfriends, of the last three years. Jerry thought she was a bit of a wildcat, with an eye for the wrong man, every time. Teresa described the painful breakup with Victor, her business partner. Rita thought she should snip off his thing. "If he's not going to have babies, he won't need it, right?"

And then Rita asked, "What about you, Jane?"

Everyone turned to look at Jane, who had no answer. She wasn't about to say anything about Peter until he was ready to be an *us*. Maybe she was supposed to tell them about Sam and how he died. But she didn't want to talk about him, either. She didn't want to blame Sam for anything. For years, she saw herself as his widow. But today, trying so hard to tell the truth to her pseudo-mother-in-law, she knew that Sam had nothing to do with this. He had been dead such a long time.

"I'm single, Mrs. Whittier. I just am."

And they took that answer, with no more poking or pushing. They rose to leave, and Ray was visibly delighted. At last, the interrogation was over.

"Well, I always say, there's a Jack for every Jill. A lid for every pot. I bet you'll find some nice divorced daddy and make a big ol' family. That's my bet."

Jane saw a different plot twist in her future, but she smiled and nodded and helped them gather their coats and bags. It was still raining, so Rita wore her clear plastic scarf and accepted an umbrella from Jane.

"You're a love! Can I give you a big hug?" Rita didn't wait for an answer, but gave Jane hugs, and kisses. Oh, there were hugs and kisses all around. Ray kept nudging them toward the door. He led the way down the stairs.

Rita turned and shouted, "We'll come visit again after the baby comes!"

"Mom!"

It took them a long time to get down the stairs.

Chapter Eleven

Peter had to go to L.A. He had to. You can't break up with your wife by voice mail. Jane knew that one already. It was only a weekend, but he had to go there and see her and tell her and maybe fall back in love with her perky perkiness. He kissed Jane sweetly and wished Jane wouldn't worry so much. Jane tried to grant his wish. After all, it was only a weekend with his wife. What's to worry about? Everything.

So Jane distracted herself for the weekend by helping Barbara assemble the materials for her big China-moms Seminar in the Living Room. Did Barbara really need a T.A. for this? Jane didn't think so. Her responsibilities included copying, stapling, and pretending to be the evil Maleficent from *Sleeping Beauty* for Rachel, who then dashed off to a playdate for the afternoon.

"So. Are you going to marry Peter?" Barbara asked during the stapling marathon. Jane remembered how Barbara always liked to start with the hard questions. She kept her students alert that way.

"I don't know."

"When is he getting his divorce?"

"I don't know."

"Do you think his wife is going to make it difficult?

She could. Are they California residents? Wouldn't that mean community property laws and all that?"

"Still with the 'Don't Know.' "

Jane stopped stapling. She figured she had just flunked a quiz about her own life. Talk about demoralizing.

"Find out," said Barbara. "You can't make plans or decisions until you know all this and a whole lot more. He's going to be in your daughter's life. But how much? And how soon? This is happening fast, Janie. Find out."

Why did Barbara have to smash her happy plans with all these petty details? Jane stapled with indignation. Eventually she ran out of paper to staple together. She looked up and saw Barbara smiling at her the same way she smiled when Rachel was deep into one of her "I can do it myself" scenes. She gingerly took the stack of papers from Jane and said, "Find out."

. . .

Barbara opened the lecture/discussion with advice about the first weeks home: stock your fridge and make sure you have someone checking on you. Jane was still seething. Find out. She trusted Peter. The man had just flown across the country to end his very Catholic marriage so that he could be with her! Find out, indeed. When are we getting married? *Are* we getting married?

"As for your daughter's potential health issues—I'm going to arrange for a separate seminar with Dr. Val. She's the top pediatrician for international adoptions. She'll prep you better than I can."

Find out. Oh, Jane would find out all right. Hey. Wait. What did Barbara just say about public school vs. private school? Jane kicked herself for missing Barbara's lecture/discussion.

". . . and those are some of the main factors to consider when you're choosing child care. Any questions?"

Karen's hand shot up.

"This sheet here about day care centers? These prices can't be right. This has to be top-of-the line, luxury day care for Kennedys. Where's the real-person day care?"

"This is it." Everyone turned and looked at Karen, who now had red splotches on her cheeks. Her eyes were wide. Was she starting to cry?

"No. This can't be it. I can't afford this. What am I doing? Why didn't someone tell me it was going to be this expensive? I can't swing this. No way."

Karen was starting to cry. Her friends circled around her and tried to make comforting sounds as they patted her back. Karen was crying full out.

"Do I have to cancel this adoption?" she managed to say.

Barbara stepped in and said, "Could everyone leave us alone? Jane? Could you take them into the kitchen? This might be a good time for a break."

Jane managed to take care of her fellow students and be the official eavesdropper for the group. She heard, "I need a better job" and "Why didn't I know this?" a few times. She heard the Microsoft melody as Barbara booted up her computer. She heard "budget," and then things got quiet for a while.

"Is she canceling her dossier?" Teresa asked.

"Shhhh!"

Jane heard "budget" a few more times, followed by "a lot of bologna sandwiches." She peeked in and saw Karen and Barbara hugging. Barbara signaled to Jane that everyone could come in. And Jane paid strict attention for the rest of the afternoon.

"Ladies, this is single motherhood you're facing. It's so hard I'm not even going to try to describe it. It's all down to you: paying the bills, helping with homework, fixing boo-boos, and playing games. And so much more. You have to know that you can do this alone. Can you?"

Jane looked around. She saw finals week exhaustion and terror on the faces of the Chinamoms. Barbara looked as if she had so much more to say but didn't have the heart to beat any more information into these tired women.

"Good night, you guys. Get some rest. While you can." And the Chinamoms climbed out of her sofa like they were climbing out of an open grave.

Teresa sighed and said, "God, I think my head's going to explode."

Karen took Jane aside and whispered, "She must have been a marvelous teacher. I think she just saved my life."

"Jane!" Barbara called. "Can I say one more thing to you?"

Jane went back to her teacher, who said, "I don't want you to be unhappy, Jane. Maybe things will work out with Peter after all. But I think you need to know that you can do this on your own if you have to. If anyone can, you can."

Jane wanted to be flattered, but she got stuck on the "maybe." Maybe things will work out? Things *will* work out with Peter. Too depleted to fight much, she only managed a quiet, "Things will work out with Peter."

To: jane.howe@argenti.com
From: petermandell@worthnet.net
Subject: How R U?

Just returned from CA. Can we meet for dinner tonight? We need to talk.

XO
Peter

He had not called or e-mailed during the trip. Okay, it was only a weekend, but still. She missed him. And now Jane prepared herself for anything, everything, nothing: Peter was going to ask her to marry him. Peter was going to pack his things and move to California. Peter was going to become a bride of Christ. Anything.

He didn't say anything for a while as he held her to his chest like a teddy bear. The good smell had survived transcontinental flights. In her list, preparing for his return, she hadn't included "Peter was going to be silent."

"Okay, Peter. Just tell me. What happened with your wife? With Bianca." Saying her name took a little effort.

Eventually Peter sat down and spoke. "She was so angry. I never heard her voice like that." Peter seemed to be starting his story in the middle, which was fine. He surprised Bianca with this visit. She took it as a romantic gesture, which led to deep, loud anger.

"This is going to be complicated, and I haven't even told my parents yet. That's when it will all become real. When I tell my father that I'm getting—" He didn't finish that sentence.

"Anyway," he resumed. "As bad as that was, telling my parents will be worse. They're old-school Catholics. Very old-school. Fish on Fridays and all that."

"My mom opted for microwave pizza on Fridays. No pepperoni, though."

Peter didn't seem to hear her.

"I'm dreading telling them. It'll be even worse than telling Bianca."

He was studying her ceilings and floors. The silence was very hard to take.

"Peter. You don't have to do anything for my sake. It's not like I'm pregnant. You don't have to make an honest woman of me. I made my own choices. You make yours."

"What? Jane. This is something I have to do."

"No, you don't have to do anything."

"Yes, I do. I love you."

Thank God.

. . .

Teresa and Karen officially invited Ray to the Melting Pot dinners. Karen stood up and declared, "Welcome to the henhouse!" when he walked over to the table. They ordered, they gossiped, they complained about the wait.

"When are we going to get our referrals? I thought we were supposed to know by now! And where's Teresa? Why is everything about waiting?"

Ray consoled them and compared the wait to enduring the four-hour *Virginia Cycle* he had just reviewed/eviscerated for the *Times*. It was a musical about the Civil War that consisted of the same story told from seven points of view, including that of an earthworm.

"I made Burton go with me, and I swear I thought he was going to divorce me."

"Speaking of divorce," said Jane. "I have news."

Ray very nearly pounced on her.

"It's about Peter, isn't it? Don't think I haven't noticed your oh-so-discreet silence on this topic. You haven't talked about him in forever. What have you been doing?"

She told them every detail, every eyelash of Peter's return, Peter's impending divorce, Peter's selfless sacrifices for Jane. She was discreetly vague about the fact that she was sleeping with Peter. She left out Barbara's "find out" and "maybe" comments.

Ray didn't try to comment. He didn't even blink. Jane knew that look. It was his analytic mode. He was going to seize some particular adjective and use it as proof positive that Jane was hopelessly neurotic, or that Peter was, or that life was pointless.

Karen was a highly satisfying audience member. She smiled, winced, and occasionally let her mouth fall open—especially when the story revealed to this single-mother-to-be that Jane was no longer a single-mother-to-be.

"So, Jane. This whole thing—it makes you sort of different from me, and from Teresa."

Jane froze. No, it didn't, she thought. Peter's presence changed nothing. Karen responded to Jane's freeze.

"It's okay. We'll be the single moms, and you'll be the married mom. We don't have to be the same. But we all need to eat. What's keeping Teresa, anyway? You know you'll have to repeat this whole sordid tale to her. But don't stop now. When is he moving in?"

Ray was still quiet. He scooted his chair over when Teresa slipped in quietly, looking rather pale. She ordered a martini.

"Jane has been telling us about her love life," Ray said quietly. "And we, who have no lives, salute her."

Jane stopped her story. She saw that Teresa's hands were shaking. Her makeup was smudged near her eyes. Something was wrong.

Teresa started telling her story to Jane, but soon everyone at the table was listening.

"For months now, I've been waiting to see who was going to drop out of this adoption. Karen, you have financial issues, but I think you've worked them out. Jane, you're so tangled up with Peter, and you think we don't know it, but my money has been on you all this time. You'll marry him and make babies the way couples do. Or you'll dump him. Or he'll dump you. Or something. Anyway, I thought you were a goner."

Jane's pale face was flushed. Was Teresa trying to start a fight? Before Jane could ask her, Teresa continued.

"But now, I put the odds on me."

At earlier dinners, she had told the story of how she let word of the adoption circulate at the office. And Victor, her ex, had given his famous speech about Chinese babies as the ultimate (returnable) accessory. Eventually, he offered a chilly "Congratulations," but they never spoke of it again. But then, their conversations were never personal anymore. He had said enough.

Everyone knew that Victor was dating someone young, someone not perimenopausal. If Teresa was bothered by this, she didn't let on. Jane thought that this had to be the acid test for mental health. After the first time Teresa saw them together, she gave a detailed description of the girl: pretty in an ornamental way, rail thin, blond, and bearing a passing resemblance to a young Teresa. This aspect was flattering, but Teresa made it clear to all the Chinamoms that she had moved on with her life. Her apartment renovation had commanded her full attention. Jane noticed that Teresa said more about her plumber than about Victor. Until tonight:

"Want to know why I'm late? Hmm? I was all set to leave, but Victor and his little chippy with the winter tan—I mean, his girlfriend—were giggling away in the lobby. So, I'm a mature adult and I decided to wait at my desk until they left, thus avoiding the awkward scene, and aren't I nice?"

She held her empty martini glass aloft and signaled the waiter for a refill.

"So I waited. I waited. But they were lingering there, because that's what truly evil people do. It was like they were never leaving. So fine. I went out."

When her waiting was done, Teresa strode out to the lobby and pushed the glass doors open. She tossed a quick "Good night" over her shoulder, proud of her cool maturity. The glass door closed, and she froze. She turned. The girlfriend was standing up, and she had a distinct belly. She was pregnant. She was very, very pregnant.

Teresa was staring. Victor shielded his young, pregnant girlfriend from Teresa's gaze. He stepped outside to Teresa.

"You're probably wondering—" was all he managed to say.

"You bastard. I quit."

And in a blink, she was an unemployed, single-mother-to-be. She rose to the top of her own list of candidates to drop out of the adoption process. But first, she had stepped out to Twenty-third Street at rush hour and cried.

After Teresa finished her story, and her third martini, Jane advised her to sue Victor for crimes against humanity. Karen, who thought that all litigation led to bad karma, thought this might be the exception. Sue him.

"Ruin him. Take the business away from him. He owes you."

Ray advised her to make no plans tonight, other than more martinis.

"Look, I don't know you very well, and I don't know Victor at all. But sure, he'll buy you out. He'll have to. And maybe you can start your own agency—"

Teresa crumbled under the exhaustion implicit in that suggestion. Ray continued.

"Or maybe you can work somewhere else. Or maybe you can take a year off and think about it all and play with a cooing little baby. Maybe you don't have to decide anything tonight. Wait."

Waiting sounded just fine to Teresa and to everyone. Jane was justifiably proud of her hubstitute. Everyone settled in for an evening of Victor-bashing. Teresa was not holding back.

"For twelve years, he didn't want to have kids. Suddenly, he meets little miss fake-tan, and he decides he's going to be a daddy? He waited until I was gone? He waited until I was in menopause? The bastard. The unbelievable bastard!"

Jane echoed, "He's a bastard."

"He's older than me. Did I tell you that?" Yes. "And he can still get that girl pregnant. He has all the time in the world. And he doesn't know what to do with it."

Karen should have echoed her friend. Instead, she said, "Will China let you adopt if you're not employed anymore?"

This question should have waited. But once it was said, Teresa nearly collapsed under the weight of it.

"I don't know. I have to fix this. And soon. If the latest statistics stay true, we'll be getting our referrals in about a month, maybe two. I'll be damned if Victor is going to ruin this for me. The bastard."

Teresa laid her head down on the table and echoed herself.

"The bastard."

Her friends took her home.

. . .

Jane called Sheila but spoke only to the crackly answering machine. This was not a saga for an answering machine. She left an insistent "Call me and you'll be glad you did" message for her sister. She hung up and studied the phone. She wanted to ask her sister: Was Betty in heaven, protecting Jane from all the turmoil her friends were experiencing? She began to see herself as the Lucky One. She had no bad ex-boyfriend to induce her to quit a job where her paycheck actually covered her living expenses plus child care.

And Peter was almost free and almost hers. Everything was so close.

. . .

Ray settled in to watch Jane empty a neatly organized drawer.

"Peter needs room for some things. He keeps piling up T-shirts on the hamper. And look." She dangled a shiny new set of keys she had made for Peter. Ray didn't smile.

"He gave me keys to his place," Jane said. "It's only fair."

"Cozy. Have you told Howard yet?"

Jane hadn't told her father yet.

"I have to tell Sheila first, and I can't seem to find her lately."

"There are no accidents . . ."

"No. Telling Dad is a lose-lose situation. Either he'll say, 'See? I was right about how you can't be single and adopt,' or he'll say, 'Jezebel! Stealing another woman's husband!' "

Ray nodded. "It's nice to know just how crazy a person is, huh?"

"Well. Isn't he right?"

"About which thing?" Ray was peeking in the boxes.

"The first. Second. Both. Is it a bad sign to start a relationship like this? With him leaving his wife like this?"

"You can't start a relationship if he doesn't. And isn't this what Bitty-Betty wanted?"

Jane was folding and putting away.

"Still."

"I know."

Ray made them tea. They settled in the kitchen, where Jane watched for Peter to come up the street.

"I wonder if I could have raised a baby all alone."

"No."

"Ouch. I thought you believed in me. I thought you supported this adoption."

"You were never going to be alone, darling. You had me. In fact, Burton thinks that he and I should adopt. I think we should start with a plant and see if we can keep that alive."

"In your place? You get no light. Get a plastic plant."

"Excellent plan. And maybe Burton's right. I had sort of gotten used to the idea of being a pseudo-dad for you and your little one. Now that I'm out of the picture—"

"When did you fall out of the picture?"

"When you emptied that drawer." Jane gave him a look of sympathy/sad/I love you, which forced him to look away. "And that's fine. I always kind of knew you'd leave me for another man. You're a hottie; you just don't dress like one. So now I'm the wacky uncle. Again. I play that part well."

"You're not out of the picture. You're still coming with me to China, aren't you?"

Now it was Ray's turn to give a look of sympathy/sad/I love you. "The three of us? What would Chairman Mao say? No, no, no. This is not a trip for the wacky uncle. I'm out."

Jane's doorbell rang, and she buzzed Peter in. She trolled around for words of comfort for Ray, but she found none. She opened her front door, and there was Peter, carrying a crazy bouquet of blue daisies.

• • •

Peter was a morning person. Jane was not. He started the day with an indecent amount of energy, whereas Jane eased into the morning. More often than not, Jane and Peter commuted together. She collapsed against his shoulder as they held hands. She knew they were looking so couply-cute when they bumped into Dick-Richard, who hurt Peter with his vigorous handshake. He was on a break from the new Martin Scorsese movie.

"I love working with Marty. He really feeds the extras well. And you? What are you up to these days?"

He was asking about someone other than himself. How was that for a sign of Divine Providence?

She replied, "I'm adopting a baby from China."

Dick-Richard said nothing. He seemed to be concentrating on something in his teeth. When he finished with his dental hygiene, he said, "Did I tell you about the showcase I'm doing next month? It's a new play, and I don't think it's very good. It's some kind of murder mystery, I think. But I have a really funny scene at the end. You should come."

Jane smiled, and Peter took a flier from him. Maybe they would actually go see this play called *The Customer Is Always Dead*.

Chapter Twelve

You have one *new message.*

"Hi, Janie, it's me." Sheila. At last. "Call me. Something happened and— I don't want to leave this on your machine, so just call me, okay? Right away."

Beep.

Jane dialed her sister's number. Sheila answered the phone in a perfect telephone-lady voice, calm and composed, but dissolved the moment she heard Jane's voice.

After Sheila caught her breath, she said, "I was pregnant, and don't be mad at me, but I didn't want to tell anyone too soon. I was afraid of bad luck. But then Raoul was telling everyone and I got mad at him and told him it was bad luck, but he doesn't believe in luck or signs or anything. I do. Especially now."

Sheila was talking quickly, and Jane had to struggle to keep up. Sheila was crying, so her words were wet and mushy. Jane pieced the story together as if it were a quilt. Pregnant. Miscarried. Distraught. Sheila was grieving and needed all the family she could get.

"I know I said all that stuff about not being sure I wanted to get pregnant. Right now, I can't believe I ever said anything so crazy. I was so happy, Janie. I was counting the days until I could tell you. Why did this happen to me? Why?"

Jane stayed on the phone with her sister for the rest of the evening. There were long stretches of crying and even longer stretches of silence. They hung up, both depleted, and that night Jane dreamed that Betty was knitting a small boat, urging her girls to get in and start rowing.

. . .

Jane and Peter were late for work. She had stayed up late with Sheila once again, and they both forgot about petty things like alarm clocks. Jane usually raced to work, hating to walk in late, hating to have everyone see her emerge from the elevator long after they had started working/surfing the Web/fake-working. But Peter's presence made even this anticipated stress more survivable.

Peter locked the apartment door as Jane began the race down the stairs. She had just a moment to notice the Open House sign posted near the mailboxes before they sped out the door. Jane tried to maintain her dignity as they did a speed-walk from the subway to the office building. They kissed good-bye as they approached their separate elevator banks. During the ride, she worked to catch her breath and make a serene entrance to workday. She entered her busy floor and stopped cold. No one was there. For a moment, she had to check that it was a workday. It was. It was a Tuesday. Jane finally found a living human being. It was Kendra, who was clutching a stack of personnel folders. She looked at her folders, then at Jane. The lines around her mouth were set and hard. Her shoulders were up high, and she looked tired.

"Jane. You're late."

Tuesday. The perfect day to lay off all the staff. Not a Monday, since everybody hates Mondays. Early enough in the week that they can start to make some progress on a job search. Not so late in the week that they end up brooding for the weekend, only to return to the office with an Uzi. Tuesday, bloody Tuesday.

"Jane? I've been waiting for you."

Walking to Kendra's office felt like wading through ice water. She sat down carefully and silently begged for this to be merciful and brief. It wasn't. Kendra had been instructed to speak only Corporate Speak today. She had a party line to say to each and every person she fired. Jane had to sift through it all and translate it to plain English.

"After careful analysis, we realized that outsourcing is going to be the best way for us to leverage resources."

This means, "We fired everyone."

"I want to manage your expectations here, but, Jane, you've always added value, and we've retained headcount for you for the rest of the fiscal year."

This means, "Don't get your hopes up, but we like you and you're not fired. Yet."

"But we'll need you to reach out to different business silos and evaluate their needs. We need to be flexible and responsive. We're redesigning your position, but we need you to architect it too."

This means, "You have to do a lot more work."

Kendra described Jane's new job—which would involve much longer hours, supervising global support in Europe and Asia. Of course, Jane would have no trouble keeping up with the time differences—just come in real early and leave real late. Oh, and be here for lots of weekend projects. Oh, and there'll be lots of travel.

Jane felt like melted wax. She chose this time to come out.

"I'm adopting a baby. I don't think I'll be able to reach out to different silos or travel all that much. Once the baby comes home, I'll need to be less flexible here at the office. I'll need to go home. On time."

Kendra gasped. There was nothing in her Corporate Speak script to address adoptions. She shook her head and said, "I think we'll need to take this off-line."

. . .

The office was depressingly quiet. Jane phoned Peter at work. After all, he worked on Wall Street too. He'd understand her situation and have good advice and insights. He was the right person to call. And okay, yes, she was longing to hear his voice again. After all, it had been minutes since they had spoken.

"I was hoping I'd get promoted before the baby came, but this isn't a promotion. It's just more work. I can't do *more* work. I can only do *less*."

"Why are you whispering?"

"Because I'm all alone here and it's creepy."

"Oh. Okay. Why don't I come over tonight? We can talk about it, and you can use your whole voice."

. . .

Jane sent out an e-mail distress signal. Teresa offered the name of a good lawyer. One strongly worded letter from him and she'd be fine. Karen offered deep-breathing exercises, push the belly out and fill up with air. Ray recommended a fake pregnancy pillow and was sure he could get one from a costume designer he knew. After all, would they do this to a pregnant woman?

When Jane and Peter returned to her apartment building that evening, there it was again: Open House. Printed with a fancy color laser printer, no doubt. With a photo of the friendly Realtor.

"Let's take a look," said Jane.

They started climbing the stairs. Peter was still not used to it.

"It's just downstairs from me," said Jane. "Let's take a look."

She sailed into the open apartment, where the Realtor gave her best spider-to-fly welcome.

"This is a terrific building. Historic, but very well maintained.

And such an up-and-coming neighborhood. Sarah Jessica Parker had dinner down the street from here just a week ago."

"Well, then," said Peter. "We'll take it."

"Really?" the Realtor was almost drooling.

"I'm kidding. Sorry. We're just having a look. Sorry." Ms. Realtor was not amused. Jane was off exploring the other room.

"Look!" she called out. "You think the apartment is done, and then there's this other room off the kitchen. I thought it was going to be a broom closet, but it's this whole big room. The layout of the space is so funky, but it's kind of cool."

Peter looked restless and hungry. Jane kept exploring. Nice hardwood floors. Crappy old kitchen appliances. Interesting.

"Jane. You have a perfectly good apartment right upstairs from this one."

Ms. Realtor had moved on to her next prospects, so Jane and Peter continued their conversation in her perfectly good apartment right upstairs.

"Because. I could climb one less flight of stairs. That's key. Did you see the nice bathroom in the place?"

Jane was too excited to notice the storm brewing over Peter's head. She was coveting that bathroom. So much marble in such a small space.

"No. We can't. I can't." Peter sounded definite.

Jane stopped coveting for a moment. Peter continued.

"Jane, honey. Your job is in flux, remember? Outsourcing? Ring a bell?"

"Oh. Yeah. That."

"And look at me. I just left my wife. I'm going to be going through a divorce. This is not a good time for me to buy an apartment. No. I just can't. If you like, I can give you a list—an actual list—of good reasons why this is a bad idea."

The joy and potential of real estate had lifted Jane's face into a wide-eyed smile that wouldn't release. Maybe she could connect the two apartments. Or maybe she could sublet the upstairs apartment for enough money to cover her nanny expenses. Perfect! She was sure she could talk Peter into this.

"Jane, how can we even be having this conversation? You're too smart to be dazzled by a marble bathroom. Come on."

Jane put water on for pasta, as she thought about this. Wouldn't this be a good investment? And, "Wouldn't it be cool to sublet this place, and we'd always have control over who our upstairs neighbors were. That's a New Yorker's dream. And we'd be the landlords. And we'd make extra money. All the work I put into this place would really pay off. Think about it."

Peter looked surprised. At what? That Jane was thinking about money? She had been thinking about it since Barbara's scary seminar. That Jane was still talking about the apartment? She didn't feel answered or defeated. Not yet. That Jane was arguing with him? She was still Irish, after all.

"Our upstairs neighbors?" he asked. "Let's be realistic here: We'll be leaving the city pretty soon. We'll be in a house. We won't have upstairs neighbors."

Jane accidentally dumped the contents of an entire box of pasta into the boiling water. It splashed and burned her wrist. Peter was right there, with an ice cube.

"Here."

There was a small pink teardrop shape on her wrist. It stung. Peter pressed the ice cube against it, and it slowly numbed. She studied the long bones that stood out against the back of his hand. Good hands and—look. No wedding ring.

"Where are we going?" she asked quietly. It took Peter a minute to catch up. She didn't mean tonight. She meant post-city.

"Well. I don't know. New Jersey, maybe." Jane pulled her arm away. She could hold her own ice cube, thank you. "Or Long Island. Or Connecticut. I don't know. I haven't really thought about it, Jane."

"You've thought about it a little."

Was Peter blushing? Why? Was he busted? For what?

"Jane. Hey. Of course. I mean. I think about the future. Of course. Hey." His blush subsided. He caught his breath. "I mean, it's not like people raise kids in the city. Not most people. And there are two of us now. I just assumed, I mean, naturally, we're going to move out. To the suburbs."

"Why?"

"Why? Schools. Backyards. All that suburban stuff. Kids love that stuff."

Jane forgot about the boiling pasta. She wasn't hungry anymore. What an awful day she was having. Why did Peter have to pick today to become Mr. Suburbia?

"Why are you Mr. Suburbia today?"

"Are you saying we should stay in the city?"

"Did I miss an e-mail? Are you saying we have to move out of the best city in the world?"

"But it's completely selfish to raise kids in the city. You don't raise kids in the city. You just don't. That's the one thing Bianca was right about."

Later, Jane would look back at the evening and see that as the moment this turned into a true fight. Bianca.

"Well, Bianca didn't factor in how much I love the city, and how close I am to Chinatown. Bianca doesn't know that my kid is *not* going to be the token Chinese kid in a white world. She's going to school in Chinatown. In the city. New York City."

"What about Catholic school?"

"Are you insane? I can't believe you're standing here, assuming that, of course, naturally, no question, my kid's going to be in a plaid uniform in Jersey. You're incredible."

"Your kid. Yours. Am I even here? Am I going to be her father? How?" Jane wanted to answer him there, but he had more to say. "And why? I mean, why bother if I have no say about anything?"

He stood there, waiting for a real answer. But Jane had none.

She noticed that her pasta was now mushy baby food. She walked away from it all. No dinner and no peace.

. . .

The next day, Kendra summoned Jane to a large conference room filled with people in dark suits and white shirts. Jane wished she could have gone to the bathroom first.

"We're ramping up a new position for you. We've factored in your work life adjustments and the demands of your new responsibilities, and we agree that you would need more coverage."

This means, "You can't be a mom and work the kind of hours we want from you."

"We would never terminate an expectant mother, and we're prepared to treat you as such. We have an alternate position for you, moving from IT Support to Help Desk. The hours are more manageable, and the compensation will reflect that. Read these documents for full granularity."

This means, "You're not fired. You're demoted, and we're going to pay you less."

Jane was too tired to translate her thoughts into Corporate Speak, so Kendra offered to revisit this topic at a future date. But Jane knew that she would have to take this demotion with a smile.

Back at her desk, Jane assembled her new budget, factoring in child care costs, and had to walk away from her Excel spreadsheet because it was so shocking. There had to be a virus screwing up the calculations. She was about to start scraping by.

Kendra ordered moving boxes. Jane was expected to vacate her office and move into a small cubicle at the Help Desk at her earliest convenience. She moved slowly. Her new, small, open space was fine. It was just small. And open. And she would have to bring home a lot of her personal touches. She packed a box for home and called for a car service.

Celeste shouted to her, "Hello, my friend! You don't work late no more? I never see you!"

Celeste's orange hair had changed to hot pink. This was probably on purpose, and it matched her lipsticked teeth. Celeste smiled broadly, then saw the box in Jane's hand. She gasped.

"Janie? They fire you? You quit? What you doing with a box?"

"I can't work late anymore. So they kind of demoted me."

"Sue them! Sue them! You sue them for every penny, baby. I got a good lawyer for you. What happened? You sick?"

"I'm going to have a baby. I can't work late and be a mom."

Celeste drove quietly for a while. Jane was too tired to read anything into Celeste's silence. Eventually Celeste spoke again.

"So, darling. When did you get pregnant? I don't see no baby-tummy on you, sweetheart. What happened? You happy? Some man do wrong by you? You sue him too."

Jane explained the adoption, and Celeste was joyously relieved.

"Ah. Good. Good. Everything is good. You can be happy now. Stop complaining."

· · ·

"Hey, Sheila. Any new news from the doctor?" It was harder to call Sheila from a cubicle. Jane had no privacy. Sometimes she spoke in code. Sometimes she spelled things, which seemed a little bit crazy.

"He said I'm okay. He said that sometimes these miscarriages happen this early when there's something really wrong. He said we can try again."

"And do you want to?"

"I do. I got your birthday present. You're sweet."

Jane had sent a spa gift to Sheila. Raoul helped make the arrangements. Sheila would spend a day being massaged, manicured, facialed, and pampered. Exactly what she needed, Jane hoped.

"Janie. I got a card from Dad. A birthday card."

"Wow."

Howard knew nothing about Sheila's pregnancy and loss, but he knew her birthday. He bought a rhyming Hallmark card and signed it, "Love, Dad." And that was all Sheila needed: a little movement in her direction.

"I'm going to call him on Sunday. Just for a few minutes. I'll thank him for the card and ask about his health. We'll probably talk about the weather. You know, the big stuff."

Wow.

• • •

"Okay, Peter. Here's the deal. My dossier is already in China, and your name isn't on it. When I get matched with a baby, *I'll* be the adoptive parent. Not you. Not yet." Jane just knew he had something highly snarky to say in response to this, so she talked a bit faster. "When we get back to the U.S., you can adopt her too. And yes, you'll be a dad. Her dad."

Jane hadn't calculated it, but the word "dad" seemed to make Peter melt. Maybe he was still thinking about the suburbs. Maybe. But look at him: See that glint in his eye? See how his whole face softened when he tried on Dadness? He wanted this baby as much as Jane did. And Jane fell in love with him all over again.

"I'll be her dad." His voice was tender. And maybe that was enough for now. They didn't talk about houses in the suburbs anymore. Jane wondered if they should close up that conversation, but she never managed to do it.

• • •

Jane had missed a handful of Melting Pot dinners as she adjusted to life as a couple, so she played catch-up at the next one. According to everyone's Web-based calculations, the group was now about a month away from referrals—that glorious day when they'd be matched with their children. Of course, Jane could be two months or even three months away, but she kept that to herself. Her dossier was just a bit later than her friends'. The tension was edible.

"Where's Charm?"

The women drew a visual short-straw to see who would tell Jane about Charm. No, she didn't come to the Melting Pot dinners anymore.

Charm's return to Dr. Laskin had resulted in a pregnancy. But the fetus was diagnosed with Down syndrome. Charm retreated to her parents' home on Long Island to think it over.

"She's done thinking. She's going to have this baby," said Arlene.

The evening turned quiet and somber, as they all ran stressful movies in their heads: *Charm Has a Down Syndrome Child.* Followed by *I Have a Down Syndrome Child.* Both movies were hard to watch.

"I spent the day with Megan and her baby." Karen changed the reel for them all. "You guys should see this little girl! Oh, Stella is just the sweetest, easiest baby!"

Teresa had to ask, "And the couch?"

"I sat on the floor. But, for the record, I changed her diaper, and it looked like a perfect little Hollywood poop."

It took some explaining, but a Hollywood poop is the perfect picture of classic poop in terms of shape, consistency, and quantity. This was happy news, although the people at nearby tables didn't appreciate the description.

"So." Teresa turned everyone's focus to Jane. "How is Peter the Great?"

"He's pretty great" was the easy answer. "It's like we've always been together. It's easy. I wonder why that is."

"It means a very deep relationship in a previous life. Probably a recent one." Karen couldn't let go of past-life theories.

"What does your father think of all this?" Teresa asked.

Jane hadn't told Howard yet. She had her reasons. A whole list of them, in fact.

"I know he likes Peter a lot. But I have to wait for Peter to tell his parents." Before Teresa could finish taking that deep breath for that snide remark, Jane added, "Which he's going to do this weekend when he goes out there to visit with them. He's a good son."

But Jane was not feeling like a good daughter. She was still angry at Howard. If she told him something personal about Peter, something glad, could he stomp on it, darken it, the way he did the adoption? She didn't want to risk it.

• • •

On Saturday, Jane offered to spend the day with Megan and baby Stella and babysit while Megan did silly, selfish things like grocery shopping. It would get Jane's mind off work woes. She invited Ray along for moral support.

"Why not me?" asked Peter. "I could always reschedule my folks." Oh, God, was there always going to be some sort of balancing act between these two? "Well?" he asked. "Why are you taking Ray?"

"Peter. I'm taking Ray. Do I really have to explain that I love you both? 'Cause I think we'll both feel stupid if I give you that speech. And I don't want that for either one of us. Okay?"

• • •

Baby Stella screeched whenever her mother was out of sight. Megan took it all in stride. She didn't blink, just raised her volume so that Jane could hear her over the din. Ray winced a lot as the baby's pitch rose.

"Those are dissonant notes even Sondheim wouldn't touch," he whispered.

"I think Stella and I are going to come to the next Melting Pot dinner," Megan shouted. "Can you hand me that bib? Thanks. I miss restaurants. But I think Stella is almost ready for it. Watch out."

And that's when Stella projectile-vomited from four feet away. Megan supplied Jane with a clean(ish) T-shirt and many apologies.

The baby was teething, and something was definitely going on with her tummy. Ray had to leave the room.

Little Stella slept now and then, for about twenty or thirty minutes, in her mother's arms. Megan needed to change out of the pajamas she'd been wearing for two days, so she slipped the sleeping child into Jane's arms. Megan was so smooth—she must have practiced this type of move before. Stella never stirred.

Ray smiled sweetly. "Look at you, little Mommy."

When Megan was holding the baby, she appeared to be filled with helium. But Jane felt she was holding Lead Baby. She looked so small, and yet she gave Jane a backache by the time she woke up and discovered that an evil stranger was keeping her far from her beloved mother. More screaming.

"It's a very intense relationship," Megan conceded as she stirred foul-smelling baby food in glass jars. "She needs me so much. I love her. It's hard. Watch out."

And that's when Stella's diaper slipped half off, and this was no Hollywood poop. While Megan changed her diaper, Stella let loose again. And again, there were no Hollywood poops and there was no sweet, easy baby. Karen must have been high when she visited Megan and little Stella. Jane was already on her third shirt of the day. Ray opened windows and leaned out.

Megan was gone for only an hour, but Jane and Ray broke a sweat trying to make Stella happy. Toward the end, Ray announced that it couldn't be done.

"It's not you, Jane. This baby is defective, and she knows it. That's why she keeps crying like that."

He sat Stella down on the floor. Jane laid down and looked up at the angry baby.

"I suck at this. I'm not even a mother yet, and I already suck at this."

"No. You may not talk like that. Take it back," Ray ordered.

"I'm sorry, baby Stella. You wanna banana?"

And Stella stopped crying. Jane froze.

"Wanna banana." Jane tried it again. Stella smiled. "Wanna banana!" More smiles. She had found a funny sound. She was a genius. Stella threw her head back and giggled.

"You found the magic words! 'Wanna banana.' You're a genius!"

When Megan returned, Ray regaled her with the wanna-banana story. Jane beamed modestly. Megan hugged Baby Stella, whose smile seemed to announce that Jane was not evil after all.

Megan, on the other hand, did not smile.

"You sat her on the floor? On the wood floor? That part's not clean. And she could get a splinter. She's a crawling baby. She only goes on the letter and number mats—I thought I made that clear."

Jane apologized, but her lack of belief that she had actually endangered the baby may have bled through. Ray watched the scene in disbelief and pretended to sneeze "Issues!" to Jane.

When they left, Jane smiled conspiratorially at Stella and knew in her heart that one day she would yell the same way at some unsuspecting friend or sitter. Maybe even at Ray, who was ready for a nap.

"Thanks for coming here today. I couldn't have done this without you." Jane collapsed against Ray's arm.

"Yes, you couldn't have."

"Thank God for Peter."

Ray stopped in his tracks, like he was shot through the heart. Jane did her best backpedaling.

"What I mean is I couldn't do what she's doing. All alone like that. All day, every day. All along, I wondered how I would do it. And after today, I know I couldn't have done it alone. This was hard, even with the two of us. Come on, don't be mad. Please?"

"Why can't I be mad at you, Jane? Can't I be mad for twelve minutes?"

Ray was louder than Jane had expected, and he kept shouting.

"You know what you are? You know what your problem is? You're the Great Underestimator. You think you can't do this. You think I can't help you, that you have to have Peter."

Ray was crying. Jane held her breath. She had seen Ray cry before, but not in the middle of a busy street. Jesus. This was bad.

"You just had to have him, didn't you? You know, this was my one chance, my one shot at sort of being a dad. But you didn't think that you and I could do it. And you took it away."

She took a chance and hugged him. He tolerated her embrace while he cried for a few more minutes.

"I'm sorry. I didn't— I mean, I knew you'd be great. And you still will be. But I fell in love with Peter. I really did."

Ray was quieter now. "I don't usually stay friends with anyone who leaves me for another man. You're the sole exception. So don't push it. And try to remember that Peter is only Peter. You could have done this alone." Ray's voice still changed when he said Peter's name, spitting out the *P*.

"I thought you and Burton were looking into adopting. What happened?"

"The way we fight? I don't know. Maybe we could adopt the off-stage kid from *Who's Afraid of Virginia Woolf.*"

"Isn't he fictional? Anyway, he's taken."

"Then we're doomed. We managed to kill a plastic cactus. Apparently you're not supposed to put them on the radiator. Who knew?"

• • •

At her new/old job, Jane had no privacy but lots of downtime, so she paid attention to the listservs more than ever. The other Help Desk staffers all seemed to have their own online missions. Jane's was the SEPT_DTC list that Karen and Teresa had discovered. There were no flame wars in this much smaller group, but Mona, the leader, posted her lack of news every Tuesday and Friday. China didn't drop any hints about when referrals were about to happen. Everyone knew that, and it really sounded like the agency was making up news, just to keep Mona happy. But the group hung on every non-word.

"The dossiers have completed the translation process and are in the matching room. *Right now!!!* We're being matched with our beautiful girls!!!!" Mona posted.

"They're assembling the medical reports!! We're matched!! It's just a matter of time now!!!!!" Mona posted.

"It's a holiday in China, so everything's on hold for a few days! I can't stand this suspense much longer!!!!!" Mona posted.

On the bigger lists, whenever batches of referrals came in, the proud parents posted with subject lines like:

!!!!!!!!REFERRAL!!!!!!!!

or

******IT'S A GIRL******

or

~~~~~~I'M A MOM~~~~~~

Jane, Karen, and Teresa began to scour all the lists for those subject headings. They were panning for gold. When all the August referrals came in, Jane pictured the Chinamoms stepping forward in a line. No one was in front of Jane, Karen, and Teresa now. Jane wanted to post one of those overpunctuated announcements.

"Who are you going to travel with?" was the big question among the Chinamoms. This was not a decision to make lightly. Your travel partner was the adoption world's version of the Lamaze coach.

Teresa was traveling with Beverly, an old friend. She had chosen her scientifically: Bev worked for NBC News and had traveled a great deal. She had an eleven-year-old son, and Teresa was very fond of the boy. The two women had traveled together previously without incident. Done. Bev would travel with Teresa.

Karen opted to travel with an ex-boyfriend. This sounded crazy, but Karen and Charles had remained friends over the years. And he would be strong enough to hoist luggage—a point that Teresa took to heart. Who would lift her heavy things?

Jane was greedy. She wanted to bring Peter and Ray. Both. Little Beth would have three grown-ups fawning over her in China, although Jane was the only official parent. Peter could bond with Beth right away, and already play the part of Dad before he adopted her later in the U.S. And Ray would be her favorite uncle at first glance, and that just had to be enough to make him happy. True, he had said he wouldn't go, but she wouldn't allow that. She would withhold love and baby time, if need be. He would always know how to help her breathe.

. . .

Jane and Ray met for breakfast before work on a stray Wednesday. He tried to convince her to play hooky from her dull, dull work and see a matinee with him. He worried that he was losing his edge as a critic and needed another perspective. He was liking too many shows these days. But she couldn't. The job might be dull, but she needed it. She had stopped worrying about looming unemployment, and that was a reason to do right by them.

Jane didn't tell him the real reason she wanted to go to the office that day. She felt too foolish. She would tell him much later, but she had a feeling that she needed to be near the phone.

Jane carried a cup of tea to her desk and made herself comfortable. She was about to take a sip when the phone rang. She put down the cup, knowing that this call was The Call she had been waiting for.

"Hello, Mommy." It was Barbara. Jane managed no words at all. Barbara understood. She had made this sort of call before, so she kept talking.

"I'm looking at your referral, and your beautiful daughter's face. Her name is Hao Wei Xian. She is in the Haozhou Social Welfare Institute in Guangdong Province. She's ten months old, and she's in very good health."

Jane tried to catch her breath. Barbara continued.

"All your girls are in the same orphanage, so you, Karen, and Teresa will definitely travel together. All the girls were given the surname Hao, for the name of the town."

Jane tried to write it down, but she couldn't hold the pen. When she finally spoke she said, "My name is Howe too."

"I know, honey. I'm going to call the others now. Congratulations, Jane, you're a mom."

Chapter Thirteen

At 10% Jane could see the red background.

25%: Come on! Oh, God, this was taking forever to open!

30%: The top of her head. A brush of black hair. Like a pagoda or a punk rocker.

44%: A blank forehead.

68%: Dark eyes. Sad. Soulful. The word "responsibility" flashed in Jane's head.

75%: A pouty mouth. Beauty.

100%: Tiny shoulders. Blue's Clues pajamas.

My Baby.

Jane sat at her computer and stared at the scanned picture of Her Daughter. The tears had subsided, and she blessed Bill Gates and all the demons of technology that had gotten this picture to her so quickly. She printed it on a printer no one is supposed to use unless they have permission from God.

• • •

The phone rang. Karen and Teresa were conferencing Jane.

"We're mommies! We're mommies!"

They composed their joyous *****REFERRAL*****

messages for the listserv and even received a handful of e-mail congratulations from kind strangers around the country. They celebrated. They were giddy. They were useless. Jane ran outside so that she could call Peter and Ray and have a good cry in the privacy of a busy street. She was coherent for Peter's message, but a blubbery mess for Ray's. No matter. Ray was one of the few people who understood Jane through sobs.

"Where are you, Jane? I can't possibly work any more today. I have to see you and all the Chinamoms."

"We're going to meet at the Melting Pot and celebrate."

. . .

Jane walked down the street, clutching the picture of Her Daughter and sneaking peeks. The Chinamoms hugged and cried and continued to stare at their photos. Long silences ended with fits of giggles.

All three babies were about ten months old and about the same size. Each was dressed in the same Blue's Clues pj's, photographed against the same red background. Jane pictured someone picking out *the* perfect photo outfit, then starting a baby assembly line on Photo Day. You look gorgeous, baby, now take off the pj's and give them to the next kid.

Ray made a grand entrance.

"Hello, Little Mamas!" He gave each photo a rave review, but had to stop when he finally held Jane's photo. He didn't say anything, then embraced Jane.

"She's a beauty," he whispered.

They ordered food and stared at that too. Karen started a small game.

"Oh, did I mention? *I got my referral!*"

Everyone feigned surprise, then Jane and Theresa announced their own referrals. They repeated this exchange more than a few times that afternoon. Lost in baby bliss, it felt like the height of funny. They repeated it too many times to be sensible.

Teresa asked, "Should we be getting ready or something? I mean, how soon 'til we travel? What do we need to do before then?"

Jane sensed a list in the making. "I've got to work on the baby's room. It's a wreck, it's full of junk, and I'll need to paint it and—"

"Not tonight," Ray announced. "For twenty-four hours, we bask. Reality will keep."

Teresa agreed, and the basking continued.

. . .

Jane was home, standing in the middle of the living room. Peter walked in, still a bit breathless from the climb up the stairs.

"I'm sorry. I tried to call you at work. Can I see her?"

Jane held up the picture. Peter's mouth fell open.

"She's so perfect. So—I don't know—complete."

"Complete?"

"Fingers and toes and eyes and ears. Complete. A complete little person. And she's ours. Yours."

"Ours."

"Jane. This is all from you. You're like this amazing gift that I got and I never deserved. Thank you. Thank you, Jane. Thank you, God. Thank you."

Little Wei Xian, soon to be known as Beth, was probably fast asleep on the other side of the planet, unaware of the family that was tugging on a red thread to bring her home.

Jane didn't want to sleep that night. Like a child, she wanted to stay awake and keep having fun. Her sleep was deep and dreamless.

. . .

Jane toned down her announcement to Sheila, who did not tone down her reaction. She screamed with delight. Jane could tell she was crying.

"You have to tell me everything that happens. If I can't get pregnant again, I'm doing this. Why doesn't everyone do this? Oh, Jane, you have a baby!"

"I haven't told Dad yet," Jane confessed.

"Yes, well, I can't really blame you. Don't tell him until Peter is legally separated or single or something. That's my two pennies. Wait."

"That's another conversation I need to have. I don't know what's happening with Peter and his divorce. He was so blue after that last trip I decided I'd tread carefully. Let him bring it up. I don't want to be that girlfriend-nag."

"Ick."

"Ick," Jane agreed.

Meanwhile, she needed to make a list. Several lists. Maybe she'd start by making a list of the necessary lists. An Über-List.

1. Paperwork to be assembled for China.
2. Pack Mommy for China.
3. Pack baby stuff for China.
4. Baby's room.
5. Baby's wardrobe and life necessities.
6. How to cope when we first come home.

Each of the list titles was a mountaintop. This was massive. What the hell had she been doing all these months? Nothing! She could have been buying baby clothes. She could have been stenciling the baby's room. She could have been gathering the many packing lists that circulated on the listserv.

Barbara assured her that none of her adoptive parents ever did any of those things during the wait. But Jane still wanted to be the A student. Barbara laughed at her.

"Janie, this is the duck-to-water part for you. This is about lists and organization. I just want you to get something: This is the easy part."

Easy? Was she being sarcastic? All the stress, all the unknowns, all the work, and this was easy? Jane wanted to answer her, but she had no words. She knew her face looked like an ad for a horror movie, but she couldn't help that.

"Never mind, never mind." Barbara's voice was soothing. "Show me your lists. Let's work through them." Jane smiled and pulled a manila folder from her bag.

"Here."

"Ah. Good." Barbara studied the list of lists, and some subsequent lists. "And, Jane? I'm glad things are working out with Peter so far." So far? Jane feared that she was developing facial tics. So far? Barbara must have seen that tic.

"What I mean is I'm glad that you're getting all this happiness. You deserve it."

Jane hated herself for ever being mean in her head to Barbara. She hugged her teacher and said, "Tell me I'll be ready."

"You'll be ready."

· · ·

Trapped at work, Jane scoured the listservs for packing lists. Some of these were a little scary. These included suggestions on how much clothing to bring and what the Chinese think of Americans who wear shorts (they don't approve). There was an intimidating list of medications, both over-the-counter and prescription, that everyone should bring to China. Peter found a list that advised everyone to pack adult diapers, in case of Mao's Revenge.

And then she knew that her boss was standing behind her. She did a quick alt-tab to something work related, as she had always seen her own staff do when she crept up from behind. She spun around.

"Oh, hi, Kendra. What's up?"

"I need to talk to you." Doom. "Let's go in my office." No! No! *Mercy!*

"Okay."

Jane was paper white when she sat in Kendra's office. She

couldn't fake calm. Kendra cried out, "Oh! Don't be scared. I just wanted to offer you my son's old baby furniture! I've got a crib, a changing table, and some other stuff you might want. It's all in my basement. Do you want them? Oh, you poor thing!"

Jane happily accepted and wondered how much more her heart could take.

· · ·

Jane and Peter took a Saturday drive to Buy-Buy Baby. Ray had assigned them decorative items to purchase for the baby's room, which he swore he would convert to a real nursery. They were parents-to-be with big shopping lists. Jane was shopping like a soldier these days, but then she saw Peter holding the cute little onesies and went weak in the knees. Peter kissed her and said another "Thank you for all this. Thank you."

As Jane and Peter debated over plain crib sheets vs. ultimate crib sheets, a saleswoman strolled by. "Do you know if you're having a boy or a girl?"

Peter didn't even pause. "A girl."

"Oh, how nice. Take a look at these John Lennon sheets. They're very popular." They looked, they cooed and threw more and more onto the pile. A whole new life was going to need a lot of stuff.

"Have you and your wife picked out a stroller yet?"

Peter replied, "Not yet."

The bubbly saleswoman had a universe of strollers, and Peter studied them carefully. He very nearly kicked the tires on them. He looked like he knew what he was doing.

"I read about this one. This is really top of the line. Jane? Look at this."

The massive triangular stroller was designed for people who want to jog while strolling their babies. Jane couldn't imagine something she would want to do less than jog while strolling a baby. She lifted the stroller, or tried to.

"No. Too heavy." And she moved to another part of the stroller galaxy. She was picking up super-light strollers when she realized that Peter was following her with the super-heavy stroller. Why?

"Peter, why do you still have that one? It's way too heavy to get up and down all those stairs."

"Here's a deluxe travel stroller," said the bubbly saleswoman. "Great for walk-ups."

And indeed, that stroller looked like a light delight. But Peter said, "Can you put this one aside for us?" And he slid the heavy jog stroller over to her. Bubbles looked just as puzzled as Jane did.

"Sir. This one might be too heavy for your wife to carry upstairs. Remember, you have to hold the baby while you do that."

"I know. But this one'll be great for when we move out of the city."

Oh, my God.

"I see!" said Bubbles. "Have you and your wife picked out baby furniture? If you're leaving the city, you can look at the larger pieces over here."

Oh. My. God.

"Great," said Peter. And then he had the nerve to add, "But we're not married."

Oh. My. God.

Jane actually growled as she pushed the jog stroller out of her way and marched to the exit. She could hear Peter bustling along behind her. He was weighed down with the bags of baby stuff they had already purchased.

"Jane! What are you doing?"

She wondered if her entire family tree possessed enough sarcasm to answer Peter.

"I'm going to join the Stepford Wives club." Jane didn't stop moving until she got to the car. "Let me help you catch up. Previously, on our life together: I'm not moving to the suburbs. I'm just not."

He looked genuinely surprised. Was he an idiot? "I thought we had this fight already. And I thought I won," he said.

Now it was Jane's turn to be surprised. "I thought *I* won."

They hustled themselves and their stuff into Peter's car. They didn't speak. They crawled through traffic for a few blocks. Still not speaking.

Not until Jane said, "And when are you getting divorced?" Okay, no one likes to sound like *The Bold and the Beautiful,* but she kept talking anyway. "And why did you have to tell that woman that we're not married?"

"Well. We're not."

Oh, damn, she didn't want to lose the logic side of the argument. She didn't know where to turn. She fell back on preadolescent repetition.

"Why did you have to tell her that we're not married?"

"What's wrong with telling the truth?"

"Okay, then." Jane could be logical too. "Why aren't we married? With a baby coming in about four weeks, don't you think you should think about it?"

They got each other. They had from the beginning. He set his jaw as if he were a bad TMJ patient and gripped the wheel. She had won the argument in some stupid, unfair way. He got it.

"You don't sound like you, Jane. You sound like one of your black-and-white movies."

"You sound like a guy who's not answering my question."

She knew perfectly well that he didn't have an answer. That didn't stop her from wanting one. They drove along in more silence.

Until Jane said, "Sometimes you're such a jerk. You should know that about yourself."

"Sometimes you're really childish." He mimicked her saying, " 'Why aren't we married?' " and then added "Come on, Jane."

She used her best bratty voice to mimic him right back. "Come on, Jane."

"Don't do that."

"Don't do that." She had grown up with brothers, remember. She had learned how to be annoying.

They arrived at her building and he said, "Fine. You win. You're the baby, so enjoy all your baby stuff. I'm going home. Hey! Maybe I'll write a list."

He wasn't going to help her lug the seven thousand pounds of baby crap up the four flights of stairs. Ouch. Winning arguments comes with a price. He sat in the car and stared straight ahead. He drove away.

She could barely lift the giant bags of baby crap. She dragged them as if she were a wayward Santa. She had to take three breathers up the stairs. After one flight, she had forgotten about Peter and their stupid argument. By the time she pulled it all into her apartment, she was completely done in.

The biggest bag spilled open. Clothes, sheets, bumper pads, bottles, nipples, diapers, diaper creams, wipes, more clothes, formula, a lamp, two diaper bags, baby shampoo, baby bath, baby-sized towel, pajamas, *What to Expect the First Year* and *What to Expect the Toddler Years,* some teething rings, baby sunscreen, socks, a bath seat, adorable soft onesies, and a huge array of baby-proofing items. And there was some other stuff too.

The apartment already looked so crowded.

"We're going to need a bigger boat," she said in full voice. She wanted to feel bad for Peter. She wanted to find a way to put all these things away. She stretched out on the floor and planned to stay there for a long time. She wanted to slap Peter and then apologize. She wanted a c-c-c-commitment.

Someone or something bumped against her door, trying to open it.

"Who's there?" Jane shouted. "Peter?" But she heard only a grunt in response, and, hey, Peter drove away. It couldn't be him. Her New York survival instincts kicked in. She needed a good blunt object, so she grabbed a pewter candlestick. Oh, but Sam gave her that. So she traded it for *What to Expect the Toddler Years,* which was a huge tome and could easily do some damage.

"You have the wrong apartment!" she shouted. The grunting intruder might believe her if she sounded forceful enough.

The lock clicked. The door opened. It was Ray, unable to speak through the mouthful of bagel he was chewing. She sat down again, ten years older than when the day began.

"Don't let China know that I'm this unstable, okay?" She sighed.

"Mmm-hmmm." And then he was out of sight. She found him in the storage room/Beth's room-to-be. The room was emptied and cleaned, with a fresh coat of paint on the walls. So much hidden space was suddenly revealed. He must have spent the whole day on this.

Ray finally spoke. "See? I told you I could turn it into a real room."

"Beth's room" was all she managed to say around the catch in her throat.

"I took the liberty of throwing away the very broken chair and the box of scary, mildewed fabric. The other stuff is in the basement. This room is bigger than I thought it was."

Jane nodded. "It's like a dream."

"What's in the bags?"

"Baby crap."

"It's a lot."

"Yeah."

• • •

Peter stayed away all afternoon. Jane had no idea he was such a brooder. There was a knock at the door, and Jane rushed to open it, thinking that Peter was making a contrite entrance. But it wasn't Peter. It was someone looking for the open house in the apartment downstairs. Still not sold. Still open housing. But there was Peter, climbing the stairs and carrying a large gift.

"Here. This was the travel stroller that you liked. The woman said it was wonderful, and lightweight and wonderful. I just carried it up four flights of stairs and it felt like nothing. So. Here."

She wanted to refuse it and warn him that he couldn't buy his way out of bad behavior. She wanted to tell him that she was sorry for being so childish. But the stroller was actually wonderful. It was a stroller for a city baby in a walk-up.

"I'm sorry," he said. "You don't like being stuck in limbo, huh?"

"So crowded in there, with all those unbaptized babies. And I'm a baby too. But a baptized one, so it's really unfair. Anyway. I'm really sorry about today. I guess you're kind of in limbo too. In a way."

They hugged for a long time. Peter finally spoke.

"I thought I won the suburbs argument. I made a better case than you. Didn't I?" he asked. "And that should count for something. See, with Bianca, I never won an argument. Never got my way. But we're partners, aren't we, Janie? Equals? And I'm getting tired of apartment life. I want to live in a house."

Jane allowed herself no sarcasm and no walking away. Hang in there and work this out with Peter. Now.

"Peter, please. My life is unrecognizable from where it was a year ago. I can't leave my island. Not right now. Here's a compromise. Can we talk about it again, after we get settled with the baby? Can I keep this down to one big change at a time? That's all I can handle."

This was mostly true. But there was one more change Jane wanted in her life. She wanted Peter to put both feet down and stay. Was he reading her mind when he said, "Bianca isn't ready for a divorce just yet. She's changing publishers, and her aunt who raised her died a few months ago, and she's really having a hard time."

Jane stared at his shoes for a minute and said, "I'm sorry about her aunt."

"Yeah. Look. Just give her some time."

"I don't have time. I'm sorry, but I don't. I'm going to China soon."

Jane's face was twisted with worry. Had she learned nothing from all those old movies? This man was never going to divorce his wife, was he? She lowered her face to hide the bad movie scenario, and Peter ducked down to see her face.

"Hey. We're going to be together. You believe that, don't you?"

"Yes." She was an awful liar, so she said, "No." She wanted to make a *Reasons to Believe Peter* list, but she was busy trying not to cry. When she finally looked up, she said, "Why are you still living in your wife's apartment?"

Peter's mouth fell open for a second, then he began to nod slowly.

"Good point."

No, he couldn't marry her, at least not yet. But why couldn't he move in with her? Why was he still just her neighbor when he should be so much more? He should be her family. Peter wandered around her apartment like a tourist, sizing up the place.

"Look, Peter, I don't have time for stupid games, and I really don't have time for you to figure things out. Be with me or be with her. Make a choice. And, okay, no pressure, but you have to decide fast." Jane made a note in her head: She needed to brag to Sheila about how strong she sounded right now, even though she felt ready to dissolve.

"Don't you have more closet space than this?" he called from the bedroom.

"Really?" Jane needed to sit down. Peter was moving in? Did she just make that happen? She floated into a chair and noticed that the tight feeling behind her eyes was gone.

She missed his packing and moving plans while she tried to figure out how many more drawers she could empty for him. It's a good thing he had no plates or furniture. She had no room for those.

But she had room for Peter. Now the cloud of what's-happening-between-us lifted. This was a commitment, wasn't it? This was together. This was *Us*.

. . .

Since babies need so much crap, it is important to have people throw parties for you. Let people give you presents whenever you can. Jane had forgotten that. It was her first baby, after all. Karen feared that a baby shower would be bad luck. Don't buy a gift for the child until she's home. She told her family to give her a welcome home party/shower. Jane's coworkers threw her a small shower at work.

The party fell on her birthday. She had loomed into thirty-eight and had barely noticed it coming. She felt like a kid. She felt like a geriatric. She wondered what her mother would say.

Her coworkers told her repeatedly how brave she was. Nothing scared her more than being told that she was brave. She didn't feel brave, and if she was doing something that required bravery, then she should really be scared. She nodded and smiled a lot.

Teresa didn't want to cope with party preparations so close to Travel Time. She hired a party planner to throw an elegant shower in the Puck Building. Jane and Karen arrived at the party and stuck together. Clearly, their silly little gifts were too silly and too little next to the various Tiffany boxes in the room.

"Teresa really has money, doesn't she?" Karen said.

Oh, yes. Teresa really had money. And so did her friends. The party was swelegant-elegant, and Jane recognized three cast members from *Law & Order*. Eventually they found Arlene, who was not intimidated by all the fame and wealth in the room.

"Have you two been reading the lists? No, of course not, how would you have time? Well, there's a big scandal going on. It's really awful."

It was nice that she had become a talker.

"What happened?" asked Jane.

"Well. This couple get their referral and they stare at the picture a lot, and then they finally get to travel, but they get to China and they get the baby and it's not her."

"What?"

"It wasn't her. It wasn't the same baby."

By now, Teresa had caught up with the Chinamoms and was locked in to this story.

"They both started freaking out and saying, 'Look, this isn't the baby that was referred to us and blah-blah-blah' and getting really upset. And at first, the orphanage director kept saying, 'Yes, it is,' but then she said, 'Okay, no, it isn't.' "

"And?" Teresa needed to know.

"Well, it was a different baby, all right. And they never found out for sure, but it sounds like their baby died."

Jane clapped a hand to her mouth so that she could stop horrible sounds from emerging. Arlene had more to say.

"So they gave the baby back to the orphanage. The mother said that she wanted the baby that was referred to her, and no other baby would do. And they came home and had a funeral."

"Not one word of that is true." Teresa needed to believe.

"It's all over the listserv. You haven't been reading it, huh?"

Arlene didn't mean to devastate her friends, but that's what happens when you talk about dead babies at a baby shower. No one should ever do that.

Karen, Teresa, and Jane were united in their desire to escape that story. They promised one another that they'd never bring it up again.

"But I'll say one thing," Karen said. "I am *not* coming home from China without a baby. If they pull a switch, I'll deal with it."

They nodded a silent amen and put the story away forever.

Chapter Fourteen

It was a beautiful, warm Saturday when Jane and Ray went to collect the baby furniture that Kendra had promised her. But Jane forgot the part where she promised to retrieve a crib for Karen. The crib was the last one in stock at Baby-O-Rama, and they were holding it for Karen until Saturday night. That task never landed on her list, and so it fell out of her head.

Kendra's seven-year-old son had the same fine features that his mother had. When he answered the door, he turned and bellowed for his mother.

"The lady is here for the baby stuff!"

The baby stuff was in the basement. A crib, a bureau that turned into a changing table (bureau! Jane had forgotten about getting one of those), a diaper genie, a collection of blankets, a few toys, and a diaper bag.

"Do you want this stroller? This is a three-hundred-dollar stroller. It's the top of the line, really great. Scott rode in this thing until he was, what, five years old?"

"Mom!"

"Actually, I've got a stroller. Really lightweight. Wonderful."

"You'll need a second one," Kendra insisted.

Jane tried to lift the stroller and knew that she'd be leaving it behind.

"I live in a walk-up," she explained. And Kendra looked at her as if she had just announced that she ate bugs.

Kendra's husband was clearly out of the picture, but Jane was shy about asking why. After lunch and her son's departure to his friend's swimming pool, Kendra volunteered the tale of her ex-husband's abuse.

"He never laid a finger on me. If he had, I wouldn't have had a child with him. No, he hit Scott. It was bad." She stopped herself. She must have remembered the working relationship she would have to maintain with Jane. She didn't switch to Corporate Speak, but she did talk cheerfully about potty training.

They packed up Ray's car. It sagged under all that weight, but it rolled toward the city.

"Peter says he's not going to hire movers. He doesn't have enough stuff to justify it. The super's going to loan him a dolly or something next weekend. He'll just roll his stuff up the street. Remind me to have my camera ready."

Ray nodded and kept his eyes on the road as he said, "So, when you and Peter go to China—"

"Whoa. Correction: When all *three* of us go to China."

"Oh, come on, Jane. How much longer can I play third wheel/fifth wheel/extra wheel?"

"Forever. You're coming to China."

"I really don't think I should go. And besides, do you realize how tough my schedule is these days at the paper? What am I going to get—a week's notice to drop everything and go to China? I'll undo all the hard work I've done there."

"You're coming to China."

"We'll look strange. Mom, Dad, Baby, and Gay Uncle."

"You're coming to China."

"I don't have enough frequent flyer miles to get all the way there."

"You're coming to China."

"Did you see my piece on the Beckett Festival? I thought of you."

"You're coming to China."

"Do you like my spray-on tan? I never get outside, but now I look like I do."

"You're coming to China."

"Bitch."

"You're coming to China."

. . .

"Jane. I lost my crib, thanks to you. Now I have to pay almost twice as much *plus* delivery *plus* I don't get the one I wanted."

"I'm sorry. I forgot. There was so much to do."

Teresa should never have stepped in. She should have let Jane grovel until Karen ran out of steam.

"It's not Jane's fault. She's not your delivery service."

"She promised."

Jane was still groveling. "I did. And I'm sorry. I screwed up."

"So buy another crib, get it delivered, and it's over. There are thousands of cribs, right here in New York City." Teresa liked tidy endings.

"You don't get it. I'm really scared here, and I needed that crib. *That* one. You let me down, Jane. You two have all this money, so you don't know what it's like to face motherhood on a really tight budget. It's scary as hell. I can't believe you did this to me."

Jane stopped groveling. She didn't have all this money and she did know what it was like to face it all on a really tight budget. Her budget was a cinch-waist, size-four, tight-tight budget.

"Not as tight as mine," Karen replied. "And you've got a husband. Hell, you've got two!"

"Money is not the point here." Yes, Teresa had money, but she was still scared. Was Karen implying that she wasn't entitled to her fear because she had Calvin Klein crib sheets?

"Look. I forgot your crib. I forgot. And I really am sorry, but if you keep yelling at me, I'm gonna run out of sorry. Understand?"

Karen walked away first. She radiated heat as she stormed down the street.

Teresa wanted to form an alliance with Jane, but she went about it like this: "Just because I have money doesn't mean I'm not scared."

Jane shook her head. She couldn't take care of anyone right now, least of all an adult. She mumbled a good-bye and left for home. Teresa went shopping.

That night, Jane kept Peter awake with her complaints. Poor tired Peter sided with her completely. Smart man.

• • •

Jane dreamed about rickety ladders that hooked together but led her nowhere. She was fighting to get out of the dream when the phone rang and woke her.

"Wake up, you lazy slug. You're a mother. You don't get to sleep in anymore. Besides, we have muffins." It was Teresa.

"This sounds like girlfriend time," said Peter. "Wake me when it's over." This time it was Jane who was bouncing through the morning. She kissed Peter on the cheek and buzzed in her friends.

Teresa and Karen appeared at her door with a large basket of muffins, a bottle of champagne, and a carton of orange juice. What problem would stand up against all that? Jane invited them in. They promised not to be quite so stupid with one another again. They moaned about the stress, stress, stress of wondering when they would travel and managing to get enough time to do everything.

She showed off Beth's room-in-progress.

"I want to do a fancy-schmancy stencil on this wall, but I need a big chunk of time to do it. And I want to do a red border thingy."

"Good luck," said Karen. They were happy. They had stepped out of their manic preparations to be happy.

That's when the phone rang, and it was Barbara with their travel dates. Really. The earth stopped spinning on its axis as Jane repeated all the information to the Chinamoms. The travel permission was completed, the consulate appointments obtained. They were set to travel in seventeen days.

"We've generally used Henry Wong's travel service in Chinatown. Call him, tell him these dates, and he'll take care of it all. Are you three going to fly together?"

Jane wanted it all to slow down, please. She wasn't ready, and it wasn't about lists or stencils or diapers. After all this time, motherhood was about to hit her like an avalanche.

Peter stepped into the living room and asked, "What did I miss?"

• • •

Saturday. Peter's move-in day. Jane could hardly wait to check this item off her Major Life Changes list. Soon, she'd be able to call Howard and say, "Hah! I'm officially not going to be a single mother. So there." Ray was about eighty percent successful at hiding his fear and jealousy from Jane.

"Come to the theater this afternoon, darling. It'll be so much harder to get out after the baby comes home. And, hey, the shows won't be any better."

Jane said yes. And she dressed up to see a matinee of *Death in Venice Beach*. Ray hated it too much to discuss it over a postshow martini.

"Besides, Burton says that liquor makes me surly. The jerk!"

So instead he came home with Jane for chamomile tea. Jane hoped that was enough incentive to climb all those stairs. She raced up the last flight as she heard her phone ringing.

"It's me." It was Peter. "Can I come over? And can I bring everything I own?"

Jane looked at Ray panting up the last few stairs and decided that everyone would be too tired to fight. "Sure. Come on over."

Within ten minutes, Peter and his possessions were barreling through Jane's front door.

"Here's my chair, and I've got two more boxes." Peter took less than an hour to move into Jane's apartment. Minimalists are good that way. Jane watched Ray for a reaction, but he was revealing nothing.

Peter made three trips to Jane's apartment. He packed a massive suitcase, a small one, three boxes, and a chair. He used Jane's shopping cart.

Ray shook his head. "I carry more stuff for a weekend getaway."

Jane had to wonder how a grown man had so few possessions. But it didn't matter. His few possessions were here, and so was he. Done.

"I have to go back for my lamp and to turn in the keys. Then I'm all done."

He kissed Jane and left once more.

Ray turned the suitcase over, then back. "You could pack a person in this thing." He pressed his ear against the side of it. "Hey, do you hear a . . . scratching sound?"

"Ha ha." Jane put on the kettle.

• • •

Barbara arranged for the Chinamoms to have their long-awaited evening session with Dr. Valerie Martinez, better known as Dr. Val. She spoke at events, she published articles on the subject. And she held travel prep sessions in her apartment for those who were about to adopt.

All the travel companions came along for this evening. Ray was a superior note-taker, so Jane could relax about retaining all the information. Peter was the happiest Jane had ever seen him. He wanted to know all about the medical needs of babies. That was how he put it.

Karen's ex, Charles, and Teresa's friend, Beverly, cooed over the photos of the babies. Beverly was Teresa's clone. They had the same outfit, the same haircut, and the same speech patterns. It was eerie.

Earlier, Karen had expressed doubt about Charles as a travel companion because he was such a "white-sugar, ambitious, corporate type." And so, the tie-dyed, bearded, Birkenstocked fellow who introduced himself as Charles was a bit of a surprise to Jane.

Ray brought Burton, who wanted to know all about the medical needs of babies too. Burton towered over everyone in the room. He seemed too big for the furniture. But he found a comfy sofa and took half of it. Jane wondered if this was going to be a Little Red Bathing Suit moment for these two. They would see these lovely babies and—

"Everyone please sit. I need quiet." Dr. Val clip-clopped into the room.

Dr. Val was tired. She had recently been profiled in *New York* magazine and was coping with new fame. Apparently she didn't like it. She didn't like the chitter-chattering people in her living room either. She gathered her props and began.

"Let's start with fungal diaper rash" was how she began, and she never got any cheerier than that. She moved on to fevers.

She urged everyone to use rectal thermometers, and then talked about the levels of fever and what a small child could tolerate. She extolled the virtues of good old soap and water. She told a story of a young man who had leprosy. He thought he might clean his diseased flesh with alcohol, but that caused it all to fall off. He should have used, you guessed it, soap and water.

Dr. Val talked about problems with nutrition, bonding, sleeping, pooping, adjusting in general. She shared disturbing Polaroids of hideous diseases, then quizzed her students to make a diagnosis.

"That's an example of rickets! Correct!" Jane wondered why Dr. Val sounded so thrilled.

Then Dr. Val gave advice for Life at Home: "I recommend you make your own baby food. Just get a blender or a food processor and throw in some chicken and veggies, and you've got a delicious meal for your child. And you'll save a fortune, believe me. Save that money for Harvard."

Teresa looked pale green. Burton's expression matched hers. Karen had stopped taking notes after the leprosy story. Jane wanted to giggle at the whole scene. She didn't know why, but she knew that the giggle would not be appreciated. Peter caught her eye and silently warned her not to giggle. Ray kept his eyes on his notepad. But he was biting his lip, clearly suppressing his sarcasm.

"The child's bedroom should be plain and simple, using quiet colors. Not overstimulating. Keep the toys down to a minimum. Simple rag dolls will do. Your daughter will love them, and you can save that money for Harvard."

Dr. Val made sense, and yet Jane wanted to do the opposite of every piece of advice offered. She didn't know why.

"Any questions?"

• • •

After the presentation, they were all outside, and Teresa spoke first.

"Drink. Now."

At the bar, they vented and laughed. Maybe Dr. Val was right about all her dire warnings, and maybe she was wrong. But they needed to escape the memory of those gruesome Polaroids.

"Is anyone else hungry? I'm going to order some food," said Arlene.

"Uh-oh. There goes Harvard."

Jane sat back and saw that it was all right here. Everyone was laughing, eating, talking. For a moment, there was no stress about travel, impending motherhood, or extra wheels on her relationship. There weren't even any lists.

Ray and Burton were holding hands. Burton whispered something in Ray's ear, which caused a head shake/eye roll from Ray. The restaurant was noisy, with all the conversation from every table rising up like a cloud and raining down on the diners. Jane had trouble hearing individual words but enjoyed the whole downpour.

Peter was holding her hand. He looked even more relaxed than when he was asleep. This was all going to work. It was all right here. His smile was wide and easy. He held one of her hands with both of his. He leaned in and kissed Jane.

"Did you hear that? I said, 'Dr. Val needs a little Dr. Valium.' Come on, that was a good one—for me."

Jane laughed. He kissed her again and looked very pleased with himself over his little joke.

And then everything changed. His face. His hands. His chair. The smile dropped, the eyes changed, and the muscles around his neck tilted his head up. He let go of Jane's hand as if it were on fire. He moved his chair away. He could only move it about an inch, but he did move it. He was now buddy-buddy next to Teresa, who didn't notice. Jane felt herself sinking into the ocean. The cold ocean. Peter turned around.

"Mom. Dad. What are you guys doing here?" Peter's parents were part of a large group that had just entered the restaurant. City Seniors.

"We just went to the reading at the Ninety-second Street Y," said Mr. Mandell. "Wallace Somebody. Duller than dishwater."

"Your father fell asleep. I had to punch him awake a couple of times to stop him from snoring. And who is this?" Mrs. Mandell looked at Jane.

Peter stood up. He looked like he wanted to move his parents away from the table. Or shield them from a hail of bullets.

"Oh, this is a bunch of friends of mine." He named everyone at the table, travel companions included. He circled the table with names, and then: "And you remember Jane. Jane Howe? We went to high school together. Sort of. We were in different classes. But the same school. High school. Can you believe it—we're neighbors."

Mr. and Mrs. Mandell hugged and kissed Jane, and of course they remembered her, because she hadn't changed a bit. Jane managed to say "Hello" and even "How are you," but she looked again at Peter, who wasn't being Peter anymore.

"Bianca told us about Christmas in Australia," said Mr. Mandell, returning his attention to his son. "You lucky duck. It'll be summer there."

Jane sank back into her chair. Ray reached across the table and held her hand. The Mandells talked about family stuff, doctor visits, and Bianca. They waved good-bye to the old high school pal that Peter had run into. Mr. and Mrs. Mandell returned to their table. Ray kept hold of Jane's hand. No one at the table spoke. Peter couldn't seem to sit back down.

"Jane. Can we talk about this? Outside maybe? Or can we go home?"

"Sure," said Jane. "After all, we're neighbors."

"Jane."

"Neighbors. Jesus."

"Please. Not here."

She pulled her hand away from Ray. She was out the door as if she were wearing a jet pack. In one of those rare New York moments, there was a cab right there, right outside the restaurant. Jane opened the door and slammed it in time to see Peter racing after her. She looked back. There were no other taxis. Hah!

She didn't want to cry in a taxi. Then again, perhaps she should cry, get it out of her system and be all cried out by the time Peter got home. Neighbor Peter. Old high school friend Peter. She let the city lights hypnotize her for a while. Traffic was light, another rare New York moment. Jane decided that she needed to look at Beth's picture for a while. That would make her feel better. Thank God she kept it in her purse.

And that was when she realized she had left the restaurant without her purse. No money. No keys. That was all she needed to push her over the edge. She began to cry. The driver looked back at her, but said nothing.

"Excuse me? Driver? I left my purse in the restaurant. I have no money on me. If you can wait a little while, my"—what should she call Peter?—"my friend will pay you. I'm sorry. I never do this. I promise I'll pay you."

• • •

Jane and the driver sat in front of Jane's building, with the meter running, for nearly fifteen minutes. Finally another cab pulled over. It was Peter. He carried Jane's purse. He walked over to Jane, who took her purse and said, "Pay the man."

Upstairs, Jane wished she had gathered thoughts or lists. Everything was a mess all around and inside her. Chaos. She hated chaos. She saw her face distorted in a window. She looked like a gargoyle. She circled the living room and let her face get uglier. Peter was walking carefully up the stairs. He looked like a penitent saint. His face was childlike and sad as he put his hands over his heart.

"What? What, Peter? What was that? Who are you? And who am I? And what's going on? Answer me!" She knew that this was a tough question to answer, but she didn't care. She sat down. Peter was still standing. It looked like she was expecting a performance. Peter looked like he had stage fright.

"I haven't told them. Obviously. They think that Bianca and I are—"

"Spending Christmas in Australia," Jane finished for him.

"You have the baby coming so soon. I didn't want to burden you with all this."

"You're quite a guy."

"I'm sorry." He said this several times. He went to the kitchen and made Jane a cup of tea. When he returned with it, Jane was ten degrees less brittle.

"I'm sorry," he said again.

"You mentioned that." Jane almost smiled. The tea was a nice gesture. Okay, so he was reluctant to tell his Catholic parents about his pending divorce. Give the guy a break.

"So"—she leaned in—"when are you going to tell them?"

Peter backed away. "See, that's the thing. Bianca and I—we haven't actually— We aren't really, legally, technically separated."

Jane was just starting to get it. Lies. All those lies. Bianca really was planning Christmas in Australia, wasn't she? Bianca knew nothing of Jane, of Beth, of anything here. Jane was a fool.

"Bianca knows that I'm not happy. She knows that I want children. But she doesn't actually know about you, or the adoption." Peter looked lighter, unburdened of all these lies. Jane was having trouble seeing over the top of them.

"My parents are really strict Catholics, Jane. I told you that. And so is Bianca. I can't just come home one day and say, 'Oh, by the way, I'm going to move in with this girl and adopt a baby with her in China.' I can't say that."

"I see. You can do it. You just can't say it."

"Look. I was scared. You wouldn't let the adoption wait for me. You wouldn't move into a house with me. I swear, if you had, I would have made the break with Bianca. But you don't need me. In fact, I bet you'll get all wrapped up in your new life as a mother and forget I'm even here. Is there room for me in your life?"

He sounded a lot less timid now. His voice had some power to it, and he kept going.

"So I kept a safety net. I admit it. I didn't want to make a break until I was sure that this—that you and I—that we were really going to work out. Is that so awful? I was scared. Is that a crime? And once everything worked out, I could end my marriage in my own time. I need it to be really gradual. In slow, small steps."

"Yes, I know what 'gradual' means. And I know what all this means. This means that you can't—"

She couldn't finish. His words were landing like an anvil on her head. And the tears she had managed to swallow in the cab took over her throat. Peter tried to console her, but she pushed him away. She wouldn't take comfort from him, since this was all his fault. Or was it all her fault? Shouldn't she have seen this? Wasn't she an idiot? Shouldn't she have known that she couldn't have all this happiness?

"Get out," she managed to say after a while.

He protested. Tried to get her to look at him. None of it was successful.

He had to leave. This married, lying Catholic man had to leave.

. . .

The good thing about having a less-wonderful job was that Jane could call in sick without guilt or fear of big work pile-up. Jane called in sick. Peter tried phoning her. From her caller ID she saw that he was back at his little studio apartment. Wait, that was Bianca's old apartment, and he had never given it up. The lying, lying liar. He couldn't even break a lease.

Jane picked up the phone when Ray called.

"I'm supposed to interview Nathan Lane at noon, but you have me for the morning. Will that do?" he asked.

"Get over here."

Jane stayed in pajamas and bathrobe for maximum pathetic effect. She took Peter's remaining belongings and packed them in trash bags.

Ray looked so clean and polished for Mr. Lane. Jane straightened her robe, but Ray just wanted to hug her for a long time. She cried some more and worried that she was ruining his beautiful shirt. They settled in the kitchen over tea and peanut butter cups, breakfast of the heartbroken.

"He can't commit to me because he can't commit to breaking his first commitment. That's it. He's under-committed because he's over-committed."

"He ought to *be* committed." Ray took the obvious one. "For letting you slip away."

"I wish I could fast-forward to 'over it' and be all okay."

"No, you don't. That's a bad wish. Just let it happen, Jane. Think about how you'll teach your daughter to deal with sadness. Don't tell her to fast-forward and—"

"My daughter?" Jane had pushed aside thoughts of motherhood, but now they were back. Peter was gone, and Jane was facing single motherhood once again.

"Maybe . . ." She didn't want to finish this sentence, but she did. "Maybe I should cancel the adoption."

Ray's whole body changed. His voice was strident as he said, "You do, and I'll never speak to you again. I mean it. I will not be friends with you if you cancel this adoption." He sounded like he meant it.

"But what about—"

"No. Sorry, I know you're all sad and abandoned and all that, but you have a bigger responsibility now. And her name is Beth. Go right ahead and feel sorry for yourself for a while. You're entitled. But you're adopting that kid, missy."

"You knew all along. You never liked Peter, did you?"

Ray let his shoulders droop as he tried a low-wattage grin. He looked under his eyebrows at Jane.

"Actually, I did like him. Maybe that's why I felt so jealous. And I thought you two were a good match. Didn't you?"

"Yes," she whispered. She cleared her throat, tried to look mature, and said, "It might not be wise for me to do this alone."

"Not wise? Jane, I wish you could hear yourself. Now, I've got a big Broadway star waiting for me, so I don't have time to walk you through this whole thing. We'll fast-forward to this one part: You can be a mother. I'll help you. Your friends will help you. Even Howard will help you. Eventually. Anyway, isn't it bad enough that Peter got to break your heart? Don't let him break this too."

"But I'm scared." Jane didn't sound mature anymore.

"All right, all right." Ray sounded like a mother. "Fall apart for a while, and then get back to your packing lists. And don't try to tell me that you don't have lists. I know you. For today, you can watch an old movie or two or seven. But starting tomorrow, you have to get on with your life."

Ray left, and Jane took the longest shower of her life. Afterward, she called Barbara.

"You need to cancel Peter out of the trip to China." She tried to make it sound like a change in dinner reservations.

Barbara sighed. "Oh, Jane. I'm sorry."

"I need a little time to fall apart."

"You don't have that kind of time. Sorry."

And with that, Barbara eased Jane into her lists. And her sub-lists. And her alternate lists. She told Jane precisely what to do for the rest of the day. And Jane obeyed.

She got dressed and read over Barbara's list for the day, organized geographically. She went outside.

She wired money to China to cover their local legal fees and the orphanage donation. She purchased gifts to give to everyone they met in China. She bought a shocking amount of Elimite cream, in case of scabies-babies. She bought jet lag cures and sleep masks for the flight. She bought disposable baby bottles for China. She tried not to think, because that would only slow her down. At home she opened a suitcase on the floor of her bedroom and dropped clothing into it from time to time.

The day ended. The lists continued.

• • •

Henry Wong was a travel agent genius. The orphanage was on the outskirts of Haozhou, which was too small to have its own airport. But it was very near Guangzhou, and that was good news. It meant that they could stay in Guangzhou for the entire adoption process and make the day trip to Haozhou to meet their daughters. The U.S. Consulate was located in Guangzhou, and a visit there was the final, necessary step for all Americans who were adopting. There, the girls would be given their visas and would be allowed to fly back to the U.S.

Still, he urged the Chinamoms to see Beijing while they could. Jane and Teresa looked sideways at Karen, expecting Karen to balk at the additional expense. Jane winced at the costs herself. But it was Karen who urged the others on.

"We have a moral obligation to take in as much Chinese culture as we can. If we don't see the Great Wall of China, we're bad mothers."

They would spend a few days in Beijing and meet their fellow adopters from other cities, then the whole group would proceed to Guangzhou and a completely new world. It was settled. Jane adjusted her request to two airline tickets instead of three. Without Peter, she and Ray would look like any other couple adopting from China. And that was good, wasn't it?

Karen wanted Jane to talk about the breakup. But none of them had time. Besides, it wasn't on Jane's list.

• • •

She had airline tickets, she was nearly packed, and finally, Jane had no more excuses for avoiding her father. She dialed.

Howard filled her in on family current events. Hearing about her nieces and nephews made her feel like part of the family again, and maybe that would suffice for a sign.

"Dad, I have news. I have good news."

"Did they promote you at work?" He wasn't going to make this easy.

"I'm traveling. Next Tuesday. I'm going to China."

She heard him sigh. She thought she could still turn him around.

"I have a picture of her. She's beautiful. She has these sad eyes and these—"

"Jane, this is not a lost puppy. This is a human being. And this is a much bigger undertaking than you can imagine. You can not do this alone. I love you too much to stay silent on this point. Leave this child to be adopted by a married couple. Oh, honey, I'm sorry that this part of life passed you by, truly I am. But you just don't get to be a mother. And you can't satisfy that need in yourself at some innocent child's expense. It's a sin."

She would never turn him around. He kept talking.

"It's not too late to fix this, sweetheart. Just don't get on that plane. You may think it has a momentum all its own, but it doesn't. This is a mistake that would cost you dearly and would cost her even more. Don't ruin your life and don't ruin hers. She's an innocent. You can stop this. Jane?"

"No."

She hung up the phone.

Chapter Fifteen

Jane and Karen were whispering across the aisle of the plane, while the sensible passengers were sleeping.

KAREN: You're killing me. Please. Tell me what happened.

JANE: Oh, God, Karen. After the hateful conversation with my father, well, I cried a lot. A lot a lot. But then there was so much to do, still. I looked at my lists—

KAREN: You and your lists. Your mom believed in early potty training. Am I right?

JANE: Never mind. Anyway, I had to prewash the baby's clothes and there was still stuff to get, and I think I checked my paperwork for the consulate about thirty times. So thank God I took off from work for this whole week. All day Monday, I was running up-town and down, and my father's voice quieted down to a buzz in my head. A kind of gnat-buzz. Very annoying. But not enough to stop me in my tracks. But then one thing did stop me. Peter. I came home on Monday and found all his stuff gone. And this really lame note. "I'm sorry, I still love you, I never meant to hurt you. Please give me a chance to make it up to you." Very unoriginal. And *so* not enough to help me. But all his stuff is gone. He's not coming back.

KAREN: You already knew that, Jane. Didn't you? I knew that.

JANE: Yes. I did. Of course I did. So. There I was on Monday night— my last actual night home, and I thought, if I don't do this stenciling, I'll never get it done. And I have to do it. It's not optional.

KAREN: This is disturbing, do you know that? Stencils are always optional in my world, Jane.

JANE: I wanted this for her room. It looked so cold and sterile. And I've been working on this stupid thing since my stupid dossier went to stupid China.

KAREN: What is this stupid stencil, anyway?

JANE: It's not stupid. It's the Chinese zodiac—all of the animals.

KAREN: Awwww.

JANE: Yeah. And let me tell you, it was hard to make a rat look cute. Anyway, so there I am, ready to do this. I put on some music and I start working and I really get into it. I'm loving the colors, and I don't know, maybe I'm stoned on all the paint, but I feel great. I get into the zen of stenciling. I work on it for a couple of hours, and it's really good anti-Peter therapy. I don't think about him. Much. I get all calm and easy. And then my buzzer rings. It's Teresa. I'm thinking, it's our last night home and what the hell is she doing at my door? She comes up and I can smell the liquor on her breath. She's kind of drunk. So I make her some instant coffee, because that's all I have, and she doesn't want any. She starts telling me about how we're about to get in way over our heads and we're all crazy. Turns out, she spent the day with Megan and baby Stella.

KAREN: Oh. She was pulling a Greta?

JANE: Yes! And I've never seen her hair messed up like that. She's so busy pacing and shaking her head, she doesn't even notice. At first she'd make sense, and then she wouldn't. So I'm sitting there, freaking out, trying to figure out what to say to her. I can't make her go through with this if she doesn't want to. On the other hand, I think she wants to. And by the way, this whole time, she's wearing jeans and a T-shirt.

KAREN: Wow!

JANE: Yes, wow. So I try to talk to her about the nursery schools where her daughter is already waitlisted and about the gaggle of nannies she'll have working for her, and she keeps shaking her head. So it's getting late and I tell her that I have to finish stenciling Beth's room.

KAREN: That is so cold. She's in crisis and you have an urgent crafts problem?

JANE: Wait. So she comes in and sees it, and I've gotten carried away with the whole red thread border thing and she likes it. I was relieved, to tell you the truth. I wasn't sure that the border worked. Anyway, she helps me finish the red thread, and that takes like a good hour and a half, and we're playing music and stenciling and—

KAREN: You got her stoned on paint.

JANE: I did not. I . . . I don't think I did. Anyway, we get really quiet toward the end and we just do the stencil. It's the middle of the night now, and we're tired. But we're doing really careful, gentle work. And it looks amazing. And when we're done, she puts on her shoes and—

KAREN: She took off her shoes? You skipped that!

JANE: She puts on her shoes and she says, "Well, the room looks lovely and I imagine our girls will have enormous fun playing here," and then she leaves. And me, I clean up and go to bed.

KAREN: Cool.

JANE: And today, I get up and my lists are down so low, and I'm running around and I know I'm going to make it. I'm fine. I can't even hear my dad anymore. Ray is going to come to my place for dinner before the car comes to pick us up for the airport, and then he calls and cancels the dinner. Fine, no problem. One less thing to take care of. But then he calls and says let's schedule the car to pick us up a little later. Big bad sign right there, and I should have known. I didn't say anything, but I should have. So it's time to go and the car gets here and Ray isn't here. So I ask the car guy to wait and he does. And I call Ray and he's not there, and that's good. That means he's on his way. And I pull my suitcases downstairs and put them in the car and I see the Christ Child, and I think this is a good sign—

KAREN: Who did you see?

JANE: The Christ Child. He's this baby and he's gorgeous and I kind of call him the Christ Child. But only in my head.

KAREN: That's so wrong on so many levels I'm going to have to let it go.

JANE: Good. So now I'm calling Ray's cell, and I'm not getting an answer, and good. That must mean that he's on the subway or something. But it's really getting late and I'm starting to feel a little tense. I go upstairs to see if he's called. He hasn't. I go downstairs to see if he's there. He's not. I go back upstairs to see if he's called. You get the idea. It's a lot of stairs, and a lot of Ray not being there. Now, this is an international flight, right? So we're supposed to check in two hours in advance, and we are now two and a half hours from takeoff, and out of nowhere I figure I can just call Peter. I'm this close to dialing his number.

KAREN: Very resourceful. In a misguided, bad kind of way.

JANE: Exactly. And I'm thinking Peter will come with me and meet Beth, and when he does, he'll snap out of his stupidity and choose me over his wife and his parents and we'll be happy. Somehow. So I call him.

KAREN: What did he say?

JANE: He wasn't there. I got his machine. I left a message. "You busy tonight? Want to go to China and get a baby?" And I hear myself sounding so crazy that I hang up. I can't have Peter in my head right now. It's him or me.

KAREN: I pick you. Go on.

JANE: Now, at this point, it's like two hours from takeoff and I tell the guy, "Drive. Just drive to the airport. I'm not missing this flight."

KAREN: This is giving me a stomachache. Please finish.

JANE: You know how it ends. We see Ray running down my street, suitcases in hand, waving and yelling, and I say, "Stop!" and Ray gets in. He's a mess and he's upset.

KAREN: So? What happened? Was it your dad?

JANE: No. He fell asleep. He's been trying to switch over to China time in advance. Anyway, he's all upset and I'm trying to stay calm but I'm thinking, "If we miss this flight, I'll hurt you so bad." And the driver knows. He can hear my thoughts or something because he gets us there. Somehow we didn't hit one red light, we didn't hit any traffic, we just flew to the airport. It felt like we never touched the ground. And then we checked in and we even got to sit in the lounge for three whole minutes before they called us to board the flight, and that's when we found you guys.

Jane's sleep mask was dangling like unfortunate jewelry. She knew she should sleep too. She consulted her list about how to avoid jet lag. She glanced at the in-flight movie. Julia Roberts was about to find love or fulfillment, or maybe even both. Peter always made fun of Julia Roberts. Jane pulled the mask over her eyes and went to sleep.

She woke up in Korea, where they had a long layover. They dominated the lounge and tried to pick out any other adopting Americans. There was the large woman who was crocheting a panda. Too easy. The very large couple who whispered into each other's ears. Possibly. The extremely large woman who looked scared. Maybe.

Oh, she was reading a baby book. Yes. Another Mommy.

Day One

Hi. Welcome to my Travel Journal. Today, we are in Beijing. I can't believe I just wrote that sentence. I never used to keep journals. But this trip is too important, so here goes:

When we arrived in Beijing, I was the last one off the plane. Barbara had told us that James Lui was going to meet us at the airport. He's going to be our tour guide/facilitator for the trip. So everybody forged ahead to find him outside, or maybe they just wanted a little sunshine. It's very hot and sunny here in Beijing. So I saw this man in the crowd. He was holding up a sign for "Foundering Mothers." Close enough.

James's English is wonderful, especially compared to my Chinese. Maybe I'm naïve, but I thought it was impressive that so many Chinese speak English. And so many speak it so well. So the whole Chinamom group boarded a private bus, and we clunked our way into the heart of the capital. Along the way, James provided fun, tour-guide facts.

"Do you see so many bicycles? In fact, you could almost say that Beijing is the Kingdom of Bicycles."

We were all nodding and smiling, but really, we were in some kind of shock. It was more than jet lag, but less than culture shock. Everyone in this group has traveled enough to be jaded and smug, but we couldn't muster any smug just then. After all, this was China. China.

James would tell us in English that "Beijing is much larger than your New York City. You will not see it all, but you will see many great and historic sites in our time together." And then he'd say something very quick and slightly hostile in Chinese to the driver.

Oh, God, the driving. The traffic was terrifying. It was a free-for-all. The Kingdom of Bicycles is in a state of anarchy. Cars blocked grids, switched lanes, and aggressively cut off anyone and anything. And yield at your own peril. So far, every time we have crossed a street has been a stunt from a bad reality show.

James told us that we were the late arrivers.

"Your other Americans were at the Winter Palace today. Tomorrow, you will see the Forbidden City also along with them. It will be beautiful."

Okay, here comes my snobbery. The other Americans in the

group were the non–New Yorkers. They lived in real places that New Yorkers emigrated from and then felt superior to. These people had arrived in Beijing earlier. I was so jealous already.

The hotel is fine, I guess. It's disappointingly Western in every way, except for the large sign in the bathroom that shouts DO NOT DRINK THE WATER!! I've been warned about this on all the list-servs. Don't drink it, don't brush your teeth with it, and keep your mouth shut tight in the shower. Got it.

I checked my answering machine at home. There was a message from Peter.

"Jane. If I'd been home, I would have come with you in a heart-beat. I miss you a lot. I hope you got to China okay. I guess since you're not picking up, you must be in China. Or still really mad at me. Or both."

I must have been still tired and jet-lagged, because I started cry-ing. I love Ray and I want him to be here, but I want Peter too. That's so disloyal to Ray. I can't believe I just wrote it.

So I told Ray I was going to call Peter back. Ray tried to talk me out of it. Aside from the fact that the call itself would cost a semes-ter's tuition at Harvard, what would be the point of returning that call right here right now? He made perfect sense. I dialed the phone.

Got his voice mail. His damn voice mail. It was a sign. I hung up without saying anything, then I told Ray that he was right.

So. We started Project Stay Awake! Why? Because you have to stay awake if you want to get over jet lag. So we all set out for a walk almost immediately.

The Most Surprising Things in Beijing Were:
1. Tiananmen Square. Everyone talks about it like it's just a place. People go there every day.
2. The crowds. Remember, I live in Manhattan, and this city made me feel like the country mouse.
3. Peter. I keep thinking about him. I keep wondering what he

would think of this place. He's here in my head. I saw a little boy in split pants. The middle seam of the pants is split open, and little kids are dangled over potties or streets to do their business. And not a pooper scooper in sight. I thought about how I would tell the story to Peter. I need to keep "don't think of Peter" on my to-do list.

James urged us all to come out to dinner with the larger group. He's a real gourmand, and he wants to show off all his favorite restaurants to his guests. Peter would absolutely love this part of the trip. Jesus. I have to stop writing about him.

I don't remember much about dinner. I was too tired for conversation. Before I forget—Ray was right: If he, Peter, and I had all traveled together, we would have freaked everyone out. After a while, I realized that everyone assumed that Ray and I were married and Karen and Charles were married, and that Teresa and Beverly were lesbians. Fine.

Day Two

It wasn't until this morning when we were in the Forbidden City that I really woke up. I am really in China. I am on the other side of the earth, and I'm coming home with a baby. Sorry if my pen slipped there, that last word was "baby." So we toured this amazing place and I studied the architecture so that I could push the b-b-b-baby part of that revelation to one side.

James is so smart. He had us all enter from the North Gate, because most tourists enter from the South. This way, it seemed as if we had the Forbidden City to ourselves for most of the tour.

He asked us if we had ever seen *The Last Emperor*. Most of us had, and I couldn't believe my eyes. This is where the little boy Emperor rode his bike. Remember?

One guy is seeing China strictly through the LCD panel of his video camera. He was adding his own narration to his videotape and, yes, this is America (or it will be when he watches it), so I guess he can do that. But he still bugged me. When James showed the house of the concubines, the American narration was "and here's where the Emperor kept his bitches." I think Teresa was actually twitching toward a confrontation, but she must have thought better of it.

The group headed into the Forbidden City Starbucks. It was real. It was in the Forbidden City. Could the Gap be far behind? Did I mention that we saw the Beijing Ikea? We did. It was disturbing.

James gave us an hour to wander on our own, and then we were supposed to reunite at a designated spot. After an hour and some miscellaneous time went by, everyone had returned except for Ray. James shook his head and said, "Jane, where is your husband?"

So I shook my head and said, "James, I have no idea." It was an honest answer. But one more time, I thought of Peter. I wanted to say, "He's married to somebody else, the dope." But then Ray snuck up behind us, and we were a couple once again.

Later, James took us all to Tiananmen Square. He was talking about the history of the place, beyond that horrible day in 1989 (and now as I write this, it looks like a long time ago). The soldiers in the square do this slow, dancelike march and I think it hypnotized me. I got pulled out of my trance when I heard a pair of Chinese girls nearby. They were pointing and laughing at our group. James heard them, but he only spoke louder and louder. Then all of a sudden, he turned and spoke sharply to the girls in Chinese. They stopped pointing, smothered their laughs, and looked at the sky. Whatever it was, it was still funny to them. They got all subversive and started pointing and giggling again, but they were quieter. I figured out what was amusing them.

A lot of the people in our travel group are overweight. The girls had been pointing at the heaviest Americans in the group and laughing. I haven't seen any fat Chinese, although I've read about them. For the rest of the day, I noticed Chinese people pointing and sneering at overweight tourists. The overweight tourists said nothing. I don't know if they noticed it, but it would have been hard to miss.

Day Three

James wanted us all to go out extremely early this morning. "Come to the park and see how Chinese people start the day." It was painfully early, and I'll confess here that I hesitated. It will probably be years before I can ever sleep in again. And I love sleep. I told Ray, "I might want to sleep some more."

And he said, "How can you even think about missing this!" He sounded really shocked.

So I was duly embarrassed, but then I told him, "I guess you got all that extra sleep while *I was waiting for you to go to the airport.*"

He stopped lecturing me. I plan to use this line until it stops working.

I'm so glad I decided to go. James had us walk to this beautiful park, and on the way we saw people sweeping spotless streets with tiny straw brooms. Some kind of government works program in progress. Cleaning clean streets.

The first group we saw in the park was doing tai chi. It was silent and graceful and serious. Mr. Annoying Video Guy started shouting, "Wax on! Wax off!" until his wife pinched him really hard. I had this vague sense of shame at the discipline I was seeing in front of me. And it only got worse. Then came the calligraphy writers. They dipped large brushes in muddy water, they bent down at the waist, and wrote on the pavement. The floor became a mosaic of Chinese characters. Their work would dry, get washed away, and they would re-create it all the next morning. They did this on purpose.

But today's big event was the Great Wall. I have now climbed the Great Wall of China. James told us that the Great Wall can *not* be seen from the moon, but maybe it can be seen by people like John

Glenn who orbit the earth. That's not a lot of people. The best way to see it is to go to it and climb it, and I speak from experience here. I don't know how to describe something this grand, so I'll paste some pictures in the journal here. I got a certificate that announces that I did indeed climb the Great Wall, so lucky, silly me.

When it was time for lunch, James had another great restaurant lined up for us. But some members of the group started shouting out:

"Can't we just get pizza or something?"

"I'm dying for a burger."

And, the one that made me grimace at my fellow travelers: "Please, anything but Chinese. I'm so sick of Chinese!"

Maybe James has a high pain threshold. If it hurt, he showed nothing. He took us to eat exotic foods instead, promising that it was "tasty, so tasty." Most of the group grumbled, ate rice, and declined a great many dishes. I wanted to compensate for their rudeness by eating everything James ordered. This included things that really didn't want to go down my throat. There were strange sauces, things with bones, and flora and fauna I have never seen before, even on Canal Street. But I ate it just to show the others that it could be done. And my reward, every time and for every dish, was a second helping.

It reminded me of Peter and the new foods he used to get me to try. Peter. Again. Why am I writing about Peter when I'm on the other side of the planet?

Peter is gone and I am in China.

Peter is gone and I am in China.

Peter is gone and I am in China. There.

For the afternoon, James wanted to show us how real Chinese live here in Beijing. The noise, the energy, the commerce all dropped away as we walked. He took us to a courtyard in a residential district. And that's when the smell hit us. If you're eating right now, put it down. Because this was an outhouse smell, amplified by stadium speakers. That's the nicest way to describe it.

Teresa just had to ask, "What is that?" And Karen was covering her mouth, but I could tell that she was gagging. It was really that bad.

James told us that this was the public bathroom, and it seemed the obvious answer. A few hundred people use it every day. After we passed it, the smell began to dissipate, or maybe we grew some tolerance toward it. I stopped worrying that Karen was going to be sick.

"This is middle-class Beijing." James sounded like a professor. "They have no indoor plumbing. They come here, and that is what you smell. It is bad, isn't it?"

There was a girl, several blocks ahead of us. She was walking toward the group, carrying some small items. Her clothes were light and casual. I thought that she was wearing pajamas. She was. And she was carrying a towel and a toothbrush. How long had she been walking?

James told us, "She is going to the bathroom. Imagine if she is sick in the night. How far must she go?"

He stopped at a gate in a stone wall. He entered and spoke to the residents, leaving us Americans outside for a bit. We barely had time to say, ewww, gross, about the bathroom situation, when James opened the door and signaled us in. We were in a Chinese courtyard.

The ground was paved with a kind of cobblestone. It looked as if we were in a fraction of some grand and wealthy person's ancient home. There were three doors, forming a semicircle around the courtyard. There were plants, bean sprouts, and other vegetation winding around the pillars of some of the entrances. The paint was peeling badly on every door and wall. We skipped the first door. Maybe no one was home. But we were invited to the next home.

It contained two rooms. A living room/kitchen and a bedroom. The living room/kitchen had a yellow velvet couch that was worn but well cared for. A little boy, eight years old, maybe nine, sat there, doing homework. He was too shy to look up. His mother was a tiny woman with high energy. She had a computer; she had nice things.

The bedroom was filled with a giant mattress, where the family slept.

In the next house, we met a small, elderly lady. She was not frail, and her house was not as accessible. The Americans backed away. She consented to photos with the Americans. She took a few pictures of us too.

Is this the life my daughter might have had? Would she have been happy? What would she have grown up to be here? What *will* she grow up to be? Someone stop me before my head explodes.

I felt like such a spoiled, pampered American. And I thought of Pete— I mean, I thought of you know who. P. When he left, it was like someone amputated a limb. But let's be honest here—my life is easy-peasy. So the guy left. So what? Get a little sense of perspective, Jane. And grow up.

For the record, the people in the courtyard were happy. They seemed to like their lives. Peter would argue with me here—just for the sake of arguing, because that's how he is and now he's arguing in my head: "What, should they move into condos and eat McDonald's?" No. But they should have flushing toilets. That's all I'm saying.

Shut up, Peter.

Day Four

Today we flew to Guangzhou, where we were to be united with our children, and oh, my God. I didn't tell anyone, but I was praying that we would *not* get the babies that day. I need one more day to get ready. Just one. Please.

James was sweet and kind with us at the Beijing airport. He gave us detailed instructions about how to board a flight, as if we were idiot children. We had a lovely short flight from Beijing to Guangzhou, on Shamian Island. This was the spot where the Chinese used to stash all the foreign traders, pirates, and other suspicious international characters. Parts of it looked like New Orleans to me. Maybe I'm crazy.

When we checked into the hotel, the White Swan, everyone was looking left, looking right, looking for a room full of babies. I was relieved that we didn't find one. But then I was upset to be relieved, so I'd look for more babies. And then I'd be relieved. And then I'd be upset. And that is the worst kind of vicious cycle.

While we unpacked, I turned on the TV, and can you believe it? They were showing *Bringing Up Baby*. Ray was worried about me when I got all weepy at the scene where Katharine Hepburn climbs the dinosaur and Cary Grant kisses her at last. He doesn't think people should cry at screwball comedies. Critics . . .

The Chinamoms gathered for dinner, and it felt like the condemned eating a hearty meal. No one said anything about being scared out of their wits. Am I the only one? Teresa said that she almost pushed Mr. Annoying Video Guy off the Great Wall. So we gossiped about our fellow travelers for a while. We argued about life in the courtyards of Beijing, and we were pretty much our same, original selves. This could have been a Melting Pot dinner, but we were on the other side of the world. Was this the last time we would be our old selves? Ever? I think so. You can count it down in hours, but I don't want to.

Tomorrow, we go get our babies.

Chapter Sixteen

When Jane woke up, Ray was still asleep in the next bed. The sun was almost up. She should sleep while she can. She turned over and saw the crib. She turned back.

After the Last Supper, she and Ray had giggled their way back to their room. But then the hotel staff wheeled in the crib, and there was a lot of general gulping from the Americans in the room. It was small, but it vacuumed the air right out of the room. Jane and Ray both reached for the minibar.

But now, she wanted to fall back asleep.

. . .

Ray was making her late. Again! He wanted to go back to the room and make sure that he had his camera. Oh, and extra rolls of film. Oh, and the toy he wanted to give to little Beth. Oh, and Jane was inches away from spontaneous combustion.

They were inches away from the breakfast bar when one of the mothers-to-be in the group found them and announced her need for a group hug and Jane broke away in an obvious break-away style.

"Oh," she said. "Somebody gets cranky without a little breakfast, huh?"

Bitch. Evil bitch. Jane raced to gather some food that she didn't want. Why were there pigs in a blanket in the breakfast buffet? It was upsetting in every way. She wrapped banana bread in a paper napkin and stashed it in the diaper bag. Already, she was a self-ish mother. They raced to catch the orphanage bus. James waved them on.

"*It's Christmas!*" Karen shouted, and a handful of people looked like they were wishing for guns. "We're getting our girls! *It's like Christmas!*"

Is it? Christmas wouldn't be so hot and so sweaty and so damn scary. Christmas wouldn't be so polluted and gray and wouldn't start so early and wouldn't happen on a bus and wouldn't include Jane wanting to strangle Karen with her hands if she said "Christmas" again.

Karen started singing, "Did you know we're riding on ba-a-by ex-press?"

It was so much worse in person. Karen had her video camera at hand to capture every precious moment. She taped the gray scenery through the dirty bus window. Jane watched as Karen put the camera in her bag while it was still recording, capturing lengthy stretches of the interior life of a camera bag.

Ray bounced a toy bunny, but with no musical accompaniment. Maybe he was starting to figure out that Jane was just a bit tense. Jane caught him watching her sideways. She worried about being the object of his worry.

The ride was ugly. Teresa and Beverly sat far from Jane and Karen, and Jane was jealous. They were quiet and exuded a kind of calm that could only come from people who actually knew what the hell they were doing. Or were hungover. Jane wanted to throw up. The scenery was so damn ugly. Haozhou seemed to consist only of tire shops. How could that be? Was this a town where you stopped only if you had a flat?

The ride took two hours. It was too short. Jane wanted to drive the length of the Great Wall and wave to John Glenn. She smiled weakly at Karen whenever she held up the potentially blackmailing video camera. Ray was quiet, dancing the toy bunny in a rhythmic, comforting way.

"Here we are," announced James.

It was a big wall. Wooden and dirty. They walked into a small parking lot/courtyard/open space.

"Does anyone need to go to the bathroom?" James asked.

Oh, God, yes. They needed to go. A pride of women followed an orphanage worker up several flights of stairs to a bathroom.

"Oh! No! Oh, ick! I can't do this!" squealed the first woman. This was a traditional, Eastern, squat bathroom. No toilets here, not like she was expecting. This was essentially a hole in the floor where one had to squat and go.

Jane decided to remain upstairs and accompany a mother who was openly nervous about the day.

"I bet they brought out the babies," said Jane as they found the stairs again.

"No!" said Nervous Mother. "They wouldn't do that!"

"They would."

They descended the stairs and found bedlam in the small courtyard. There were babies, parents, and every kind of noise.

"I held your baby already!" Teresa shouted. "I held her! Where have you been?"

While they were upstairs, a parade of nannies had brought the babies to all the waiting parents. This was the result.

Jane scanned the crowd and saw Ray holding the doe-eyed beauty whom Jane had studied for months in a tiny photo with a red background. Beth. That was Beth. Jane would know her anywhere. Jane's chest felt like a door that was opening, rusty and old. It was Beth, and she loved her.

"Hi, baby girl. Hi. Hi. Hi." She said that a lot. And she said, "Oh, you're so beautiful. You're so sweet. Look at you. Hi."

The baby clung to Ray. Jane wanted to snatch her and run. She wanted to pull her away and shout, "This is *my* baby!" but that would be unwise. Right? Better to wait. Take it easy. Take it slow. She waited. Finally Ray couldn't justify holding the girl anymore.

"Hi, sweetheart. Hi. Are you okay?" Jane said to the fifteen pounds of panic and fear in her arms. The baby didn't cry, but she dug her fingers into Jane's arm and held on. Jane read "whoever you are, don't let go" in her body language. There was an ocean of eleven babies and who knows how many grown-ups cavorting about this tiny courtyard where Jane and Beth held on to each other. Jane was having a Tony and Maria experience: Everyone else was a gauzy soft focus as these two danced and discovered how much they loved each other. It would be a while before the Jets and the Sharks came into focus. There was no noise in their misty world, only quiet colors and soft textures.

Years might have passed before Jane looked up from the baby. When she finally did, she saw that the grown-ups were the ones crying. Most of the babies were quiet. One was wailing enough for the whole zoo of infants. It was Karen's baby, Ariel. She was frantic to comfort the baby. Nothing was working.

James held Karen's crying baby, and the crying stopped instantly. He whispered to her in Cantonese, and the baby even managed a smile. But she screamed and cried when she was handed back to her new mother. Karen's face was red, she was sweaty, she was an inch away from crying herself. How could a baby reject her so quickly and so completely?

"It's okay," James reassured her. "Baby has strong ties here. This means that she knows how to love. She will love you just as much. You will see."

The whole crowd was summoned into a large room. Jane found a seat far from the madding crowd and sat Beth on her lap to get a look at her child, beyond the wisps of hair and the cherubic face. Despite the heat, Beth was wearing a long-sleeved terry cloth sleeper. It was blue and had some stains on it. It may have been a little small; she seemed to be working hard to straighten her legs and push her feet through the terry cloth footsies. She felt substantial and real. She looked good.

The room had two old couches and some large folding tables, now covered in diaper bags and other goods. Everyone had brought a clothing donation for the unseen children who would remain in the orphanage. There were bottles everywhere, filled with a heavy, lumpy kind of formula. Jane took one. It was very hot, and the bottle's nipple had been widened to accommodate the thick meal inside. Beth grabbed it and chowed down.

Ray was crying. He had taken dozens of photos and hoped that they were in focus. He couldn't see.

Teresa's face had changed. She looked softer, more available. A set of muscles around her mouth unclenched. She was bouncing her girl, Grace, on her lap and singing to her. Karen was pale. She was rocking Ariel, who maintained a steady cry until she had her bottle.

Mrs. Wu, the orphanage director, stepped forward. She was warm but very serious looking. She had a lot of information for the new families, and she launched into it. She described sleep schedules and eating schedules and described general living conditions for the girls during their time here at the Haozhou Social Welfare Institute. She was on the other side of the room, and Jane missed every word of it. Ray was trying to take notes, but he still couldn't see very well.

Beth finished her bottle and smacked her lips a few times. Her eyes were at half-mast. Jane didn't know whether or not the child needed a burp, but she opted to try. Beth was starting to drowse, and sleep made her heavier. That would become a significant law of physics in the days to come. Sleep Makes Children Heavier. Beth nodded out, and Jane was complete. She had everything she wanted. Peter didn't exist in this gossamer world.

"What's that?" asked Ray. He was pointing to a large red scab on the back of Beth's head. It was the size of a poker chip and looked like a recent injury.

Each family stepped forward to give their clothing donation to the orphanage. They took pictures with Mrs. Wu. They said thank you in English and Cantonese. She smiled and nodded graciously.

"Can we go in and see the other babies?" a father asked.

"No. I'm sorry, no." Mrs. Wu never allowed anyone inside the orphanage. Years before, a Canadian filmmaker had brought a hidden camera into an orphanage, and the subsequent documentary had rattled China and the adoption world. It would not happen again.

When Jane stepped up, she pointed to the wound on her daughter's head and asked Mrs. Wu, "What's this? What happened?"

"It's getting better," Mrs. Wu replied. And she moved on to the next family.

Karen's baby was finally starting to calm down. Jane floated over to them.

"Beth, this is Karen and her baby, Ariel. When you wake up, you guys can have a playdate," Jane offered.

Ariel didn't like the sound of that and threw her head back for another cry. Karen was losing more color.

"Can I help?" Jane asked.

"You can back off," Karen answered in a voice Jane had never heard before. She backed off.

James announced that all the parents should change their baby's diapers before they boarded the bus. Jane bit her lip and wished that she had practiced this move at least once before she had to do it for real. Why had she never put that on a list?

The large folding table became a diaper changing world. Most of the babies were awake now and screaming at the prospect of a clean diaper. Jane settled her sleeping girl on the couch and opened the terry cloth sleeper. Beth was hot and sweaty, so her dutiful mother would change her into a cool, clean new outfit.

There were three large red rings on Beth's stomach. They almost looked like welts. The red skin flaked. Jane stared in disbelief. She couldn't remember any of Dr. Val's Polaroids looking like this. What was it?

"Hurry, please! The bus must go!" James shouted.

Beth woke up and screamed. Tears rolled around her head. Her tongue wavered in her mouth, and she looked a lot like the killer plant in *Little Shop of Horrors*. Jane snapped out of her haze and grabbed Ray.

"I need a diaper! I need a wipe! Stat! What are those red things on her belly?"

Jane's hands were shaking, and Beth knew she was in the hands of an amateur. She screamed even louder. She could belt. Jane lifted her legs and slipped the diaper underneath. She almost looked like she knew what was doing, until she realized that the diaper was backward. Or was it? Did it matter? She switched it. She switched it back. Beth had no patience for this indecision. Jane closed the diaper, closed the too-hot sleeper, and clutched the baby to her chest.

"There. That wasn't easy at all, was it?" she said to the sniffly kid.

Jane, Beth, and Ray were the last ones out of the orphanage. They scrambled to catch up with the crowd ahead of them. They exited the courtyard into the bustling streets of Haozhou. It was noisy and busy and in full motion, except for the young Chinese woman across the street. She stood still and was impeccably dressed, watching the Americans toting the babies, and she was weeping. Jane froze and held Beth a little too tightly. Beth wriggled as they went to the bus.

• • •

Karen took Ariel to the back of the bus, where she screamed for the entire ride. Teresa bounced little Grace recklessly but happily. Grace squealed with joy.

"I got her to laugh! She actually laughed. Did you hear that?" Teresa was now about twelve years younger.

It took nearly three hours to drive back to the hotel, as they were trapped in a traffic debacle. Beth stayed awake but didn't cry again. She studied. Her eyes were impossibly large. Jane smiled without stopping. Beth clutched her mother.

. . .

Jane was living in a pink bubble. And then, at the hotel, it popped. Ray, Jane, and Beth rode the elevator and everything was so far, so good. But Jane couldn't find her hotel room key. She was holding the baby, a purse, and a large diaper bag. She couldn't do something as simple as find her key. She couldn't even tell you where her key was. Not a clue. She fumbled for it in her bag and nearly strangled herself on her purse straps.

"It's okay. I've got it." But Ray didn't get it. It wasn't about having the key. It wasn't that simple. Ray wouldn't always be by her side with a key. Duh! How would she ever accomplish the simple task of entering a room on her own? She wouldn't! Jane saw all the petty details of daily life in one big montage with loud music and crying and, just like that, she knew that *nothing would ever be simple again.*

. . .

In the hotel room, Beth finally got to wear a cool, new outfit and relax. Jane laid down on a bed, because she had to. So Beth explored her, smushing Jane's mouth, drumming on her chest. She scratched at the polyester bedspread.

"Textures!" said Ray. "She likes textures."

Beth's movements gained energy and speed, so the adults created a pillow fort around the bed. She could still fall, but they'd get a little more warning this way. Jane bent her legs, and Beth tried to climb over them.

"Climbing Mt. Mommy!" said Jane. They stayed this way until it was time to meet the larger group for lunch. This time, Jane planned her petty details a bit, in order to keep them simple. That was all she wanted: simple. Simple sounded like a Mediterranean paradise. She got her keys, her money, the diaper bag, some lip balm, a toy, another toy, the camera, the teething biscuits, a bottle. Simple was not available at this time.

She must have been insane for thinking that she could do this motherhood thing alone. She wanted to fix this problem. Now. Should she propose to Ray?

"Let's eat!" Ray declared. Jane snapped out of her feverish planning and followed him to the restaurant. She must have been wearing blinders on her previous visits to the hotel restaurant. Virtually every table was populated by American or European parents with Chinese babies. This view certainly made the children look like an export. She didn't enjoy thinking that.

At lunch, she had no appetite. Beth, a highly perceptive child, picked up on the maternal anxiety and began to fuss.

"She has gas."

"She's hungry."

"She's having bonding issues."

There was unlimited advice from people who had been parents for a handful of hours. Jane nodded quietly at it all. She handed Beth to Ray and excused herself to the restroom, where she let it all out. Locked in a little stall, Jane cried and sobbed as hard as she had at her own mother's funeral. It was done. She was a mother. A single mother. Forever. Her father was providing a deadly voice-over: *You have ruined your life. You have ruined her life, and she is an innocent.*

By the time Jane returned to the table, everyone was gone except Ray and Beth. Perhaps young Beth had given him some pointers on handling maternal anxiety. He was careful and quiet.

• • •

There was an afternoon meeting with James, where he gave instructions and warnings about their activity for the next day.

"Tomorrow is the legal adoption. I need you all on the bus at seven A.M. We will spend the morning at the Haozhou Notary Office. And then you are legal parents. It is done."

Someone shouted out, "Do we bring the babies?"

James scowled. "Yes, of course you bring the babies."

• • •

At bedtime, Jane read *Goodnight Moon* to her daughter, who kept trying to flip the pages to the end.

"Hey! Don't ruin the ending for me!" Jane was pushing hard to be more lighthearted. In the background, Ray played a CD of Tibetan children singing the chants of the Joyous Mantras. He reasoned that the sound of children would be comforting to a girl who had been in an orphanage, and he may have been right. Beth was drooping with fatigue, and when she finished her bottle, Jane lowered her into the crib. Peace.

Then Beth screamed. She did *not* want to go to sleep, she did *not* want to sleep in that crib, she did *not* like any of this. Jane rocked her without a rocking chair until Ray detected rapid eye movement from Beth. Jane lowered the baby into the crib so slowly she looked like she was posing for a camera.

Beth slept. Jane gasped. She had put the baby to sleep on her stomach, and everyone knows that babies need to sleep on their backs. SIDS. Ray didn't know that, but he warned Jane not to move this baby. Eventually Jane remembered that at ten months Beth really wasn't in much danger of SIDS. She let Beth sleep.

The room was dark and quiet. Ray waited a respectable interval and then said, "You can do this. You're going to be just fine." And doesn't that sound helpful, encouraging, and sweet? Jane wanted to tell him to shut up. Jane wanted to hug him and kiss him. Instead, she started shaking.

"Is it cold in here?"

It wasn't cold. Not at all.

"I'm freezing. I'm really cold."

Ray hugged her and kissed her. He drew her a bath, with special scented oils that Burton had designed to counter a new mother's anxiety attacks. Burton was so smart. It would be wrong to steal his boyfriend. Jane took the phone with her to the bathroom.

• • •

"Hi, Peter. It's Jane. Listen, I'm a mother now, and I'm completely useless. But that's not why I'm calling. You know, you might not have told any technical lies, in a Bill Clinton it-depends-on-what-'is'-is kind of way. But you made me think that we were going to be doing this together, and now we're not. So that was a continent-sized lie, and I see that now. But that's not why I'm calling. Beth is so amazing already, and she's been through so much more than I have. It's a shame she drew the short straw and got the incompetent mother. She deserves someone who knows how to cope. And I don't. But that's not why I'm calling. I'm calling because I miss you. I miss you so much. I'm still mad at you and I still love you, which proves that I'm permanently dumb. Because I have to live without you and, goddamn it, that's exactly what I'm going to do. This is my first day as a mother, and I'm going to get through it. And I'll get through the next one and the next one and the next one. I'm going to do it because I have to. I just wanted to hear your voice. This call is costing me my entire 401(k). So. Sorry for the long message. Bye."

The call helped. The bath helped even more. It wasn't a cure, but it helped. Jane went to bed, shivering under the covers. Exhaustion trumped fear, and she slept.

• • •

Beth was crying. It was 6:05 A.M., and this was some kind of victory, wasn't it? They had both slept through the night. Jane picked Beth up and brought her into her bed.

"Good morning. Hey, we're late already. We better move."

The acid-fear wasn't leaving. She tried to hide it, but she was really bad at it. They arrived at the Notary Office and the whole squirmy group sat in a hot waiting room so that they could wait.

They weren't sure what they were waiting for. Jane was waiting for cool air, a breeze, anything. All this heat. Jane couldn't remember the last time she felt so sweaty and oppressed.

Teresa, Karen, and Jane all compared notes on their first night as mothers.

Teresa spoke: "Grace basically didn't sleep, or maybe she did, but it wasn't much. She ate. Oh, God, did she eat. That calmed her down whenever she thought we were trying to put her to bed. But sleep didn't really happen. And you?"

Grace looked peaceful and Buddha-like.

Karen spoke: "Ariel slept, but not in the crib. I tried putting her in there, and she got so mad. I'm not sure, but I think there was swearing in Cantonese. Anyway, the bed is kind of small and narrow, but we managed."

Ariel looked alert and curious.

Jane spoke: "Beth slept through the night. She fought it, at first, but she slept until six."

Beth looked worried.

"You're so lucky!" They seemed so genuine. Why didn't Jane feel lucky? Why didn't anyone else hear the paternal voice-over in the room? It was booming: *You've ruined your life. You've ruined her life, and she is an innocent. Ruined. Ruined. Ruined.*

"You look sort of green. Are you okay?" Ray asked as Beth lunged for Jane.

"No."

"Howe family?" the photographer called.

Jane held Beth on her lap, then had to bring her up higher, so that their faces were almost side by side.

"Smile, please!"

Sweat was stinging Jane's eyes and making her hands slippery. Beth still looked worried. They finished the photo, and James gathered the parents for a sort of swearing-in ceremony. An official from the Notary Office addressed the families. He spoke over the yelling, crying, and squealing. He spoke over Howard's booming voice-over.

It looked like a casual-dress, Moonie, mass-wedding when he asked for their vows:

"Do you wish to adopt this child?"

"Do you promise to care for her and give her all the benefits that you would give to biological children?"

"Do you promise never to abandon or abuse her?"

"I do," said the delirious parents.

"I congratulate you, new Mommies and Daddies."

And there was much rejoicing.

James distributed gifts on behalf of the Notary Office or the China Center of Adoption Affairs or Mao's illegitimate children. Jane had trouble hearing him over the babies' cries and her father's "Ruined Lives" aria.

When James reached Jane, he presented her with a stack of white booklets. Jane glanced at the first one, a birth certificate. The second one was an abandonment certificate. She sat Beth on her lap, opened it, and read. Beth—Wei Xian—was alone in the parking lot of the local train station. She was found by a policeman and brought to the Haozhou Social Welfare Institute. They guessed her age to be about six weeks old and assigned her a birthday. A search for her birth parents brought no results. Little Wei Xian was an orphan. Jane stopped reading. The image of six-week-old Beth alone in a parking lot was too painful. She held Beth a little closer.

James gave her a beautiful necklace with a small jade heart. It had Beth's name and birthday engraved on it. The heart was attached to a strong cord of red thread. There was a vinyl booklet. The official family photo was attached to a certificate enclosed inside the booklet. It was an adoption certificate.

Chapter Seventeen

James led a parade of new families to a medical office, where the children were to be examined. The waiting room looked like a corral of nervous rabbits. Jane wondered if she could get a diagnosis of the red circles on her daughter's tummy. And what about the scab on her head?

Picture babies being drafted into the military and undergoing the basic physical exam involved. Subtract the command to turn and cough, and that was mass physical exam of the day.

Jane pointed to the red circles on Beth's abdomen, and the doctors waved it away. It wouldn't stop her from serving her country. Jane became more insistent about the scab on Beth's head. What was it? Finally, through a translator, a doctor answered her, "It's getting better." The nurse must have seen that Jane was pale and tense. Maybe she saw Jane's white knucklebones through the skin on her hands. Maybe she had seen this before. She handed Jane a package of herbs and instructed her to make tea from them. "To relax you," she said through her cotton mask. Jane wanted to hug her.

Ray stepped in and showed the red circles on Beth's tummy to the nurse. She nodded her head and said, "Yes. Lingworm." She thrust a tube of cream into his hand.

"Daddy put on tummy." A diagnosis. A cure. All things were possible.

In the comfort of her room, Jane mixed the herbs with hot water and drank. The herbal tea tasted like tar. Jane did her best to consume an entire sip of tar tea.

. . .

Good news: They had only one task left to complete, and that was the Consulate appointment. There, the adoption would be approved, a visa issued, federal blessings bestowed.

Bad news: The Consulate appointment was ten long days away.

Pick up an atlas and you'll learn that Guangzhou is on the same parallel as Havana, Cuba. Jane began to appreciate how tropically hot Guangzhou was. And how smelly the city was when you walked by the Pearl River Canal. There were no restrictions on car or factory emissions. It showed, and it smelled.

. . .

The Chinamoms made an attempt at a playdate in Teresa's room. Jane was sitting, legs akimbo. She let the floor support her, and let the bed hold up her spine. She had nothing left. The three mothers compared travel partners.

Teresa was delighted with Bev. "She watches the baby while I get a massage. This is the life."

"Ray does everything any human being can do to help me. He's a world-class human being."

Karen was not as happy as her friends. Charles refused to help with Karen's baby. He barely tolerated the baby. Karen was certain she had seen him coo at babies back when they were dating. Maybe those were sleeping babies. Ariel was not a sleeper. Ariel was a crier. He became angry when the crying got too loud, and that may be why little Ariel cried so often. He would not hold her and made Karen promise that she would never leave him alone with the baby for more than twenty minutes.

"He tracks how much time I spend in the shower," Karen complained.

"What?" Teresa looked ready to call the cops or a talk-show host.

"Ariel cries the whole time. He doesn't know what to do with her. So he watches the clock. I come out of the shower, and she's in the crib. All red-faced and loud."

Jane tried to picture it. It wasn't pretty. Karen kept talking.

"So now he's really mad because I was in the gift shop for almost forty-five minutes. He was all alone with her. See, she was asleep when I left, so I thought I could get a little extra time. But she woke up. When I came back she was howling."

Charles decided to move into his own room. Karen would be on her own. Jane tried to use this to keep some sense of perspective on her own troubles. She tried hard.

"Jane? I think your daughter is doing something," Teresa warned.

Yes, Beth was offering her first poop and making sure everyone knew it. Teresa wasn't enjoying the heady scent that was settling into her hotel room. Jane pounced.

"Have you got a changing table set up?"

There was a makeshift changing table on a bench with a vinyl pad that Teresa usually carried in her diaper bag.

"Help yourself."

Jane had gotten some practice at this. She whipped off the old diaper, whoosh, and had the wipe ready, 1-2-3. She was doing a masterful diaper changing. And then she saw that she was doing it *too* well, or at least too quickly. Beth wasn't done yet.

"She's not done yet. What do I do? What do I do?" It was too late to save the pad or anyone's dignity.

• • •

There were so many Americans at the White Swan Hotel that Jane should have anticipated seeing someone who looked too much like Peter. She should have prepared herself. But for about seventeen seconds she lived out a fantasy. She walked down the hallway, and who was that walking toward her? It was Peter. He had made the grandest of gestures. He had flown halfway around the world to find her. Jane's prayers were answered.

But the not-Peter-fantasy-man kept walking. Up close, he didn't look much like Peter at all. The features didn't fit together the right way. The eyes were the wrong color. He was too neat, too angular. No. Not Peter.

To: stepmom@mynet.com
From: janie38@quickmail.com
Subject: The Way We Live Now

Dear Sheila,

I'm here in the hotel business center with a wriggling baby on my lap. Now I know why no parent can ever spell anything correctly on those listservs. I'm impressed that I've gotten online.

Oh Sheila, what have I done? Pretty soon, I'll be all alone with FOUR FLIGHTS OF STAIRS and this kid on my hip.

That's the bad part. The good part is that she's so beautiful (shallow me?) and I can make her laugh pretty much any time I want to. And she clings to me and she wants to belong to me and I want to belong to her. I just hope I'm up to it.

I alternate between waves of confidence and waves of despair. Please write back to me if you can and tell me how a real mother handles a situation like this. That's silly and selfish of me, because I'll be home in less than a week, but please, please write back anyway.

And how are things with you and Raoul and the boys?

XXOO
J

PS: What if I can't do this?

To: janie38@quickmail.com
From: stepmom@mynet.com
Subject: Re: The Way We Live Now

Oh, Janie,

Alternating between confidence and despair? You sound
like a real mom to me. Sweetie, you're it. You're the mom
here.

I love Dad, and I've actually had a phone conversation with
him since my birthday. And I want us to be close again, if we
can. So please remember that when I say that he needs to SHUT
UP. Shut him up. Sorry. I know that's a little harsh, but I had
to say it.

I have a husband, yes, but I have twin boys, so the ratio of
parent to kid is the same for me. Man-to-man defense. So, I can
sort of identify with your life. Please cut yourself lots of slack right
now, honey. This is all new. This is hard, you're right about that.
But it's going to get better. I promise you.

Did you ever wonder why I didn't tell you that I was eloping
with Raoul? This might sound crazy (I've never said all this out
loud—or typed it in an e-mail), but here goes: I needed to know
that I was strong enough to do it on my own. I needed to do it
without anyone's permission. Even yours. I needed to grow up a
little bit.

And now it's your turn: you can do this. You can, because you
have to.

I can't wait to see you and that baby!

Love,
Sheila

PS: Yes, you can do this.

To: janie38@quickmail.com
From: petermandell@worthnet.net
Subject: You're In China

J,

I can't believe you called me from China and I wasn't here. You sounded really upset in your message, but I don't believe a word of what you said about being incompetent. I bet you're a brilliant mother already.

How is little Beth? Do you sing to her all the time? What a lucky kid. I should be there with you. I'll confess: I went to the airport and tried to find you. But you had left, and China is a big country. And I'm an idiot.

Are you ever going to forgive me? What can I do to prove how sorry I am? I made one mistake, and yes it was a big one, but I'm so sorry and I wish I could talk to you. There has to be a way to make it up to you.

If you want me to go away, I will, but I don't want to. You wouldn't believe how much I miss you.

Love,
Peter

She printed her e-mails to bring back to Ray. As she passed through the hotel restaurant, she saw her friends. She dashed in to share Peter's e-mail, but before she could read one word, she got the news: Charles left. He was gone for a full day before Karen knew it. He had arranged for an earlier flight, because why not? Hey, he had no reason to wait around for a Consulate appointment that he had no intention of attending. Karen trudged into the hotel dinner buffet and filled her plate with the evening's special: pigs in a blanket. She ate them with a dramatic, I-dare-you-to-talk-to-me expression. Teresa offered to share Beverly, who didn't know that she was shareable.

"I sort of thought that Charles and I would, you know, spark. And he would see Ariel and me and think, 'I want that.' Why wouldn't he want that? Instead, he looked at us and said, 'I need a boarding pass.'"

In the old days, Charles's sudden departure would have called for retail therapy, margaritas, spa treatments, or any one of a list of healing indulgences. In the old days, there was time to tend to these wounds. But the old days ended with a bus ride to Haozhou. Karen didn't need to be told. She fed her daughter a better dinner than the cocktail weenies she was munching.

Jane put away her printed e-mails.

. . .

Consulate Day. Jane flashed back to the homestudy and was tempted to clean the hotel room, even though no one was going to see it. She had packed one nice dress, specifically for this event, and because she had imagined lovely dinners with her friends at restaurants where cooperative babies served as nice background props. She pulled out a Baby Ralph Lauren dress that fit Beth like an evening gown.

"Okay, Cinderella. Let's have a ball."

The Consulate was a short walk from the hotel. There was a mass of Chinese citizens who wanted to get in and get to America. They had no appointments, it seemed. When James shepherded his Americans and their Chinese babies forward, the crowd parted like bad choreography. James spoke briefly to the guard, and the group entered. Someone in the crowd of Chinese shouted, "Lucky Baby! Lucky Baby!"

There was a Consulate assembly line already in progress. Several Consulate workers were sitting at several tables interviewing several parents. They stamped official-looking stamps and called for the next family. Each interview lasted several minutes.

Jane had all her paperwork ready a second before it was asked for. She answered the questions clearly and intelligently. She bounced Beth on her knee and kept her happy all the while. There was no trace of gut-wrenching fear left in Jane's voice.

That night they celebrated, or at least they tried. The whole group had dinner in the hotel restaurant. It had only been ten days, but the girls had all changed so much. To Jane, it seemed that they had been covered with a thin coat of gray paint, but now that paint was washing away. The girls were emerging, and so were the mothers.

Later Ray arranged the dark and quiet room for Jane to begin tonight's bedtime routine for Beth. Story, bottle, and rocking. It was starting to seem so natural. Even Beth seemed to get it. Jane rocked her daughter and saw a flicker of a smile on her face as she rolled her eyes back and fought sleep. Jane kept rocking. This was her daughter. They belonged to each other. This was where she was meant to be. Jane kept rocking. Her back hurt. She was tired. But she was a mother now. Jane kept rocking. And she knew in her heart that she could do this. She could be a mother to her daughter. Beth was asleep.

. . .

She returned to her beloved lists and that rejuvenated her. There was a separate packing list for What to Bring on the Plane to Keep the Baby Happy on an Eighteen-Hour Flight. The flight would be long, but, hey, it was finite and therefore manageable. Jane did a lot of belly breathing whenever she thought about it.

As the Chinamoms waited to board the plane, they were already laughing and being wise and philosophical about their trip to China. Remember when Charles left? Remember how much Ariel cried every night? Good times!

When they boarded the flight, Jane settled Beth into her tray/bed with a bottle, and she promptly fell asleep. So Jane ate dinner like a person. Yes, it was airplane food, but that's not the point.

She was sitting up and feeding herself with both hands. And then she could just plain go to sleep. This flight had reached Cloud Nine.

Jane dreamed that she was riding a roller coaster, up and down hills. The dream rolled along until she heard a siren. No, it wasn't a siren—it was a baby. She jolted awake and saw Beth still peaceful. It was Ariel.

The plane was dark, everyone was sleeping or pretending to. But Karen was pacing the aisle with a writhing, kicking, crying, loud baby. She covered the length of the plane, sharing the wealth with one and all.

Jane rose and took Ariel up and down the aisle for a half hour, so that Karen could rest her arms and cry too. After a painfully long while, Ariel quieted down. Her eyelids began to droop, and she followed them. The squall had depleted her. Karen whispered a quiet "Thank you" and returned to her seat.

Teresa was watching the whole scene from her seat. She smiled at Jane and winked.

"You're a natural," she said quietly.

Jane smiled back. She returned to her seat and found Ray holding Beth, whose wide eyes were wide open and showed no signs of fatigue.

"Ariel?" Ray asked.

"Mmm-hmm. You want me to take Beth?"

"No, we're fine."

Jane sat back. Beth discovered the texture of Ray's shirt and began to gnaw on his shoulder.

"Ready for home?" he asked.

"Yes. No. Yes. I actually am."

"Did you ever write back to Peter?"

"No. That's too dangerous. I'm not allowed to see him or speak to him anymore. And fine. Whatever. We'll be okay."

Ray sighed and shifted Beth to the other shoulder. She seemed delighted to have a new surface to explore and soak.

"Duh," said Ray. "I could have told you that. But then, you had to learn it for yourself, Dorothy. Speaking of which, I checked my e-mail," said Ray. "The paper is sending me to cover the Oscars this year."

"Is that good?"

Ray tried to shrug it off, but the grin on his face betrayed him. "It's excellent."

"Are you branching out to cover movies?"

"A little. Maybe. It's more flexible, so I can be there for you and Beth. I mean, I realize that I'm not Peter, but I think I help."

"Slow down, mister. 'I'm not Peter.' Ick. Try again."

So Ray tried again. "I want this part. I want to play Sort-of-Dad for you two. God, I sound like those needy actors. Cast me! Cast me!"

"Ray. You got the part. You're our Sort-of-Dad. You're doing it. You're a star."

"Bah!" shouted Beth. Several other passengers stared for a while. Was this kid going to be the next screamer? But she went quiet again almost immediately, hypnotized by the bumpy in-flight uphol-stery.

"Remember when I overslept and I was late for the plane to China?"

"That's on my list of Stuff I'll Never Forget. So, yes. I remember."

"I didn't oversleep. Burton and I were breaking up. He changed his mind about adoption and that was a deal-breaker for me. It's over."

"Oh, God, Ray. I'm so sorry," Jane whispered.

"I didn't want to tell you before. No offense, but you were offi-cially freaked out for a while there. But now. Well. You're not. And anyway. I talk too much. I could probably spend a lot of years with Burton. He's a good one. But the whole baby thing scared him."

"I thought he wanted to have a baby. Didn't you say that?"

"I did, and he did. But now I think that he was just dreaming. Ba-bies were a remote, straight-couple, pipe dream. Real babies are much scarier. He's never been the same since I came home from that day with baby Stella and there was poop on my Hugo Boss shirt. Hey, maybe I should hook him up with Peter's wife."

Ray stopped talking. He didn't cry. He didn't cry. He didn't cry. And then he cried. Jane tried to hug him, around sleepy Beth. It was awkward at best, but Jane stayed with it. Eventually Ray sniffed and said, "Just as well. He thinks that you're going to bogart me." Jane started to protest. Oh, the guilt she was feeling. It wasn't pretty. But Ray stopped her.

"And so what if you do? That's my choice."

They both noticed that each time Beth blinked was slower than the time before. She was falling, so slowly, asleep.

"There she goes," Jane whispered.

Beth was draped at an awkward angle across Ray's chest. He had to support her full weight with his arms. And sleeping children get So Heavy.

"Are you sure you don't want me to take her?" Jane put some voice behind her whisper.

"Nah. You know, I still have some upper body strength from all that time I spent at the gym."

Jane nodded. She closed her eyes and tried to relax. She thought that Ray was doing the same until he said, "I can't stand this."

"Do you want me to take her?"

"No, not that. I told you. I'm fine with holding her."

"What can't you stand?"

Beth stirred, so Ray had to drop his voice back down to a whisper.

"Me. I mean, what's going on here? Who am I? I'm a gym rat, then I'm a spiritual guy. And then I'm a workaholic. And even that— I'm a theater critic, then I'm a movie critic. What am I going to be when I grow up?"

He frowned, but Jane smiled. She was not worried about Ray. Not really.

"You *are* grown up, silly. Who else could be strong enough to hold her, patient enough to cope with me, and make enough money

288 · Judy Sheehan

to come with me to China? And you even know show tunes, so you can sing to Beth and keep us both happy. And whatever comes next, well, I'm sure you can use that too."

Ray had to think about that one for a while. Jane saw his forehead ease. He even smiled a bit. She got it. Maybe he did too.

• • •

They arrived at JFK late at night. The air was beautiful, if only because it was invisible. Jane gulped it and wanted to kiss the tarmac. She carried her daughter on her hip as they moved through the airport.

"Welcome home, Chinamoms!" Barbara and Rachel formed a tired little welcome wagon. Barbara handed each mom a list (!) entitled, Making the Adjustment to Home.

"You need fresh air and sunshine to help the girls get used to the time change." Jane heard vague plans for a playdate the next day at Teresa's. But she stopped listening when she saw him.

She thought that she may have seen him before he saw her. Peter. He was separate from the crowd of mothers, standing by the door, blocking it. She thought he looked perfect—the way all the features fell into place, forming Peter's face exactly. Still tousled and hazel and warm. Her heart leapt into her mouth. She couldn't speak. It would have taken seconds to run to him there. But then she remembered: This was over. This had to be over. She felt like an addict meeting a mountain of cocaine. She didn't dare go near him. Danger. She looked for a way to dodge him, but then he saw her.

"Jane!" he shouted. And everyone heard him. Beth, the Chinamoms, everyone in JFK. Why was this man smiling? Didn't he know that they were broken up? What was he doing here?

He was walking toward her. Jane wanted to stop this scary movie. But her feet were locked in six inches of cement. Her mouth was wired shut. Her eyes were taped open.

"Is this Beth?" Was he actually speaking to her? "She's so beautiful."

"No. Sorry, Peter. But, no."

"Just let me explain—"

"Don't. Just go away."

And before Jane knew what was happening, the entire fleet of Chinamoms, travel companions, little children, and Ray had formed a circle around her.

"You heard her," Ray said. "Go."

"But, please!" was as much as Peter got to say. Jane and Beth were now the Beatles, and their entourage sped them along to where the Chinamoms each had a car waiting. Their farewells were quick. They would be together again, and soon. Jane looked back. There was no sign of Peter. She looked in front of her and saw the neon yellow glow of Celeste's hair as she shouted, "Welcome home, darling! Welcome home!"

Celeste covered Beth with kisses before buckling the child into the five-point harness of the car seat. It looked complicated. Jane was too tired to tell the story of her trip to China, and Celeste understood. "Relax, Little Mama. I get you home soon." Jane and Ray collapsed on either side of Beth and her car seat.

The lights on the Long Island Expressway felt like Christmas.

Chapter Eighteen

In her old life, Jane always looked forward to the first few days home from a trip. She would rediscover the world she had left behind and find the comfort of her version of normal. That couldn't happen this time. Her new life was unrecognizable.

Ray planned to stay with her that first night. She was going to need a slow weaning from his assistance. He had to make two trips up the stairs to pull all their luggage into the apartment. Jane carried Beth, who clung to her tightly. Stairs? What are stairs?

Inside the apartment, Jane said, "Welcome home, love. We're going to bed in a little while. Tomorrow we have a playdate at Auntie Teresa's."

And with that, she set Beth to crawling around the apartment. The price for Beth's good sleep on the plane was her alertness here at home. She couldn't be reasoned with. She was staying awake. She liked her room but was unimpressed with the stenciling. Ray supplied a few oohs of appreciation.

By 3 A.M., the baby showed signs of fatigue, while the adults showed signs of nervous collapse. They offered some familiar sights and sounds: *Goodnight Moon* and the Tibetan children chanting. Jane held her and rocked her until she could do the slo-mo, one-degree-per-minute descent into the crib. Her shoulders were burning with pain. Her arms were starting to shake. But it was all worth it. Beth slipped into her crib and *slept*.

"Good job, Mommy. Now, let's both of us get some sleep," Ray whispered.

"Oh, I thought I'd unpack a little bit and—"

"Sleep. Trust me."

. . .

The next day, Jane heeded Barbara's advice and dragged her tired little family to a playdate. Beth, Ariel, and Grace got to hang out together while their mothers said things like, "This baby is kicking my ass."

"Tell me again why we did this?" Teresa asked. The three mothers and their daughters were in Teresa's living room. Ray scrambled around the room, trying to keep the babies away from all the glass.

"We had too much time, too much sleep, too much money. Take your pick," Jane answered.

"You know what I figured out in China?" Karen ventured. "Besides the fact that I choose toxic men? Babies are a little bit—can I say this?—boring. It's so relentless."

"I know! It's all that repetition," Teresa agreed. "It wears you down. I mean, it's not like they're great conversationalists. Yet."

"It's the sleep deprivation. Beth wakes up, oh, three or four times a night. I jump out of bed and I rock her, and she goes back to sleep, but oh, God. It takes me forever to fall back asleep. And then she's up again."

Ray called over, "This is how they torture political prisoners, you know. They make them crazy from lack of sleep."

Karen took the confession session a step forward.

"I can't believe I'm going to say this out loud. I'm half looking forward to going back to work. That sounds awful, doesn't it?"

"Yes, it does, and that's why you must only say it within the confines of my home and this playdate. I understand completely," Teresa answered. "The hardest job on earth is easy compared to this. I've been working since I was seventeen, which was a long time ago, and it was all tea and scones compared to motherhood. I want to wear a nice watch again."

"So," said Karen. "Peter? Have you heard from him today? I thought that was pretty bold—showing up at the airport like that."

"That was a gesture. So that he can look good when he tells the story later. He wanted a sort of 'last word' I think. I won't hear from him again. I'd bet her college fund on it. That reminds me. I need to start her college fund. Anyway, it's over. I'm sure of that. I think."

Ray agreed. "Good. You don't want to have to get over this guy twice, do you?"

Karen agreed. "Break the cycle!"

Teresa agreed. "Be strong. For yourself and for your daughter."

Beth said, "Abrrrrr! Agah!"

Jane and her friends revisited the What Every Single Mother Needs list. They still endorsed every entry on the original list, but they expanded it just a bit:

1. The Perfect Apartment. At last, they defined this fantasy. This now consisted of: three bedrooms (the extra one would become a playroom or a guest room or a maid's room—each woman had a different use for it), doorman, elevator, lots of sun, too many closets, good schools within walking distance, good parks within walking distance, washer/dryer/dishwasher/new everything, no sharp corners anywhere, and heavily soundproofed walls and self-cleaning floors. At this, the definition of Perfect was complete and impossible.
2. Lots of pockets.
3. A strong immune system, and a thick skin.
4. A very light and small video camera.
5. Membership at the zoo.

6. A cheap hairstylist who will take last-minute appointments and still make you feel gorgeous.
7. A massage therapist who will take last-minute appointments and still make you feel better.
8. At least two back-up babysitters (although none of them had used any babysitters just yet—the thought of leaving the baby anywhere with anyone was actually shocking).
9. TiVo.
10. An enormous sense of humor.

The best part about being so busy and tired today was: no time to moon over lost Peter. Peter who was gone and should stay gone. Peter whom she sent packing. Peter. Nope. Not thinking about him at all. And when the phone rang, she was absolutely not secretly hoping that it was Peter.

"Janie? It's me. It's your old dad."

There was entirely too much to say to this man. Curses and blessings. In truth, she was surprised he called at all. She expected him to behave as Betty would have, stubborn to the end. Betty could hold a grudge. She could nurse it and keep it alive. And that was part of what killed her.

"Hi, Dad."

"Look. I said a few things when you were leaving, and I know you didn't like to hear them."

"You were wrong. You were way out of line, Dad."

"I had to listen to my conscience. I had to. I hope you understand that."

"Not really."

"But this little girl is now a member of our family, and I want to welcome her and give my blessing, if you'll let me."

How did he manage that? He had changed. And that was so not-Irish. Jane was wrestling with her squirmy daughter while she squeezed the phone between her ear and shoulder.

"She's a great little girl, Dad. I love her so much."

They talked about the trip to China. Jane whitewashed it a whole lot, and Howard sounded relieved that Jane accepted his olive branch. Jane was relieved that he offered it. It was late, and he was saying his good-byes and best wishes.

"But, Dad. You haven't even asked her name yet."

"You're right, I haven't. What is it?"

"Elizabeth. Beth. I call her Beth."

His voice held steady, almost.

"That's lovely."

. . .

Was this the longest day in history? Did the sun stop in the middle of the sky? And didn't Jane see that in an old movie? How was she supposed to survive the first day home if it was going to last 327 hours? That was grossly unfair. She would just have to coax Beth into a nap. Beth seemed to think that this was a deeply flawed plan. No, no, no, no, zzzzzzzzz. Beth napped.

As soon as Beth was asleep, Jane raced to the phone. She couldn't wait to tell Sheila about their father's change of heart. She picked up the phone and reenacted the entire conversation. Sheila was quiet and happy.

"Sheila, you have to come to New York and meet her. She's amazing. She's beautiful. She knows how to hail a taxi. She puts her arm up and every cab in town stops for us."

"I'll come soon. I will. But I have to wait just a while. I don't feel well enough to fly right now."

"What's the matter?"

"Nothing's the matter. I'm pregnant. It's okay to tell you now."

"Oh, Sheila!"

Jane tried to stay on the phone and get every detail about the pregnancy, but there was urgent loud noise coming from downstairs, and it woke Beth, who responded with genteel screeching. This developed into full-blown bellowing, and Jane was right by her side.

"Beth? What's the matter? It's just a big noisy noise. You don't need to be scared."

Beth didn't look like she was buying that. She looked very upset about the noisy noise.

"Let's go investigate. You'll see."

She parked Beth on her hip, and this seemed to be pretty comforting already. Jane and Beth headed downstairs, and Jane said, "See? It's movers. Someone is moving in. They're our neighbors. Can you say neighbors? Can you say mama? Can you say anything? No? That's okay."

The movers dropped something very thuddy and Beth started creeping toward another big cry. Jane sat down on the stairs and began to sing new words to Brahms's lullaby.

"Lullaby and good night, I love you, my Be-eth.
That was just a big noise, and you do-on't need to cry.
It's okay. You are safe, and we're going upstairs now.
I love you. Yes, I do. I love you, my Beth."

And that's when she saw Peter. Right in the hall of her building. How did he get in? Didn't she get his keys back? She could have sworn she did. Damn. She flinched enough to scare Beth a little. How did he get in? Jane was tired, remember. She was slow at putting things together.

"You do sing to her. I knew you would."

He stooped to Beth's eye level. "Hello, Beth." She reached out and grabbed his thumb. "Strong grip! You're a strong girl, aren't you?"

He looked dangerously good. Jane wanted to run, but Beth held on to Peter's thumb. Jane reached down to pry them apart, but that required touching Peter's hand. A staggering task, but she did it.

And then, oh, God, he tried to hold on to her hand. She made sure he failed.

"What?" Jane's voice was shrill. "You saw her, you saw me, and you saw that we're fine. We're more than fine. We're goddamn happy. How do you like that? I'm doing this without you, and did I mention that we're as fine as we can be?"

"I see that. Hi, Beth. I'm Peter. I'm your neighbor."

Beth seized his thumb again. "Let go of him, honey. We have to go now."

"Please, Jane, just hear me out."

Jane felt a cry in her throat.

"You lied to me."

"Yes. And I'm sorry. I missed China, I hurt you, and I let you get away. I was scared, but now the only thing that scares me is you walking away again."

Jane's breathing was shallow. How could he expect her to trust him? He hurt her. A lot.

"Do you expect me to trust you? You hurt me. A lot."

"I'm sorry. But I'm here now for good. I'll do whatever it takes. Because I have to," he said as Beth twisted his thumb in a direction it wasn't meant to go.

Jane shook her head. She wasn't going to be this stupid. "No. See, I'm not just me anymore. I have a child. I can't just jump in and out of love. I can't have you here and then not here, bouncing off your latest whim. You should have stayed gone. It's too late now."

Jane turned her attention to Beth. "Come on, sweetheart, let's go back upstairs."

"Wait!" Peter shouted. But she didn't wait. She climbed the stairs, and with each step, Jane imagined crushing Peter under her feet. And that was the perfect final cure for Peter. Oh, sure, Peter. Let's do this *your* way. Commitment? Who needs that. Stability? Overrated. Trust? An illusion. Hope? A nightmare. Love? A marketing tool.

Jane was so busy crushing Peter's bones she forgot to maintain her New York peripheral vision. She would have seen Peter signing a clipboard presented by the movers. He finished signing and started to climb the stairs after Jane. She swung around and used a voice she had learned in self-defense class.

"Are you stalking me? I'll call the cops. I'm not afraid to scream."

Peter stopped short. Jane fumbled through her pockets.

"I've got my phone right here. Somewhere. I'll call 911 right now, I swear. You leave me and my daughter alone." She began to fumble through her pockets, but then she remembered leaving the cell phone upstairs. Damn.

"Jane. I'm not stalking you. In fact—" He reached out to her and moved closer.

"Don't take another step." Jane's fumbling produced a set of keys. Hah!

Peter had keys too. "This is what I was trying to tell you. I bought the apartment. The one you wanted to buy before."

Beth reached for his interesting thumb once again. Peter kept talking.

"And I bought dishes and furniture and everything. I'm dug in here, Jane. Truly. What can I do to show you that I'm here to stay?"

Jane and Beth sat down on the stairs.

"Go ahead and be mad at me, Jane. I've got that coming. But you need to know what I know. In fact, I made a list. It's called What I Know. Here goes:

1. I love you.
2. We belong together.
3. I was an idiot for leaving.
4. I'm not leaving again.
5. I told my parents that I moved here for you.
6. I love you.

That needed two spots on the list. Extra important, you know. Jane. Do you get it yet? I'll do whatever it takes."

Beth was now exploring the rest of Peter's hand. Jane shifted her daughter to the other hip, vainly hoping that it would distract her from the tears that she was absolutely not going to let fall. But they fell. He reached his free hand to brush them from her cheek. She thought she was pushing his hand away, but she was letting her hand rest on his.

He moved slowly and took her hand. She touched his cheek. He kissed her open palm.

. . .

Ray had wanted to throw Jane a baby shower, but their travel plans to China had gotten the best of him. Instead, he threw Beth's first birthday party. The Chinamoms came, of course, old friends, new friends. Arlene was there with her referral picture.

"I travel in three weeks! Any words of advice?"

Arlene didn't realize what she was asking. Teresa talked directly into her ear for an hour. Arlene looked tired after that.

Megan and her toddler/baby Stella came to the party. Stella was walking, saying a few words, and taking every toy from every baby. The babies looked confused, but Stella looked determined. Charm brought her gorgeous baby boy, Seth. He seemed like the peaceful king of the harem.

Karen introduced her handsome friend Raj to Ray.

"Raj and I dated a long time ago, but that was before Raj knew he liked boys better than girls. Which explained a whole lot. Anyway, I thought you two should meet. And here you are. Meeting."

"A suave fix up. Very cool." Ray either liked this guy a lot or was mortified. Jane couldn't tell. But she wasn't accustomed to seeing Ray blush.

All the babies gathered around Celeste, who had changed her hair to pumpkin orange. She clapped, sang songs, and could probably lead them all out of town if she wanted to. Celeste spoke exclusively to the children. She could see adults any day. She did reserve a minute or two for Jane, though.

"Darling. You will be happy in this baby for the rest of your life. Every minute of every day. You hear me? Some days will be hard, but still you will be happy."

Peter arrived late. He carried a bouquet of pink balloons that declared, "It's a girl!" in glittery letters. Jane didn't notice him right away. Beth did, and she shouted, "A Bah!"

All the babies bounced the balloons, and Beth managed to pop one with a newly erupting tooth. Peter mingled with the group and tried not to step on any children. None of the Chinamoms actually talked to him. Yet. But they watched him. And Jane watched them watching him, while Peter watched her watching them watching him.

"Peter? Could you give me a hand in the kitchen?" Ray asked.

Peter followed him, but this was such an obvious Invitation to an Inquisition. Ray, Karen, and Teresa cornered him in Jane's tiny kitchen. Jane saw the parade and pressed her ear to the kitchen door. She heard:

"What are your intentions toward our girl?" Ray asked.

"We simply won't allow you to hurt her again," said Teresa.

"Do you think you knew her in a previous life?" asked Karen.

"Well?" Ray commanded.

Jane peeked through the doorway. Peter's smile went on forever.

"I picked the right girl to fall in love with, didn't I?"

Jane matched his smile. There was already so much love in her life, such fierce protection. What a lucky girl she was. What a happy life they could have together. Jane kissed her daughter.

• • •

The weather was turning cold, but then had the odd snap of a warm day. Jane took Beth to the park. It was a sort of Mardi Gras/make hay while the sun doth shine afternoon. Jane was not the only parent to have this thought. Washington Square Park was overflowing with children and parents.

Jane had been alternating between two parks. At Tompkins Square Park, she felt like the old parent. There, everyone had tattoos and piercings and let their kids eat the dirt, and so? Why not?

In Washington Square, Jane felt like the poor parent. There were jewels, cell phone calls to film stars, nannies to watch the kids even while the parents were there, and rich-family conversations:

"Honey, if we can't find a present for Mommy at Tiffany's, we'll have to go back to Cartier. Sorry."

"Mommy! Tad is wearing a shirt he's worn before!"

"Daddy, when are you going to buy another island—I'm bored with the old one."

Jane was a gate-crasher, or at least that was how it felt. Her baby couldn't walk yet, so the playground seemed unnecessary. And it was so *Lord of the Flies* in so many ways. The larger children tormented the smaller ones for sport.

"Beth, this is what you have to look forward to."

"Oh, now, it's not so bad."

Wow. No, it wasn't Beth speaking. It was another mom, sitting on the park bench. She looked familiar. Beth had probably seen her here before.

She called to her toddling son, "Hi, Joshua! I see you, my big walking boy!"

"Mommy!" he cried. He said that a lot as he circled a stone turtle nearby. He used it for balance.

"How old is your daughter?"

"Twelve months."

At this age, the answer is always in months. It stays that way until they're two years old. No one tells you this, but now you know.

The wind picked up, and Beth wanted her mother's lap. Jane wanted to hold her. They snuggled on the park bench. Beth gazed up at her mother and absently curled her hair around one finger.

"That's nice," said the other mother.

"What is?"

"The way she plays with your hair. Like she's the one who's cuddling you. It's all so delightful, isn't it?"

"Yes. It wasn't at first. I thought I'd made a mistake."

"You didn't."

"No, I didn't. But I was so scared. I'm still scared, but now we just move through the days. She keeps learning things, keeps changing. It's shocking."

"Are you okay now?"

"I think . . ." She had not asked herself that question since China, so she didn't really think anything. She had to find the answer.

"Yes."

"I'm glad. Joshua! Time for din-din!" She scooped up a beautiful boy, her Christ Child.

"Bye-bye!" he called and waved.

Epilogue

And that's how Jane came to be my mom. It was a weird and twisted journey, but we both got here. And please don't think that it was all soft ice cream after she got a good night's sleep and Peter came back. Oh. My. God.

I remember Cathy, the nanny, and she was so great. I loved her, I think. But then she went to school and became a dental hygienist. We had a couple of nannies after that, but Mom got a nanny cam, and none of them lasted very long. She stressed. I survived.

Then Mom got so freaked about schools. She had to get me into a school in Chinatown, so I could be at one with my Chinese heritage. I have to learn Mandarin, but she can't speak one word of Gaelic. But don't get me started on that. I actually like my school, but I don't like her to know it. Mom's Irish, and a little suffering does her some good, I think.

You should have seen how much she suffered when they were building the stairs. We have an upstairs and a downstairs, like a real house-house. But Mom and Peter actually had to build the stairs and fix all sorts of things. Mom was pretty good at it. Peter mostly kept me away from sharp things. Then he'd make dinner and they'd watch movies together. The movies they like are really old and they're not even in color. I don't get it. But they do. He makes the best mac and cheese in the world, and he knows exactly what to say to Mom when I get in trouble. He even took the blame when my art project accidentally got glued to the lampshade and accidentally left a hole that looked like Australia. What a guy. Someday, when they get married, I want to be a flower girl and throw petals in the air.

Ray is one of my favorite human beings. Please don't tell Mom, but he is going to get me a kitten for my birthday. We went to the shelter and picked her out, and right now she's at Ray's house. He's starting to love the kitten and all, but he said he'll still give her to me. He promised. We go to these Daddy and Me classes, which are hilarious, but I'm not sure if they're supposed to be. So I try not to laugh.

My grandfather is this quiet old guy in New Jersey. We go for visits. He has a backyard and he doesn't even use it. Can you believe that? A whole backyard to himself, and it only gets used by his grandkids. Unbelievable.

Last winter we went to visit my aunt Sheila and all my cousins and they live near the beach, which is so unfair. Aunt Sheila has four kids and they're two sets of twins. Uncle Raoul plays the guitar, and he says he's going to teach me someday when my hands are big enough. Mom and Aunt Sheila can talk for hours and hours and hours and hours and hours. It's crazy.

When I'm here in New York, I go play with Ariel and Grace. Grace has a sandbox on her patio and Ariel has cool dress-up clothes. I like the guy that Aunt Teresa dates. He's totally good and funny. Aunt Karen doesn't date at all, which is cool too.

Mom sings a lot, and I love it. She sings songs you know and songs nobody knows. She makes up songs. She's really good at it. She sings for Peter when they're cooking, and sometimes she kisses him. When I'm upset about something, I ask her to sing to me. She always does. I love her singing. I love her.

So, things move along here, and we're all okay. Thanks.

JUDY SHEEHAN started her career as one of the original cast members and creators of the long-running stage hit *Tony n' Tina's Wedding*. Currently Sheehan is the playwright-in-residence at New York City's prestigious Looking Glass Theatre, which produces her work every season. Excerpts from her plays have appeared in the popular anthologies *Monologues for Women by Women* and *Even More Monologues for Women by Women*. In 2000, Sheehan joined the growing ranks of adoptive parents when she traveled to China to adopt a ten-month-old girl. Judy and her daughter, Annie, live in New York City.

ABOUT THE TYPE

This book was set in Fairfield, the first typeface from the hand of the distinguished American artist and engraver Rudolph Ruzicka (1883–1978). Ruzicka was born in Bohemia and came to America in 1894. He set up his own shop, devoted to wood engraving and printing, in New York in 1913 after a varied career working as a wood engraver, in photoengraving and banknote printing plants, and as an art director and freelance artist. He designed and illustrated many books, and was the creator of a considerable list of individual prints—wood engravings, line engravings on copper, and aquatints.